In Another Country and Other Short Novels

In Another Country and Other Short Novels

Robert Silverberg

Five Star • Waterville, Maine

This collection is a work of fiction. Names, characters, places, and incidents are either the product of the author's imagination, or, if real, used fictitiously.

Five Star First Edition Science Fiction and Fantasy Series.

Published in 2002 in conjunction with Tekno Books and Ed Gorman.

Set in 11 pt. Plantin by Minnie B. Raven.

Printed in the United States on permanent paper.

Library of Congress Cataloging-in-Publication Data

Silverberg, Robert.
In another country, and other short novels /
Robert Silverberg.
p. cm.—(Five Star first edition science fiction and fantasy series)
Contents: In another country—The way to spook city—They hide, we seek—This is the road.
ISBN 0-7862-3876-3 (hc : alk. paper)
1. Science fiction, American. I. Title. II. Series.
PS3569.I472 I6 2002
813′.54—dc21 2001055739

Table of Contents

Introduction

The short novel—or "novella," as some prefer to call it—is one of the richest and most rewarding of literary forms, and has long been a personal favorite of mine. Spanning twenty to thirty thousand words, usually, it permits more extended development of theme and character than the short story does, without making the elaborate structural demands of the full-length book. It is particularly well suited to science fiction, since it allows the writer to create a strikingly original world in powerful detail but does not require the elaborate and lengthy working out of plot and sub-plot that all too often can blur the focus of the concept.

Some of the greatest works of modern literature fall into the novella class—Mann's "Death in Venice," Joyce's "The Dead," Faulkner's "The Bear," Conrad's "Heart of Darkness," Melville's "Billy Budd," and many more. The roster of great science-fictional short novels is also a distinguished one: James Blish's "A Case of Conscience," Robert A. Heinlein's "By His Bootstraps," Jack Vance's "Telek," Roger Zelazny's "A Rose for Ecclesiastes," Wyman Guin's "Beyond Bedlam," and dozens more come to mind immediately.

In my own career, prolific as it has been, I've made something of a specialty of the novella. Perhaps the most successful of my early ones was "Hawksbill Station" of 1966, followed a few years later by the Hugo-winning "Nightwings," then the Nebula-winning "Born with the

Dead" and "Sailing to Byzantium," and a good many others. I've brought together in this volume four of my best longer stories, representing a twenty-year period of work and a variety of moods and modes.

—Robert Silverberg

Introduction to *In Another Country*

Writing *In Another Country* was one of the strangest and most challenging things I've ever done in my forty-five years of professional writing.

The impetus to do it came from the anthologist Martin H. Greenberg, who told me one wintry day in 1988 that he was editing a series of books for which contemporary science fiction writers would be asked to produce companions to classic SF novellas of the past. The new story and the old one would then be published in the same volume. He invited me to participate; and after hardly a moment's thought I chose C. L. Moore's *Vintage Season* as the story I most wanted to work with.

Now and then I have deliberately chosen to reconstruct some classic work of literature in a science-fictional mode, as a kind of technical exercise. My novel *The Man in the Maze* of twenty years ago is based on the *Philoctetes* of Sophocles, though you'd have to look hard to find the parallel. *Downward to the Earth*, about the same time, was written with a nod to Joseph Conrad's *Heart of Darkness*. My story "To See the Invisible Man" develops an idea that Jorge Luis Borges threw away in a single sentence. In 1989 I reworked Conrad's famous story "The Secret Sharer," translating it completely into an SF context.

But in all those cases, though I was using the themes and patterns of earlier and greater writers, the stories themselves, and the worlds in which they were set, were entirely my own inventions. Essentially I was running my own variation on classic themes, as Beethoven did with the themes of Mozart, or Brahms with Haydn. The task this time was to enter a world already created by a master artist—the world of Moore's classic 1946 story, *Vintage Season*—and work with *her material,* finding something new to say about a narrative situation that had already been triumphantly, and, one would think, completely, explored in great depth.

The solution was not to write a sequel to *Vintage Season*—that would have been pointless, a mere time-travelog to some other era—but to produce a work interwoven with hers the way a lining of a cape is interwoven with the cape itself. My story is set during the same few weeks as hers, and builds towards the same climax. I used many of her characters, but not as major figures; they move through the background, and the people in the foreground are mine. She told her story from the point of view of a man of the twentieth century who finds himself in the midst of perplexing strangers from the future; I went around to the far side and worked from the point of view of one of the visitors. Where I could, I filled in details of the time-traveling society that she had not provided, and clarified aspects of her story that she had chosen to leave undeveloped, thus providing a kind of Silverbergian commentary on Moore's concepts. And though I made no real attempt to write in Moore's style, I adapted my own as well as I could to match the grace and elegance of her tone.

There is perhaps an aspect of real *lèse-majeste* in all of this, or perhaps the word I want is *hubris*. Readers of my autobiographical anthology, *Robert Silverberg's Worlds of Wonder*, will know that C. L. Moore is one of the writers I most revere in our field, that I have studied her work with respect verging on awe. To find myself now going back over the substance of her most accomplished story in the hope of adding something to it of my own was an odd and almost frightening experience. I suspect I would not have dared to do any such thing fifteen or twenty years ago, confident though I was then of my own technical abilities. But now, when my own science-fiction-writing career has extended through a period longer than that of Moore's own, I found myself willing to risk the attempt, if only to see whether I could bring it off.

It was an extraordinary thing for me to enter Moore's world and feel, for the weeks I was at work, that I was actually writing, if not *Vintage Season*, then something as close to it as could be imagined. I was there, in that city, at that time, and it all became far more vivid for me than even my many readings of the original story over a 40-year period had been able to achieve. I hope that the result justifies the effort and that I will be forgiven for having dared tinker with a masterpiece this way. And most profoundly do I wish that C. L. Moore could have seen my work and perhaps found a good word or two to say for it.

In Another Country

The summer had been Capri, at the villa of Augustus, the high summer of the emperor at the peak of his reign, and the autumn had been the pilgrimage to golden Canterbury. Later they would all go to Rome for Christmas, to see the coronation of Charlemagne. But now it was the springtime of their wondrous journey, that glorious May late in the twentieth century that was destined to end in sudden roaring death and a red smoking sky. In wonder and something almost like ecstasy Thimiroi watched the stone walls of Canterbury fade into mist and this newest strange city take on solidity around him. The sight of it woke half-formed poems in his mind. He felt amazingly young, alive, open . . . vulnerable.

"Thimiroi's in a trance," Denvin said in his light, mocking way, and winked and grinned. He stood leaning casually against the rail of the embankment, a compact, elegant little man, looking back at his two companions.

"Let him alone," said Laliene sharply. In anger she ran her hands over the crimson nimbus of her hair and down the sides of her sleek tanned cheeks. Her gray-violet eyes flashed with annoyance. "Can't you see he's overwhelmed by what he sees out there?"

"By the monstrous ugliness of it?"

"By its beauty," Laliene said, with some ferocity. She touched Thimiroi's elbow. "Are you all right?" she whispered.

Thimiroi nodded.

She gestured toward the city. "How wonderfully discordant it is! How beautifully strident! No two buildings alike. And the surfaces of everything so flat. But colors, shapes, sizes, textures, all different. Not even the trees showing any sort of harmony."

"And the noise," said Denvin. "Don't forget the noise, if you're delighted by discordance. Machinery screeching and clanging and booming, and giving off smelly fumes besides—oh, it's marvelous, Laliene! Those painted things are vehicles, aren't they? Those boxy looking machines. Honking and bellowing like crazed oxen with wheels. That thing flying around up there, too, the shining thing with wings—listen to it! Just listen!"

"Stop it," Laliene said. "You're going to upset him."

"No," Thimiroi said. "He's not bothering me. But I do think it's very beautiful. Beautiful in its ugliness. Beautiful in its discordance. There's energy here. Whatever else this place may be, it's a place of tremendous energy. And energy is always beautiful." His heart was pounding. It had not pounded like this when they had arrived at any of the other places of their tour through antiquity. But the twentieth century was special: an apocalyptic time, a time of such potent darkness that it cast an eerie black radiance across half a dozen centuries to come. And this was its most poignant moment, when the century was at its highest point, all its earlier turmoil far behind—the moment when splendor and magnificence would be transformed in an instant, by nature's malevolent prank, into stunning catastrophe. "Besides," he said, "not everything here is ugly or discordant, anyway. Look at the sky."

"Yes," Laliene said. "That's a sky to remember. It's a sky that absolutely demands a great artist to capture, wouldn't you say? Someone on the order of Nivander, or even Sathimon. Those blues, and the white of the clouds. And then those streaks of gold and purple and red."

"You mean the pollution?" Denvin asked.

She glowered at him. "Don't. Please. If you don't want to be here, tell Kadro when he shows up, and he'll send you home. But don't spoil it for the rest of us."

"Sorry," said Denvin, in a chastened tone. "I do have to admit that that sky is fantastic."

"So intense," Laliene said. "It comes right down and wraps itself around the tops of the buildings like a shimmering blue cloak. And everything so sharp, so vivid, so clear. The sun was brighter back in these days, someone said. That must be why. And the air more transparent, a different mix of elements. Of course, this was an unusual season even for here. That's well known. They say there had never been a month like this one, a magical springtime, everything perfect, almost as if it had been arranged that way for maximum contrast with—with—"

Her voice trailed away.

Thimiroi shook his head. "You both talk too much. Can't you simply stand here and let it all come flooding into your souls? We came here to *experience* this place, not to talk about it. We'll have the rest of our lives to talk about it."

They looked abashed. He grasped their hands in his and laughed—his rich, exuberant, pealing laugh, which some people thought was too much for their delicate sensibilities—to take the sting out of the rebuke. Denvin, after a moment, managed a smile. Laliene gave Thimiroi a curiously impenetrable stare; but then she too, smiled, a warmer and more sincere one than Denvin's. Thimiroi nodded and released them, and stepped forward to peer over the edge of the embankment.

They had materialized just a few moments earlier, in what seemed to be a park on the highest slopes of a lush green hillside overlooking a broad, swiftly flowing river. The city was on the far side, stretching out before them in dizzying vastness. Where they stood was in a sort of overlook point, jutting out of the hill, protected by a dark metal railing. Their luggage was beside them. The hour appeared to be midday; the sun was high; the air was mild, and very still and clear. The park was almost empty, though Thimiroi could see a few people strolling on the paths below. Natives of this time and place, he thought. His heart went out to them. He would have run down to them and embraced them, if he could. He longed to know what they were really like, these ancients, these rough earthy primitives, these people of lost antiquity.

Primitives, he thought? Well, yes, what else could they be called? They lived so long ago. But this city is no trifling thing. This is no squalid village of mud-and-wattle huts that lies before us.

In silence Thimiroi stared across the river at the massive blocky gray towers and wide, busy streets of the great metropolis, and at the shimmering silvery bridges to his right and to his left, and at the endless rows of small white and pink houses that rose up and up and up through the green hills on the other side. The weight and size and power of the place were extraordinary. His soul quivered with—what? Joy? Amazement? Fear?—at such immensity. How many people lived here? A million? Five million? He could scarcely conceive of such a number, all packed into a single place. The other ancient cities they had visited on this tour, imperial capitals though they were, were mere citylets—towns, even; piddling little medieval settlements—however grand they might have imagined themselves to be. But the great cities of the twentieth century, he had always been told, marked the high point in human urban concentration: cities of ten million, fifteen million, twenty million people. Unimaginable. This one before him was not even the biggest one, not even close to the biggest. Never before in history had cities grown to this size—and never again, either. Never again. What an extraordinary sight! What an astounding thing to contemplate, this great humming throbbing hive of intense human activity, especially when one knew—when one knew—

—when one knew the fate that was soon to befall it—

"Thimiroi?" Laliene called. "Kadro's here!"

He turned. The tour leader, a small, fragile-looking man with thick flame-red hair and eerie blue-violet eyes, held out his arms to them. He could only just have arrived himself—they had all been together mere minutes before, in Canterbury—but he was dressed already in twentieth-century costume, curious and quaint and awkward-looking, but oddly elegant on him. Thimiroi had no idea how that trick had been accomplished, but he accepted it untroubledly: The Travel was full of mysteries of all sorts, detours and overlaps and side-jaunts through time. It was Kadro's business to understand such things, not his.

"You'd better change," Kadro said. "There's a transport vehicle on the way up here to take you into town."

He touched something at his hip and a cloud of dark mist sprang up around them. Under its protective cover they opened their suitcases—their twentieth-century clothes were waiting neatly inside, and some of the strange local currency—and set about the task of making themselves look like natives.

"Oh, how wonderful!" Laliene cried, holding a gleaming, iridescent green robe in front of herself and dancing around with it. "How did they think of such things? Look at how it's cut! Look at the way it's fitted together!"

"I've seen you wearing a thousand things more lovely than those," said Denvin sourly.

She made a face at him. Denvin himself had almost finished changing: he was clad now in gray trousers, scarlet shirt open at the throat, charcoal-colored jacket cut with flaring lapels. Like Kadro, he looked splendid in his costume. But Kadro and Denvin looked splendid in anything they wore. The two of them were men of the same sort, Thimiroi thought, both of them dandyish, almost dainty. Perfect men of fashion. He himself, much taller than they and very muscular, almost rawboned, had never quite mastered their knack of seeming at utter ease in all situations. He often felt out of place among such smooth types as they, almost as though he were some sort of throwback, full of hot, primordial passions and drives rarely seen in the refined era into which he had happened to be born. It was, perhaps, his creative intensity, he often thought. His artistic nature. He was too earthy for them, too robust of spirit, too much the primitive. As he slipped into his twentieth-century clothes, the tight yellow pants, the white shirt boldly striped in blue, the jet-black jacket, the tapering black boots, he felt a curious sense of having returned home at last, after a long journey.

"Here comes the car," Kadro said. "Hold out your hands, quickly! I have your implants."

Thimiroi extended his arm. Something silvery-bright, like a tiny gleaming beetle, sparkled between two of Kadro's fingers. He pressed it gently against Thimiroi's skin, just above the long rosy scar of the inoculation, and it made the tiniest of whirring sounds.

"This is their language," said Kadro. He touched it to

Denvin's arm also, and to Laliene's. "And this one, the technology and social customs. And this is your medical booster, just in case." Buzz, buzz, buzz. Kadro smiled. He was very efficient. "You're all ready for the twentieth century now. And just in time, too."

A vehicle had pulled up in the roadway behind them, yellow with black markings, and odd projections on its roof. Thimiroi felt a quick faint stab of nausea as a breeze, suddenly stirring out of the quiescent air, swept a whiff of the vehicle's greasy fumes past his face.

The driver hopped out. He was very big, bigger even than Thimiroi, with immense heavy shoulders and a massive column of a neck. His face was unusual, the lips strongly pronounced, the cheekbones broad and jutting like blades. His hair was black and woolly and grew very close to his skull. But the most surprising thing about him was the color of his skin. It was dark brown, almost black: his eyes were bright as beacons against that astonishing chocolate-hued backdrop. Thimiroi had never imagined that anyone might have skin of such a color. Was that what they all were like in the twentieth century? Skin the color of night? No one on Capri had looked like that, or in Canterbury.

"You the people called for a taxi?" the driver asked. "Here—let me put those suitcases in the trunk—"

Perhaps it is a form of ornamentation, Thimiroi thought. They have it artificially done. They think it makes them look more beautiful when they change their skins, when they change their faces, so that they are like this.

And it *was* beautiful. There was a brooding somber power about this black man's face. He was like something carved from a block of some precious and recalcitrant stone.

"I'll ride up front," Kadro said. "You three get in back." He turned to the driver. "The Montgomery House is where we are going. You know where that is?"

The driver laughed. "Ain't no one in town who don't know the Montgomery House. But you sure you don't want a hotel that's a little cheaper?"

"The Montgomery House will do," said Kadro.

They had ridden in mule-drawn carts on the narrow winding paths of hilly Capri, and in wagons drawn by oxen on the rutted road to Canterbury. That had been charming and pretty, to ride in such things, to feel the jouncing of the wheels and see the sweat glistening on the backs of the panting animals. There was nothing charming or pretty about traveling in this squat glass-walled wheeled vehicle, this *taxi*. It rumbled and quivered as if it were about to explode. It careered alarmingly around the sharp curves of the road, threatening at any moment to break free of the driver's tenuous control and go spurting over the edge of the embankment in a cataclysmic dive through space. It poured forth all manner of dark noxious gases. It was an altogether terrifying thing.

And yet fascinating and wonderful. Crude and scary though the taxi was, it was not really very different in fundamental concept or design from the silent, flawless vehicles of Thimiroi's world. Contemplating that, Thimiroi had a keen sense of the kinship of this world to his own. We are not that far beyond them in time, he thought. They exist at the edge of the modern era, really. The Capri of the Romans, the Canterbury of the pilgrimage—those are truly alien places, set deep back in the pre-technological past. But there is not the same qualitative difference between our epoch and this twentieth century. The gulf is not so great.

The seeds of our world can be found in theirs. Or so it seems to me, Thimiroi told himself, after five minutes' acquaintance with this place.

Kadro said, "Omerie and Kleph and Klia are here already. They've rented a house just down the street from the hotel where you'll be staying."

Laliene smiled. "The Sanciscos! Oh, how I look forward to seeing them again! Omerie is such a clever man. And Kleph and Klia—how beautiful they are, how refreshing to spend time with them!"

"The place they've taken is absolutely perfect for the end of the month," said Kadro. "The view will be supreme. Hollia and Hara wanted to buy it, you know. But Omerie got to it ahead of them."

"Hollia and Hara are going to be here?" Denvin said, sounding surprised.

"*Everyone* will be here. Who would miss it?" Kadro's hands moved in a quick playful gesture of malicious pleasure. "Hollia was beside herself, of course. She couldn't believe that Omerie had beaten her to that house. But, as you say, Laliene, Omerie is such a clever man."

"Hollia is ruthless," said Denvin. "If the place is that good, she'll try to get it away from the Sanciscos. Mark my words, Kadro. She'll try some slippery little trick."

"She may very well. Not that there's any real reason to. I understand that the Sanciscos are planning to invite all of us to watch the show from their front window. Including Hollia and Hara, naturally. So they won't be the worse for it. Except that Hollia would have preferred to be the hostess herself. Cenbe will be coming, you know."

"Cenbe!" Laliene cried.

"Exactly. To finish his symphony. Hollia would have wanted to preside over that. And instead it will be Omerie's party, and Kleph's and Klia's, and she'll just be one of the crowd." Kadro giggled. "Dear Hollia. My heart goes out to her."

"Dear Hollia," Denvin echoed.

"Look there," said Thimiroi, pointing out the side window of the taxi. He spoke brusquely, his voice deliberately rough. All this gossipy chatter bored and maddened him. Who cared whether it was Hollia who gave the party, or the Sanciscos, or the Emperor Augustus himself? What mattered was the event that was coming. The experience. The awesome, wondrous, shattering calamity. "Isn't that Lutheena across the street?" he asked.

They had emerged from the park, had descended to the bank of the river, were passing through a district of venerable-looking three-story wooden houses. One of the bridges was just ahead of them, and the towers of the downtown section rose like huge stone palisades on the other side of the river. Now they were halted at an intersection, waiting for the colored lights that governed the flow of traffic to change; and in the group of pedestrians waiting also to cross was an unmistakably regal figure—yes, it was Lutheena, who else could it be but Lutheena?—who stood among the twentieth-century folk like a goddess among mortals. The difference was not so much in her clothes, which were scarcely distinguishable from the street clothes of the people around her, nor in her features or her hair, perfect and flawless though they were, as in the way she bore herself: for though she was slender and of a porcelain frailty, and no more than ordinary in height, she held herself with such self-contained majesty, such imperious grace, that she seemed to tower above the others, coarse and clumsy with a thick-ankled peasant cloddishness about them, who waited alongside her.

"I thought she was coming here *after* Charlemagne," Denvin said. "And then going on to Canterbury."

Thimiroi frowned. What was he talking about? Whether she came here first and then went to Canterbury, or journeyed from Canterbury to here as they had done, would they not all be here at the same time? He would never understand these things. This was another of the baffling complexities of The Travel. Surely there was only one May like this one, and one 1347 November, and one 800 December? Though everyone seemed to make the tour in some private order of his own, some going through the four seasons in the natural succession, others hopping about as they pleased, certainly they must all converge on the same point in time at once—was that not so?—

"Perhaps it's someone else," he suggested uneasily.

"But of *course* that's Lutheena," said Laliene. "I wonder what she's doing all the way out here by herself."

"Lutheena is like that," Denvin pointed out.

"Yes," Laliene said. "She is, yes." She rapped on the window. Lutheena turned, and stared gravely, and after a moment burst into that incandescent smile of hers, though her luminous eyes remained mysteriously solemn. Then the traffic light changed, the taxi moved forward, Lutheena was lost in the distance. In a few minutes they were on the bridge, and then passing through the heart of the city, alive in all its awesome afternoon clangor, and then upward, up into the hills, up to the lofty street, green with the tender new growth of this heartbreakingly perfect springtime, where they would all wait out that glorious skein of May days that lay between this moment and the terrible hour of doom's arrival.

After the straw-filled mattresses and rank smells of the

lodges along the way to Canterbury, and the sweltering musty splendors of their whitewashed villas on the crest of Capri, the Montgomery House was almost palatial.

The rooms had a curious stiffness and angularity about them that Thimiroi was already beginning to associate with twentieth-century architecture in general, and of course there was no sweep-damping, no mood insulation, no gravity gradients, none of the little things that one took for granted when one was in one's own era. All the same, everything seemed comfortable in its way, and with the proper modifications he knew he would have no trouble feeling at home here. The rooms were spacious, the ceilings were high, the windows were clean, no odors invaded from neighboring chambers. There was indoor plumbing: a blessing, after Canterbury. He had a suite of three rooms, furnished in the strange but pleasant late-twentieth-century way that he had seen in museums. There was a box in the main sitting room that broadcast images in color, flat ones, with no sensory augmentation other than sonics. There were paintings on the wall, maddeningly motionless. The walls themselves were painted—how remarkable!—with some thick substance so porous that he could almost make out its molecular structure if he looked closely.

Laliene's suite was down the hall from his; Denvin was on a different floor. That struck him as odd. He had assumed they were lovers and would be sharing accommodations. But, he reflected, it was always risky to assume things like that.

Thimiroi spent an hour transforming his rooms into a more familiar and congenial environment. From his suitcase he drew carpeting and draperies and coverlets of his own time, all of them supple with life and magic, to replace the harsh, flat, dead ones that they seemed to prefer here.

He pulled out the three little tripod tables of fine, intricately worked Sipulva marquetry that went with him everywhere: he would read at the golden one, sip his euphoriac at the copper-hued one, write his poetry at the one that was woven in scarlet and amber. He hung an esthetikon on the wall opposite the window and set it going, filling the room with warm, throbbing color. He set a music sphere on the dresser. To provide some variation in psychological tonality he activated a little subsonic that he had carried with him, adjusting it to travel through the entire spectrum of positive moods over a twenty-four hour span, from *anticipation* through *excitation* to *culmination* in imperceptible gradations. Then he stood back, surveying the results, and nodded. That would do for now. The room had been made amiable; the room was *civilized* now. He could bring out other things later. The suitcase was infinitely capacious. All it was, after all, was a pipeline to his own era. At the far end they would put anything in it that he might requisition.

Now at last he could begin to explore the city.

That evening they were supposed to go to a concert. Denvin had arranged it; Denvin was going to take care of all the cultural events. The legendary young violinist Sandra di Santis was playing, in what would turn out to be her final performance, though of course no one of this era could know that yet. But that was hours away. It was still only early afternoon. He would go out—he would savor the sights, the sounds, the smells of this place—

He felt just a moment of hesitation.

But why? Why? He had wandered by himself, unafraid, through the trash-strewn alleys of medieval Canterbury, though he knew that cutthroats and roisterers lurked everywhere. He had scrambled alone across the steep gullied cliffs of Capri, looking down without fear at the blue rock-rimmed Mediterranean, far below, into which a single misstep could plunge him. What was there to be cautious about here? The noisy cars racing so swiftly through the streets, perhaps. But surely a little caution and common sense would keep him from harm. If Lutheena had been out by herself, why not he? But still—still, that nagging uneasiness—

Thimiroi shrugged and left his room, and made his way down the hall to the elevator, and descended to the lobby.

At every stage of his departure wave upon wave of unsettling strangeness assailed him. The simplest act was a challenge. He had to call upon the resources of his technology implant in order to operate the lock of his room door, to summon the elevator, to tell it to take him to the lobby. But he met each of these minor mysteries in turn with a growing sense of accomplishment. By the time he reached the lobby he was moving boldly and confidently, feeling almost at home in this strange land, this unfamiliar country, that was the past.

The lobby, which Thimiroi had seen only briefly when he had arrived, was a somber, cavernous place, intricately divided into any number of smaller open chambers. He studied, as he walked calmly through it toward the brightness at the far end, the paintings, the furnishings, the things on display. Everything had that odd stiffness of form and flatness of texture that seemed to be the rule in this era: nothing appeared to have any inner life or movement. Was that how they had really liked it to be? Or was this curious deadness merely a function of the limitations of their materials? Probably some of each, Thimiroi decided. These were an artful, sophisticated folk. Of course, he thought, they had not had the advantage of many of our modern materials and devices. All the same, they would not have made everything so drab unless their esthetic saw beauty in the drabness. He would have to examine that possibility more deeply as this month went along, studying everything with an artist's shrewd and sympathetic eye, not interested in finding fault, only in understanding.

People were standing about here and there in the lobby, mainly in twos and threes, talking quietly. They paid no attention to him. Most of them, he noticed, had fair skin much like his own. A few, Thimiroi noticed, were black-skinned like the taxi driver, but others had skin of still another unusual tone, a kind of pale olive or light yellow, and their features too were unusual, very delicate, with an odd tilt to the eyes.

Once again he wondered if this skin-toning might be some sort of cosmetic alteration: but no, no, this time he queried his implant and it told him that in fact in this era there had been several different races of humanity, varying widely in physical appearance.

How lovely, Thimiroi thought. How sad for us that we are all so much alike. Another point for further research: had these black and yellow people, and the other unusual races, been swept away by the great calamity, or was it rather that all mankind had tended toward a uniformity of traits as the centuries went by? Again, perhaps, some of each. Whatever the reason, it was a cause for regret.

He reached the grand doorway that led to the street. A woman said, entering the hotel just as he was leaving it, "How I hate going indoors in weather like this!"

Her companion laughed. "Who doesn't? Can it last much longer, I wonder?"

Thimiroi stepped past them, into the splendor of the soft golden sunlight.

The air was miraculous: amazingly transparent, clear

with a limpidity almost beyond belief, despite all the astonishing impurities that Thimiroi knew were routinely poured into it by the unthinking people of this era. It was as though for the long blessed moment of this one last magnificent May all the ordinary rules of nature had been suspended, and the atmosphere had become invulnerable to harm. Beyond that sublime zone of clarity rose the blue shield of the sky, pulsingly brilliant; and from its throne high in the distance the sun sent forth a tranquil, steady radiance that was like no sunlight Thimiroi had ever seen. Small wonder that those who had planned the tour had chosen this time and this place to be the epitome of springtime, he thought. There might never have been such beauty before. There might never be again.

He turned to his left and began to walk, hardly knowing or caring where he might be going.

From all sides came powerful sensory signals: the honking of horns, the sharp spicy scent of something cooking nearby, the subtler fragrance of the light breeze. Great gray buildings soared far into the dazzling sky. Billboards and posters blared their messages in twenty colors. The impact was immediate and profound. Thimiroi beheld everything in wonder and joy.

What richness! What complexity!

And yet there was a paradox here. What he took to be complexity in this street scene was really only a studied lack of harmony. As it had in the hotel lobby, a second glance revealed the true essence of this world's vocabulary of design: a curious rough-hewn plainness, even a severity, that made clear to him how far in the past he actually was. The extraordinary May light seemed to dance along the rooftops, giving the buildings an intricacy of texture they did not in fact possess. These ancient styles were fundamentally simple and harsh, and could all too easily be taken to be primitive and crude. In Thimiroi's own era every surface vibrated in at least half a dozen different ways, throbbing and rippling and pulsating and shimmering and gleaming and quivering. Here everything was flat, stolid, static. The strangeness of that seemed oppressive at first encounter; but now, as he ventured deeper and deeper into this unfamiliar world, Thimiroi came to see the underlying majesty of it. What he had mistaken for deadness was in fact strength. The people of this era were survivors: they had come through monstrous wars, tremendous technological change, immense social upheaval. Those who had outlasted the brutal tests of this taxing century were rugged, hearty, deeply optimistic. Their style of building and decoration showed that plainly. Nothing quivering and shimmery for them—oh, no! Great solid slabs of buildings, constructed out of simple, hard, unadorned materials that looked you straight in the eye—that was the way of things, here in the late twentieth century, in this time of assurance and robust faith in even better things to come.

Of course, Thimiroi thought, there was savage irony in that, considering what actually *was* to come. For a moment he was swept by deep and shattering compassion that brought him almost to tears. But he forced himself to fight the emotion back. Would Denvin weep for these people? Would Omerie, would Cenbe, would Kadro? The past is a sealed book, Thimiroi told himself forcefully. What has happened has happened. The losses are totaled, the debits are irretrievable. We have come here to experience the joys of jarring contrasts, as Denvin might say, not to cry over spilled milk.

He crossed the street. The next block was one of older-looking single-family houses, each set apart in a little garden plot where bright flowers bloomed and the leaves of the trees were just beginning to unfold under springtime's first warmth.

There was music coming from an upstairs window three houses from the corner. He paused to listen.

It was simple straightforward stuff, monochromatic in tone. The instrument, he supposed, was the piano, the one that made its sound by the action of little mallets striking strings stretched across a resonating board. The melodic line was both sinuous and stark, carried in the treble with a little commentary in the bass: music a child could play. Perhaps a child was indeed playing. The simplicity of it made him smile. It was quaint stuff, charming but naïve. He began to move onward.

And yet—yet—

Suddenly he felt himself caught and transfixed by a simple, magical turn of phrase that came creeping almost surreptitiously out of the bass line. It held him. Unexpectedly, it touched him. He remained still, unable to go on, listening while the lovely phrase fled, waiting in hope for its return. Yes, there it was again! And as it came and went, it cast startling illumination over the entire musical pattern. He saw its beauty and its artfully hidden depth now, and he grew angry at himself for having responded at first in that patronizing way, that snide, condescending Denvin-like way. Quaint? Naïve? Hardly. Simple, yes: this music achieved its effects with a minimum of means. But what was naïve about that? Was a quartet for strings naïve, because it did not make use of the resources of a full symphony orchestra? There was something about this music—its directness, its freedom—that the composers of his own time might well want to study, might even look upon with a certain degree of envy. For all their colossal technical resources, could the best of them—yes, even Cenbe—manage to equal the quiet force, Thimiroi wondered, of that easy, graceful little tune?

He stood listening until the music rolled to a gentle climax and a pleasant resolution and came to a halt. Its sudden absence brought him up short. He looked up imploringly at the open window. Play it again, he begged silently. Play it again! But there was no more music.

Impulsively he burst into applause, thinking that that might encourage an encore.

A woman's face appeared at the window. Thimiroi was aware of pale skin, long straight golden hair, warm blue-green eyes. "Very lovely," he called. "Thank you. Thank you very much."

She looked at him in apparent surprise, perhaps frowning a little. Then the frown was replaced for a moment by a quick amiable smile of pleasure; and then, just as quickly, she was gone. Thimiroi remained before her house a while longer, still hoping the music would begin again. But there was no more of it.

He returned to the hotel an hour later, dazzled, awed, weary, his mind full of wonders great and small. Just as he entered his suite, a small machine on the table beside the bed set up a curious insistent tinkling sound: the telephone, it was, so his technology implant informed him. He picked up the receiver.

"This is Thimiroi."

"Back at last." The voice was Laliene's. "Was it an interesting walk?"

"One revelation after another. Certainly this year is going to be the high point of our trip."

Laliene laughed lazily. "Oh, darling Thimiroi, didn't you

say the same thing when we came to Canterbury? And when we had the audience with the emperor on Capri?"

He did not reply.

"Anyway," she continued. "We're all going to gather in my suite before we go to the concert. Would you like to come? I've brewed a little tea, of course."

"Of course," he said. "I'll be right there."

She, too, had redone her rooms in the style of their own period. Instead of the ponderous hotel bed she had installed a floater, and in the sitting room now was a set of elegant turquoise slopes mounted around a depth baffle, so that one had the illusion of looking down into a long curving valley of ravishing beauty. Her choice of simso screens was, as usual, superb: wondrous dizzying vistas opened to infinity on every wall. Laliene herself looked sumptuous in a brilliant robe of woven silver mesh and a pair of scarlet gliders.

What surprised him was that no one else was there.

"Oh," she said lightly, "they'll all be coming along soon. We can get a head start."

She selected one of the lovely little cups on the table beside her, and offered it to him. And as he took it from her he felt a sudden transformation of the space between them, an intensification, an amplification. Without warning, Laliene was turning up the psychic voltage.

Her face was flushed, her eyes were glistening. The rich gray of them had deepened almost to purple. There was no mistaking the look. He had seen it many times before: Laliene in her best flirtatious mode, verging on the frankly seductive. Here they were, a man, a woman, well known to one another, together in a hotel room in a strange and distant city, about to enjoy a friendly sip or two of euphoriac tea—well, of course, Laliene could be expected to put on her most inviting manner, if only for the sport of it. But something else was going on here besides mere playful flirtation, Thimiroi realized. There was an odd eagerness to the set of her jaw, a peculiar quirk in the corners of her mouth. As though she *cared,* he thought. As though she were *serious.*

What was this? Was she trying to change the rules of the game?

Deftly she turned a music sphere on without looking away from him. Some barely audible melodikia came stealing like faint azure vapor into the air, and very gradually began to rise and throb. One of Cenbe's songs, he wondered? No. No, too voluptuous for Cenbe: more like Palivandrin's work, or Athaea's. He sipped his euphoriac. The sweet coiling fumes crept sinuously about him. Laliene stood close beside him, making it seem almost as if the music were coming from her and not the sphere. Thimiroi met her languid invitation with a practiced courteous smile, one which acknowledged her beauty, her grace, the intimacy of the moment, the prospect of delights to come, while neither accepting nor rejecting anything that was being proposed.

Of course they could do nothing now. At any moment the others would come trooping in.

But he wondered where this unexpected offer was meant to lead. He could, of course, put down the cup, draw her close: a kiss, a quick caress, an understanding swiftly arrived at, yes. But that did not seem to be quite what she was after, or at least that was not all she was after. And was the offer, he asked himself, all that unexpected? Thimiroi realized abruptly that there was no reason why he should be as surprised by this as he was. As he cast his mind back over the earlier weeks of their journey across time, he came to see that in fact Laliene had been moving steadily toward him since the beginning—in Canterbury, in Capri, a touch of the hand here, a quick private smile there, a quip, a glance. Her defending him so earnestly against Denvin's snobbery and Denvin's sarcasm, just after they had arrived here: what was that, if not the groundwork for some subtle treaty that was to be established subsequently between them? But why? Why? Such romance as could ever have existed for Laliene and him had come and gone long, long ago. Now they were merely friends. Perhaps he was mistaking the nature of this transaction. But no . . . no. There was no mistake.

Sparring for time, he said, keeping his tone and style carefully neutral, "You should come walking with me tomorrow. I saw marvelous things just a few blocks from here."

"I'd love to, Thimiroi. I want you to show me everything you've discovered."

"Yes. Yes, of course, Laliene."

But as he said it, he felt a deep stab of confusion. Everything? There was the house where that music had been playing. The open window, the simple, haunting melody. And the woman's face, then: the golden hair, the pale skin, the blue-green eyes. Thinking of her, thinking of the music she had played, Thimiroi found himself stirred by powerful and inexplicable forces that made him want to seize Laliene's music sphere and hurl it, and with it the subtle melodikia that it was playing, into the street. How smug that music sounded to him now, how overcivilized, how empty! And Laliene herself, so perfect in her beauty, the crimson hair, the flawless features, the sleek slender body—she was like some finely crafted statue, some life-sized doll: there was no reality to her, no essence of humanity. That woman in the window had shown more vital force in just her quick little half-frown and half-smile than Laliene displayed in all her repertoire of artful movements and expressions.

He stared at her, astounded, shaken.

She seemed shaken too. "Are you all right, Thimiroi?" she whispered.

"A little—tired, perhaps," he said huskily. "Stretched myself farther today than I really knew."

Laliene nodded toward the cup. "The tea will heal you."

"Yes. Yes."

He sipped. There was a knocking at the door. Laliene smiled, excused herself, opened it.

Denvin was there, and others behind him.

"Lutheena—Hollia—Hara—come in, come in, come in all of you! Omerie, how good to see you—Kleph, Klia—dear Klia—come in, everyone! How wonderful, how wonderful! I have the tea all ready and waiting for you!"

The concert that night was an extraordinary experience. Every moment, every note, seemed freighted with unforgettable meaning. Perhaps it was the poignancy of knowing that the beautiful young violinist who played so brilliantly had only a few weeks left to live, and that this grand and sumptuous concert hall itself was soon to be a smoking ruin. Perhaps it was the tiny magical phrase he had heard while listening in the street, which had somehow sensitized him to the fine secret graces of this seemingly simple twentieth-century music. Perhaps it was only the euphoriac they had had in Laliene's room before setting out. Whatever it was, it evoked a mood of unusual, even unique, attentiveness in Thimiroi, and as the minutes went by he knew that this evening at the concert hall would surely resonate joyously in his soul forever after.

That mood was jarred and shaken and irrevocably shattered at intermission, when he was compelled to stand with his stunningly dressed companions in the vestibule and listen to their brittle chirping chatter. How empty they all seemed, how foolish! Omerie stalking around in his most virile and commanding mode, like some sort of peacock, and imperious Lutheena matching him swagger for swagger, and Klia looking on complacently, and Kleph even more complacent, mysteriously lost in mists like some child who has found a packet of narcotic candies. And then of course there was the awesome Miss Hollia, who seemed older than the Pyramids, glowering at Omerie in unconcealed malevolence even while she complimented him on his mastery of twentieth-century costuming, and Hollia's pretty little playmate Hara as usual saying scarcely anything, but lending his support to his owner by glaring at Omerie also—and Denvin, chiming in with his sardonic, too-too-special insights from time to time—

What a wearying crew, Thimiroi thought. These precious connoisseurs of history, these tireless voyagers of the eons. His head began to ache. He stepped away from them and began to walk back toward the auditorium. For the first time he noticed how the other members of the audience were staring at the little group. Wondering what country they came from, no doubt, and how rich they might be. Such perfection of dress, such precision of movement, such elegance of speech—foreign, obviously foreign, but mystifyingly so, for they seemed to belong to no recognizable nationality, and spoke with no recognizable accent. Thimiroi smiled wearily. "Do you want to know the truth about us?" he imagined himself crying. "We are visitors, yes. Tourists from a far country. But where we live is not only beyond your reach, it is beyond even your imaginations. What would you say, if I revealed to you that we are natives of the year—"

"Bored with the concert?" Laliene asked. She had come up quietly beside him, without his noticing it.

"Quite the contrary."

"Bored with us, then." It was not a question.

Thimiroi shrugged. "The intermission's an unfortunate interruption. I wish the music hadn't stopped."

"The music always stops," she said, and laughed her throatiest, smokiest laugh.

He studied her. She was still offering herself to him, with her eyes, her smile, her slightly sidewise stance. Thimiroi felt almost guilty for his willful failure to accept the gambit. Was he infuriating her? Was he wounding her?

But I do not want her, he told himself.

Once again, as in her room that afternoon while they were sipping euphoriac together, he was struck by the puzzling distaste and even anger that the perfection of her beauty aroused in him. Why this violent reaction? He had always lived in a world of perfect people. He had been accustomed all his life to Laliene's sort of flawlessness. There was no need for anyone to have blemishes of face or form any more. One took that sort of thing for granted; everyone did. Why should it trouble him now? What strange restlessness was this century kindling in his soul?

Thimiroi saw the strain, the tension, the barely suppressed impatience in Laliene's expression, and for a moment he was so abashed by the distress he knew he must be causing her that he came close to inviting her to join him in his suite after the concert. But he could not bring himself to do it. The moment passed; the tension slackened; Laliene made an elegant recovery, smiling and slipping her arm through his to lead him back to their seats, and he moved gratefully into a round of banter with her, and with Kleph, who drifted back up the aisle with them. But the magic and wonder of the concert were forever lost. In the second half he sat in a leaden slump, barely listening, unable to find the patterns that made the music comprehensible.

That night Thimiroi slept alone, and slept badly. After some hours of wakefulness he had to have recourse to one of his drugs. And even that brought him only partial solace, for with sleep came dark dreams of a singularly ominous and disruptive kind, full of hot furious blasts of anguish and panic, and he felt too drained of energy to get up again and rummage through his kit for the drug that banishes dreams. Morning was a long time in coming.

Over the next few days Thimiroi kept mostly to himself. He suspected that his fellow voyagers were talking about him—that they were worried about him—but he shied away from any sort of contact with them. The mere sight of them was something that caused him a perceptible pain, almost like the closing of a clamp about his heart. He longed to recapture that delicious openness to experience, that wonderful vulnerability, that he had felt when he had first arrived here, and he knew that so long as he was with any of them he would never be able to attain it.

By withdrawing from them in this morose way, he realized, he was missing some of the pleasures of the visit. The others were quite serious, as serious as such frivolous people ever could be, about the late twentieth century, and they spent each day moving busily about the city, taking advantage of its wealth of cultural opportunities—many of them obscure even to the natives of the era themselves. Kleph, whose specialty was Golconda studies, put together a small festival of the films of that great actor, and for two days they all, even Hollia, scurried around town seeing him at work in actual original prints. Omerie discovered, and proudly displayed, a first edition of Martin Drexel's *Lyrical Journeys*. "It cost me next to nothing," Omerie declared in vast satisfaction. "These people don't have the slightest idea of what Drexel achieved." A day or two later, Klia organized a river trip to the birthplace of David Courtney, a short way north of the city. Courtney would not be born, of course, for another seventy years, but his birthplace already existed, and who could resist making the pilgrimage? Thimiroi resisted. "Come with us," Laliene pleaded, with a curious urgency in her voice that he had never heard in it before. "This is one trip you really must not miss." He told her, calmly at first and then more forcefully, as she continued to press the point, that he had no desire to go. She looked at him in a stricken way, as though he had slapped her; but at that point she yielded. The others went on the river journey and he stayed behind, drifting through the streets of the downtown section without purpose, without goal.

Troubled as he was, he found excitement nevertheless in the things he saw on his solitary walks. The vigor and intensity of this era struck resonances in his own unfashionably robust spirit. The noise here, the smells, the colors, the expansive, confident air of the people, who obviously knew that they were living at one of history's great peak periods—everything startled and stimulated him in a way that Roman Capri and Chaucerian Canterbury had not been able to do.

Those older places and times had been too remote in spirit and essence from his native epoch to be truly comprehensible: they were interesting the way a visit to an alien planet can be interesting, but they had not moved him as this era moved him. Possibly the knowledge of impending doom that he had here had something to do with that. But there was something else. Thimiroi sensed, as he had not in any way sensed during the earlier stops, that he might actually be able to *live* in this era, and feel at home in it, and be happy here. For much of his life he had felt somehow out of place in his own world, unable all too often to come to terms with the seamlessness of everything, the impeccability of that immaculate era. Now he thought he understood why. As he wandered the streets of this booming, brawling, far-from-perfect city—taking joy in its curious mixture of earthy marvelous accomplishment and mysterious indifference to its own shortcomings, and finding himself curiously at ease in it—he began to perceive himself as a man of the late twentieth century who by some bewildering prank of the gods had been born long after his own proper time. And with that perception came a kind of calmness in the face of the storm that was to come.

Toward the end of the first week—it was the day when the others made their pilgrimage up the river to David Courtney's birthplace—Thimiroi encountered the golden-haired woman who had been playing the piano in the house down the block from the hotel. He caught sight of her downtown while he was crossing a plaza paved with pink cobblestones, which linked twin black towers of almost unthinkable height and mass near the river embankment.

Though he had only seen her for a moment, that one other time, and that time only her face and throat at the window, he had no doubt that it was she. Her blue-green eyes and long straight shining hair were unmistakable. She was fairly tall and very slender, with a tall woman's quick way of walking, ankles close together, shoulders slightly hunched forward. Thimiroi supposed that she was about thirty, or perhaps forty at most. She was young, at any rate, but not *very* young. He had no clear idea of how quickly people aged in this era. The first mild signs of aging seemed visible on her. In his own time that would mean nothing—there, a woman who looked like this might be anywhere between fifty and a hundred and fifty—but he knew that here they had no significant way of reversing the effects of time, and what she showed was almost certainly an indication that she had left her girlhood behind by some years but had not yet gone very far into the middle of the journey.

"Pardon me," he said, a little to his own surprise, as she came toward him.

She peered blankly at him. "Yes?"

Thimiroi offered her a disarming smile. "I'm a visitor here. Staying at the Montgomery House."

The mention of the famous hotel—and, perhaps, his gentle manner and the quality of his clothing—seemed to ease whatever apprehensions she might be feeling. She paused, looking at him questioningly.

He said, "You live near there, don't you? A few days ago, when I was out for a walk—it was my first day here—I heard you playing the piano. I'm sure it was you. I applauded when you stopped, and you looked out the window at me. I think you must have seen me. You frowned, and then you smiled."

She frowned now, just a quick flicker of confusion; and then again she smiled.

"Just like that, yes," Thimiroi said. "Do you mind if we talk? Are you in a hurry?"

"Not really," she said, and he sensed something troubled behind the words.

"Is there some place near here where we could have a

drink? Or lunch, perhaps?" That was what they called the meal they ate at this time of day, he was certain. Lunch. People of this era met often for lunch, as a social thing. He did not think it was too late in the day to be offering her lunch.

"Well, there's the River Cafe," she said. "That's just two or three blocks. I suppose we—" She broke off. "You know, I never ever do anything like this. Let myself get picked up in the street, I mean."

"Picked up? I do not understand."

"What don't you understand?"

"The phrase," Thimiroi said. "Pick up? To lift? Am I lifting you?"

She laughed and said, "Are you foreign?"

"Oh, yes. Very foreign."

"I thought your way of speaking was a little strange. So precise—every syllable perfectly shaped. No one really speaks English that way. Except computers, of course. You aren't a computer, are you?"

"Hardly."

"Good. I would never allow myself to be picked up by a computer in First National Plaza. Or anyplace else, as a matter of fact. Are you still interested in going to the River Cafe?"

"Of course."

She was playful now. "We can't do this anonymously, though. It's too sordid. My name's Christine Rawlins."

"And I am called Thimiroi."

"Timmery?"

"Thimiroi," he said.

"Thim-i-roi," she repeated, imitating his precision. "A very unusual name, I'd say. I've never met anyone named Thimiroi before. What country are you from, may I ask?"

"You would not know it. A very small one, very far away."

"Iran?"

"Farther away than that."

"A lot of people who came here from Iran prefer not to admit that that's where they're from."

"I am not from Iran, I assure you."

"But you won't tell me where?"

"You would not know it," he said again.

Her eyes twinkled. "Oh, you *are* from Iran! You're a spy, aren't you? I see the whole thing: they're getting ready to have a new revolution, there's another Ayatollah on his way from his hiding place in Beirut, and you're here to transfer Iranian assets out of this country before—" She broke off, looking sheepish. "I'm sorry. I'm just being weird. Have I offended you?"

"Not at all."

"You don't have to tell me where you're from if you don't want to."

"I am from Stiinowain," he said, astounded at his own daring in actually uttering the forbidden name.

She tried to repeat the name, but was unable to manage the soft glide of the first syllable.

"You're right," she said. "I don't know anything about it at all. But you'll tell me all about it, won't you?"

"Perhaps," he said.

The River Cafe was a glossy bubble of pink marble and black glass cantilevered out over the embankment, with a semicircular open-air dining area, paved with shining flagstones, that jutted even farther, so that it seemed suspended almost in mid-river. They were lucky enough to find one vacant table that was right at the cafe's outermost edge, looking down on the swift blue river-flow. "Ordinarily the outdoor section doesn't open until the middle of June," Christine told him. "But this year it's been so warm and dry that they opened it a month early. We've been breaking records every day. There's never been a May like this, that's what they're all saying. Just one long run of fabulous weather day after day after day."

"It's been extraordinary, yes."

"What is May like in Stiin—in your country?" she asked.

"Very much like this. As a matter of fact, it is rather like this all the year round."

"Really? How wonderful that must be!"

It must have seemed like boasting to her. He regretted that. "No," he said. "We take our mild climate for granted and the succession of beautiful days means nothing to us. It is better this way, sudden glory rising out of contrast, the darkness of winter giving way to the splendor of spring. The warm sunny days coming upon you like—like the coming of grace, shall I say?—like—" He smiled. "Like that heavenly little theme that came suddenly out of the music you were playing, transforming something simple and ordinary into something unforgettable. Do you know what I mean?"

"Yes," she said. "I think I do."

He began to hum the melody. Her eyes sparkled, and she nodded and grinned warmly, and after a moment or two she started humming along with him. He felt a tightness at his throat, warmth along his back and shoulders, a throbbing in his chest. All the symptoms of a rush of strong emotion. Very strange to him, very primitive, very exciting, very pleasing.

People at other tables turned. They seemed to notice something also. Thimiroi saw them smiling at the two of them with that unmistakable proprietorial smile that strangers will offer to young lovers in the springtime. Christine must have seen those smiles too, for color came to her face, and for a moment she looked away from him as though embarrassed.

"Tell me about yourself," he said.

"We should order first. Are you familiar with our foods? A salad might be nice on a beautiful warm day like this—and then perhaps the cold salmon plate, or—" She stopped abruptly. "Is something wrong?"

Thimiroi struggled to fight back nausea. "Not a salad, no, please. It is—not good for me. And in my country we do not eat fish of any sort, not ever."

"Forgive me."

"But how could you have known?"

"Even so—you looked so distressed—"

"Not really. It was only a moment's uneasiness." He scanned the menu desperately. Nothing on it made sense to him. At home, he would only have to touch the screen beside anything that seemed to be of interest, and he would get a quick flavor-analog appercept to guide his choice. But that was at home. Here he had been taking most of his meals in his room, meals prepared many centuries away by his own autochef and sent to him down the time conduit. On those few occasions when he ate in the hotel dining room with his fellow travelers, he relied on Kadro to choose his food for him. Now, plunging ahead blindly, he selected something called carpaccio for his starter, and vichyssoise to follow.

"Are you sure you don't want anything warm?" Christine asked gently.

"Oh, I think not, not on such a mild day," Thimiroi said casually. He had no idea what he had ordered; but he was determined not to seem utterly ignorant of her era.

The carpaccio, though, turned out to be not merely cold but raw: red raw meat, very thinly sliced, in a light sauce. He stared at it in amazement. His whole body recoiled at the thought of eating raw meat. His bones themselves protested. He saw Christine staring at him, and wondered how much of his horror his expression was revealing to her. But there was no helping it: he slipped his fork under one of the paper-thin slices and conveyed it to his mouth. To his amazement it was delicious. Forgetting all breeding, he ate the rest without pausing once, while she watched in what seemed like a mixture of surprise and amusement.

"You liked that, didn't you?" she said.

"Carpaccio has always been one of my favorites," he told her shamelessly.

Vichyssoise turned out to be a cold dish too, a thick white soup, presumably made from some vegetable. It seemed harmless and proved to be quite tasty. Christine had ordered the salmon, and he tried not to peer at her plate, or to imagine what it must be like to put chunks of sea-creatures in one's mouth, while she ate.

"You promised to tell me something about yourself," he reminded her.

She looked uneasy. "It's not a very interesting story, I'm afraid."

"But you must tell me a little of it. Are you a musician by profession? Surely you are. Do you perform in the concert hall?"

Her look of discomfort deepened. "I know you don't mean to be cruel, but—"

"Cruel? Of course not. But when I was listening there outside the window I could feel the great gift that you have."

"Please."

"I don't understand."

"No, you don't, do you?" she said gently. "You weren't trying to be funny, or to hurt me. But I'm not any sort of gifted pianist, Thimiroi. Believe me. I'm just a reasonably good amateur. Maybe when I was ten years old I dreamed of having a concert career some day, but I came to my senses a long time ago."

"You are too modest."

"No. No. I know what I am. And what the real thing is like. Even *they* don't have an easy time of it. You can't believe how many concert-quality pianists my age there are in this country. With so many genuine geniuses out there, there's no hope at all for a decent third-rater like me."

He shook his head in amazement, remembering the magical sounds that had come from her window. "Third-rater!"

"I don't have any illusions about that," she said. "I'm the sort of pianist who winds up giving piano lessons, not playing in Carnegie Hall. I have a couple of pupils. They come and go. It's not possible to earn a living that way. And the job that I did have, with an export-import firm—well, they say that this is the most prosperous time this country has seen in the past forty years, but somehow I managed to get laid off last week anyway. That's why I'm downtown today—another job interview. You see? Just an ordinary woman, an ordinary life, ordinary problems—"

"There is nothing ordinary about you," said Thimiroi fervently. "Not to me! To me you are altogether extraordinary, Christine!" She seemed almost about to weep as he said that. Compassion and tenderness overwhelmed him, and he reached out to take her hand in his, to comfort her, to reassure her. Her eyes widened and she pulled back instantly, catching her breath sharply, as though he had tried to stab her with his fork.

Thimiroi looked at her sadly. The quickness and vehemence of her reaction mystified him.

"That was wrong?" he said. "To want to touch your hand?"

Awkwardly Christine said, "You surprised me, that's all. I'm sorry. I didn't mean—it was rude of me, actually—oh, Thimiroi, I can't explain—it was just automatic, a kind of dumb reflex—"

Puzzled, he turned his hand over several times, examining it, searching for something about it that might have frightened or repelled her. He saw nothing. It was simply a hand. After a moment she took it lightly with her own, and held it.

He said, "You have a husband? Is that why I should not have done that?"

"I'm not married, no." She glanced away from him, but did not release his hand. "I'm not even—involved. Not currently." Her fingers were lightly stroking his wrist. "I have to confess something," she said, after a moment. "I saw you at Symphony Hall last week. The De Santis concert."

"You did?"

"In the lobby. With your—friends. I watched you all, wondering who you were. There was a kind of glow about the whole group of you. The women were all so beautiful, every one of them. Immaculate. Perfect. Like movie stars, they were."

"They are nothing compared with you."

"Please. Don't say any more things like that. I don't like to be flattered, Thimiroi. Not only does it make me uncomfortable but it simply isn't effective with me. Whatever else I am, I'm a realistic woman. Especially about myself."

"And I am a truthful man. What I tell you is what I feel, Christine." Her hand tightened on his wrist at that. He said, "So you knew who I was, when I approached you in the plaza up above just now."

"Yes," she murmured.

"But pretended you did not."

"I was frightened."

"I am not frightening, Christine."

"Not frightened of you. Of me. When I saw you that first day, standing outside my house—I felt—I don't know, I felt something strange, just looking at you. Felt that I had seen you before somewhere, that I had known you very well in some other life, perhaps, that—oh, Thimiroi, I'm not making any sense, am I? But I knew you had been *important* to me at some other time. Or *would* be important. It's crazy, isn't it? And I don't have any room in my life for craziness. I'm just trying to hold my own, don't you see? Trying to maintain, trying to hang on and not get swept under. In these wonderful prosperous times, I'm all alone, Thimiroi, I'm not sure where I'm heading, what's going to come next for me. Everything seems so uncertain. And so I don't want any extra uncertainties in my life."

"I will not bring you uncertainty," he said.

She stared and said nothing. Her hand still touched his.

"If you are finished with your food," he said, "perhaps you would like to come back to the hotel with me."

There was a long tense silence. After a time she drew her hand away from him and knotted her fingers together, and sat very still, her expression indecipherable.

"You think it was inappropriate of me to have extended such an invitation," he said finally.

"No. Not really."

"I want only to be your friend."

"Yes. I know that."

"And I thought, since you live so close to the hotel, I

could offer you some refreshment, and show you some treasures of my own country that I have brought with me. I meant nothing more than that, Christine. Please. Believe me."

She seemed to shed some of her tension. "I'd love to stop off at your hotel with you for a little while," she said.

He had no doubt at all that it was much too soon for them to become lovers. Not only was he completely unskilled in this era's sociosexual rituals and procedures, so that it was probably almost impossible for him to avoid offending or displeasing her by this or that unintentional violation of the accepted courtship customs of her society, but also at this point he was still much too uncertain of the accuracy of his insight into her own nature. Once he knew her better, perhaps he would be less likely to go about things incorrectly, particularly since she already gave him the benefit of many doubts because she knew he came from some distant land.

There was also the not inconsiderable point to consider that it was a profound violation of the rules of The Travel to enter into any kind of emotional or physical involvement with a native of a past era.

That, somehow, seemed secondary to Thimiroi just now. He knew all about the importance of avoiding distortion or contamination of the time-line; they drilled it into you endlessly before you ever started to Travel. But suddenly such issues seemed unreal and abstract to him. What mattered was what he felt: the surge of delight, eagerness, passion, that ran through him when he turned to look at this woman of a far-off time. All his life he had been a stranger among his own people, a prisoner within his own skin; now, here, at last, it seemed to him that he had a chance of breaking through the net of brittle conventions that for so long had bound his spirit, and touching, at last, the soul of another human being. He had read about love, of course—who had not?—but here, he thought, he might actually experience it. Was that a reckless ambition? Well, then, he would be reckless. The alternative was to condemn himself to a lifetime of bitter regret.

Therefore he schooled himself to patience. He dared not be too hasty, for fear of ruining everything.

Christine appeared astounded by what she saw in his rooms. She wandered through them like a child in a wonderland, hardly breathing, pausing here and there to look, to reach out hesitantly, to hold her hand above this or that miraculous object as though afraid actually to touch it but eager to experience its texture.

"You brought all this from your own country?" she asked. "You must have had fifty suitcases!"

"We get homesick very easily. We wish to have our familiar things about us."

"The way a sultan would travel. A pasha." Her eyes were shining with awe. "These little tables—I've never seen anything like them. I try to follow the weave, but the pattern won't stand still. It keeps sliding around its own corners."

"The woodworkers of Sipulva are extremely ingenious," Thimiroi said.

"Sipulva? Is that a city in your country?"

"A place nearby," he said. "You may touch them if you wish."

She caressed the intricately carved surfaces, fingers tracing the weave as it went through its incomprehensible convolutions. Thimiroi, smiling, turned the music sphere on—one of Mirtin's melodikias began to come from it, a shimmering crystalline piece—and set about brewing some tea. Christine drifted onward, examining the draperies, the glistening carpets, the pulsating esthetikon that was sending waves of color through the room, the simso screens with their shifting views of unknown worlds. She was altogether enthralled. It would certainly be easy enough to seduce her now, Thimiroi realized. A little sensuous music, a few sips of euphoriac, perhaps some surreptitious adjustments of the little subsonic so that it sent forth heightened tonalities of *anticipation* and *excitation*—yes, that was all that it would take, he knew. But easy conquest was not what he wanted. He did not intend to pass through her soul like a frivolous tourist drifting through a museum in search of an hour's superficial diversion.

One cup of tea for each of them, then, and no more. Some music, some quick demonstrations of a few of the little wonders that filled his rooms. A light kiss, finally, and then one that was more intense: but a quick restoration, afterward, of the barriers between them. Christine seemed no more willing to breach those barriers today than he was. Thimiroi was relieved at that, and pleased. They seemed to understand each other already.

"I'll walk you home," he said, when they plainly had reached the time when she must either leave or stay much longer.

"You needn't. It's just down the street." Her hand lingered in his. Her touch was warm, her skin faintly moist, pleasantly so. "You'll call me? Here's my number." She gave him a smooth little yellow card. "We could have dinner, perhaps. Or a concert—whatever you'd like to see—"

"Yes. Yes, I'll call you."

"You'll be here at least a few more days, won't you?"

"Until the end of the month."

She nodded. He saw the momentary darkening of her expression, and guessed at the inward calculations: reckoning the number of days remaining to his visit, the possibilities that those days might hold, the rashness of embarking on anything that would surely not extend beyond the last day of May. Thimiroi had already made the same calculations himself, though tempered by information that she could not conceivably have, information which made everything inconceivably more precarious. After the smallest of pauses she said, "That's plenty of time, isn't it? But call me soon, Thimiroi. Will you? Will you?"

A little while later there was a light knocking at the door, and Thimiroi, hoping with a startling rush of eagerness that Christine had found some pretext for returning, opened it to find Laliene. She looked weary. The perfection of her beauty was unmarred, of course, every shining strand of hair in its place, her tanned skin fresh and glistening. But beneath the radiant outer glow there was once again something drawn and tense and ragged about her, a subliminal atmosphere of strain, of fatigue, of devitalization, that was not at all typical of the Laliene he had known. This visit to the late twentieth century did not seem to be agreeing with her.

"May I come in?" she asked. He nodded and beckoned to her. "We've all just returned from the Courtney birthplace," she said. "You really should have gone with us, Thimiroi. You can feel the aura of the man everywhere in the place, even this early, so many years before he even existed." Taking a few steps into the room, Laliene paused, sniffed the air lightly, smiled. "Having a little tea by yourself just now, were you, Thimiroi?"

"Just a cup. It was a long quiet afternoon."

"Poor Thimiroi. Couldn't find anything at all interesting

to do? Then you certainly should have come with us." He saw her glance flicking quickly about, and felt pleased and relieved that he had taken the trouble to put the teacups away. It was in fact no business of Laliene's that he had had a guest in here this afternoon, but he did not want her, all the same, to know that he had.

"Can I brew a cup for you?" he asked.

"I think not. I'm so tired after our outing—it'll put me right to sleep, I would say." She turned toward him, giving him a direct inquisitorial stare that he found acutely discomforting. In a straightforward way that verged on bluntness she said, "I'm worried about you, you know, Thimiroi. Keeping off by yourself so much. The others are talking. You really should make an effort to join the group more often."

"Maybe I'm bored with the group, Laliene. With Denvin's snide little remarks, with Hollia's queenly airs, with Hara's mincing inanity, with Omerie's arrogance, with Klia's vacuity—"

"And with my presumptuousness?"

"You said that. Not I."

But it was true, he realized. She was crowding him constantly, forever edging into his psychic space, pressing herself upon him in a strange, almost incomprehensible way. It had been that way since the beginning of the trip: she never seemed to leave him alone. Her approach toward him was an odd mix of seductiveness, protectiveness, and—what?—inquisitiveness? She was like that strangest of antique phenomena, a jealous lover, almost. But jealous of what? Of whom? Surely not Christine. Christine had not so much as existed for him, except as a mysterious briefly glimpsed face in a window, until this afternoon, and Laliene had been behaving like this for many weeks. It made no sense. Even now, covertly snooping around his suite, all too obviously searching for some trace of the guest who had only a short while before been present here—what was she after?

He took two fresh cups from his cabinet. "If you don't mind, Laliene, I'll put up a little more tea for myself. And it would be no trouble to make some for you."

"I said I didn't want any, Thimiroi. I don't enjoy gulping the stuff down, you know, the way Kleph does."

"Kleph?"

"Certainly you know how heavily she indulges. She's euphoric more often than not these days."

Thimiroi shrugged. "I didn't realize that. I suppose Omerie can get on anyone's nerves. Even Kleph's."

Laliene studied him for a long moment. "You don't know about Kleph, then?" she asked finally. "No, I suppose you don't. Keeping to yourself this way, how would you?"

This was maddening. "What about Kleph?" he said, his voice growing tight.

"Perhaps you should fix some tea for me after all," Laliene said. "It's quite a nasty story. It'll be easier for me with a little euphoriac."

"Very well."

He busied himself over the tiny covered cups. In a short while the fragrant coiling steam began to rise through the fine crescent opening. His hands trembled, and he nearly swept the cups from the tray as he reached for them; but he recovered quickly and brought them to the table. They sipped the drug in silence. Watching her, Thimiroi was struck once more by the inhuman superfluity of Laliene's elegance. Laliene was much too perfect. How different from Christine, whose skin had minute unimportant blemishes here and there, whose teeth were charmingly irregular, whose hair looked like real hair and not like something spun by machines. Christine probably *perspired,* he thought. She endured the messiness of menstruation. She might even snore. She was wonderfully real, wonderfully human in every regard. Whereas Laliene—Laliene seemed—scarcely real at all—

"What's this about Kleph, now?" Thimiroi said, after a time.

"She's become involved with the man that the Sanciscos are renting their house from."

"Involved?"

"An affair," said Laliene acidly. Her glistening eyes were trained remorselessly on his. "He goes to her room. She gives him too much tea, and has too much herself. She plays music for him, or they watch the simsos. And then—then—"

"How do you know any of this?" Thimiroi asked.

Laliene took a deep draught of the intoxicating tea, and her brow grew less furrowed, her dark rich-hued eyes less troubled. "She told Klia. Klia told me."

"And Omerie? Does he know?"

"Of course. He's furious. Kleph can sleep with anyone she cares to, naturally—but such a violation of the Travel rules, to get involved with one of these ancient people! And so stupid, too—spending so much of the precious time of her visit here letting herself get wrapped up in a useless diversion with some commonplace and extremely uninteresting man. A man who isn't even alive, who's been dead for all these centuries!"

"He doesn't happen to be dead right now," Thimiroi said.

Laliene gave him a look of amazement. "Are you defending her, Thimiroi?"

"I'm trying to comprehend her."

"Yes. Yes, of course. But certainly Kleph must see that although he may be alive at the present moment, technically speaking, the present moment itself isn't really the present moment. Not if you see it from our point of view, and what other point of view is appropriate for us to take? What's past is past, sealed and finished. In absolute reality this person of Kleph's died long ago, at least so far as we're concerned." Laliene shook her head. "No, no, Thimiroi, completely apart from the issue of transgression against the rules of The Travel, it's an unthinkably foolish adventure that Kleph's let herself get into. Unthinkably foolish! It's purely a waste of time. What kind of pleasure can she possibly get from it? She might as well be coupling with—with a donkey!"

"Who is this man?" Thimiroi asked.

"What does that matter? His name is Oliver Wilson. He owns that house where they are, the one that Hollia is trying to buy, and he lives there, too. Omerie neglected to arrange for him to vacate the premises for the month. You may have seen him: a very ordinary-looking pleasant young man with light-colored hair. But he isn't important. What's important is the insane, absurd, destructive thing Kleph is doing. Which particular person of this long-gone era she happens to be doing it with is completely beside the point."

Thimiroi studied her for a time.

"Why are you telling me this, Laliene?"

"Aren't you interested in what your friends are getting themselves mixed up in?"

"Is Kleph my friend?"

"Isn't she?"

"We have come to the same place at the same time, Kleph and I," Thimiroi said. "Does that make us friends? We *know* each other, Kleph and I. Possibly we were even lovers once, possibly not. My relationship with the Sanciscos in general and with Kleph in particular isn't a close one nowadays. So far as this matters to me, Kleph can do what she likes with anyone she pleases."

"She runs the risk of punishment."

"She was aware of that. Presumably she chooses not to be troubled by it."

"She should think of Omerie, then. And Klia. If Kleph is forbidden to Travel again, they will be deprived of her company. They have always Traveled together. They are accustomed to Traveling together. How selfish of her, Thimiroi."

"Presumably she chooses not to be troubled by that, either," said Thimiroi. "In any case, it's no concern of yours or mine." He hesitated. "Do you know what I think *should* trouble her, Laliene? The fact that she's going to pay a very steep emotional price for what she's doing, if indeed she's actually doing it. That part of it ought to be on her mind, at least a little."

"What do you mean?" Laliene asked.

"I mean the effect it will have on her when the meteor comes, and this man is killed by it. Or by what comes after the meteor, and you know what that is. If the meteor doesn't kill him, the Blue Death will take him a week or two later. How will Kleph feel then, Laliene? Knowing that the man she loves is dead? And that she has done nothing, nothing at all, to spare him from the fate that she knew was rushing toward him? Poor Kleph! Poor foolish Kleph! What torment it will be for her!"

"The man she *loves?*"

"Doesn't she?"

Laliene looked astounded. "What ever gave you that idea? It's a game, Thimiroi, only a silly game! She's simply playing with him. And then she'll move along. He won't be killed by the meteor—obviously. He'll be in the same house as all the rest of us when it strikes. And she'll be at Charlemagne's coronation by the time the Blue Death breaks out. She won't even remember his *name,* Thimiroi. How could you possibly have thought that she—she—" Laliene shook her head. "You don't understand a thing, do you?"

"Perhaps I don't." Thimiroi put his cup down and stared at his fingers. They were trembling. "Would you like some more tea, Laliene?"

"No, I—yes. Yes, another, if you will, Thimiroi."

He set about the task of brewing the euphoriac. His head was throbbing. Things were occurring to him that he had not bothered to consider before. While he worked, Laliene rose, roamed the room, toyed with this artifact and that, and drifted out into the hall that led to the bedroom. Did she suspect anything? Was she searching for something, perhaps? He wondered whether Christine had left any trace of her presence behind that Laliene might be able to detect, and decided that probably she had not. Certainly he hoped not. Considering how agitated Laliene seemed to be over Kleph's little fling with her landlord, how would she react if she knew that he, too, was involved with someone of this era?

Involved?

How involved are you, really? he asked himself.

He thought of all that they had said just now about Kleph and her odd little affair with Oliver Wilson. A cold, inescapable anguish began to rise in him. How sorry he had felt for Kleph, a moment ago! The punishment for transgression against the rules, yes—but also the high emotional price that he imagined Kleph would pay for entangling herself with someone who lay under sentence of immediate death—the guilt—the sense of irretrievable loss—

The meteor—the Blue Death—

"The tea is ready," Thimiroi announced, and as he reached for the delicate cups he knocked one into the other, and both of the pretty things went tumbling from the tray, landing at the carpet's edge and cracking like eggshells against the wooden floor. A little rivulet of euphoriac came swirling from them. He gasped, shocked and appalled. Laliene, emerging from one of the far rooms, looked down at the wreckage for a moment, then swiftly knelt and began to sweep the fragments together.

"Oh, Thimiroi," she said, glancing upward at him. "Oh, how sad, Thimiroi, how terribly sad—"

After lunch the next day, he telephoned Christine, certain that she would be out and a little uneasy about that; but she answered on the second ring, and there was an eagerness in her voice that made him think she had been poised beside the phone for some time now, waiting for him to call. Did she happen to be free this afternoon? Yes, yes, she said, she was free. Did she care to—his mind went blank a moment—to go for a walk with him somewhere? Yes, yes, what a lovely idea! She sounded almost jubilant. A perfect day for a walk, yes!

She was waiting outside her house when Thimiroi came down the street. It was a day much like all the other days so far, sharp cloudless sky, brilliant sun, gold blazing against blue. But there was a deeper tinge of warmth in the air, for May was near its end now and spring was relinquishing its hold to the coming summer. Trees which had seemed barely into leaf the week before now unfurled canopies of rich deep green.

"Where shall we go?" she asked him.

"This is your city. I don't know the good places."

"We could walk in Baxter Park, I suppose."

Thimiroi frowned. "Isn't that all the way on the other side of the river?"

"Baxter Park? Oh, no, you must be thinking of Butterfield Gardens. Up on the high ridge, you mean, over there opposite us? The very big park, with the botanical gardens and the zoo and everything? Baxter Park's right near here, just a few blocks up the hill. We could be there in ten minutes."

Actually it was more like fifteen, and no easy walk, but none of that mattered to Thimiroi. Simply being close to Christine awoke unfamiliar sensations of contentment in him. They climbed the steep streets side by side, saying very little as they made the difficult ascent, pausing now and again to catch their breaths. The city was like a giant bowl, cleft by the great river that ran through its middle, and they were nearing its rim.

Baxter Park, like its counterpart across the river that Thimiroi had seen when he first arrived in the twentieth century, occupied a commanding position looking out and down toward the heart of the urban area. But apart from that the two parks were very different, for the other was intricately laid out, with roads and amusement sectors scattered through it, and this one seemed nothing more than a strip of rough, wild semi-forest that had been left undeveloped at the top of the city. Simple paths crudely paved led through its dense groves and tangles of underbrush.

"It isn't much, I know—" Christine said.

"It's beautiful here. So wild, so untamed. And so close to the city. We can look down and see houses and office buildings and bridges, and yet back here it's just as it must have been ten thousand years ago. There is nothing like this where I come from."

"Do you mean that?"

"We took our wilderness away a long time ago. We should have kept a little—just a little, a reminder, the way you have here. But it's too late now. It has been gone so long, so very long." Thimiroi peered into the hazy distance. Shimmering in the mid-afternoon heat, the city seemed a fairytale place, enchanted, wondrous. Shading his eyes, he peered out and downward, past the residential district to the metropolitan center by the river, and beyond it to the bridges, the suburbs on the far side, the zone of parks and recreational areas barely visible on the opposite slope. How beautiful it all was, how majestic, how grand! The thought that it all must perish in just a matter of days brought the taste of bile to his mouth, and he turned away, coughing, sputtering.

"Is something the matter?" Christine asked.

"Nothing—no—I'll be all right—"

He wondered how far they were right now from the path along which the meteor would travel.

As he understood it, it was going to come in from this side of the city, traveling low across the great urban bowl like a stone that a boy has sent skimming across a stream and striking somewhere midway down the slope, between the zone of older houses just below the Montgomery House hotel and the business district farther on. At the point of impact, of course, everything would be annihilated for blocks around. But the real devastation would come a moment later, so Kadro had explained: when the shock wave struck and radiated outward, flattening whole neighborhoods in a steadily widening circle, as if they had been swatted by a giant's contemptuous hand.

And then the fires, springing up everywhere—

And then, a few days later, when the invading microbes

had had a chance to spread through the contaminated water supply of the shattered city, the plague—

"You look so troubled, Thimiroi," Christine said, nestling up beside him, sliding her arm through his.

"Do I?"

"You must miss your homeland very much."

"No. No, that isn't it."

"Why so sad, then?"

"I find it extremely moving," he said, "to look out over your whole city this way. Taking it all in in a single sweep. Seeing it in all its magnificence, all its power."

"But it's not even the most important city in the—"

"I know. But that doesn't matter. The fact that there may be bigger cities takes nothing away from the grandeur of this one. Especially for me. Where I come from, there are no cities of any size at all. Our population is extremely small . . . *extremely* small."

"But it must be a very wealthy country, all the same."

Thimiroi shrugged. "I suppose it is. But what does that mean? I look at your city here and I think of the transience of all that is splendid and grand. I think of all the great empires of the past, and how they rose, and fell, and were swept away and forgotten. All the empires that ever were, and all those that will ever be."

To his surprise, she laughed. "Oh, how strange you are!"

"Strange?"

"So terribly solemn. So philosophical. Brooding about the rise and fall of empires on a glorious spring day like this. Standing here with the most amazing sunlight pouring down on us and telling me in those elocution-school tones of yours that empires that don't even exist yet are already swept away and forgotten. How can something be forgotten that hasn't yet even happened? And how can you even bother to think about anything morbid in a season like this one?" She moved closer to him, nuzzling against his side almost like a cat. "Do you know what I think, standing here right this minute looking out at the city? I think that the warmth of the sun feels wonderful and that the air is as fresh as new young wine and that the city has never seemed more sparkling or prosperous and that this is the most beautiful spring day in at least half a million years. And the last thing that's going to cross my mind is that the weather may not hold or that the time of prosperity may not last or that great empires always crumble and are forgotten. But perhaps you and I are just different, Thimiroi. Some people are naturally gloomy, and always see the darkest side of everything, and then there are the people who couldn't manage to be moody and broody even if their lives depended on—" She broke off suddenly. "Oh, Thimiroi, I don't mean to offend you. You know that."

"You haven't offended me." He turned to her. "What's an elocution-school voice?"

"A trained one," she said, smiling. "Like the voice of a radio or TV announcer. You have a marvelous voice, you know. You speak right from the center of your diaphragm, and you always pause for breath in the right places, and the tone is so rich, so perfect—a singer's voice, really. You can sing very well, can't you? I know you can. Later, perhaps, I could play for you, and you could sing for me, back at my place, some song of Stiino—of your own country—"

"Yes," he said. "We could try that, yes."

He kissed her, then, and it was a different sort of kiss from either of the two kisses of the day before, very different indeed; and as he held her his hands ran across her back, and over the nape of her neck, and down the sides of her arms, and she pressed herself close against him. Then after a long moment they moved apart again, both of them flushed and excited, and smiled, and looked at each other as though they were seeing each other for the first time.

They walked hand in hand through the park, neither of them saying anything. Small animals were everywhere, birds and odd shiny bright-colored little insects and comical four-legged grayish beasts with big shaggy tails galloping behind them. Thimiroi was amazed by the richness of all this wildlife, and the shrubs and wildflowers dazzling with early bloom, and the huge thick-boled trees that rose so awesomely above them. What an extraordinary place this century was, he told himself: what a fantastic mixture of the still unspoiled natural world and the world of technology and industry. They had these great cities, these colossal buildings, these immense bridges—and yet, also, they still had saved room for flowers, for beetles and birds, for little furry animals with enormous tails. When the thought of the meteor, and the destruction that it would cause, crept back into his mind, he forced it furiously away. He asked Christine to tell him the names of things: this is a squirrel, she said, and this is a maple tree, and this a grasshopper. She was surprised that he knew so little about them, and asked him what kinds of insects and trees and animals they had in his own country.

"Very few," he told her. "All our wild things went from us long ago."

"Not even squirrels left? Grasshoppers?"

"Nothing like that," he said. "Nothing at all. That is why we travel—to experience life in places such as this. To experience squirrels. To experience grasshoppers."

"Of course. Everyone travels to see things different from what they have at home. But it's hard to believe that there's any country that's done such ecological damage to itself that it doesn't even have—"

"Oh, the problem is not ecological damage," said Thimiroi. "Not as you understand the term. Our country is very beautiful, in its way, and we care for it extremely well. The problem is that it is an extremely civilized place. Too civilized, I think. We have everything under control. And one thing that we controlled, a very long time ago, is the very thing that this park is designed to provide: the world of nature, as it existed before the cities ever were."

She stared. "Not even a squirrel."

"Not even a squirrel, no."

"Where is this country of yours? Did you say it was in Arabia? One of the oil kingdoms?"

"No," he said. "Not in Arabia."

They went onward. The afternoon's heat was at its peak, now, and Thimiroi felt the moisture of the air clinging close against his skin, a strange and unusual sensation for him. Again they paused, after a while, to kiss, even more passionately than before.

"Come," Christine said. "Let's go home."

They hurried down the hillside, taking it practically at a jog. But they slowed as the Montgomery House came into view. Thimiroi thought of inviting her to his room once again, but the thought of Laliene hovering nearby—spying on him, scowling her disapproval as he entered into the same transgression for which she had so sternly censured Kleph—displeased him. Christine reminded him, though, that she had offered to play the piano for him, and wanted him to sing for her. Gladly, eagerly, Thimiroi accepted the invitation to go with her to her house.

But as they approached it he was dismayed to see Kleph standing on the steps of a big, rambling old house just opposite

Christine's, on the uphill side of the street. She was talking to a sturdy square-shouldered man with a good-natured, open face, and she did not appear to notice Thimiroi.

Christine said, "Do you want to say hello to her?"

"Not really."

"She's one of your friends, isn't she? Someone from your country?"

"She's from my country, yes. But not exactly a friend. Just someone who's taking the same tour I am. Is that the house where she's staying?"

"Yes," Christine said. "She and another woman, and a tall somber-looking man. I saw them all with you, that night at the concert hall. They've rented the house for the whole month. That man's the owner, Oliver Wilson."

"Ah." Thimiroi drew his breath in sharply.

So that was the one. Oliver. Kleph's twentieth-century lover. Thimiroi felt a stab of despair. Looking across the way now at Kleph, deep in conversation with this Oliver, it seemed to him suddenly that Laliene's scorn for Kleph had not been misplaced, that it was foolish and pathetic and even a little sordid for any Traveler to indulge in such doomed and absurd romances as this. And yet he was on the verge of embarking on the same thing Kleph was doing. Was that what he really wanted? Or should he not leave such adventures to shallow, trivial people like Kleph?

Christine said, "You're looking troubled again."

"It's nothing. Nothing." Thimiroi gazed closely at her, and her warmth, her directness, her radiant joyous eyes, swept away all the sudden doubts that had come to engulf him. He had no right to condemn Kleph. And in any case what he might choose to do, or Kleph, was no concern of Laliene's. "Come," he said. He caught Christine lightly by the arm. "Let's go inside."

Just as he turned, Kleph did also, and for an instant their eyes met as they stood facing each other on opposite sides of the street. She gave him a startled look. Thimiroi smiled to her; but Kleph merely stared back intently in a curiously cold way. Then she was gone. Thimiroi shrugged.

He followed Christine into her house.

It was an old, comfortable-looking place with a great many small, dark, high-ceilinged rooms on the ground floor and a massive wooden staircase leading upstairs. The furnishings looked heavy and unstylish, as though they were already long out of date, but everything had an appealing, well-worn feel.

"My family's lived in this house for almost a hundred years," Christine said, as though reading his mind. "I was born here. I grew up here. I don't know what it's like to live anywhere else." She gestured toward the staircase. "The music room is upstairs."

"I know. Do you live here by yourself?"

"Basically. My sister and I inherited the house when my mother died, but she's hardly ever here. The last I heard from her, she was in Oaxaca."

"Wah-ha-ka?" Thimiroi said carefully.

"Oaxaca, yes. In Mexico, you know? She's studying Mexican handicrafts, she says. I think she's actually studying Mexican men, but that's her business, isn't it? She likes to travel. Before Mexico she was in Thailand, and before that it was Portugal, I think."

Mexico, Thimiroi thought. Thailand. Portugal. So many names, so many places. Such a complex society, this world of the twentieth century. His own world had fewer places, and they had different names. So much had changed, after the time of the Blue Death. So much had been swept away, never to return.

Christine said, "It's a musty old house, I know. But I love it. And I could never have afforded to buy one of my own. Everything's so fantastically expensive these days. If I hadn't happened to have lived here all along, I suppose I'd be living in one of those poky little studio apartments down by the river, paying umpty thousand dollars a month for one bedroom and a terrace the size of a postage stamp."

Desperately he tried to follow what she was saying. His implant helped, but not enough. Umpty thousand dollars? Studio apartment? Postage stamp? He got the sense of her words, but the literal meanings eluded him. How much was umpty? How big was a postage stamp?

The music room on the second floor was bright and spacious, with three large windows looking out into the garden and the street beyond. The piano itself, against the front wall between two of the windows, was larger than he expected, a splendid, imposing thing, with ponderous, ornately carved legs and a black, gleaming wooden case. Obviously it was old and very valuable and well cared for; and as he studied it he realized suddenly that this must not be any ordinary home musical instrument, but more likely one that a concert performer would use; and therefore Christine's lighthearted dismissal of his question about her having a musical career must almost certainly conceal bitter defeat, frustration, the deflection of a cherished dream. She had wanted and expected more from her music than life had been able to bring her.

"Play for me," he said. "The same piece you were playing the first time, when I happened to walk by."

"The Debussy, you mean?"

"I don't know its name."

Thimiroi hummed the melody that had so captured him.

She nodded and sat down to play.

It was not quite as magical, the second time. But nothing ever was, he knew. And it was beautiful all the same, haunting, mysterious in its powerful simplicity.

"Will you sing for me now?" Christine asked.

"What should I sing?"

"A song of your own country?"

He thought a moment. How could he explain to her what music was like in his own time—not sound alone, but a cluster of all the arts, visual, olfactory, the melodic line rising out of a dozen different sensory concepts? But he could improvise, he supposed. He began to sing one of his own poems, putting a tune to it as he went. Christine, listening, closed her eyes, nodded, turned to the keyboard, played a few notes and a few more, gradually shaping them into an accompaniment for him. Thimiroi was amazed at the swiftness with which she caught the melody of his tune—stumbling only once or twice, over chordal structures that were obviously alien to her—and traveled along easily with it. By the time he reached the fifth cycle of the song, he and she were joined in an elegant harmony, as though they had played this song together many times instead of both improvising it as they went. And when he made the sudden startling key-shift that in his culture signaled the close of a song, she adapted to it almost instantaneously and stayed with him to the final note.

They applauded each other resoundingly.

Her eyes were shining with delight. "Oh, Thimiroi—Thimiroi—what a marvelous singer you are! And what a marvelous song!"

"And how cunningly you wove your accompaniment into it."

"That wasn't really hard."

"For you, perhaps. You have a great musical gift, Christine."

She reddened and looked away.

"What language were you singing in?" she asked, after a time.

"The language of my country."

"It was so strange. It isn't like any language I've ever heard. Why won't you tell me anything about where you come from, Thimiroi?"

"I will. Later."

"And what did the words mean?"

"It's a poem about—about journeying to far lands, and seeing great wonders. A very romantic poem, perhaps a little silly. But the poet himself is also very romantic and perhaps a little silly."

"What's his name?" she asked.

"Thimiroi."

"You?" she said, grinning broadly. "Is that what you are? A poet?"

"I sometimes write poetry, yes," he said, beginning to feel as uneasy as she had seemed when he was trying to praise her playing. They looked at each other awkwardly. Then he said, "May I try the piano?"

"Of course."

He sat down, peered at the keys, touched one of the white ones experimentally, then another, another. What were the black ones? Modulators of some sort? No, no, their function was very much like that of the white ones, it seemed. And these pedals here—

He began to play.

He was dreadful at first, but quickly he came to understand the relationship of the notes and the range of the keyboard and the proper way of touching the keys. He played the piece that she had played for him before, exactly at first, then launching into a set of subtle variations that carried him farther and farther from the original, into the musical modes of his own time. The longer he played, the more keenly he appreciated the delicacy and versatility of this ancient instrument; and he knew that if he were to study it with some care, not merely guess his way along as he was doing now, he would be able to draw such wonders from it as even great composers like Cenbe or Palivandrin would find worthwhile. Once again he felt humbled by the achievements of this great, lost civilization of the past. Which to brittle, heartless people like Hollia or Omerie must seem a mere simple primitive age. But they understood nothing. Nothing.

He stopped playing, and looked back at Christine.

She was staring at him in horror, her face pale, her eyes wide and stricken, tears streaking her cheeks.

"What's wrong?" he asked.

"The way you play—" she whispered. "I've never heard anyone play like that."

"It is all very bad, I know. But you must realize, I have had no formal training in this instrument, I am simply inventing a technique as I go—"

"No. Please. Don't tell me that. You mustn't tell me that!"

"Christine?"

And then he realized what the matter was. It was not that he had played badly; it was that he had played so well. She had devoted all her life to this instrument, and played it with great skill, and even so had never been able to attain a level of proficiency that gave her any real satisfaction. And he, never so much as having seen a piano in his life, could sit down at it and draw from it splendors beyond her fondest hope of achieving. His playing was unorthodox, of course, it was odd and even bizarre, but yet she had seen the surpassing mastery in it, and had been stunned and chagrined and crushed by it, and stood here now bewildered and confounded by this stranger she had brought into her own home—

I should have known better, Thimiroi thought. I should have realized that this is *her* art, and that I, with all the advantages that are mine purely by virtue of my having been born when I was, ought never to have presumed to invade her special territory with such a display of skills that are beyond her comprehension. Without even suspecting what I was doing, I have humiliated her.

"Christine," he murmured. "No. No, Christine."

Thimiroi went to her and pulled her close against him, and kissed the tears away, and spoke softly to her, calming her, reassuring her. He could never tell her the truth; but he could make her understand, at least, that he had not meant to hurt her. And after a time he felt the tension leave her, and felt her press herself tight to him, and then their lips met, and she looked up, smiling. And took him lightly by the hand, and drew him from the room and down the hall.

Afterward, as he was dressing, she touched the long, fading red scar on his arm and said, "Were you in some kind of accident?"

"An inoculation," he told her. "Against disease."

"I've never seen one like that before."

"No," he said. "I suppose you haven't."

"A disease of your country?"

"No," he said, after a time. "Of yours."

"But what kind of disease requires a vaccination like—"

"Do we have to talk of diseases just now, Christine."

"Of course not," she said, smiling ruefully. "How foolish

of me. How absurd." She ran her fingers lightly, almost fondly, over the inoculation scar a second time. "Of all things for me to be curious about!" Softly she said, "You don't have to leave now, you know."

"But I must. I really must."

"Yes," she said. "I suppose you must." She accompanied him to the front door. "You'll call me, won't you? Very soon?"

"Of course," Thimiroi said.

Night had fallen. The air was mild and humid, but the sky was clear and the stars glittered brilliantly. He looked for the moon but could not find it.

How many days remain, he wondered?

Somewhere out there in the airless dark a lump of dead rock was falling steadily toward earth, falling, falling, inexorably coming this way. How far away was it now? How soon before it would come roaring over the horizon to bring unimaginable death to this place?

I must find a way of saving her, he told himself.

The thought was numbing, dizzying, intolerably disturbing.

Save her? How? Impossible. Impossible. It was something that he must not even allow himself to consider.

And yet—

Again it came. *I must find a way of saving her.*

There was a message for him at his hotel, just a few quick scrawled sentences:

Party at Lutheena's. We're all going. See you there?

Laliene's handwriting, which even in her haste was as beautiful as the finest calligraphy. Thimiroi crumpled the note and tossed it aside. Going to a party tonight was very close to the last thing he would want to do. Everyone in glittering clothes, making glittering conversation, trading sparkling anecdotes, no doubt, of their latest adventures among the simple sweaty blotchy-skinned folk of this interestingly raucous and crude century—no. No. No. Let them trade their anecdotes without him. Let them sip their euphoriac and exchange their chatter and play their little games. He was going to bed. Very likely, without him there, they would all be talking about him. How oddly he had been behaving, how strange and uncouth he seemed to be becoming since their arrival in this era. Let them talk. What did it matter?

He wished Kleph had not seen him going into Christine's house, though.

But how would Kleph know whose house it was? And why would Kleph—Kleph, with her own Oliver Wilson entanglement preoccupying her—want to say anything to anyone about having seen some other member of the tour slipping away for an intimate hour with a twentieth-century person? Better for her to be silent. The subject was a delicate one. She would not want to raise it. She of all people would be unlikely to disapprove, or to want to bring down on him the disapproval of the others. No, Thimiroi thought. Kleph will say nothing. We are allies in this business, Kleph and I.

He slept, and dark dreams came that he could not abide: the remorseless meteor crossing the sky, the city aflame and shrieking, Christine's wonderful old house swept away by a searing blast of destruction, the piano lying tumbled in the street, split in half, golden strings spilling out.

Wearily Thimiroi dosed himself with the drug that banishes dreams, and lay down to sleep again. But now sleep evaded him. Very well: there was the other drug, the one that brings sleep. He hesitated to take it. The two drugs taken in the wrong order exacted a price; he would be jittery and off balance emotionally for the next two or three days. He was far enough off balance as it was already. So he lay still, hoping that he would drift eventually into sleep without recourse to more medication; and gradually his mind grew easier, gradually he began the familiar descent toward unconsciousness.

Suddenly the image of Laliene blazed in his mind.

It was so vivid that it seemed she was standing beside him in the darkness and light was streaming from her body. She was nude, and her breasts, her hips, her thighs, all had a throbbing incandescent glow. Thimiroi sat up, astonished, swept with waves of startling feverish excitement.

"Laliene?"

How radiant she looked! How splendid! Her eyes were glowing like beacons. Her crimson hair stood out about her head like a bright corona. The scent of her filled his nostrils. He trembled. His throat was dry, his lips seemed gummed together.

Wave after wave of intense, overpowering desire swept through him.

Helplessly Thimiroi rose, lurched across the room, reached gropingly toward her. This was madness, he knew, but there was no holding himself back.

The shimmering image retreated as he came near it. He stumbled, nearly tripped, regained his balance.

"Wait, Laliene," he cried hoarsely. His heart was pounding thunderously. It was almost impossible for him to catch his breath. He was choking with his need. "Come here, will you? Stop edging away like that."

"I'm not here, Thimiroi. I'm in my own room. Put your robe on and come visit me."

"What? You're not here?"

"Down the hall. Come, now. Hurry!"

"You are here. You have to be."

As though in a daze, brain swathed in thick layers of white cotton, he reached for her again. Like a love-struck boy he yearned to draw her close, to cup her breasts in his hands, to run his fingers over those silken thighs, those satiny flanks—

"To my room," she whispered.

"Yes. Yes."

His flesh was aflame. Sweat rolled down his body. She danced before him like a shining will-o'-the-wisp. Frantically he struggled to comprehend what was happening. A vision? A dream? But he had drugged himself against dreams. And he was awake now. Surely he was awake. And yet he saw her—he wanted her—he wanted her beyond all measure—he was going to slip his robe on, and go to her suite, and she would be waiting for him there, and he would slip into her bed—into her arms—

No. No. No.

He fought it. He caught the side of some piece of furniture, and held it, anchoring himself, struggling to keep himself from going forward. His teeth chattered. Chills ran along his back and shoulders. The muscles in his arms and chest writhed and spasmed as he battled to stay where he was.

He was fully awake now, and he was beginning to understand. He remembered how Laliene had gone wandering around here the other day while he was brewing the tea—examining the works of art, so he had thought. But she could just as easily have been planting something. Which now was broadcasting monstrous compulsions into his mind.

He switched on the light, wincing as it flooded the room.

Now Thimiroi could no longer see that mocking, beckoning image of Laliene, but he still felt her presence all around him, the heat of her body, the pungency of her fragrance, the strength of her urgent summons.

Somehow he managed to find the card with Christine's telephone number on it, and dialed it with tense, quivering fingers. The phone rang endlessly until, finally, he heard her sleepy voice, barely focused, saying, "Yes? Hello?"

"Christine? Christine, it's me, Thimiroi."

"What? Who? Don't you know it's four in the morn—" Then her tone changed. The sleepiness left it, and the irritation. "What's wrong, Thimiroi? What's happening?"

"I'll be all right. I need you to talk to me, that's all. I'm having a—kind of an attack."

"No, Thimiroi!" He could feel the intensity of her concern. "What can I do? Shall I come over?"

"No. That's not necessary. Just talk to me. I need to stir up—cerebral activity. Do you understand? It's just an—an electrochemical imbalance. But if I talk—even if I listen to something—speak to me, say anything, recite poetry—"

"Poetry," she said. "All right. Let me think. *'Four score and seven years ago—'* " she began.

"Good," he said. "Even if I don't understand it, that's all right. Say anything. Just keep talking."

Already Laliene's aura was ebbing from the room. Christine continued to speak; and he broke in from time to time, simply to keep his mental level up. In a few minutes Thimiroi knew that he had defeated Laliene's plan. He slumped forward, breathing hard, letting his stiff, anguished muscles uncoil.

He still could feel the waves of mental force sweeping through the room. But they were pallid now, they were almost comical, they no longer were capable of arousing in him the obsessive obedience that they had been able to conjure into his sleeping mind.

Christine, troubled, still wanted to come to him; but Thimiroi told her that everything was fine, now, that she should go back to sleep, that he was sorry to have disturbed her. He would explain, he promised. Later. Later.

Fury overtook him the moment he put the receiver down.

Damn Laliene. Damn her! What did she think she was doing?

He searched through the sitting room, and then the bedroom, and the third room of the suite. But it was almost dawn before he found what he was looking for: the tiny silvery pellet, the minute erotic broadcaster that she had hidden beneath one of his Sipulva tables. He pulled it loose and crushed it against the wall, and the last faint vestige of Laliene's presence went from the room like water swirling down a drain. Slowly Thimiroi's anger receded. He put on some music, one of Cenbe's early pieces, and listened quietly to it until he saw the first pale light of morning streaking the sky.

Casually, easily, with a wonderful recklessness he had not known he had in him, he said to Christine, "We go anywhere we want. Anywhere. They run tours for us, you see. We were in Canterbury in Chaucer's time, to make the pilgrimage. We went to Rome and then to Emperor Augustus' summer palace on the island of Capri, and he invited us to a grand banquet, thinking we were visitors from a great kingdom near India."

Christine was staring at him in a wide-eyed gaze, as though she were a child and he were telling her some fabulous tale of dragons and princes.

He had gone to her at midday, when the late May sun was immense overhead and the sky seemed like a great curving plate of burnished blue steel. She had let him in without a word, and for a long while they looked at each other in silence, their hands barely touching. She was very pale and her eyes were reddened from sleeplessness, with dark crescents beneath them. Thimiroi embraced her, and assured her that he was in no danger, that with her help he had been able to fight off the demon that had assailed him in the night. Then she took him upstairs, to the room on the second floor where they had made love the day before, and drew him down with her on the bed, almost shyly at first, and then, casting all reserve aside, seizing him eagerly, hungrily.

When finally they lay back, side-by-side, all passion slaked for the moment, Christine turned toward him and said, "Tell me now where your country is, Thimiroi."

And at last he began—calmly, unhesitatingly—to tell her about The Travel.

"We went to Canterbury in the autumn of 1347," he said. "Actually Chaucer was still only a boy, then. The poem was many years away. Of course we read him before we set out. We even looked at the original Old English text. I suppose the language would be strange even to you. *'When that Aprill with his shoures soote/The droghte of March hath perced to the roote.'* I suppose we really should have gone in April ourselves, to be more authentic; but April was wet that year, as it usually is at that time in England, and the autumn was warm and brilliant, a season much like the one you are having here, a true vintage season. We are very fond of warm, dry weather, and rain depresses us."

"You could have gone in another year, then, and found a warmer, drier April," Christine said.

"No. The year had to be 1347. It isn't important why. And so we went in autumn, in beautiful October."

"Ah."

"We began in London, gathering in an inn on the south side of the river, just as Chaucer's pilgrims did, and we set out with a band of pilgrims that must have been much like his, even one who played a bagpipe the way his Miller did, and a woman who might almost have been the Wife of Bath—" Thimiroi closed his eyes a moment, letting the journey come rushing back from memory, sights and sounds, laughter, barking dogs, cool bitter ale, embroidered gowns, the mounds of straw in the stable, falling leaves, warm dry breezes. "And then, before that, first-century Capri. In the time of Augustus. In high summer, a perfect Mediterranean summer, still another vintage season. How splendid Capri is. Do you know it? No? An island off Italy, very steep, a mountaintop in the water, with strange grottos at its base and huge rocks all about. There comes a time every evening when the sky and the sea are the same color, a pale blue-gray, so that it is impossible to tell where one ends and the other begins, and you stand by the edge of the high cliff, looking outward into that gray haze, and it seems to you that all the world is completely still, that time is not moving at all."

"The—first century—?" Christine murmured.

"The reign of the Emperor Augustus, yes. A surprisingly short man, and very gentle and witty, extremely likable, although you can feel the ruthlessness of him just behind the gentleness. He has amazing eyes, utterly penetrating, with a kind of light coming from them. You look at him and you see Rome: the Empire embodied in one man, its beginning and its end, its greatness and its power."

"You speak of him as though he is still alive. 'He

has amazing eyes,' you said."

"I saw him only a few months ago," said Thimiroi. "He handed me a cup of sweet red wine with his own hands, and recommended it, saying there certainly was nothing like it in my own land. He has a palace on Capri, nothing very grand—his stepson Tiberius, who was there also, would build a much greater one later on, so our guide told us—and he was there for the summer. We were guests under false pretenses, I suppose, ambassadors from a distant land, though he never would have guessed *how* distant. The year was—let me think—no, not the first century, not *your* first century, it was what you call B.C., the last century *before* the first century—I think the year was 19, the 19 *before*—such a muddle, these dating systems—"

"And in your country?" Christine asked. "What year is it now in your country, Thimiroi? 2600? 3100?"

He pondered that a moment. "We use a different system of reckoning. It is not at all analogous. The term would be meaningless to you."

"You can't tell me what year it is there?"

"Not in your kind of numbers, no. There was—a break in the pattern of numbering, long before our time. I could ask Kadro. He is our tour guide, Kadro. He knows how to compute the equivalencies."

She stared at him. "Couldn't you guess? Five hundred years? A thousand?"

"Perhaps it is something like that. But even if I knew, I would not tell you the exact span, Christine. It would be wrong. It is forbidden, absolutely forbidden." Thimiroi laughed. "Everything I have just told you is absolutely forbidden, do you know that? We must conceal the truth about ourselves to those we meet when we undertake The Travel. That is the rule. Of course, you don't believe a thing I've just been telling you, do you?"

Color flared in her cheeks. "Don't you think I do?" she cried.

Tenderly Thimiroi said, "There are two things they tell us about The Travel, Christine, before we set out for the first time. The first, they say, is that sooner or later you will feel some compulsion to reveal to a person of ancient times that you are a visitor from a future time. The second thing is that you will not be believed."

"But I believe you, Thimiroi!"

"Do you? Do you really?"

"Of course it all sounds so terribly strange, so fantastic—"

"Yes. Of course."

"But I want to believe you. And so I do believe you. The way you speak—the way you dress—the way you look—everything about you is *foreign,* Thimiroi, totally foreign beyond any ordinary kind of foreignness. It isn't Iran or India or Afghanistan that you come from, it has to be some other world, or some other time. Yes. Yes. Everything about you. The way you played the piano yesterday." She paused a moment. "The way you touch me in bed. You are like no man I have ever—like no man—" She faltered, reddened fiercely, looked away from him a moment. "Of course I believe that you are what you say you are. Of course I do!"

When he returned to the Montgomery House late that afternoon he went down the hall to Laliene's suite and rapped angrily at the door. Denvin opened it and peered out at him. He was dressed in peacock splendor, an outfit exceptional even for Denvin, a shirt with brilliant red stripes and golden epaulets, tight green trousers flecked with scarlet checks.

He gave Thimiroi a long cool malevolent glance and exclaimed, "Well! The prodigal returns!"

"How good to see you, Denvin. Am I interrupting anything?"

"Only a quiet little chat." Denvin turned. "Laliene! Our wandering poet is here!"

Laliene emerged from deeper within. Like Denvin she was elaborately clothed, wearing a pale topaz-hued gown fashioned of a myriad shimmering mirrors, shining metallic eye-shadow, gossamer finger-gloves. She looked magnificent. But for an instant, as her eyes met Thimiroi's, her matchless poise appeared to desert her, and she seemed startled, flustered, almost frightened. Then, regaining her equilibrium with a superb show of control, she gave him a cool smile and said, "So there you are. We tried to reach you before, but of course there was no finding you. Maitira, Antilimoin, and Fevra are here. We've just been with them. They've been holding open house all afternoon, and you were invited. I suppose it's still going on. Lesentru is due to arrive in about an hour, and Kuiane, and they say that Broyal and Hammin will be getting here tonight also."

"The whole clan," Thimiroi said. "That will be delightful. Laliene, may I speak with you privately?"

Again a flicker of distress from her. She glanced almost apologetically at Denvin.

"Well, excuse me!" Denvin said theatrically.

"Please," Laliene said. "For just a moment, Denvin."

"Certainly. Certainly, Laliene." He favored Thimiroi with a strange grimace as he went out.

"Very well," said Laliene, turning to face Thimiroi squarely. Her expression had hardened; she looked steely, now, and prepared for any sort of attack. "What is it, Thimiroi?"

He drew forth the little silvery pellet that he had found

attached to the underside of the Sipulva table, and held it out to her in the palm of his hand.

"Do you know what this is, Laliene?"

"Some little broken toy, I assume. Why do you ask?"

"It's an erotic," he said. "I found it in my rooms, where someone had hidden it. It began broadcasting when I went to sleep last night. Sending out practically irresistible waves of sexual desire."

"How fascinating. I hope you were able to find someone to satisfy them with."

"The images I was getting, Laliene, were images of you. Standing naked next to my bed, whispering to me, inviting me to come down the hall and make love to you."

She smiled icily. "I had no idea you were still interested, Thimiroi!"

"Don't play games with me. Why did you plant this thing in my room, Laliene?"

"I?"

"I said, don't play games. You were in my room the other day. No one else of our group has been. The erotic was specifically broadcasting your image. How can there be any doubt that you planted it yourself, for the particular purpose of luring me into your bed?"

"You're being absurd, Thimiroi. Anyone could have planted it. Anyone. Do you think it's hard to get into these rooms? These people have no idea of security. You ask a chambermaid in the right way and you can enter anywhere. As for the images of me that were being broadcast to you, why, you know as well as I do that erotics don't broadcast images of specific individuals. They send out generalized waves of feeling, and the recipient supplies whatever image seems appropriate to him. In your case evidently it was my image that came up from your unconscious when—"

"Don't lie to me, Laliene."

Her eyes flashed. "I'm not lying. I deny planting anything in your room. Why on earth would I, anyway? Could going to bed with you, or anyone else, for that matter, possibly be that important to me that I would connive and sneak around and make use of some kind of mechanical amplifying device in order to achieve my purpose? Is that plausible, Thimiroi?"

"I don't know. What I do know is that what happened to me during the night happened to me, and that I found this when I searched my rooms." He thought for a moment to add, *And that you've been pressing yourself upon me ever since we began this trip, in the most embarrassing and irritating fashion.* But he did not have the heart to say that to her. "I believe that you hid this when you visited me for tea. What your reason may have been is something I can't begin to imagine."

"Of course you can't. Because I had no reason. And I didn't do it."

Thimiroi made no reply. Laliene's face was firmly set. Her gaze met his unwaveringly. She was certainly lying: he knew that beyond any question. But they were at an impasse. All he could do was accuse; he could not prove anything; he was stymied by her denial, and there was no way of carrying this further. She appeared to know that also. There was a long tense moment of silence between them, and then she said, "Are you finished with this, Thimiroi? Because there are more important things we should be discussing."

"Go ahead. What important things?"

"The plans for Friday night."

"Friday night," Thimiroi said, not understanding.

She looked at him scornfully. "Friday—tomorrow—is

the last day of May. Or have you forgotten that?"

He felt a chill. "The meteor," he said.

"The meteor, yes. The event which we came to this place to see," Laliene said. "Do you recall?"

"So soon," Thimiroi said dully. "Tomorrow night."

"We will all assemble about midnight, or a little before, at the Sanciscos' house. The view will be best from there, according to Kadro. From their front rooms, upstairs. Kleph, Omerie, and Klia have invited everyone—everyone except Hollia and Hara, that is: Omerie is adamant about their not coming, because of something slippery that Hollia tried to do to him. Kleph would not discuss it, but I assume it had to do with trying to get the Sanciscos evicted, so that they could have the Wilson house for themselves. But all the rest of us will be there. And you are particularly included, Thimiroi. Kleph made a point of telling me that. Unless you have other plans for the evening, naturally."

"Is that what Kleph said? Or are you adding that part of it yourself, about my having other plans?"

"That is what Kleph said."

"I see."

"*Do* you have other plans?"

"What other plans could I possibly have, do you think? Where? With whom?"

Christine seemed startled to see him again so soon. She was still wearing an old pink robe that she had thrown on as he was leaving her house two hours before, and she looked rumpled and drowsy and confused. Behind him the sky held the pearl-gray of early twilight on this late spring evening, but she stood in the half-opened doorway blinking at him as though he had awakened her once again in the middle of the night.

"Thimiroi? You're back?"

"Let me in. Quickly, please."

"Is there something wrong? Are you in trouble?"

"Please."

He stepped past her into the vestibule and hastily pushed the door shut behind him. She gave him a baffled look. "I was just napping," she said. "I didn't think you'd be coming back this evening, and I had so little sleep last night, you know—"

"I know. We need to talk. This is urgent, Christine."

"Go into the parlor. I'll be with you in a moment."

She pointed to Thimiroi's left and vanished into the dim recesses at the rear of the entrance hall. Thimiroi went into the room she had indicated, a long, oppressively narrow chamber hung with heavy brocaded draperies and furnished with the sort of low-slung clumsy-looking couches and chairs, probably out of some even earlier era, that were everywhere in the house. He paced restlessly about the room. It was like being in a museum of forgotten styles. There was something eerie and almost hieratic about this mysterious furniture: the dark wood, the heavy legs jutting at curious angles, the coarse, intricately worked fabric, the strange brass buttons running along the edges. Someone like Denvin would probably think it hideous. To him it was merely strange, powerful, haunting, wonderful in its way.

At last Christine appeared. She had been gone for what felt like hours: washing her face, brushing her hair, changing into a robe she evidently considered more seemly for receiving a visitor at nightfall. Her vanity was almost amusing. The world is about to come to an end, he thought, and she pauses to make herself fit for entertaining company.

But of course she could have no idea of why he was here.

He said, "Are you free tomorrow night?"

"Free? Tomorrow?" She looked uncertain. "Why—yes, yes, I suppose. Friday night. I'm free, yes. What did you have in mind, Thimiroi?"

"How well do you trust me, Christine?"

She did not reply for a moment. For the first time since that day they had had lunch together at the River Cafe, there was something other than fascination, warmth, even love for him, in her eyes. She seemed mystified, troubled, perhaps frightened. It was as if his sudden breathless arrival here this evening had reminded her of how truly strange their relationship was, and of how little she really knew about him.

"Trust you how?" she said finally.

"What I told you this afternoon, about Capri, about Canterbury, about The Travel—did you believe all that or not?"

She moistened her lips. "I suppose you're going to say that you were making it all up, and that you feel guilty now for having fed all that nonsense to a poor simple gullible woman like me."

"No."

"No what?"

"I wasn't making anything up. But do you believe that, Christine? Do you?"

"I said I did, this afternoon."

"But you've had a few hours to think about it. Do you still believe it?"

She made no immediate reply. At length she said, glancing at him warily, "I've been napping, Thimiroi. I haven't been thinking about anything at all. But since it seems to be so important to you: Yes. Yes, I think that what you told me, weird as it was, was the truth. There. If it was just a joke, I swallowed it. Does that make me a simpleton in your eyes?"

"So you trust me."

"Yes. I trust you."

"Will you go away with me, then? Leave here with me tomorrow, and possibly never come back?"

"Tomorrow?" The word seemed to have struck her like an explosion. She looked dazed. "Never—come—back—?"

"In all likelihood."

She put the palms of her hands together, rubbed them against each other, pressed them tight: a little ritual of hers, perhaps. When she looked up at him again her expression had changed: the confusion had cleared from her face and now she appeared merely puzzled, and even somewhat irritated.

In a sharp tone she said, "What is all this about, Thimiroi?"

He drew a deep breath. "Do you know why we chose the autumn of 1347 for our Canterbury visit?" he asked. "Because it was a season of extraordinarily fine weather, yes. But also because it was a peak time, looking down into a terrible valley, the last sweet moment before the coming of a great calamity. By the following summer the Black Death would be devouring England, and millions would die. We chose the timing of our visit to Augustus the same way. The year 19—19 B.C., it was—was the year he finally consolidated all imperial power in his grasp. Rome was his; he ruled it in a way that no one had ruled that nation before. After that there would be only anticlimax for him, and disappointments and losses; and indeed just after we went to him he would fall seriously ill, almost to the edge of death, and for a time it would seem to him that he had lost everything in the very moment of attaining it. But when we visited him in 19 B.C., it was the summit of his time."

"What does this have to do with—"

"This May, here, now, is another vintage season, Christine. This long golden month of unforgettable weather—it will end tomorrow, Christine, in terror, in destruction, a frightful descent from happiness into disaster, far steeper than either of the other two. That is why we are here, do you see? As spectators, as observers of the great irony—visiting your city at its happiest moment, and then, tomorrow, watching the catastrophe."

As he spoke, she grew pale and her lips began to quiver; and then color flooded into her face, as it will sometimes do when the full impact of terrible news arrives. Something close to panic was gleaming in her eyes.

"Are you saying that there's going to be nuclear war? That after all these years the bombs are finally going to go off?"

"Not war, no."

"What then?"

Without answering, Thimiroi drew forth his wallet and began to stack currency on the table in front of him, hundreds of dollars, perhaps thousands, all the strange little strips of green-and-black paper that they had supplied him with when he first had arrived here. Christine gaped in astonishment. He shoved the money toward her.

"Here," he said. "I'll get more tomorrow morning, and give you that too. Arrange a trip for us to some other country, France, Spain, England, wherever you'd like to go, it makes no difference which one, so long as it is far from here. You will understand how to do such things, with which I have had no experience. Buy airplane tickets—is that the right term, airplane tickets?—get us a hotel room, do whatever is necessary. But we must depart no later than this time tomorrow. When you pack, pack as though you may never return to this house: take your most precious things, the things you would not want to leave behind, but only as much as you can carry yourself. If you have money on deposit, take it out, or arrange for it to be transferred to some place of deposit in the country that we will be going to. Call me when everything is ready, and I'll come for you and we'll go together to the place where the planes take off."

Her expression was frozen, her eyes glazed, rigid. "You won't tell me what's going to happen?"

"I have already told you vastly too much. If I tell you more—and you tell others—and the news spreads widely, and the pattern of the future is greatly changed by the things that those people may do as a result of knowing what is to come—no. No. I do not dare, Christine. You are the only one I can save, and I can tell you no more than I have already told you. And you must tell no one else at all."

"This is like a dream, Thimiroi."

"Yes. But it is very real, I assure you."

Once again she stared. Her lips worked a moment before she could speak.

"I'm so terribly afraid, Thimiroi."

"I understand that. But you do believe me? Will you do as I ask? I swear to you, Christine, your only hope lies in trusting me. *Our* only hope."

"Yes," she said hesitantly.

"Then will you do as I ask?"

"Yes," she said, beginning the single syllable with doubt in her voice, and finishing it with sudden conviction. "But there's something I don't understand."

"What is that?"

"If something awful is going to happen here, why must

we run off to England or Spain? Why not take me back to your own country, Thimiroi? Your own time."

"There is no way I can do that," he said softly.

"When you go back, then, what will happen to me?"

He took her hand in his. "I will not go back, Christine. I will stay here with you, in this era—in England, in France, wherever we may go—for the rest of my life. We will both be exiles. But we will be exiles together."

She asked him to stay with her at her house that night, and he refused. He could see that the refusal hurt her deeply; but there was much that he needed to do, and he could not do it there. They would have many other nights for spending together. Returning to his hotel, he went quickly to his rooms to contemplate the things that would have to be dealt with.

Everything that belonged to his own era, of course, packed and sent back via his suitcase: no question about that. He could keep some of his clothing with him here, perhaps, but none of the furniture, none of the artifacts, nothing that might betray the technology of a time yet unborn. The room would have to be bare when he left it. And he would have to requisition more twentieth-century money. He had no idea how much Christine might have above what he had already given her, nor how long it would last; but certainly they would need more as they began their new lives. As for the suitcase, his one remaining link to the epoch from which he came, he would have to destroy that. He would have to sever all ties. He would—

The telephone rang. The light jingling of its bell cut across his consciousness like a scream.

Christine, he thought. To tell him that she had reconsidered, that she saw now that this was all madness, that if he did not leave her alone she would call the police—

"Yes?" he said.

"Thimiroi! Oh, I *am* glad you're there." A warm, hearty, familiar masculine voice. "Laliene said I might have difficulty finding you, but I thought I'd ring your room anyway—"

"Antilimoin?"

"None other. We've just arrived. Ninth floor, the Presidential suite, whatever that may be. Maitira and Fevra are here with me, of course. Listen, old friend, we're having a tremendous blast tonight—oh, pardon me, that's a sick thing to say, isn't it?—a tremendous gathering, you know, a *soiree,* to enliven the night before the big night—do you think you can make it?"

"Well—"

"Laliene says you've been terribly standoffish lately, and I suppose she's right. But look, old friend, you can't spend the evening moping by yourself, you absolutely can't. Lesentru'll be here, do you know that? And Kuiane. Maybe even Broyal and Hammin, later on. And a rumor of Cenbe, too, though I suspect he won't show up until the very last minute, as usual. Listen, there are all sorts of stories to tell. You were in Canterbury, weren't you? And we've just done the Charlemagne thing. We have some splendid tips on what to see and what to avoid. You'll come, of course. Room 941, the end of the hall."

"I don't know if I—"

"Of course you will! Of course!"

Antilimoin's gusto was irresistible. It always was. The man was a ferociously social being: when he gave a party, attendance was never optional. And Thimiroi realized, after a moment, that it was better, perhaps, for him to go than to lurk here by himself, tensely awaiting the ordeals that tomorrow would bring. He had already brought more than enough suspicion upon himself. Antilimoin's party would be his farewell to his native time, to his friends, to everything that had been his life.

He spent a busy hour planning what had to be planned.

Then he dressed in his formal best—in the clothes, in fact, that he had planned to wear tomorrow night—and went upstairs. The party was going at full force. Antilimoin, dapper and elegant as always, greeted him with a hearty embrace, and Fevra and Maitira came gliding up from opposite sides of the room to kiss him, and Thimiroi saw, farther away, Lesentru and Kuiane deep in conversation with Lutheena, Denvin, and some others. Everyone seemed buoyant, excited, energetic. There was tension, too, the undercurrent of keen excitement that comes on the eve of a powerful experience. Voices were pitched a little too high, gestures were a trifle too emphatic. A great screen on one wall was playing one of Cenbe's finest symphonias, but no one seemed to be watching or listening. Thimiroi glanced at it and shivered. Cenbe, of course: that connoisseur of disaster, assembling his masterpieces out of other people's tragedies—he was the perfect artist for this event. Doubtless he was in the city already, skulking around somewhere looking for the material he would need to complete his newest and surely finest work.

I will never see any of these people again after tonight, Thimiroi thought, and the concept was so difficult to accept that he repeated it to himself two or three more times, without being able to give it any more reality.

Laliene appeared beside him. There was no sign on her face of the earlier unpleasantness between them; her eyes were glowing and she was smiling warmly, even tenderly, as though they were lovers.

"I'm glad you came," she murmured. "I hoped you would."

"Antilimoin is very persuasive."

"You must have some tea. You look so tense, Thimiroi."

"Do I?"

"Is it because of our talk before?"

He shrugged. "Let's forget all about that, shall we?"

Laliene let the tips of her fingers rest lightly on his arm. "I should never have put that transmitter in your room. It was utterly stupid of me."

"It was, yes. But that's all ancient history."

Her face rose toward his. "Come have some tea with me."

"Laliene—"

Softly she said, "I wanted you to come to me so very badly. That was why I did it. You were ignoring me—you've ignored me ever since this trip began—oh, Thimiroi, Thimiroi, I'm trying to do the right thing, don't you see? And I want you to do the right thing too."

"What are you trying to tell me, Laliene?"

"Be careful, is what I'm trying to tell you."

"Careful of what?"

"Have some tea with me," she said.

"I'll have some tea," he told her. "But not, I think, with you."

Tears welled in her eyes. She turned her head to the side, but not so quickly that Thimiroi did not see them.

That was new, he thought. Tears in Laliene's eyes! He had never known her to be so overwrought. Too much euphoriac, he wondered? She kept her grip on his arm for a long moment, and then, smiling sadly, she released him and moved away.

"Thimiroi!" Lesentru called, turning and grinning broadly at him and waving his long thin arms. "How absolutely splendid to see you! Come, come, let's sip a little together!" He crossed the room as if swimming through air. "You look so gloomy, man! That can't be allowed. "Lutheena! Fevra! Everybody! We must cheer Thimiroi up! We can't let anyonc go around looking as bleak as this, not tonight."

They swept toward him from every direction, six, eight, ten of them, laughing, whooping, embracing him, holding fragrant cups of euphoriac tea out at him. It began almost to seem that the party was in his honor. Why were they making such a fuss over him? He was starting to regret having come here at all. He drank the tea that someone put in his hand, and almost at once there was another cup there. He drank that too.

Laliene was at his side again. Thimiroi was having trouble focusing his eyes.

"What did you mean?" he asked. "When you said to be careful."

"I'm not supposed to say. It would be improperly influencing the flow of events."

"Be improper, then. But stop talking in riddles."

"Are they such riddles, then?"

"To me they are."

"I think you know what I'm talking about," Laliene said.

"I do?"

They might have been all alone in the middle of the room. I have had too much euphoriac, he told himself. But I can still hold my own. I can still hold my own, yes.

Laliene said in a low whisper, leaning close, her breath warm against his cheek, "Tomorrow—where are you going to go tomorrow, Thimiroi?"

He looked at her, astounded, speechless.

"I know," she said.

"Get away from me."

"I've known all along. I've been trying to save you from—"

"You're out of your mind, Laliene."

"No, Thimiroi. *You* are!"

She clung to him. Everyone was gaping at them.

Terror seized him. I have to get out of here, he thought. Now. Go to Christine. Help her pack, and go with her to the airport. Right now. Whatever time it is, midnight, one in the morning, whatever. Before they can stop me. Before they *change* me.

"No, Thimiroi," Laliene cried. "Please—please—"

Furiously he pushed her away. She went sprawling to the floor, landing in a flurried heap at Antilimoin's feet. Everyone was yelling at once.

Laliene's voice came cutting through the confusion. "Don't do it, Thimiroi! *Don't do it!*"

He swung around and rushed toward the door, and through it, and wildly down the stairs, and through the quiet hotel lobby and out into the night. A brilliant crescent moon hung above him, and behind it the cold blaze of the stars in the clear darkness. Looking back, he saw no pursuers. He headed up the street toward Christine's, walking swiftly at first, then breaking into a light trot.

As he reached the corner, everything swirled and went strange around him. He felt a pang of inexplicable loss, and a sharp stab of wild fear, and a rush of anger without motive. The darkness closed bewilderingly around him, like a great glove. Then came a feeling of motion, swift and impossible to resist. He had a sense of being swept down a vast river toward an abyss that lay just beyond.

The effect lasted only a moment, but it was an endless moment, in which Thimiroi perceived the passage of time in sharp discontinuous segments, a burst of motion followed by a deep stillness and then another burst, and then stillness again. All color went from the world, even the muted colors of night: the sky was a startling blinding white, the buildings about him were black.

His eyes ached. His head was whirling.

He tried to move, but his movements were jerky and futile, as though he were fighting his way on foot through a deep tank of water. It must be the euphoriac, he told himself. I have had much too much. But I have had too much before, and I have never felt anything like—like—

Then the strangeness vanished as swiftly as it had come.

Everything was normal again, the whiteness gone from the sky, time flowing as it had always flowed, and he was running smoothly, steadily, down the street, like some sort of machine, arms and legs pumping, head thrown back.

Christine's house was dark. He rang the bell, and when there was no answer he hammered on the door.

"Christine! Christine, it's me, Thimiroi! Open the door, Christine! Hurry! Please!"

There was no response. He pounded on the door again.

This time a light went on upstairs.

"Here," he called. "I'm by the front door!"

Her window opened. Christine looked out and down at him.

"Who are you? What do you want? Do you know what time it is?"

"Christine!"

"Go away."

"But—Christine—"

"You have exactly two seconds to get away from here, whoever you are. Then I'm calling the police." Her voice was cold and angry. "They'll sober you up fast enough."

"Christine, I'm *Thimiroi.*"

"Who? What kind of name is that? I don't know anybody by that name. I've never seen you before in my life." The window slammed shut. The light went out above him. Thimiroi stood frozen, amazed, dumbstruck.

Then he began to understand.

Laliene said, "We all knew, yes. We were told before we ever came here. Nothing is secret to those who operate The Travel. How could it be? They move freely through all of time. They see everything. We were warned in Canterbury that you were going to try an intervention, and that there would be a counter-intervention if you did. So I tried to stop you. To prevent you from getting yourself into trouble."

"By throwing your body at me?" Thimiroi said bitterly.

"By getting you to fall in love with me," she said. "So that you wouldn't want to get involved with *her.*"

He shook his head in wonder. "All along, throughout the whole trip. Everything you did, aimed at ensnaring me into a romance, just as I thought. What I didn't realize was that you were simply trying to save me from myself."

"Yes."

"I suppose you didn't try hard enough," Thimiroi said. "No. No, that isn't it. You tried too hard."

"Did I?"

"Perhaps that was it. At any rate I didn't want you, not at any point. I wanted her the moment I saw her. It couldn't have been avoided, I suppose."

"I'm sorry, Thimiroi."

"That you failed?"

"That you have done such harm to yourself."

He stood there wordlessly for a time. "What will happen to me now?" he asked finally.

"You'll be sent back for rehabilitation, Kadro says."

"When?"

"It's up to you. You can stay and watch the show with the rest of us—you've paid for it, after all. There's no harm, Kadro says, in letting you remain in this era another few hours. Or you can let them have you right now."

For an instant despair engulfed him. Then he regained his control.

"Tell Kadro that I think I'll go now," he said.

"Yes," said Laliene. "That's probably the wisest thing."

He said, "Will Kleph be punished too?"

"I don't think so."

He felt a surge of anger. "Why not? Why is what I did any different from what she did? All right, I had a twentieth-century lover. So did Kleph. You know that. That Wilson man."

"It was different, Thimiroi."

"Different? How?"

"For Kleph it was just a little diversion, an illicit adventure. What she was doing was wrong, but it didn't imperil the basic structure of things. She doesn't propose to save this Wilson. She isn't going to intervene with the pattern. You were going to run off with yours, weren't you? Live with her somewhere far from here, spare her from the calamity, possibly change all time to come? That couldn't be tolerated, Thimiroi. I'm astonished that you thought it would be. But of course you were in love."

Thimiroi was silent again. Then he said, "Will you do me one favor, at least?"

"What is that?"

"Send word to her. Her name's Christine Rawlins. She

lives in the big old house right across the street from the one where the Sanciscos are. Tell her to go somewhere else tonight—to move into the Montgomery House, maybe, or even to leave the city. She can't stay where she is. Her house is almost certainly right in the path of—of—"

"I couldn't possibly do that," Laliene said quietly.

"No?"

"It would be intervention. It's the same thing you're being punished for."

"She'll die, though!" Thimiroi cried. "She doesn't deserve that. She's full of life, full of hopes, dreams—"

"She's been dead for hundreds of years," said Laliene coolly. "Giving her another day or two of life now won't matter. If the meteor doesn't get her, the plague will. You know that. You also know that I can't intervene for her. And you know that even if I tried, she'd never believe me. She'd have no reason to. No matter what you may have told her before, she knows nothing of it now. There's been a counter-intervention, Thimiroi. You understand that, don't you? She's never known you, now. Whatever may have happened between you and she has been unhappened."

Laliene's words struck him like knives.

"So you won't do a thing?"

"I can't," she said. "I'm sorry, Thimiroi. I tried to save you from this. For friendship's sake. For love's sake, even. But of course you wouldn't be swerved at all."

Kadro came into the room. He was dressed for the evening's big event already.

"Well?" he said. "Has Laliene explained the arrangement? You can stay on through tonight, or you can go back now."

Thimiroi looked at him, and back at Laliene, and to Kadro again. It was all very clear. He had gambled and lost.

He had tried to do a foolish, romantic, impossible sort of thing, a twentieth-century sort of thing, for he was in many ways a twentieth-century sort of man; and it had failed, as of course, he realized now, it had been destined to do from the start. But that did not mean it had not been worth attempting. Not at all. Not at all.

"I understand," Thimiroi said. "I'll go back now."

The chairs had all been arranged neatly before the windows in the upstairs rooms. It was past midnight. There was euphoria in the air, thick and dense. A quarter moon hung over the doomed city, but it was almost hidden now by the thickening clouds. The long season of clear skies was ending. The weather was changing, finally.

"It will be happening very soon now," Omerie said.

Laliene nodded. "I feel almost as though I've lived through it several times already."

"The same with me," said Kleph.

"Perhaps we have," said Klia, with a little laugh. "Who knows? We go round and round in time, and maybe we travel over the same paths more than once."

Denvin said, "I wonder where Thimiroi is now. And what they're doing to him."

"Let's not talk of Thimiroi," Antilimoin said. "It's too sad."

"He won't be able to Travel again, will he?" asked Maitira.

"Never again. Absolutely forbidden," Omerie said. "But he'll be lucky if that's the worst thing they throw at him. What he did was unforgivable. Unforgivable!"

"Antilimoin's right," said Laliene. "Let's not talk of Thimiroi."

Kleph moved closer to her. "You love him, don't you?"

"Loved," Laliene said.

"Here. Some more tea."

"Yes. Yes." Laliene smiled grimly. "He wanted me to send a warning to that woman of his, do you know? She lives right across the way. Her house will be destroyed by the shock wave, almost certainly."

Lutheena said, looking shocked, "You didn't think of doing it, did you?"

"Of course not. But I feel so sad about it, all the same. He loved her, you know. And I loved him. And so, for his sake, entirely for his sake—" Laliene shook her head. "But of course it was inconceivable. I suppose she's asleep right at this minute, not even suspecting—"

"Better the meteor than the Blue Death that follows," said Omerie. "Quicker. The quick deaths are the good ones. What's the point of hiding from the meteor only to die of the plague?"

"This is too morbid," Klia said. "I almost wish we hadn't come here. We could have skipped it and just gone on to Charlemagne's coronation—"

"We'll be there soon enough," said Kleph. "But we're here, now. And it's going to be wonderful—wonderful—"

"Places, everybody!" Kadro called. "It's almost time! Ten—nine—eight—"

Laliene held her breath. This all seemed so familiar, she thought. As though she had been through it many times already. In a moment the impact, and the tremendous sound, and the first flames rising, and the first stunned cries from the city, and the dark shapes moving around in the distance, blind, bewildered—and then the lurid sky, red as blood, the long unending shriek coming as though from a single voice—

"Now," said Kadro.

There was an astounding stillness overhead. The onrushing meteor might almost have been sucking all sound from the city toward which it plummeted. And after the silence the cataclysmic crash, the incredible impact, the earth itself recoiling with the force of the collision.

Poor Thimiroi, Laliene thought. And that poor woman, too.

Her heart overflowed with love and sorrow, and her eyes filled with tears, and she turned away from the window, unable to watch, unable to see. Then came the cries. And then the flames.

The Way to Spook City

The air was shining up ahead, a cold white pulsing glow bursting imperiously out of the hard blue desert sky. That sudden chilly dazzle told Demeris that he was at the border, that he was finally getting his first glimpse of the place where human territory ended and the alien-held lands began.

He halted and stood staring for a moment, half expecting to see monsters flying around overhead on the far side of the line; and right on cue something weird went flapping by, a blotch of darkness against the brilliant icy sheen that was lighting everything up over there in the Occupied Zone. It was a heavy thing the size of a hawk and a half, with a lumpy greenish body and narrow wings like sawblades and a long snaky back that had a little globular purple head at the end of it. The creature was so awkward that Demeris had to laugh. He couldn't see how it stayed airborne. The bird, if that was what it was, flew on past, heading north, dropping a line of bright turquoise turds behind it. A little burst of flame sprang up in the dry grass where each one fell.

"Thank you kindly for that pretty welcome," Demeris called out after it, sounding jauntier than he felt.

He went a little closer to the barrier. It sprang straight up out of the ground like an actual wall, but one that was intangible and more or less transparent: he could make out vague outlines of what lay beyond that dizzying shield of light, a blurry landscape that should have been basically the same on the Spook side of the line as it was over here, low sandy hills, gray splotches of sagebrush, sprawling clumps of prickly pear, but which was in fact mysteriously touched by strangeness—unfamiliar serrated buttes, angular chasms with metallic blue-green walls, black-trunked leafless trees with rigid branches jutting out like horizontal crossbars. Everything was veiled, though, by the glow of the barrier that separated the Occupied Zone from the fragment of the former United States that lay to the west of it, and he couldn't be sure how much he was actually seeing and how much was simply the product of his expectant imagination.

A shiver of distaste ran through him. Demeris's father, who was dead now, had always regarded the Spooks as his personal enemy, and that had carried over to him. "They're just biding their time, Nick," his father would say. "One of these days they'll come across the line and grab our land the way they grabbed what they've got already. And there won't be a goddamned thing we can do about it." Demeris had dedicated himself ever since to maintaining the order and prosperity of the little ranch near the eastern border of Free Country that was his family heritage, and he loathed the Spooks, not just for what they had done but simply because they were hateful—unknown, strange, unimaginable, alien. Not-us. Others were able to take the aliens and the regime they had imposed on the old U.S.A. for granted: all that had happened long ago, ancient history. In any case there had never been a hint that the elder Demeris's fears were likely to be realized. The Spooks kept to themselves inside the Occupied Zone. In a hundred fifty years they had shown no sign of interest in expanding beyond the territory they had seized right at the beginning.

He took another step forward, and another, and waited

for things to come into better focus. But they didn't.

Demeris had made the first part of the journey from Albuquerque to Spook Land on muleback, with his brother Bud accompanying him as far as the west bank of the Pecos. But when they reached the river Demeris had sent Bud back with the mules. Bud was five years younger than Demeris, but he had three kids already. Men who had kids had no business going into Spook territory. You were supposed to go across when you were a kid yourself, for a lark, for a stunt.

Demeris had had no time for larks and stunts when he was younger. His parents had died when he was a boy, leaving him to raise his two small sisters and three younger brothers. By the time they were grown he was too old to be very interested in adventures in the Occupied Zone. But then this last June his youngest brother Tom, who had just turned eighteen, an unpredictable kid whose head seemed stuffed with all sorts of incomprehensible fantasies and incoherent yearnings, had gone off to make his Entrada. That was what New Mexicans called someone's first crossing of the border—a sort of rite of passage, the thing you did to show that you had become an adult. Demeris had never seen what was particularly adult about going to Spook Land, but he saw such things differently from most people. So Tom had gone in.

He hadn't come out, though.

The traditional length of time for an Entrada was thirty days. Tom had been gone three months now. Worry over Tom nagged at Demeris like an aching tooth. Tom was his reckless baby. Always had been, always would be. And so Demeris had decided to go in after him. Someone had to fetch Tom out of that place, and Demeris, the head of the family, the one who had always seemed to seek out responsibilities the way other people looked for shade on a sunny day, had appointed himself the one to do it. His father would have expected that of him. And Demeris was the only member of the family besides Tom himself who had never married, who had no kids, who could afford to take a risk.

What you do, Bud had said, is walk right up to the barrier and keep on going no matter what you may see or feel or think you want to do. "They'll throw all sorts of stuff at you," Bud had told him. "Don't pay it any mind. Just keep on going."

And now he was there, at the barrier zone itself.

You walk right up to it and keep on going, that was what you had to do. No matter what it did, what it threw at you.

Okay. Demeris walked right up to it. He kept on going.

The moment he stepped through the fringes of the field he felt it starting to attack him. It came on in undulating waves, the way he imagined an earthquake would, shaking him unrelentingly and making him slip and slide and struggle to stay upright. The air around him turned thick and yellow and he couldn't see more than a couple of yards in any direction. Just in front of him was a shimmering blood-hued blur that abruptly resolved itself into an army of scarlet caterpillars looping swiftly toward him over the ground, millions of them, a blazing carpet. They spread out all around him. Little teeth were gnashing in their pop-eyed heads and they made angry, muttering sounds as they approached. There was no avoiding them. He walked in among them and it was like walking on a sea of slime. A kind of growling thunder rose from them as he crushed them under foot. "Bad dreams," Bud was saying, in his ear, in his brain. "All they are is a bunch of bad dreams." Sure.

Demeris forged onward. How deep was the boundary strip, anyway? Twenty yards? Fifty? He ached in a dozen places, his eyes were stinging, his teeth seemed to be coming loose. Beyond the caterpillars he found himself at the edge of an abyss of pale quivering jelly, but there was no turning back. He compelled himself into it and its substance rose up around him like a soft blanket, and a wave of pain swept upward through him from the scrotum to the back of his neck: to avoid it he pivoted and twisted, and he felt his backbone bending as if it was going to pop out of his flesh the way the fishbone comes away from the filleted meat. Stinking rain swept horizontally over him, and then hot sleet that raked his forehead and drew howls of rage from him. No wonder you couldn't get a mule to cross this barrier, he thought. Head down, gasping for breath, he pushed himself forward another few steps. Something like a crab with wings came fluttering up out of a steaming mud hole and seized his arm, biting it just below the elbow on the inside. A stream of black blood spurted out. He yelled and flapped his arm until he shook the thing off. The pain lit a track of fire all along his arm, up to the shoulder and doubling back to his twitching fingers. He stared at his hand and saw just a knob of raw meat with blackened sticks jutting from it. Then it flickered and looked whole again.

He felt tears on his cheeks, and that amazed him: the last time he had wept was when his father died, years ago. Suddenly the urge arose in him to give up and turn back while he still could. That surprised him too. It had always been his way to go plugging ahead, doing what needed to be done, even when others were telling him, Demeris, don't be an asshole, Demeris, don't push yourself so hard, Demeris, let someone else do it for once. He had only shrugged. Let others slough off if they liked: he just didn't have the knack of it. Now, here, in this place, when he absolutely *could not* slough off, he felt the temptation to yield and go back. But he knew it was only the barrier playing devil-tricks with him. So he encapsulated the desire to turn back into a hard little shell and hurled it from him and watched it burn up in a puff of flame. And went onward.

Three suns were blazing overhead, a red one, a green one, a blue. The air seemed to be melting. He heard incomprehensible chattering voices coming out of it like demonic static, and then disembodied faces were hovering all around him suddenly, jittering and shimmering in the soupy murk, the faces of people he knew, his sisters Ellie and Netta, his nieces and nephews, his friends. He cried out to them. But everyone was horridly distorted, blobby-cheeked and bug-eyed, grotesque fun-house images. They were pointing at him and laughing. Then he saw his father and mother pointing and laughing too, which had to be impossible, and he understood. Bud was right: these were nothing but illusions or maybe delusions. The images he was seeing were things that he carried within him. Part of him. Harmless.

He began to run, plunging on through a tangle of slippery threads, a kind of soft, spongy curtain. It yielded as he ripped at it and he fell face down onto a bank of dry sandy soil that was unremarkable in every way: mere desert dirt, real-world stuff, no fancy colors, no crazy textures. More trickery? No. No, this was real. The extra suns were gone and the one that remained was the yellow one he had always known. A fresh wind blew against his face. He was across. He had made it.

He lay still for a minute or two, catching his breath.

Hot stabs of pain were coming from his arm, and when he looked down at it he saw a jagged bloody cut high up near the inside of the elbow, where he had imagined the crab-thing had bitten him. But the crab-thing had been only a dream, only an illusion. Can an illusion bite? he wondered. The pain, at any rate, was no illusion. Demeris felt it all the way up through the back of his throat, his nostrils, his forehead. A nasty pulsation was running through the whole arm, making his hand quiver rhythmically in time with it. The cut was maybe two inches long, and deep enough to see into. Fresh blood came dribbling from it every time his heart pumped. Fine, he thought, I'll bleed to death from an imaginary cut before I'm ten feet inside the Occupied Zone. But after a moment the wound began to clot over and the bleeding stopped, though the pain remained.

Shakily he stood up and glanced about.

Behind him was the vertical column of the barrier field, looking no more menacing than a searchlight beam from this side. Dimly he saw the desert flatlands of Free Country beyond it, the scrubby ordinary place from which he had just come.

On this side, though, everything was a realm of magic and mysteries.

He was able more or less to make out the basic raw material of the landscape, the underlying barren dry New Mexico/Texas nowheresville that he had spent his entire life in. But here on the far side of the barrier the invaders had done some serious screwing around with the look of the land. The jag-edged buttes and blue-green arroyos that Demeris had glimpsed through the barrier field from the other side were no illusions; somebody had taken the trouble to come out here and redesign the empty terrain, sticking in all sorts of bizarre structures and features. He saw strange zones of oddly colored soil, occasional ramshackle metal towers, entire deformed geological formations—twisted cones and spiky spires and uplifted layers—that made his eyes hurt. He saw groves of unknown wire-leaved trees and arroyos crisscrossed by sinister glossy black threads like stitches across a wound. Everything was solid and real, none of it wiggling and shifting about the way things did inside the barrier field. Wherever he looked there was evidence of how the conquerors had put their mark on the land. Some of it was actually almost beautiful, he thought; and then he recoiled, astonished at his own reaction. But there *was* a strange sort of beauty in the alien landscape. It disgusted him and moved him all at once, a response so complex that he scarcely knew how to handle it.

They must have been trying to make the landscape look like the place they had originally come from, he told himself. The idea of a whole world looking that way practically nauseated him. What they had done was a downright affront. Land was something to live on and to use productively, not to turn into a toy. They didn't have any right to take part of ours and make it look like theirs, he thought, and anger rose in him again.

He thought of his ranch, the horses, the turkeys, the barns, the ten acres of good russet soil, the rows of crops ripening in the autumn sun, the fencing that he had made with his own hands running on beyond the line of virtually identical fencing his father had made. All that was a real kind of reality, ordinary, familiar, solid—something he could not only understand but love. It was home, family, good clean hard work, sanity itself. This, though, this—this lunacy, this horror—

He tore a strip of cloth from one of the shirts in his backpack and tied it around the cut on his arm. And started walking east, toward the place where he hoped his brother Tom would be, toward the big settlement midway between the former site of Amarillo and the former site of Lubbock that was known as Spook City.

He kept alert for alien wildlife, constantly scanning to front and rear, sniffing, watching for tracks. The Spooks had brought a bunch of their jungle beasts from their home world and turned them loose in the desert. "It's like Africa out there," Bud had said. "You never know what's going to come up and try to gobble you." Once a year, Demeris knew, the aliens held a tremendous hunt on the outskirts of Spook City, a huge apocalyptic round-up where they surrounded and killed the strange beasts by the thousands and the streets ran blue and green with rivers of their blood. The rest of the time the animals roamed free in the hinterlands. Some of them occasionally strayed across the border barrier and went wandering around on the Free Country side: while he was preparing himself for his journey Demeris had visited a ranch near Bernalillo where a dozen or so of them were kept on display as a sort of zoo of nightmares, grisly things with red scaly necks and bird-beaks and ears like rubber batwings and tentacles on their heads, huge ferocious animals that seemed to have been put together randomly out of a stock of miscellaneous parts. But so far out here he had encountered nothing more threatening-looking than jackrabbits and lizards. Now and again a bird that was not a bird passed overhead—one of the big snake-necked things he had seen earlier, and another the size of an eagle with four transparent veined wings like a dragonfly's but a thick moth-like furry body between them, and a third one that had half a dozen writhing prehensile rat-tails dangling behind it for eight or ten feet, trolling for food. He watched it snatch a shrieking blue jay out of the air as though it were a bug.

When he was about three hours into the Occupied Zone

he came to a cluster of bedraggled little adobe houses at the bottom of a bowl-shaped depression that had the look of a dry lake. A thin fringe of scrubby plant growth surrounded the place, ordinary things, creosote bush and mesquite and yucca. Demeris saw some horses standing at a trough, a couple of scrawny black and white cows munching on prickly pears, a few half-naked children running circles in the dust. There was nothing alien about them, or about the buildings or the wagons and storage bins that were scattered all around. Everyone knew that Spooks were shapeshifters, that they could take on human form when the whim suited them, that when the advance guard of infiltrators had first entered the United States to prepare the way for the invasion they were all wearing human guise. But more likely this was a village of genuine humans. Bud had said there were a few little towns between the border and Spook City, inhabited by the descendants of those who had chosen to remain in the Occupied Zone after the conquest. Most people with any sense had moved out when the invaders came, even though the aliens hadn't formally asked anyone to leave. But some had stayed.

The afternoon was well along and the first chill of evening was beginning to creep into the clear dry air. The cut on his arm was still throbbing and he didn't feel much like camping in the open if he didn't have to. Perhaps these people would let him crash for the night.

When he was halfway to the bottom of the dirt road a gnomish little leathery-skinned man who looked to be about ninety years old stepped slowly out from behind a gnarled mesquite bush and took up a watchful position in the middle of the path. A moment later a boy of about sixteen, short and stocky in torn denim pants and a frayed undershirt, emerged from the same place. The boy was carrying what might have been a gun, which at a gesture from the older man he raised and aimed. It was a shiny tube a foot and a half long with a nozzle at one end and a squeeze-bulb at the other. The nozzle pointed squarely at the middle of Demeris's chest. Demeris stopped short and put his hands in the air.

The old man said something in a language that was full of grunts and clicks, and some whistling snorts. The denim boy nodded and replied in the same language.

To Demeris the boy said, "You traveling by yourself?" He was dark-haired, dark-eyed, mostly Indian or Mexican, probably. A ragged red scar ran up along his cheek to his forehead.

Demeris kept his hands up. "By myself, yes. I'm from the other side."

"Well, sure you are. Fool could see that." The boy's tone was thick, his accent unfamiliar, the end of each word clipped off in an odd way. Demeris had to work to understand him. "You making your Entrada? You a little old for that sort of thing, maybe." Laughter sparkled in the boy's eyes, but not anywhere else on his face.

"This is my first time across," Demeris said. "But it isn't exactly an Entrada."

"Your first time, that's an Entrada." The boy spoke again to the old man and got a long reply. Demeris waited patiently. Finally the boy turned back to him and said, "Okay. Remigio here says we should make it easy for you. You want to stay here your thirty days, we let you do it. You work as a field hand, that's all. We even sell you some Spook things you can take back and show off like all you people do. Okay?"

Demeris's face grew hot. "I told you, this isn't any Entrada. Entradas are fun and games for kids. I'm not a kid."

"Then what are you doing here?"

"Trying to find my brother."

The boy frowned and spat into the dusty ground, not quite in Demeris's direction. "You think we got your brother here?"

"He's in Spook City, I think."

"Spook City. Yeah. I bet that's where he is. They all go there. For the hunt, they go." He put his finger to his head and moved it in a circle. "You do that, you got to be a little crazy, you know? Going there for the hunt. Sheesh! What dumb crazy fuckers." He laughed and said, "Well, come on, I'll show you where you can stay."

The place where they put him up was a tottering weather-beaten shack made of wooden slats with big stripes of sky showing through, off at the edge of town, a hundred yards or so from the nearest building. There was nothing in it but a mildewed bundle of rags tied together for sleeping on. Some of the rags bore faded inscriptions in the curvilinear Spook script, impenetrable to Demeris. A ditch out back served as a latrine. A little stream, hardly more than a rivulet, ran nearby. Demeris crouched over it and washed out his wound, which was still pulsing unpleasantly but didn't look as bad as it had at first. The water seemed reasonably safe. He took a long drink and filled his canteens. Then he sat quietly in the open doorway of the shack for a time, not thinking of anything at all, simply unwinding from his long day's march and the border crossing.

As darkness fell the boy reappeared and led him to the communal eating hall. Fifty or sixty people were sitting at long benches in family groups. A few had an Anglo look, most seemed mixed Mexican and Indian. There was little conversation, and what there was was in the local language, all clicks and snorts and whistles. Almost nobody paid any attention to him. It was as if he was invisible; but a few did stare at him now and then and he could feel the force of their hostility, an almost intangible thing.

He ate quickly and went back to his shack. But sleep was a tough proposition. He lay awake for hours, listening to the wind blowing in out of Texas and wishing he was home, on his own ten acres, in his familiar adobe house, with the houses of his brothers and sisters around him. For a while there was singing—chanting, really—coming up from the village. It was harsh and guttural and choppy, a barrage of stiff angular sounds that didn't follow any musical scale he knew. Listening to it, he felt a powerful sense of the strangeness of these people who had lived under Spook rule for so long, tainted by Spook ways, governed by Spook ideas. How had they survived? How had they been able to stand it, the changes, the sense of being owned? But somehow they had adapted, by turning themselves into something beyond his understanding.

Later, other sounds drifted to him, the night sounds of the desert, hoots and whines and screeches that might have been coming from owls and coyotes, but probably weren't. He thought he heard noise just outside his shack, people moving around doing something, but he was too groggy to get up and see what was going on. At last he fell into a sort of stupor and lay floating in it until dawn. Just before morning he dreamed he was a boy again, with his mother and father still alive and Dave and Bud and the girls just babies and Tom not yet even born. He and his dad were out on the plains hunting Spooks, vast swarms of gleaming vaporous Spooks that were drifting overhead as thick as mosquitoes, two brave men walking side by side, the big one and the smaller one, killing the thronging aliens with dart guns that popped them like balloons. When they died they gave off a screeching sound like metal on metal and released a smell like rotting eggs and plummeted to the ground, covering it with a glassy scum that quickly melted away and left a scorched and flaking surface behind. It was a very satisfying dream. Then a flood of morning light broke through the slats and woke him.

Emerging from the shack, he discovered a small tent pitched about twenty yards away that hadn't been there the night before. A huge mottled yellow animal was tethered nearby, grazing on weeds: something that might have been a camel except there weren't any camels the size of elephants, camels with three shallow humps and great goggling green eyes the size of saucers, or knees on the backs of their legs as well as in front. As he gaped at it a woman wearing tight khaki slacks and a shirt buttoned up to the collar came out of the tent and said, "Never seen one of those before?"

"You bet I haven't. This is my first time across."

"Is it, now?" she said. She had an accent too. It wasn't as strange to Demeris as the village boy's but there was some other kind of spin to it, a sound like that of a tolling bell beneath the patterns of the words themselves.

She was youngish, slender, not bad-looking: long straight brown hair, high cheekbones, tanned Anglo face. It was hard to guess her age. Somewhere between 25 and 35 was the best he could figure. She had very dark eyes, bright, almost glossy, oddly defiant. It seemed to him that there was a kind of aura around her, a puzzling crackle of simultaneous attraction and repulsion.

She told him what the camel-thing was called. The word was an intricate slurred sound midway between a whistle and a drone, rising sharply at the end. "You do it now," she said. Demeris looked at her blankly. The sound was impossible to imitate. "Go on. Do it."

"I don't speak Spook."

"It's not all that hard." She made the sound again. Her eyes flashed with amusement.

"Never mind. I can't do it."

"You just need some practice."

Her gaze was focused right on his, strong, direct, almost aggressive. At home he didn't know many women who looked at you like that. He was accustomed to having women depend on him, to draw strength or whatever else they needed from him until they were ready to go on their way and let him go on his.

"My name's Jill," she said. "I live in Spook City. I've been in Texas a few weeks and now I'm on my way back."

"Nick Demeris. From Albuquerque. Traveling up that way too."

"What a coincidence."

"I suppose," he said.

A sudden hot fantasy sprang up just then out of nowhere within him: that instant sexual chemistry had stricken her like a thunderbolt and she was going to invite him to travel with her, that they'd ride right off into the desert together, that when they made camp that evening she would turn to him with parted lips and shining eyes and open her arms and beckon him toward her—

The urgency and intensity of the idea surprised him as much as its adolescent foolishness. Had he really let himself get as horny as that? She didn't even seem that interesting to him.

In any case he knew it wasn't going to happen. She looked cool, self-sufficient, self-contained. She wouldn't have any need for his companionship on her trip home and probably not for anything else he might have to offer.

"What brings you over here?" she asked him.

He told her about his missing brother. Her eyes narrowed thoughtfully as he spoke. She was taking a good long look, studying his face with great care, staring at him as though peering right through his skull into his brain. Turning her head this way and that, checking him out.

"I think I may know him, your brother," she said calmly, after a time.

He blinked. "You do? Seriously?"

"Not as tall as you and stockier, right? But otherwise he looks pretty much like you, only younger. Face a lot like yours, broader, but the same cheekbones, the same high forehead, the same color eyes, the same blond hair, but his is longer. The same very serious expression all the time, tight as a drum."

"Yes," Demeris said, with growing wonder. "That's him. It has to be."

"Don, that was his name. No, Tom. Don, Tom, one of those short little names."

"Tom."

"Tom, right."

He was amazed. "How do you know him?" he asked.

"Turned up in Spook City a couple of months back. June, July, somewhere back then. It isn't such a big place that you don't notice new people when they come in. Had that Free Country look about him, you know. Kind of big-eyed, raw-boned, can't stop gawking at things. But he seemed a little different from most the other Entrada kids, like there was something coiled up inside him that was likely to pop out any minute, that this trip wasn't just a thing he was doing for the hell of it but that it had some other meaning for him, something deeper that only he could understand. Peculiar sort of guy, actually."

"That was Tom, yes." The side of Demeris's face was starting to twitch. "You think he might still be there?"

"Could be. More likely than not. He was talking about staying quite a while, at least until fall, until hunt time."

"And when is that?"

"It starts late next week."

"Maybe I can still find him, then. If I can get there in time."

"I'm leaving here this afternoon. You can ride with me to Spook City if you want."

"With you?" Demeris said. He was astonished. The good old instant chemistry after all? His whole little adolescent fantasy coming to life? It seemed too neat, too slick. The world didn't work like this. And yet—yet—

"Sure. Plenty of room on those humps. Take you at least a week if you walk there, if you're a good walker. Maybe longer. Riding, it'll be just a couple of days."

What the hell, he thought.

It would be dumb to turn her down. That Spook-mauled landscape was an evil place when you were on your own.

"Sure," he said, after a bit. "Sure, I'd be glad to. If you really mean it."

"Why would I say it if I didn't mean it?"

Abruptly the notion came to him that this woman and Tom might have had something going for a while in Spook City. Of course. Of course. Why else would she remember in such detail some unknown kid who had wandered into her town months before? There had to be something else there. She must have met Tom in some Spook City bar, a couple of drinks, some chatter, a night or two of lively bed games, maybe even a romance lasting a couple of weeks. Tom wouldn't hesitate, even with a woman ten, fifteen years older than he was. And so she was offering him this ride now as a courtesy to a member of the family, so to speak. It wasn't his tremendous masculine appeal that had done it, it was mere politeness. Or curiosity about what Tom's older brother might be like.

Into his long confused silence she said, "The critter here needs a little more time to feed itself up. Then we can take off. Around two o'clock, okay?"

After breakfast the boy went over to him in the dining hall and said, "You meet the woman who come in during the night?"

Demeris nodded. "She's offering me a ride to Spook City."

Something that might have been scorn flickered across the boy's face. "That nice. You take it?"

"Better than walking there, isn't it?"

A quick knowing glance. "You crazy if you go with her, man."

Demeris said, frowning, "Why is that?"

The boy put his hand over his mouth and muffled a laugh. "That woman, she a Spook, man. You mean you don't see that? Only a damn fool go traveling around with a Spook."

Demeris was stunned for a moment, and then angry. "Don't play around with me," he said, irritated.

"Yeah, man. I'm playing. It's a joke. Just a joke." The boy's voice was flat, chilly, bearing its own built-in contradiction. The contempt in his dark hard eyes was unmistakable now. "Look, you go ride with her if you like. Let her do whatever she wants with you once she got you out there in the desert. Isn't none of my goddamn business. Fucking Free Country guys, you all got shit for brains."

Demeris squinted at him, shaken now, not sure what to

believe. The kid's cold-eyed certainty carried tremendous force. But it made no sense to him that this Jill could be an alien. Her voice, her bearing, everything about her, were too convincingly real. The Spooks couldn't imitate humans that well, could they?

Had they?

"You know this thing for a fact?" Demeris asked.

"For a fact I don't know shit," the boy said. "I never see her before, not that I can say. She come around and she wants us to put her up for the night, that's okay. We put her up. We don't care what she is if she can pay the price. But anybody with any sense, he can smell Spook on her. That's all I tell you. You do whatever you fucking like, man."

The boy strolled away. Demeris stared after him, shaking his head. He felt a tremor of bewilderment and shock, as though he had abruptly found himself looking over the edge of an abyss.

Then came another jolt of anger. Jill a Spook? It couldn't be. Everything about her seemed human.

But why would the boy make up something like that? He had no reason for it. And maybe the kid *could* tell. Over on the other side, really paranoid people carried witch-charms around with them to detect Spooks who might be roaming Free Country in disguise, little gadgets that were supposed to sound an alarm when aliens came near you, but Demeris had never taken such things seriously. It stood to reason, though, that people living out here in Spook Land would be sensitive to the presence of a Spook among them, however well disguised it might be. They wouldn't need any witch-charms to tell them. They had had a hundred fifty years to get used to being around Spooks. They'd know the smell of them by now.

The more Demeris thought about it, the more uneasy he got.

He needed to talk to her again.

He found her a little way upstream from his shack, rubbing down the shaggy yellow flanks of her elephantine pack animal with a rough sponge. Demeris halted a short distance away and studied her, trying to see her as an alien being in disguise, searching for some clue to otherworldly origin, some gleam of Spookness showing through her human appearance.

He couldn't see it. He couldn't see it at all. But that didn't necessarily mean she was real.

After a moment she noticed him. "You ready to go?" she asked, over her shoulder.

"I'm not sure."

"What?"

He was still staring.

If she *is* a Spook, he thought, why would she want to pretend she was human? What would a Spook have to gain by inveigling a human off into the desert with her?

On the other hand, what motive did the kid have for lying to him?

Suddenly it seemed to him that the simplest and safest thing was to opt out of the entire arrangement and get to Spook City on his own, as he had originally planned. The kid might just be telling the truth. The possibility of traveling with a Spook, of being close to one, of sharing a campsite and a tent with one, sickened and repelled him. And there might be danger in it as well. He had heard wild tales of Spooks who were soul-eaters, who were energy vampires, even worse things. Why take chances?

He drew a deep breath. "Listen, I've changed my mind, okay? I think I'd just as soon travel by myself."

She turned and gave him a startled look. "You serious?"

"Yep."

"You really want to walk all the way to Spook City by yourself rather than ride with me?"

"Yep. That's what I prefer to do."

"Jesus Christ. What the hell *for?*"

Demeris could detect nothing in the least unhuman in her exasperated tone or in the annoyed expression on her face. He began to think he was making a big, big mistake. But it was too late to back off. Uncomfortably he said, "Just the way I am, I guess. I sort of like to go my own way, I guess, and—"

"Bullshit. I know what's really going on in your head."

Demeris shifted about uneasily and remained silent. He wished he had never become entangled with her in the first place.

Angrily she said, "Somebody's been talking to you, right? Telling you a lot of garbage?"

"Well—"

"All right," she said. "You dumb bastard. You want to test me, is that it?"

"Test?"

"With a witch-charm."

"No," he said. "I'm not carrying any charms. I don't have faith in them. Those things aren't worth a damn."

"They'll tell you if I'm a Spook or not."

"They don't work, is what I hear."

"Some do, some don't." She reached into a saddlepack lying near her on the ground and pulled out a small device, wires and black cords intricately wound around and around each other. "Here," she said harshly. "This is one. You point it and push the button and it emits a red glow if you're pointing it at a Spook. Take it. A gift from me to you. Use it to check out the next woman you happen to meet."

She tossed the little gadget toward him. Demeris grabbed it out of the air by reflex and stood watching helplessly as she slapped the elephant-camel's flank to spur it into motion and started off downstream toward her tent.

Shit, he thought.

He felt like six kinds of idiot. The sound of her voice, tingling with contempt for him and his petty little suspicions, still echoed in his ears.

Baffled and annoyed—with her, with himself, with the boy for starting all this up—he flipped the witch-charm into the stream. There was a hissing and a bubbling around it for a moment and then the thing sank out of sight. Then he turned and walked back to his shack to pack up.

She had already begun to take down her tent. She didn't so much as glance at him. But the elephant-camel thing peered somberly around, extended its long purple lower lip, and gave him a sardonic toothy smirk. Demeris glared at the great beast and made a devil-sign with his upraised fingers. From you, at least, I don't have to take any crap, he thought.

He hoisted his pack to his shoulders and started up the steep trail out of town.

He was somewhere along the old boundary between New Mexico and Texas, he figured, probably just barely on the New Mexico side of the line. The aliens hadn't respected state boundaries when they had carved out their domain in the middle of the United States halfway through the 21st century, and some of New Mexico had landed in alien territory and some hadn't. Spook Land was roughly triangular, running from Montana to the Great Lakes along the Canadian border and tapering southward through what had been Wyoming, Nebraska, and Iowa down to Texas and Louisiana, but they had taken a little piece of eastern New Mexico too. Demeris had learned all that in school long ago. They made you study the map of the United States that once had been: so you wouldn't forget the past, they said, because some day the old United States was going to rise again.

Fat chance. The Spooks had cut the heart right out of the country, both literally and figuratively. They had taken over with scarcely a struggle and every attempt at a counterattack had been brushed aside with astonishing ease: America's weapons had been neutralized, its communications networks were silenced, its army of liberation had disappeared into the Occupied Zone like raindrops into a lake. Now there was not one United States of America but two: the western one, which ran from Washington State and Idaho down to the Mexican border and liked to call itself Free Country, and the other one in the east, along the coast and inland as far as the Mississippi, which still insisted on using the old formal name. Between the two lay the Occupied Zone, and nobody in either United States had much knowledge of what went on in there. Nor did anyone Demeris knew take the notion of a reunited United States very seriously. If America hadn't been able to cope with the aliens at the time of the invasion, it was if anything less capable of defeating them now, with much of its technical capacity eroded away and great chunks of the country having reverted to a pastoral, pre-industrial condition.

What he had to do, he calculated, was keep heading more or less easterly until he saw indications of Spook presence. Right now, though, the country was pretty empty, just barren sandy wastes with a covering of mesquite and sage. He saw more places where the aliens had indulged in their weird remodeling of the landscape, and now and again he was able to make out the traces of some little ancient abandoned human town, a couple of rusty signs or a few crumbling walls. But mainly there was nothing at all.

He was about an hour and a half beyond the village when what looked like a squadron of airborne snakes came by, a dozen of them flying in close formation. Then the sky turned heavy and purplish-yellow, like bruised fruit getting ready to rot, and three immense things with shining red scales and sail-like three-cornered fleshy wings passed overhead, emitting bursts of green gas that had the rank smell of old wet straw. They were almost like dragons. A dozen more of the snake-things followed them. Demeris scowled and waved a clenched fist at them. The air had a tangible pressure. Something bad was about to happen. He waited to see what was coming next. But then, magically, all the ominous effects cleared away and he was in the familiar old Southwest again, untouched by strangers from the far stars, the good old land of dry ravines and big sky that he had lived in all his life. He relaxed a little, but only a little.

Almost at once he heard a familiar snorting sound behind him. He turned and saw the ponderous yellow form of the elephant-camel looming up, with Jill sitting astride it just back of the front hump.

She leaned down and said, "You change your mind yet about wanting that ride?"

"I thought you were sore at me."

"I am. Was. But it still seems crazy for you to be doing this on foot when I've got room up here for you."

He stared up at her. You don't often get second chances in this life, he told himself. But he wasn't sure what to do.

"Oh, Christ," she said, as he hesitated. "Do you want a ride or don't you?"

Still he remained silent.

She shot him a quick wicked grin. "Still worried that I'm a Spook? You can check me out if you like."

"I threw your gadget in the stream. I don't like to have witch-things around me."

"Well, that's all right." She laughed. "It wasn't a charm at all, just an old power core, and a worn-out one at that. It wouldn't have told you anything."

"What's a power core?"

"Spook stuff. You could have taken it back with you to prove you were over here. Look, do you want a ride or not?"

It seemed ridiculous to turn her down again.

"What the hell," Demeris said. "Sure."

Jill spoke to the animal in what he took to be Spook language, a hiccuping wheeze and a long indrawn whistling sound, and it knelt for him. Demeris took her hand and she drew him on top of the beast with surprising ease. An openwork construction made of loosely woven cord, half poncho and half saddle, lay across the creature's broad back, with the three humps jutting through. Her tent and other possessions were fastened to it at the rear. "Tie your pack to one of those dangling strings," she said. "You can ride right behind me."

He fitted himself into the valley between the second and third humps and got a secure hold on the weaving, fingers digging down deep into it. She whistled another command and the animal began to move forward.

Its motion was a rolling, thumping, sliding kind of thing, very hard to take. The sway was both lateral and vertical and with every step the ground seemed to rise and plunge around him in lunatic lunges. Demeris had never seen the ocean or any other large body of water, but he had heard about seasickness, and this was what he imagined it was like. He gulped, clamped his mouth shut, gripped the saddle even more tightly.

Jill called back to him, "How are you doing?"

"Fine. Fine."

"Takes some getting used to, huh?"

"Some," he said.

His buttocks didn't have much padding on them. He could feel the vast bones of the elephant-camel grinding beneath him like the pistons of some giant machine. He held on tight and dug his heels in as hard as he could.

"You see those delta-winged things go by a little while ago?" she asked, after a while.

"The big dragons that were giving off the green smoke?"

"Right. Herders is what they are. On their way to Spook City for the hunt. They'll be used to drive the game toward the killing grounds. Every year this time they get brought in to help in the round-up."

"And the flying snakes?"

"They herd the herders. Herders aren't very smart. About like dogs, maybe. The snake guys are a lot brighter. The snakes tell the herders where to go and the herders make the game animals go there too."

Demeris thought about that. Level upon level of intelligence among these creatures that the Spooks had transported to the planet they had partly conquered. If the herders were as smart as dogs, he wondered how smart the snakes were. Dogs were pretty smart. He wondered how smart the Spooks were, for that matter.

"What's the hunt all about? Why do they do it?"

"For fun," Jill said. "Spook fun."

"Herding thousands of exotic wild animals together and butchering them all at once, so the blood runs deep enough to swim through? That's their idea of fun?"

"Wait and see," she said.

They saw more and more transformation of the landscape: whorls and loops of dazzling fire, great opaque spheres floating just above ground level, silvery blades revolving in the air. Demeris glared and glowered. All that strangeness made him feel vulnerable and out of place, and he spat and murmured bitterly at each intrusive wonder.

"Why are you so angry?" she asked.

"I hate this weird shit that they've strewn all over the place. I hate what they did to our country."

"It was a long time ago. And it wasn't your country they did it to, it was your great-great-grandfather's."

"Even so."

"Your country is over there. It wasn't touched at all."

"Even so," he said again, and spat.

When it was still well before dark they came to a place where bright yellow outcroppings of sulphur, like foamy stone pillows, marked the site of a spring. Jill gave the command to make her beast kneel and hopped deftly to the ground. Demeris got off more warily, feeling the pain in his thighs and butt from his ride.

"Give me a hand with the tent," she said.

It wasn't like any tent he had ever seen. The center post was nothing more than a little rod that seemed to be made of white wax, but at the touch of a hand it tripled in height and an elaborate strut-work sprang out from it in five directions to provide support for the tent fabric. A Spook tent, he supposed. The tent pegs were made of the same waxy material, and all you had to do was position them where you wanted them around the perimeter of the tent and they burrowed into the ground on their own. Faint pinging sounds came from them as they dug themselves in.

"What's that?" he asked.

"Security check. The pegs are setting up a defensive zone for a hundred yards around us. Don't try to go through it in the night."

"I'm not going anywhere," Demeris said.

The tent was just about big enough for two. He wondered whether she was going to invite him to sleep inside it.

Together they gathered mesquite brush and built a fire, and she produced some packets of powdered vegetables and a slab of dried meat for their dinner. While they waited for things to cook Jill went to the spring, which despite the sulphurous outcroppings gave fresh, pure water, and crouched by it, stripping to the waist to wash herself. Seeing her like that was unsettling. He flicked a quick glance at her as she bathed, but she didn't seem to care, or even to notice. That was unsettling too. Was she being deliberately provocative? Or did she just not give a damn?

He washed himself also, splashing handfuls of the cold water into his face and over his sweaty shoulders. "Dinner's ready," she said a few minutes later.

Darkness descended swiftly. The sky went from deep blue to utter black in minutes. In the clear desert air the stars began quickly to emerge, sharp and bright and unflickering. He looked up at them, trying to guess which of them might be the home star of the Spooks. They had never troubled to reveal that. They had never revealed very much of anything about themselves.

As they ate he asked her whether she made this trip often. "Often enough," she said. "I do a lot of courier work for my father, out to Texas, Louisiana, sometimes Oklahoma." She paused a moment. "I'm Ben Gorton's daughter," she said, as though she expected him to recognize the name.

"Sorry. Who?"

"Ben Gorton. The mayor of Spook City, actually."

"Spook City's got a human mayor?"

"The human part of it does. The Spooks have their administration and we have ours."

"Ah," Demeris said. "I'm honored, then. The boss's daughter. You should have told me before."

"It didn't seem important," she said.

They were done with their meal. She moved efficiently around the campsite, gathering utensils, burying trash. Demeris was sure now that the village boy had simply been playing with his head. He told himself that if Jill was really a Spook he'd have sensed it somehow by this time.

When the cleanup work was done she lifted the tent flap and stepped halfway inside. He held back, unsure of the right move. "Well?" she asked. "It's okay to come in. Or would you rather sleep out there?"

Demeris went in. Though the temperature outside was plunging steeply with the onset of night, it was pleasantly warm inside. There was a single bedroll, just barely big enough for two if they didn't mind sleeping very close together. He heard the sounds she made as she undressed, and tried in the absolute darkness to guess how much she was taking off. It wasn't easy to tell. He removed his own shirt and hesitated with his jeans; but then she opened the flap again to call something out to the elephant-camel, which she had tethered just outside, and by starlight he caught a flashing glimpse of bare thigh, bare buttock. He pulled off his trousers and slipped into the bedroll. She joined him a moment later. He lay awkwardly, trying to avoid rubbing up against her. For a time there was a tense expectant silence. Then her hand reached out in the darkness and grazed his shoulder, lightly but clearly not accidentally. Demeris didn't need a second hint. He had never taken any vows of chastity. He reached for her, found the hollow of her clavicle, trailed his hand downward until he was cupping a small, cool breast, resilient and firm. When he ran his thumb lightly across the nipples she made a little purring sound, and he felt the flesh quickly hardening. As was his. She turned to him. Demeris had some difficulty locating her mouth in the darkness, and she had to guide him, chuckling a little, but when his lips met hers he felt the immediate flicker of her tongue coming forth to greet him.

And then almost as though he was willing his own downfall he found himself perversely wondering if he might be embracing a Spook after all; and a wave of nausea swept through him, making him wobble and soften. But she was pressing tight against him, rubbing her breasts from side to side on him, uttering small eager murmuring sounds, and he got himself quickly back on track, losing himself in her fragrance and warmth and banishing completely from his thoughts anything but the sensations of the moment. After that one attack of doubt everything was easy. He located her long smooth thighs with no problem whatever, and when he glided into her he needed no guidance there either, and though their movements together had the usual first-time clumsiness her hot gusts of breath against his shoulder and her soft sharp outcries told him that all was going well.

He lay awake for a time when it was over, listening to the reassuring pinging of the tent pegs and the occasional far-off cry of some desert creature. He imagined he could hear the heavy snuffling breathing of the elephant-camel too, like a huge recirculating device just outside the tent. Jill had curled up against him as if they were old friends and was lost in sleep.

* * * * *

She said out of the blue, after they had been riding a long while in silence the following morning, "You ever been married, Nick?"

The incongruity of the question startled him. Until a moment ago she had seemed to be a million miles away. His attempt to make love to her a second time at dawn had been met with indifference and she had been pure business, remote and cool, all during the job of breaking camp and getting on the road.

"No," he said. "You?"

"Hasn't been on my program," she said. "But I thought everybody in Free Country got married. Nice normal people who settle down early and raise big families." The elephant-camel swayed and bumped beneath them. They were following a wide dirt track festooned on both sides with glittering strands of what looked like clear jelly, hundreds of feet long, mounted on spiny black poles that seemed to be sprouting like saplings from the ground.

"I raised a big family," he said. "My brothers and sisters. Dad got killed in a hunting accident when I was ten. Possibly got mixed up with a Spook animal that was on the wrong side of the line: nobody could quite figure it out. Then my mother came down with Blue Fever. I was fifteen then and five brothers and sisters to look after. Didn't leave me a lot of time to think about finding a wife."

"Blue Fever?"

"Don't you know what that is? Infectious disease. Kills you in three days, no hope at all. Supposed to be something the Spooks brought."

"We don't have it over here," she said. "Not that I ever heard."

"Spooks brought it, I guess they must know how to cure

it. We aren't that lucky. Anyway, there were all these little kids to look after. Of course, they're grown by now."

"But you still look after them. Coming over here to try to track down your brother."

"Somebody has to."

"What if he doesn't want to be tracked down, though?"

Demeris felt a tremor of alarm. He knew Tom was restless and troubled, but he didn't think he was actually disturbed. "Have you any reason to think Tom would want to stay over here for good?"

"I didn't say I did. But he might just prefer not to be found. A lot of boys come across and stay across, you know."

"I didn't know. Nobody I ever heard of did that. Why would someone from Free Country want to live on the Spook side?"

"For the excitement?" she suggested. "To run with the Spooks? To play their games? To hunt their animals? There's all sorts of minglings going on these days."

"Is that so," he said uneasily. He stared at the back of her head. She was so damned odd, he thought, such a fucking mystery.

She said, sounding very far away, "I wonder about marrying." Back to that again. "What it's like, waking up next to the same person every day, day after day. Sharing your life, year after year. It sounds very beautiful. But also kind of strange. It isn't easy for me to imagine what it might be like."

"Don't they have marriage in Spook City?"

"Not really. Not the way you people do."

"Well, why don't you try it and see? You don't like it, there are ways to get out of it. Nobody I know thinks that being married is any way strange. Christ, I bet whatever the

Spooks do is five hundred times as strange, and you probably think that it's the most normal thing in the world."

"Spooks don't marry. They don't even have sex, really. What I hear, it's more like the way fishes do it, no direct contact at all."

"That sounds terrifically appealing. I'd really love to try something like that. All I need is a cute Spook to try it with." He attempted to keep it light. But she glanced around at him.

"Still suspicious, Nick?"

He let that go by. "Listen, you could always take a fling at getting married for a while, couldn't you?" he said. "If you're all that curious about finding out what it's like."

"Is that an offer, Nick?"

"No," he said. "Hardly. Just a suggestion."

An hour after they set out that morning they passed a site where there was a peculiar purple depression about a hundred yards across at its thickest point. It was vaguely turtle-shaped, a long oval with four stubby projections at the corners and one at each end. "What the devil is that?" Demeris asked. "A Spook graveyard?"

"It's new," she said. "I've never seen it before."

Some vagrant curiosity impelled him. "Can we look?"

She halted the elephant-camel and they jumped down. The site might almost have been a lake, deep-hued and dense against the sandy earth, but there was nothing liquid about it: it was like a stain that ran several yards deep into the ground. Together they walked to the edge. Demeris saw something moving beneath the surface out near the middle, a kind of corkscrew effect, and was about to call it to her attention when abruptly the margin of the site started to quiver and a narrow rubbery arm rose up out of the purpleness and wrapped itself around her left leg. It started to pull her forward. She shrieked and made an odd hissing sound.

Demeris yanked his knife from the scabbard at his belt and sliced through the thing that had seized her. There was a momentary twanging sound and he felt a hot zing go up his arm to the shoulder. The energy of it ricocheted around inside his shirt collar briefly; then it ceased and he staggered back a little way. The part of the ropy arm that had been wrapped around Jill fell away; the rest writhed convulsively before them. He caught her by one wrist and pulled her back.

"It's got to be some kind of trap for game," he said. "Or for passing travelers stupid enough to go close. Let's get the hell out of here."

She was pale and shaky. "Thanks," she said simply, as they ran toward the elephant-camel.

Not much of a show of gratitude, he thought.

But at least the incident told him something about her that he needed to know. A Spook trap wouldn't have gone after one of their own, would it?

Would it?

At midday they stopped for lunch in a cottonwood grove that the Spooks had redecorated with huge crystalline mushroom-shaped things. The elephant-camel munched on one and seemed to enjoy it, but Demeris and Jill left them alone. There was a brackish little stream running through the trees, and once again she stripped and cleaned herself. Bathing seemed very important to her and she had no self-consciousness about her nudity. He watched her with cool pleasure from the bank.

Once in a while, during the long hours of the ride, she

would break the silence with a quirky sort of question: "What do people like to do at night in Free Country?" or "Are men closer friends with men than women are with women?" or "Have you ever wished you were someone else?" He gave the best answers he could. She was a strange, unpredictable kind of woman, but he was fascinated by the quick darting movements of her mind, so different from that of anyone he knew in Albuquerque. Of course he dealt mainly with ranchers and farmers, and she was a mayor's daughter. And a native of the Occupied Zone besides: no reason why she should be remotely like the kind of people he knew.

They came to places that had been almost incomprehensibly transformed by the aliens. There was an abandoned one-street town that looked as though it had been turned to glass, everything eerily translucent—buildings, furniture, plumbing fixtures. If there had been any people still living there you most likely could see right through them too, Demeris supposed. Then came a sandy tract where a row of decayed rusting automobiles had been arranged in an overlapping series, the front of each humped up on the rear end of the one in front of it, like a string of mating horses. Demeris stared at the automobiles as though they were ghosts ready to return to life. He had never actually seen one in use. The whole technology of internal combustion devices had dropped away before he was born, at least in his part of Free Country, though he had heard they still had cars of some sort in certain privileged enclaves of California.

After the row of cars there was a site where old human appliances, sinks and toilets and chairs and fragments of things Demeris wasn't able even to identify, had been fused together to form a dozen perfect pyramids fifty or sixty feet in height. It was like a museum of antiquity. By now Demeris was growing numb to the effects of seeing all this Spook meddling. It was impossible to sustain anger indefinitely when evidence of the alien presence was such a constant impingement.

There were more frequent traces now of the aliens' living presence, too: glows on the horizon, mysterious whizzing sounds far overhead that Jill said were airborne traffic, shining roadways through the desert parallel to the unpaved track they were following. Demeris expected to see Spooks go riding by next, but there was no sign of that. He wondered what they were like. "Like ghosts," Bud had said. "Long shining ghosts, but solid." That didn't help much.

When they camped that night, Demeris entered the tent with her without hesitation, and waited only a moment or two after lying down to reach for her. Her reaction was noncommittal for the first instant. But then he heard a sort of purring sound and she turned to him, open and ready. There had been nothing remotely like affection between them all afternoon, but now she generated sudden passion out of nothing at all, pulling it up like water from an artesian well; and he rode with her swiftly and expertly toward sweaty, noisy climaxes. He rested a while and went back to her a second time, but she said simply, "No. Let's sleep now," and turned her back to him. A very strange woman, he thought. He lay awake for a time, listening to the rhythm of her breathing just to see if she was asleep, thinking he might nuzzle up to her anyway if she was still conscious and seemed at all receptive. He couldn't tell. She was motionless, limp: for all he knew, dead. Her breathing-sounds were virtually imperceptible. After a time Demeris rolled away. He dreamed of a bright sky streaked with crimson fire, and dragons flying in formations out of the south.

* * * * *

Now they were distinctly nearing Spook City. Instead of following along a dusty unpaved trail they had moved onto an actual road, perhaps some old United States of America highway that the aliens had jazzed up by giving it an internal glow, a cool throbbing green luminance rising in eddying waves from a point deep underground. Other travelers joined them here, some riding wagons drawn by alien beasts of burden, a few floating along on silent flatbed vehicles that had no apparent means of propulsion. The travelers all seemed to be human.

"How do Spooks get around?" Demeris asked.

"Any way they like," said Jill.

A corroded highway sign that looked five thousand years old announced that they had reached a town called Dimmitt. There wasn't any town there, only a sort of checkpoint of light like a benign version of the border barrier: a cheerful shimmering sheen, a dazzling moiré pattern dancing in the air. One by one the wagons and flatbeds and carts passed through it and disappeared. "It's the hunt perimeter," Jill explained, while they were waiting for their turn to go through. "Like a big pen around Spook City, miles in diameter, to keep the animals in. They won't cross the line. It scares them."

He felt no effect at all as they crossed it. On the other side she told him that she had some formalities to take care of, and walked off toward a battered shed a hundred feet from the road. Demeris waited for her beside the elephant-camel.

A grizzled-looking weather-beaten man of about fifty came limping up and grinned at him.

"Jack Lawson," he announced. He put out his hand. "On my way back from my daughter's wedding, Oklahoma City."

"Nick Demeris."

"Interesting traveling companion you got, Nick. What's it like, traveling with one of those? I've always wondered about that."

"One of what?" Demeris said.

Lawson winked. "Come on, friend. You know what I mean."

"I don't think I do."

"Your pal's a Spook, friend. Surely you aren't going to try to make me believe she's anything else."

"Friend, my ass. And she's as human as you or me."

"Right."

"Believe me," Demeris said flatly. "I know. I've checked her out at very close range."

Lawson's eyebrows rose a little. "That's what I figured. I've heard there are men who go in for that. Some women, too."

"Shit," Demeris said, feeling himself beginning to heat up. He didn't have the time or the inclination for a fight, and Lawson looked about twice his age anyway. As calmly as he could he said, "You're fucking wrong, just the way that Mex kid down south who said she was a Spook was wrong. Neither of you knows shit about her."

"I know one when I see one."

"And I know an asshole when I see one," said Demeris.

"Easy, friend. Easy. I see I'm mistaken, that you simply don't understand what's going on. Okay. A thousand pardons, friend. Ten thousand." Lawson gave him an oily, smarmy smile, a courtly bow, and started to move away.

"Wait," Demeris said. "You really think she's a Spook?"

"Bet your ass I do."

"Prove it, then."

"Don't have any proof. Just intuition."

"Intuition's not worth much where I come from."

"Sometimes you can just tell. There's something about her. I don't know. I couldn't put it into words."

"My father used to say that if you can't put something into words, that's on account of you don't know what you're talking about."

Lawson laughed. It was that same patronizing I-know-better-than-you laugh that the kid in the village had given him. Anger welled up again in Demeris and it was all he could do to keep from swinging on the older man.

But just then Jill returned. She looked human as hell as she came walking up, swinging her hips. Lawson tipped his hat to her with exaggerated courtesy and went sauntering back to his wagon.

"Ready?" Demeris asked her.

"All set." She glanced at him. "You okay, Nick?"

"Sure."

"What was that fellow saying to you?"

"Telling me about his daughter's wedding in Oklahoma."

He clambered up on the elephant-camel, taking up his position on the middle hump.

His anger over what Lawson had said gradually subsided. They all knew so much, these Occupied Zone people. Or thought they did. Always trying to get one up on the greenhorn from Free Country, giving you their knowledgeable looks, hitting you with their sly insinuations.

Some rational part of him told him that if two people over here had said the same thing about Jill, it might just be true. A fair chance of it, in fact. Well, fuck it. She looked human, she smelled human, she felt human when he ran his hands over her body. That was good enough for him. Let these Spook Land people say what they liked. He intended to go on accepting her as human no matter what anyone might try to tell him. It was too late for him to believe anything else. He had had his mouth to hers; he had been inside her body; he had given himself to her in the most intimate way there was. There was no way he could let himself believe that he had been embracing something from another planet, not now. He absolutely could not permit himself to believe that now.

And then he felt a sudden stab of wild, almost intoxicating temptation: the paradoxical hope that she *was* a Spook after all, that by embracing her he had done something extraordinary and outrageous. A true crossing of borders: his youth restored. He was amazed. It was a stunning moment, a glimpse of what it might be like to step outside the prisons of his soul. But it passed quickly and he was his old sober self again. She is human, he told himself stolidly. Human. Human.

A little closer in, he saw one of the pens where the hunt animals were being kept. It was like a sheet of lightning rising from the ground, but lightning that stayed and stayed and stayed. Behind it Demeris thought he could make out huge dark moving shapes. Nothing was clear, and after a few moments of staring at that fluid, rippling wall of light he started to feel the way he had felt when he was first pushing through the border barrier.

"What kind of things do they have in there?" he asked her.

"Everything," she said. "Wait and see, when they turn them loose."

"When is that?"

"Couple of days from now." She swung around and pointed. "Look there, Nick. There's Spook City."

They were at the crest of a little hill. In the valley below lay a fair-sized sprawling town, not as big as he had expected, a mongrel place made up in part of little boxy houses and in part of tall, tapering, flickering constructions that didn't seem to be of material substance at all, ghost-towers, fairy castles, houses fit for Spooks. The sight of them gave him a jolt, the way everything was mixed together, human and non. A low line of the same immaterial stuff ran around the edge of the city like a miniature border barrier, but softer in hue and dancing like little swamp-fires.

"I don't see any Spooks," he said to her.

"You want to see a Spook? There's a Spook for you."

An alien fluttered up into view right then and there, as though she had conjured it out of empty air. Demeris, caught unprepared, muttered a whispered curse and his fingers moved with desperate urgency through the patterns of protection-signs that his mother had taught him more than twenty years before and that he had never had occasion to use. The Spook was incorporeal, elegant, almost blindingly beautiful: a sleek cone of translucence, a node of darkness limned by a dancing core of internal light. He had expected them to be frightening, not beautiful: but this one, at least, was frightening in its beauty. Then a second one appeared, and it was nothing like the first, except that it too had no solidity. It was flat below and almost formless higher up, and drifted a little way above the ground atop a pool of its own luminescence. The first one vanished; the second one revolved and seemed to spawn three more, and then it too was gone; the newest three, which had s-shaped curves and shining blue eye-like features at their upper tips, twined themselves together almost coquettishly and coalesced into a single fleshy spheroid crisscrossed by radiant purple lines. The spheroid folded itself across its own equator, taking on a half-moon configuration, and slipped downward into the earth.

Demeris shivered.

Spooks, yes. Well named. Dream-beings. No wonder there had been no way of defeating them. How could you touch them? How could you injure them in any way, when they mutated and melted and vanished while you were looking at them? It wasn't fair, creatures like that coming to the world and taking a big chunk of it the way they had, simply grabbing, not even bothering to explain why, just moving in, knowing that they were too powerful to be opposed. All his ancient hatred of them sprang into new life. And yet they were beautiful, almost godlike. He feared and loathed them but at the same time he found himself fighting back an impulse to drop to his knees.

He and Jill rode into town without speaking. There was a sweet little tingle when they went through the wall of dancing light, and then they were inside.

"Here we are," Jill said. "Spook City. I'll show you a place where you can stay."

The city's streets were unpaved—the Spooks wouldn't need sidewalks—and most of the human-style buildings had windows of some kind of semi-clear oiled cloth instead of glass. The buildings themselves were of slovenly construction and were set down higgledy-piggledy without much regard for order and logic. Sometimes there was a gap between them out of which a tall Spook structure sprouted like nightmare fungus, but mainly the Spook sectors of the city and the human sectors were separate, however it had seemed when he had been looking down from the hill. All manner of flying creatures that had been gathered for the hunt were in busy circulation overhead: the delta-winged herders, the flying snakes, a whole host of weirdities traversing the air above the city with such demonic intensity that it seemed to sizzle as they passed through it.

Jill conveyed him to a hotel of sorts made out of crudely squared logs held together clumsily by pegs, a gigantic ramshackle three-story cabin that looked as if it had been designed by people who were inventing architecture from scratch, and left him at the door. "I'll see you later," she told him, when he had jumped down. "I've got some business to tend to."

"Wait," he said. "How am I going to find you when—"

Too late. The elephant-camel had already made a massive about-face and was ambling away.

Demeris stood looking after her, feeling puzzled and a little hurt. But he had begun to grow accustomed to her brusqueness and her arbitrary shifts by now. Very likely she'd turn up again in a day or two, he told himself. Meanwhile, though, he was on his own, just when he had started to count on her help in this place.

He shrugged and went inside.

The place had the same jerry-built look within: a long dark entry hall, exposed rafters, crazily leaning walls. To the left, from behind a tattered curtain of red gauze, came the sounds of barroom chatter and clinking glasses. On the right was a cubicle with a pale, owlish-looking heavyset woman peering out of a lopsided opening.

"I need a room," Demeris told her.

"We just got one left. Busy time, on account of the hunt. It's five labor units a night, room and board and a drink or two."

"Labor units?"

"We don't take Free Country money here, chumbo. An hour cleaning out the shithouse, that's one labor unit. Two hours swabbing grease in the kitchen, that's one. Don't worry, we'll find things for you to do. You staying the usual thirty days?"

"I'm not on an Entrada," Demeris said. "I'm here to find my brother." Then, with a sudden rush of hope: "Maybe you've seen him. Looks a lot like me, shorter, around eighteen years old. Tom Demeris."

"Nobody here by that name," she said, and shoved a square metal key toward him. "Second floor on the left, 103. Welcome to Spook City, chumbo."

The room was small, squalid, dim. Hardly any light came through the oilcloth window. A strangely shaped lamp sat on the crooked table next to the bare cot that would be his bed. It turned on when he touched it and an eerie tapering glow rose from it, like a tiny Spook. He saw now that there were hangings on the wall, coarse cloth bearing cryptic inscriptions in Spook script.

Downstairs, he found four men and a parched-looking woman in the bar. They were having some sort of good-natured argument and gave him only the quickest of glances. Sized him up, wrote him off: he could see that. Free Country written all over his face. His nostrils flared and he clamped his lips.

"Whiskey," Demeris told the bartender.

"We got Shagback, Billyhow, Donovan, and Thread."

"Donovan," he said at random. The bartender poured him a shot from a lumpy-looking blue bottle with a garish yellow label. The stuff was inky-dark, vaguely sour smelling, strong. Demeris felt it hit bottom like a fishhook. The others were looking at him with more interest now. He took that for an opening and turned to them with a forced smile to tell them what they plainly already knew, which was that he was a stranger here, and to ask them the one thing he wanted to know, which was could they help him discover the whereabouts of a kid named Tom Demeris.

"How do you like the whiskey?" the woman asked him.

"It's different from what I'm accustomed to. But not bad." He fought back his anger. "He's my kid brother, that's the thing, and I've come all this way looking for him, because—"

"Tom what?" one of the men said.

"Demeris. We're from Albuquerque."

They began to laugh. "Abblecricky," the woman said.

"Dabblecricky," said one of the other men, sallow-skinned with a livid scar across his cheek.

Demeris looked coldly from one face to another. "Albuquerque," he said with great precision. "It used to be a big city in New Mexico. That's in Free Country. We still got eight, ten thousand people living there, maybe more. My brother was on his Entrada, only he didn't come back. Been gone since June. I think he's got some idea of settling here, and I want to talk to him about that. Tom Demeris is his name. Not quite as tall as I am, a little heavier set, longer hair than mine."

But he could see that he had lost their attention. The woman rolled her eyes and shrugged, and one of the men gestured to the bartender for another round of drinks.

"You want one too?" the bartender asked Demeris.

"A different kind this time."

It wasn't any better. He sipped it morosely. A few moments later the others began to file out of the room. "Abblekirky," the woman said, as she went past Demeris, and laughed again.

He spent a troubled night. The room was musty and dank and made him feel claustrophobic. The little bed offered no comfort. Sounds came from outside, grinding noises, screeches, strange honkings. When he turned the lamp off the darkness was absolute and ominous, and when he turned it on the light bothered him. He lay stiffly, waiting watchfully for sleep to take him, and when it failed to arrive he rose and pulled the oilcloth window-cover aside to stare into the night. Attenuated streaks of brightness were floating through the air, ghostly will-o'-the-wisp glowings, and by that faint illumination he saw huge winged things pumping stolidly across the sky, great dragons no more graceful than flying oxen, while in the road below the building three flickering columns of light that surely were Spooks went past, driving a herd of lean little square-headed monsters as though they were so many sheep.

In the morning, after the grudging breakfast of stale bread and some sort of coffee-like beverage with an undertaste of barley that the hotel bar provided, he went out into Spook City to look for Tom. But where was he supposed to begin? He had no idea.

It was a chaotic, incomprehensible town. The unpaved streets went squiggling off in all directions, no two of them parallel. Wagons and flatbeds of the kind he had seen at the perimeter checkpoint, some of them very ornate and bizarre, swept by constantly, stirring up whirlwinds of gray dust. Ethereal shimmering Spooks drifted in and among them, ignoring the perils of the busy traffic as though they were operating on some other plane of existence entirely, which very likely they were. Now and again came a great bleating of horns and everyone moved to the side of the street to allow a parade of menacing-looking beasts to pass through, a dozen green-scaled things like dinosaurs with high-stepping big-taloned feet or a procession of elephant-camels linked trunk to tail or a string of long slithery serpentine creatures moving on scores of powerful stubby legs.

Demeris felt a curious numbness coming over him as one enormity after another presented itself to his eyes. These few days across the border were changing him, creating a kind of dreamy tolerance in him. He had absorbed all the new alien sights and experiences he could and he was overloaded now, no room left for reactions of surprise or fear or even of loathing. The crazy superabundance of strangeness in Spook City was quickly starting to appear normal to him. Albuquerque in all its somnolent ordinariness seemed to him now like a static vision, a mere photograph of a city rather than an actual thriving place. There was still the problem of Tom, though. Demeris walked for hours and found no clue, no starting place: no building marked Police Station or City Hall or Questions Answered Here. What he really hoped to come upon was someone who was recognizably a native of Free Country, someone who could give him an inkling of how to go about tracing his brother through the network of kids making Entradas that must exist on this side. But he saw no one like that either. Where the hell was Jill? She was his only ally, and she had left him to cope with this lunacy all by himself, abandoning him as abruptly as she had picked him up in the first place.

But she, at least, could be located. She was the mayor's daughter, after all.

He entered a dark, squalid little building that seemed to be some sort of shop. A small hunched-looking woman who could have been made of old leather gave him a surly look from behind a warped counter. He met it with the best smile he could manage and said to her, "I'm new in town and I'm trying to find Jill Gorton, Ben Gorton's daughter. She's a friend of mine."

"Who?"

"Jill Gorton? Ben Gorton's—"

She shook her head curtly. "Don't know anybody by that name."

"Ben Gorton, then. Where can he be found?"

"Wherever he might happen to be," she said. "How would I know?" And slammed shut on him like a trapdoor. He peered at her in astonishment. She had turned away from him and was moving things around behind her counter as though no one was there.

"Doesn't he have an office?" Demeris asked. "Some kind of headquarters?"

No response. She got up, moving around in the shadows, ignoring him.

"I'm talking to you," Demeris said.

She might just as well have been deaf. He quivered with frustration. It was midday and he had had practically nothing to eat since yesterday afternoon and he hadn't accomplished anything all this day and it had started to dawn on him that he had no idea how he was going to find his way back to his hotel through the maze of the city—he didn't even know its name or address, and the streets bore no signs anyway—and now this old bitch was pretending he was invisible. Furiously he said, "Jesus Christ, what's the matter with you people? Haven't you ever heard of common courtesy here? Have the fucking Spooks drained everything that's human out of you all? All I want to know is how to find the goddamned mayor. Can't you tell me that one little thing? Can't you?"

Instead of answering him, she looked back over her shoulder and made a sound in Spook language, a wheezing whistling noise, the kind of sound that Jill might have directed to her elephant-camel. Almost instantly a tall flat-faced man of about thirty with the same sort of dark leathery skin as hers came out of a back room and gave Demeris a black, threatening stare.

"What the hell you think you're doing yelling at my mother?"

"Look," Demeris said, "I just asked her for a little help, that's all." He was still churning with rage. "I need to find the mayor. I'm a friend of his daughter Jill's, and she's supposed to help me track down my brother Tom, who came across from Free Country a few months ago, and I don't know one goddamned building from the next in this town, so I stopped in here hoping she could give me some directions and instead—"

"You yelled at her. You cursed at her."

"Yeah. Maybe so. But if you people don't have any decency why the hell should I? All I want to know—"

"You cursed at my mother."

"Yeah," Demeris said. "Yeah, I did." It was all too much. He was tired and hungry and far from home and the streets were full of monsters and nobody would give him the time of day here and he was sick of it. He had no idea who moved first, but suddenly they were both on the same side of the counter and swinging at each other, butting heads and pummeling each other's chests and trying to slam each other against the wall. The other man was bigger and heavier, but Demeris was angrier, and he got his hands to the other man's throat and started to squeeze. Dimly he was aware of sounds all around him, doors slamming, rapid footsteps, people shouting, a thick incoherent babble of sound. Then someone's arm was bent around his chin and throat and hands were clamped on his wrists and he was being pulled to the floor, kicking as he went and struggling to reach the knife at his waist. The confusion grew worse after that: he had no idea how many of them there were, but they were sitting on him, they were holding his arms, they were dragging him out into the daylight. He thought he saw a Spook hovering in the air above him, but perhaps he was wrong about that. There was too much light everywhere around. Nothing was clear. "Listen," he said, "The only thing I want is—" and they hit him in the mouth and kicked him in the side, and there was some raucous laughter and he heard them speaking in the Spook language; and then he came to understand that he was in a wagon, a cart, some kind of moving contrivance. His hands and feet were tied. A flushed sweaty face looked down at him, grinning.

"Where are you taking me?" Demeris asked.

"Ben Gorton. That's who you wanted to see, isn't it? Ben Gorton, right?"

He was in a basement room somewhere, windowless, lit by three of the little Spook-lamps. It was the next day, he supposed. Certainly a lot of time had gone by, perhaps a whole night. They had given him a little to eat, some sort of bean mush. He was still bound, but two men were holding him anyway.

"Untie him," Gorton said.

He had to be Gorton. He was around six feet seven, wide as a slab, with a big bald head and a great beaky nose, and everything about him spoke of power and authority. Demeris rubbed his wrists where the cord had chafed them and said, "I wasn't interested in a fight. That's not the sort of person I am. But sometimes when it builds up and builds up and builds up, and you can't stand it any more—"

"Right. You damn near killed Bobby Bridger, you know that? His eyes were bugging right out of his head. This is hunt season here, mister. The Spooks will be turning the critters loose any minute now and things are going to get real lively. It's important for everybody to stay civil so things don't get any more complicated than they usually are when the hunt's going on."

"If Bridger's mother had been a little more civil to me, it would all have been a lot different," Demeris said.

Gorton gave him a weary look. "Who are you and what are you doing here, anyway?"

Taking a deep breath, Demeris said, "My name's Nick Demeris, and I live in Free Country, and I came over here to find my kid brother Tom, who seems to have gotten side-tracked coming back from his Entrada."

"Tom Demeris," Gorton said, lifting his eyebrows.

"Yes. Then I met your daughter Jill at some little town near the border, and she invited me to travel with her. But when we got to Spook City she dropped me at some hotel and disappeared, so—"

"Wait a second," said Gorton. His eyebrows went even higher. "My daughter Jill?"

"That's right."

"Shit," the big man said. "What daughter? I don't have no fucking daughter."

"No daughter," said Demeris.

"No daughter. None. Must have been some Spook playing games with you."

The words fell on Demeris like stones. "Some Spook," he repeated numbly. "Pretending to be your daughter. You mean that? For Christ's sake, are you serious, or are you playing games with me too?"

Something in Demeris's agonized tone seemed to register sympathetically on Gorton. He squinted, he blinked, he tugged at the tip of his great nose. He said in a much softer voice, "I'm not playing any games with you. I can't say for sure that she was a Spook but she sure as hell wasn't my daughter, because I don't have any daughter. Spooks doing masks will tell you anything they damn please, though. Chances are, she was a Spook."

"Doing masks?"

"Spooks going around playing at being human. It's a big thing with them these days. The latest Spook fad."

Demeris nodded. Doing masks, he thought. He considered it and it began to sink in, and sink and sink and sink.

Then quietly he said, "Maybe you can help me find my brother, at least."

"No. I can't do that and neither can anybody else. Tom Demeris, you said his name is?"

"That's right."

Gorton glanced toward one of his men. "Mack, how long ago was it that the Demeris kid took the Spooks' nickel?"

"Middle of July, I think."

"Right." To Demeris Gorton said, "What we call 'taking the Spooks' nickel' means selling yourself to them, do you know what I mean? You agree to go with them to their home planet. They've got a kind of plush country club for humans there where you live like a grand emperor for the rest of your life, comfort, luxury, women, anything you damn please, but the deal is that in return you belong to them forever, that they get to run psychological experiments on you to see what makes you tick, like a mouse in a cage. At least that's what the Spooks tell us goes on there, and we might as well believe it. Nobody who's sold himself to the Spooks has ever come back. I'm sorry, man. I wish it wasn't so."

Demeris looked away for a moment. He felt like smashing things, but he held himself perfectly still. My brother, he thought, my baby brother.

"He was just a kid," he said.

"Well, he must have been a damned unhappy kid. Nobody with his head screwed on right would take the nickel. Hardly anybody ever does." Something flashed momentarily in Gorton's eyes, and Demeris sensed that to these people selling yourself to the Spooks was the ultimate surrender, the deepest sort of self-betrayal. They had all sold themselves to the Spooks, in a sense, by choosing to live in the Occupied Zone; but even here there were levels of yielding to the alien conqueror, he realized, and in the eyes of Spook City people the thing that Tom had done was the lowest level of all. He felt the weight of Gorton's mingling of contempt for Tom and pity for him, suddenly, and hated it, and tried to throw it back with a furious glare. Gorton watched him quietly, not reacting.

After a little while Demeris said, "All right. There's nothing I can do, is there? I guess I'd better go back to Albuquerque now."

"You'd better go back to your hotel and wait until the hunt is over," said Gorton. "It isn't safe wandering around in the open while the critters are loose."

"No," said Demeris. "I suppose it isn't."

"Take him to wherever he's staying, Mack," Gorton said to his man. He stared for a time at Demeris. The sorrow in his eyes seemed genuine. "I'm sorry," Gorton said again. "I really am."

Mack had no difficulty recognizing Demeris's hotel from the description he gave, and took him to it in a floating wagon that made the trip in less than fifteen minutes. The streets were practically empty now: no Spooks in sight and hardly any humans, and those who were still out were moving quickly.

"You want to stay indoors while the hunt is going on,"

Mack said. "A lot of dumb idiots don't, but some of them regret it. This is one event that ought to be left strictly to the Spooks."

"How will I know when it starts?"

"You'll know," Mack said.

Demeris got out of the wagon. It turned immediately and headed away. He paused a moment in front of the building, breathing deeply, feeling a little light-headed, thinking of Tom on the Spook planet, Tom living in a Spook palace, Tom sleeping on satin Spook sheets.

"Nick? Over here, Nick! It's me!"

"Oh, Christ," he said. Jill, coming up the street toward him, smiling as blithely as though this were Christmas Eve. He scanned her, searching for traces of some Spook gleam, some alien shimmer. When she reached him she held out her arms to him as though expecting a hug. He stepped back just far enough to avoid her grasp.

In a flat tight voice he said, "I found out about my brother. He's gone off to the Spook world. Took their nickel."

"Oh, Nick. Nick!"

"You knew, didn't you? Everybody in this town must have known about the kid who came from Free Country and sold himself to the Spooks." His tone turned icy. "It was your father the mayor that told me. He also told me that he doesn't have any daughters."

Her cheeks blazed with embarrassment. It was so human a reaction that he was cast into fresh confusion: how could a Spook learn to mimic a human even down to a blush? It didn't seem possible. And it gave him new hope. She had lied to him about being Ben Gorton's daughter, yes, God only knew why; but there was still the possibility that she was human, that she had chosen to put on a false identity but the body he saw was really her own. If only it was so, he thought. His anger with her, his disdain, melted away in a flash. He wanted everything to be all right. He was rocked by a powerful rush of eagerness to be assured that the woman he had embraced those two nights on the desert was indeed a woman; and with it, astonishingly, came a new burst of desire for her, of fresh yearning stronger than anything he had felt for her before.

"What he told me about was that you were a Spook," Demeris said in a guarded tone. He looked at her hopefully, waiting for her to deny it, praying for her to deny it, ready to accept her denial.

"Yes," she said. "I am."

It was like a gate slamming shut in his face.

Serenely she said, "Humans fascinate me. Their emotions, their reactions, their attitudes toward things. I've been studying them at close range for a hundred of your years and I still don't know as much as I'd like to. And finally I thought, the only way I can make that final leap of understanding is to become one myself."

"Doing masks," Demeris said in a hollow voice. Looking at her, he imagined he could see something cold and foreign peering out at him from behind her eyes for a moment, and it seemed to him that great chilly winds were sweeping through the empty caverns of his soul. He began to see now that somewhere deep within him he must have been making plans for a future that included this woman, that he had wanted her so much that he had stubbornly refused to accept for long any of the evidence that had been given him that that was unthinkable. And now he had been given the one bit of evidence that was impossible to reject.

"Right," she said. "Doing masks."

He knew he should be feeling fury, or anguish, or something, at this final revelation that he had slept with a Spook. But he hardly felt anything at all. He was like a stone. Perhaps he had already done the anger and pain, on some level below his consciousness. Or else he had somehow transcended it. The Spooks are in charge here. All right. We are their toys. All right. All right. You could go only so far into despair and then you stopped feeling it, he supposed. Or hatred. Hating the Spooks was useless. It was like hating an avalanche, like hating an earthquake.

"Taking human men as your lovers, too: that's part of doing masks, isn't it?" he asked. "Was my brother Tom one of them?"

"No. Never. I saw him only once or twice."

He believed that. He believed everything she was saying, now.

She seemed about to say something else. But then suddenly a flare of lightning burst across the sky, a monstrous forking shaft of flame that looked as though it could split the world in two. It was followed not by thunder but by music, an immense alien chord that fell like an avalanche from the air and swelled up around them with oceanic force. The vault of the sky rippled with colors: red, orange, violet, green.

"What's happening?" Demeris asked.

"The hunt is starting," she said. "That's the signal."

Yes. In the wake of the lightning and the rippling colors came swarming throngs of airborne creatures, seeming thousands of them, the delta-winged dragon-like herders and their snake-like pilots, turning the midday sky dark with their numbers, like a swarm of bees overhead, colossal ones whose wings made a terrible droning sound as they beat the air; and then Demeris heard gigantic roaring, bellowing sounds from nearby, as if monsters were approaching. There were no animals in the streets, not yet, but they couldn't be very far away. Above him, Spooks by the dozens flickered in the air. Then he heard footsteps, and a pack of humans came running frantically toward them out of a narrow street, their eyes wild, their faces weirdly rigid. Did the Spooks hunt humans too? Demeris wondered. Or was one of the monsters chasing after them? The runners came sweeping down on him. "Get out of the way, man!" one of them cried. "Out of the *way!*"

Demeris stepped back, but not fast enough, and the runner on the inside smacked hard into his shoulder, spinning him around a little. For one startling moment Demeris found himself looking straight into the man's eyes, and saw something close to madness there, but no fear at all—only eagerness, impatience, frenzied excitement—and he realized that they must be running not from but *to* the hunt, that they were on their way to witness the crazy slaughter at close range or even to take part in it themselves, that they lived just as did the Spooks for this annual moment of apocalyptic frenzy.

Jill said, "It'll be berserk here now for two or three days. You ought to be very careful if you go outdoors."

"Yes. I will."

"Listen," she said, putting an edge on her voice to make it cut through the roaring coming from overhead, "I've got a proposition for you, now that you know the truth." She leaned close to him. "Let's stay together, you and me. Despite all the problems. I like you a lot, Nick."

He peered at her, utterly astounded.

"I really think we can work something out," she went on. Another horde of winged things shot by just above them, making raspy tearing sounds as they flailed the air, and a new gush of color stained the sky. "Seriously, Nick. We can stay in Spook City if you want to, but I don't suppose you do. If you don't I'll go back across the border with you and live with you in Free Country. In my mind I've already crossed over. I don't want just to study you people from the outside. I want to *be* one of you."

"Are you crazy?" Demeris asked.

"No. Not in the least, I swear. Can you believe me? Can you?"

"I've got to go inside," he said. He was trembling. "It isn't smart to be standing out here while the hunt is going on."

"What do you say, Nick? Give me an answer."

"It isn't possible for us to be together. You know it isn't."

"You want to. Some part of you does."

"Maybe so," he said, amazed at what he was saying, but unable to deny it despite himself. "Just maybe. One little fraction of me. But it isn't possible, all the same. I don't want to live here among the Spooks, and if I take you back with me, some bastard with a sharp nose will sniff you out sooner or later and expose you for what you are, and stand up before the whole community and denounce me for what I am. I'm not going to take that risk. I'm just not, Jill."

"That's your absolute decision."

"My absolute decision, yes."

Something was coming down the street now, some vast hopping thing with a head the size of a cow and teeth like spears. A dozen or so humans ran along beside it, practically within reach of the creature's clashing jaws, and a covey of Spooks hovered over it, bombarding it with flashes of light. Demeris took a step or two toward the door of the hotel. Jill did nothing to hold him back.

He turned when he was in the doorway. She was still

standing there. The hunters and their prey sped right past her, but she took no notice. She waved to him.

Sure, he thought. He waved back. Goodbye, Jill.

He went inside. There was a clatter on the stairs, people running down, a woman and some men. He recognized them as the ones who had mocked him in the bar when he had first arrived. Two of the men ran past him and out the door, but the woman halted and caught him by the crook of the arm.

"Hey, Abblecricky!"

Demeris stared at her.

She leaned into his face and grinned. She was flushed and wild looking, like the ones who had been running through the streets. "Come on, man! It's the hunt! The hunt, man! You're heading the wrong way. Don't you want to be there?"

He had no answer for that.

She was tugging at him. "Come *on!* Live it up! Kill yourself a dragon or two!"

"Ella!" one of the men called after her.

She gave Demeris a wink and ran out the door.

He swayed uncertainly, torn between curiosity about what was going on out there and a profound wish to go upstairs and shut the door behind him. But the street had the stronger pull. He took a step or two after the woman, and then another, and then he was outside again. Jill wasn't there. The scene in the street was wilder than ever: people running back and forth yelling incoherently, colliding with each other in their frenzy, and overhead streams of winged creatures still swarming, and Spooks like beams of pure light moving among them, and in the distance the sounds of bellowing animals and thunderous explosions and high keening cries of what he took to be Spook pleasure. Far off to the south he saw a winged something the size of a small hill circling desperately in the sky, surrounded by implacable flaring pinpoints of Spook-light, and suddenly halting and plummeting like a falling moon toward the ground. He could smell the smell of charred flesh in the air, with a salty underflavor of what he suspected was the blood of alien beasts.

At a sleepwalker's dreamy pace Demeris went to the corner and turned left. Abruptly he found himself confronted with a thing so huge and hideous that it was almost funny—a massive long-snouted frog-shaped thing, sloping upward from a squat base, with a moist-looking greenish-black hide pocked with little red craters and a broad, gaping, yellow-rimmed mouth. It had planted itself in the middle of the street with its shoulders practically touching the buildings at either side and was advancing slowly and clumsily toward the intersection.

Demeris drew his knife. What the hell, he thought. He was here at hunt time, he might as well join the fun. The creature was immense but it didn't have any visible fangs or talons and he figured he could move in at an angle and slash upward through the great baggy throat, and then step back fast before the thing fell on him. And if it turned out to be more dangerous than it looked, he didn't give a damn. Not now.

He moved forward, knife already arcing upward.

"Hey!" someone cried behind him. "You out of your mind, fellow?"

Demeris glanced around. The bartender had come out of the hotel and was staring at him.

"That critter's just a big sack of acid," he said. "You cut it open, it'll pour all over you."

The frog-thing made a sound like a burp, or perhaps a

sardonic chuckle. Demeris backed away.

"You want to cut something with that," the bartender said, "you better know what you're cutting."

"Yeah." Demeris said. "I suppose so." He put the knife back in its sheath, and headed back across the street, feeling all the craziness of the moment go from him like air ebbing from a balloon. This hunt was no business of his. Let the people who live here get mixed up in it if they liked. But there was no reason why he should. He'd just be buying trouble, and he had never seen any sense in that.

As he reached the hotel entrance he saw Spook-light shimmering in the air at the corner—hunters, hovering above—and then there was a soft sighing sound and a torrent of bluish fluid came rolling out of the side street. It was foaming and hissing as it edged along the gutter.

Demeris shuddered. He went into the building.

Quickly he mounted the stairs and entered his room, and sat for a long while on the edge of the cot, gradually growing calm, letting it all finish sinking in while the din of the hunt went on and on.

Tom was gone, that was the basic thing he had to deal with. Neither dead nor really alive, but certainly gone. Okay. He faced that and grappled with it. It was bitter news, but at least it was a resolution of sorts. He'd mourn for a while and then he'd be all right.

And Jill—

Doing masks. Taking humans as lovers. The whole thing went round and round in his mind, all that he and she had done together, had said, everything that had passed between them. And how he had always felt about Spooks and how—somehow, he had no idea how—his time with Jill had changed that a little.

He remembered what she had said. I don't just want to study you. I want to *be* one of you.

What did that mean? A tourist in the human race? A sightseer across species lines?

They are softening, then. They are starting to whore after strange amusements. And if that's so, he thought, then we are beginning to win. The aliens had infiltrated Earth in the first place; but now Earth was infiltrating them. This yearning to do masks, to look and act like humans, to experience human feelings and human practices and human follies: it meant the end for them. There were too many humans on Earth and not enough Spooks, and the Spooks would eventually be swallowed up. One by one, they would succumb to the temptation of giving up their chilly godliness and trying to imitate the messy, contradictory, troublesome creatures that humans are. And, Demeris thought, over the course of time—five hundred years, a thousand, who could say?—Earth would complete the job of absorbing the invaders and something new would emerge from the mixture of the species. That was an interesting thing to consider.

But then something clicked in his mind and he felt himself being flooded by some strange interior light, a light as weird and intense as the Spook-light in the skies over the city now or the glow of the border barrier, and he realized there was another way of looking at these things altogether. Jill dropped suddenly into a new perspective and instead of thinking of her as a mere sightseer looking for forbidden thrills, he saw her for what she really was—a pioneer, an explorer, a border-jumper, a defiant enemy of boundaries and limitations and rules. The same for Tom. They were two of a kind, those two; and he had been slow to recognize it because he simply wasn't of their sort. Demeris recognized now how little he had understood his youngest brother. To him, Tom was a disturbed kid. To Ben Gorton, he was a contemptible sellout. But the real Tom, Tom's own Tom, might be something entirely different: someone looking not just to make a little thirty-day Entrada but to carry out a real penetration into the alien, to jump deep and far into otherness to find out what it was like. The same with this Jill, this alien, this Spook—she was of that kind too, but coming from the other direction.

And she had wanted his help. She had needed it all along, right from the start. She had missed her chance with Tom, but maybe she thought that Tom's brother might be the same sort of person, someone who lived on the edge, who pushed against walls.

Well, well, well. How wrong she was. That was too bad.

For an instant Demeris felt another surge of the strange excitement that had come over him back at the checkpoint, when he had considered the possibility that Jill might be a Spook and had, for a moment, felt exhilarated by the thought. Could he take her back with him? Could he sneak her into the human community and live happily ever after with her, hiding the astonishing truth like the man in the old story who had married a mermaid? He saw himself, for a moment, lying beside her at night while she told him Spook stories and whispered weird Spook words and showed him sly little Spook shapeshifting tricks as they embraced. It was an astonishing thought. And he began to quiver and sweat as he thought about it.

Then, as it had before, the moment passed.

He couldn't do it. It just wasn't who he was, not really. Tom might have done it, but Tom was gone, and he wasn't Tom or anything like him. Not one of the leapers, one of the soarers, one of the questers. Not one of the adventurous kind at all: just a careful man, a builder, a planner, a preserver, a protector. Nothing wrong with that. But not of any real use to Jill in her quest.

Too bad, he thought. Too damned bad, Jill.

He walked to the window and peered out, past the oilcloth cover. The hunt was reaching some sort of peak. The street was more crowded than ever with frantic monsters. The sky was full of Spooks. Scattered bands of Spook City humans, looking half crazed or more than half, were running back and forth. There was noise everywhere, sharp, percussive, discordant. Jill was nowhere to be seen out there. He let the oilcloth flap drop back in place and lay down on his cot and closed his eyes.

Three days later, when the hunt was over and it was safe to go out again, Demeris set out for home. For the first ten blocks or so a glow that might have been a Spook hovered above him, keeping pace as he walked. He wondered if it was Jill.

She had given him a second chance once, he remembered. Maybe she was doing it again.

"Jill?" he called up to it. "That you?"

No answer came.

"Listen," he called to the hovering glow. "Forget it. It isn't going to work out, you and me. I'm sorry, but it isn't. You hear me?"

A little change in the intensity of the flicker overhead, perhaps. Or perhaps not.

He looked upward and said, "And listen, Jill—if that's you, Jill, I want to tell you: thanks for everything, okay?" It was strange, talking to the sky this way. But he didn't care. "And good luck. You hear? Good luck, Jill! I hope you get what you want."

The glow bobbed for a moment, up, down. Then it was gone.

Demeris, shading his eyes, looked upward for a time, but there was nothing up there to see. He felt a sharp little momentary pang, thinking of the possibilities. But what could he have done? She had wanted something from him that he wasn't able to give. If he had been somebody else, things might have been different. But he was who he was. He could go only so far toward becoming someone else, and then he had to pull back and return to being who he really was, and that was all there was to it.

He moved onward, toward the edge of the city.

No one gave him any trouble at all on his way out, and the return trip through the western fringe of the Occupied Zone was just as smooth. Everything was quiet, all was peaceful, clear on to the border.

The border crossing itself was equally uncomplicated. The fizzing lights and the weird hallucinatory effects of the barrier were visible, but they had no impact from this side. Demeris passed through them as though they were so much smoke, and kept on walking. In hardly any time he was across the border and back in Free Country again.

They Hide, We Seek

Nobody had any great interest in altering the long-established galactic balance of power, least of all Captain Hayn Wing-Marra of the *Achilles*. But one thing does lead to another, and immense consequences have a way sometimes of hinging on very small pivots. In this case, the pivot was nothing more than the fact that Captain Wing-Marra had spent one lifetime as an organic chemist and another as an archaeologist before he had gone to space.

It was the passion for organic chemistry, still alive in him after all those years, that had brought his Erthuma-registry starship and its crew of nine, seven Erthumoi and two Naxians, to the vicinity of the gaseous nebula W49. What they had set out to do was to explore a large molecular cloud, a space-going soup of complex hydrocarbons, which was certainly of scientific interest and probably had some economic value as well.

What they found nearby, hidden on the far side of the cloud, was a main-sequence star, which had four or five planets, most of which had moons. That was unexpected but not particularly surprising. The galaxy is full of stars, hundreds of millions of them, and nearly all of them have planets.

At first glance neither the star nor its planets nor any of the moons seemed particularly out of the ordinary, either, though one of the planets was close enough to Earth-type to be of potential use to Erthumoi. There are, however, plenty of worlds like that.

But a second glance revealed that a Locrian ship was already present in the unknown star-system. It was parked in orbit around the second planet and Locrian scouting parties were apparently at work both on the planet and its moon. That didn't make a great deal of sense, because the second planet, was the Earth-type one, with a dense oxygen-nitrogen atmosphere very low in neon and other noble gases. Locrians are not at all comfortable in places like that. Nor would the airless moon be any more inviting to them.

So it seemed appropriate for Captain Wing-Marra to take a third and rather less casual glance. Which he did; and after that nothing would ever be quite the same for any of the six races of the galaxy that were capable of interstellar travel.

Until the discovery that a Locrian exploration force was working the same territory he was, the molecular cloud—nearly thirty light-years across and laden with marvels—had seemed quite interesting enough for Captain Wing-Marra.

"Do you see?" he said to Jorin Murry-Balff, who was his Communications. "Not just piddling little hydroxyls and ammonias. That's cyano-octa-tetrayne there—HB_9N. Eleven-atom chains, Murry-Balff! And there! That's methanol, by all the stars! CH_3OH!" Wing-Marra reached toward the spectrometer's dazzling screen, shining with swirls of amber and topaz and carnelian and amethyst, and tapped this brilliant swirl and that one. "And this—and this—"

Murry-Balff didn't seem impressed. "Doesn't every molecular cloud have stuff like that in it?"

"Not this intricate, most of them. Those are very big molecules out there. Formaldehyde—H_2CO. Vinyl cyanide—H_2CCHCN."

"Formaldehyde? Cyanide? Sounds pretty deadly to me."

"Don't be an idiot. Those are the chemicals of life, man!" Wing-Marra leaned close, staring into the screen. Information moved in dizzying whorls before him. The spectrometer, whipping its scan-beam tirelessly across the vastness of the molecular cloud, provided color-analog displays of each organic compound it detected, reports on mass configuration, a three-dimensional distribution arc, and an assortment of other quantifiable factors. "Look, there's formic acid. And five or six amino acids, or I miss my guess. You and I and the snakes downstairs and everything else that breathes and metabolizes are built out of that stuff. And for all we know, we're alive at this moment only because wandering clouds like this seeded the newborn planets they encountered with just this sort of organic material."

Murry-Balff shrugged. "I'll take your word for it, Captain. Chemistry was never my field. Cosmology neither." A red glow blossomed on his wristband. "If you'll excuse me, sir—there's data coming in now from our planetary probes—"

"Dismissed," Wing-Marra murmured.

It was embarrassing for him to see the speed with which Murry-Balff, who ordinarily was in no rush, left the observation deck. Perhaps I was too ebullient for him just now, Wing-Marra thought. Or too intemperate. Certainly I was running off at the mouth a little about those molecules.

He wondered whether an apology was in order. They were old friends, after all. Murry-Balff and Wing-Marra were natives of the same Erthuma world, Hesperia in the St. Dominic's Star system. The other five Erthumoi on board came from five different worlds, none within a hundred light-years of any other; that fact alone gave the two Hesperians a certain sense of fellowship that went beyond the pseudo-military shipboard formalities. On the other hand, Wing-Marra thought, it's Murry-Balff's problem, not mine, if the contents of that molecular cloud don't interest him. The cloud is what we came here to investigate. Before we're through with it he'll have had to learn the formulas for a hundred different hydrocarbons, like it or not.

Wing-Marra peered at the spectrometer screen once again, and within moments he was lost in wonder.

His capacity for wonder—exultant, transcendent intellectual excitement—was one of the many contradictions out of which he was constructed. Wing-Marra was quiet and self-contained, a tall, pale, ascetic-looking man who believed in setting limits and abiding by them. To some that seemed odd and even quaint, considering that he had spent the last three cycles of his long life roaming the virtually limitless reaches of the galaxy. Wing-Marra himself saw no inconsistency in that. The way to cope with the crushing weight of infinity, he thought, was to behave as though one were capable of setting boundaries to it.

And though he seemed in many ways a passionless man, his fascination with the intricacy of the organic molecules was intense to the point of obsessiveness.

Six cycles back—his life now had encompassed eleven all told, a span of nearly a thousand Erthuma years—he had been struck suddenly by a waking vision, a startling hallucinatory display. He was living then on the sultry world called Atatakai, where the air seemed as thick as fur. Suddenly in the red evening sky he saw inexplicable pulsing points of light, which cavorted and leaped about in a wild whirling dance.

As he watched, astounded, he saw two of the shimmering light-sources come together to form a pair, and then a third and larger one seize them both, and then even more complicated unions take form. And all the while the giddy dance went on. The whirling lights were strung like serpents across the sky. He had never seen anything so awesome. The patterns of their sinuous movements were elegant, compelling, sublimely beautiful. It was a revelation. It seemed to him that he was looking right into the heart of the universe, into the deepest secrets of creation.

Then, to his even greater amazement, one serpent seized its own tail in its mouth, and, ringlike now, began a fierce gyration so imperious that he fell to his knees before it, stunned and shaken. There was a powerful truth in that furiously whirling serpentine form—the truth of what, he had not the vaguest idea—and under the impact of that vision of the innerness of all things he trembled like a leaf in a storm. After a time he could no longer bear to watch. He closed his eyes; and when he opened them again he beheld only the cloud-choked crimson sky of Atatakai.

But the memory of the bewildering, overwhelming vision would not leave Wing-Marra's mind; and in the end he had had to seek help in regaining his mental balance. A zigzag trail through a variety of therapists and therapies brought him at last to a flat-faced dome of silvery metal that listened to him for a time and said finally, in a brusque impersonal voice, "Your hallucination is not original. You are not the first to experience it."

Wing-Marra felt as though the autoshrink had spat in his eye.

"Not—original? What the hell do you mean?"

"Another has had this vision before you, in early times, in the very distant past. It is the dream of Kekule. This is true. I have consulted the archives."

"Kekule?"

"You are a chemist. This is true."

"Why—no," said Wing-Marra, puzzled. "Not true. Not at all."

"Then you have studied chemistry," said the machine, sounding a little irritated. "This is true."

Wing-Marra thought. "I suppose so, yes. Long ago. In my first cycle, when I was at the university. But—"

"A datum buried since your student days has surfaced in you. You have recapitulated the dream of Kekule," the machine told him again. "Such things happen. It is not a sign of serious mental disturbance. This is true."

"Kekule," Wing-Marra said wonderingly. "Who's that?"

There was the momentary hum of data-search. "Friedrich August Kekule. Erthuma of the Earthborn. Professor of chemistry at Ghent and later at Bonn."

"Where?"

"Ancient Earth-places. Do not pursue irrelevances. Kekule, pondering questions of molecular structure, saw atoms dancing before his eyes, forming a chain. Later he dreamed again and perceived the pattern of the benzene ring. This is true. The episode is well known."

"To chemists, maybe," said Wing-Marra. "I'm not a chemist." He felt disgruntled and obscurely let down at having paid good money to discover that the vision that had so irradiated his consciousness was a second-hand one. On the other hand, he told himself, probably it was better to hear that a phantom memory had come floating up out of some lecture of his student days than to be informed that he was going out of his mind. Still, he was in a sour mood as he left the autoshrink's cubicle.

His annoyance passed, though, and his fascination with the images that had so spontaneously leaped from the recesses of his brain remained and even deepened. He looked up Kekule and his work. Nineteenth century—my God, practically prehistoric! The dawn of science! A forgotten man, but for one great accomplishment, the theory of organic molecular structure. Kekule had demonstrated the tendency of carbon atoms to link together and to share other atoms in their quadrivalent embrace.

And so that vision, second-hand or not, led Wing-Marra from one thing to another and another, forging ever deeper throughout all the years that remained to him in that lifetime into the study of organic chemistry. It was his hope to recapture some of the splendor and wonder of those dancing lights in the sky. It was his hope to know again that sense of being in contact with unarguable truth. His head was aswim with isomers and polymers, with alkanes and olefins, with aromatics and heterocyclics and aliphatics, with esters, ethers, aldehydes, ketones. The crisp symmetries of their bonding patterns offered him ineffable joy and held him in an ineluctable grip. And here he was, five lifetimes later, still pursuing the mysteries of the carbon compounds out here in this remote arm of the galaxy, 40,000 light-years from the home world of all Erthumoi and even farther from the planet of his own birth.

Now, throat dry, eyes wide and scarcely flickering, Wing-Marra gripped the handles of the spectrometer screen and guided its scanner this way and that across the face of the great molecular cloud. Radiant bands of colored light leaped out at him from the smoky vastness. He was staring into the miraculous core of creation.

Stars were being born in that dense black pit. Future worlds were coalescing. The unimaginable life-forms of a billion years hence would be assembled from those rich whorls of molecular soup.

Wing-Marra felt his spirit soaring, felt his soul expanding, going forth into the cloud, walking among the drifting wonders. It was an almost godlike sensation.

"Sir?"

Murry-Balff. The intrusion was maddening, painful.

Scowling, Wing-Marra made an impatient gesture without turning away from the screen. Whatever Murry-Balff wanted, it could wait.

"Sir, this is important."

"So is this. I'm scanning the cloud."

"And we've been scanning this nearby solar system, sir. The planetary probes have pulled in something very strange. Seems that we have company."

Wing-Marra spun around swiftly.

"Company?"

"Let me show you," Murry-Balff said. He touched his wrist-plate to a wall terminal. Instantly a data screen came to life across the room. It showed a green planetary ball. Another, somewhat smaller ball, bleak and lifeless-looking, orbited it at an inclination of about sixty degrees.

"This is the second planet of the system," said Murry-Balff. "And its moon. I call your attention to the right side of the screen, near the planetary equator."

Wing-Marra thought he could see a dark speck.

Murry-Balff fingered his wrist-plate. The screen zoomed into enlargement mode. Now the green world filled nearly all of the picture. Something like a black spider hung beside it. Murry-Balff made another tuning adjustment, and the spider occupied the center of the screen.

It wasn't a spider. It looked more like some narrow-waisted wasp now: three dark, gleaming elongated cylinders, linked by narrow communication tubes. Six fragile leg-like appendages trailed from the hindmost cylinder. At the other end were two faceted domes, rising like huge insect eyes from the front. Spiral rows of hexagonal ports wound across each cylinder's sides.

The thing was a starship. And not of Erthuma design.

"Locrians," Murry-Balff said quietly.

"So I see." Wing-Marra pressed his fists together until his knuckles cracked, and swore. Murry-Balff brought the magnification up to the next level. It was pretty grainy, but at this level Wing-Marra thought he could actually make out the insect-like figures of the aliens moving about behind the ports. He shook his head. "What in God's name would Locrians be doing *here?*"

The crew assembled fast, all but the Naxians, who needed more time. Snakes *always* needed more time, no matter what. Wing-Marra didn't feel like waiting for them. He kept the data screen lit and ordered Murry-Balff to maintain real-time tracking surveillance of the Locrian ship.

"We're under no obligation to withdraw," Wing-Marra said. "This is unclaimed territory and remains that way until they've established valid possession. Simply being the first to get here doesn't constitute valid possession."

"They aren't under any obligation to withdraw either," Linga Hyath, his Cosmography, pointed out.

"Understood."

"They might not agree that they don't have valid possession," said his Diplomacy, Ayana Sanoclaro.

Hyath and Sanoclaro looked at each other and exchanged quick, smug nods of satisfaction. Wing-Marra could usually count on them to think the same way and to express essentially the same ideas at approximately the same time. They were both wiry, long-limbed women with the gaunt, attenuated look that natives of low-gravity worlds generally have, and they appeared to be not merely sisters but twins: the same pale blue eyes, the same immense cascades of golden hair, the same thin, pinched features. The odd thing was that they were not at all related, but came, in fact, from worlds a thousand light-years apart. Some genotypes are strikingly persistent.

Wing-Marra said, "Are you suggesting that they might make trouble for us?"

"They might have serious objections to our hanging around here," Sanoclaro said.

"If they think there's something really worthwhile here, they might defend their claim in a way we wouldn't like," said Hyath.

Mikoil Karpov, the Biochemistry, said, "You imply that they'd take hostile action?"

"They might," said Sanoclaro.

Karpov blinked. He was a squat, broad-shouldered man, heavy-jowled, densely bearded, from the chilly world of Zima, and his Erthumat was thickened by strong Russkiye inflections. "You are talking about acts of war? And you are actually serious? The idea's absurd. Nobody makes war."

"Erthumoi used to, not all that long ago."

Karpov gestured emphatically. "It was plenty long ago. Nobody fires on peaceful ships."

"Especially across species lines," said the Navigation, a dark, soft, tiny, deceptively feminine-looking woman named Eslane Ree, who came from Doppler IV. "The Locrians can see that this is an Erthuma ship. Maybe the Crotonites still like to squabble among themselves, or, from what I hear from our two, the Naxians. But those are Locrians over there. They don't even have a history of intraspecies warfare—why would they take a shot at us? I'm with Karpov here. We're spinning horrors out of nothing at all."

"Maybe so. But what are Locrians doing here, though?" Linga Hyath asked. "Locrians don't ordinarily go sniffing around high-oxygen worlds. And from the looks of it, this one is particularly badly suited for them. Six gulps of that atmosphere and they'd be drunk for a month. They must have seen something out of the usual here that got their attention in a big way."

"Who says?" Eslane Ree demanded. "Have we?"

Hyath shrugged. "We've only just arrived."

"Perhaps so have they."

"But they'd have taken one look and moved on, since this world is plainly useless to them," said Ayana Sanoclaro. "Unless they've spotted something. And if they have, my guess is that they'll go to great lengths, maybe to surprisingly great lengths, to keep us away from it."

Eslane Ree gave the elongated blond woman a sour glare. "Paranoia! Hyperdefensiveness!"

"Foresight," Sanoclaro retorted. "Prudence."

"What are you advocating?" asked the Maintenance, Septen Bolangyr, who came from a high-ultraviolet world in the Nestor Cluster and whose skin, artificially hyped with melanin, was a lustrous purple-green. "Should I activate the defensive screens, sir? Do you want me to get the cannons ready? If we are to go on a war footing, Captain, then tell me so right now. But I want the order in writing, and I want it with a date and a seal."

"Stay easy," Wing-Marra said. "We're a long way from fighting any space battles. What I'm going to do is contact these Locrians and find out whether we have a problem with them. But I hope you'll go along with my feeling that we ought to take a firm position about staying here, regardless of what they say."

"Even if they threaten us?" Hyath asked.

"They won't," said Karpov. Eslane Ree nodded in vigorous agreement.

"If they do?" Wing-Marra asked.

Eslane Ree said, "It would depend on the nature of the threat. We'd be foolish to stay here if they're willing to blow us out of the sky."

"Locrians?" Karpov said incredulously.

"Sufficient greed can turn any species warlike," Ayana Sanoclaro said, looking to her friend Hyath for support. "Even Locrians. The fact that the Six Races have avoided serious conflict with each other up till now is irrelevant. The evolutionary imperatives that have carried all six species this far have plenty of aggression buried in them, and the right motivation surely can bring that aggression to life. Locrians or no, if what they've found here is so valuable that—"

"We don't know that they've found anything, and—"

"How can we assume—"

"The unmotivated adolescent belligerence of these arguments is utterly—"

"The naïveté of—"

"More than fifteen hundred years of peaceful space exploration behind us and we still regard ourselves as capable of reverting to the level of—"

"Not us, *them!*"

"Us too! Who began this whole—"

"Enough!" Wing-Marra said sharply. "Sanoclaro, tell those two snakes of ours—excuse me, those two Naxians—to get themselves on deck without any further delay. Brief them on what's going on. Murry-Balff, I want to be talking to those Locrians in five minutes or less. Bolangyr, work up an inventory of our battle stores, just for the hell of it, but don't activate anything, you hear, not a thing. The rest of you stand by and hold your peace, will you?" He glowered at the spectrometer screen, where clumps of gorgeous amide radicals and polyhydric alcohols were circling in a stately sarabande of astonishing colors. Whatever the Locrians were doing here, he thought, it ought to be possible to work out some kind of territorial agreement with them in half an hour or so, and then he would be able to get down to his real work. We are all rational beings. Reason will prevail. We of the Six Races have all managed to coexist in interstellar space for a very long time without any serious conflicts of interest. Why start now?

Why, indeed?

The Locrian gave its name as Speaker-to-Erthumoi. Murry-Balff had asked to talk to Ship-Commander, but Speaker-to-Erthumoi was the best he was able to get. Of course, they might be the same person, Wing-Marra knew. Locrians change their names as often as they change functions. Perhaps it was not even legitimate to regard Locrian "names" as names.

He put the transmission into image-stasis, freezing the communication channel. The Locrian would simply have to sit there on hold until the Erthuma captain had a clearer idea of the situation. Turning to one of his Naxians, Wing-Marra said, "Is this meant as an insult, Blue Sphere? Should I insist on speaking to Ship-Commander?"

The Naxian studied the motionless image of the Locrian that glittered from the frozen screen for a long while, assessing the information visible to it-her on the insectoid creature's seemingly impassive face. It is the extraordinary gift of Naxians to be able to read the emotional output—not the minds, only the emotions—of any life-form, no matter how alien to it. Greed, anger, lust, shame, compassion, whatever: all creatures are open books to Naxians. Even when all they have to work with is a static image on a screen. How they did it, no Erthuma knew. The various stargoing species of the galaxy had many sorts of intuitive powers that were difficult for Erthumoi to comprehend.

The Naxian seemed to be working hard, though. Meditative ripples and quivers ran the length of its-her pink, narrow snakelike body. So intense was Blue Sphere's concentration that it-she went into flipper mode for a few moments, extruding stubby fringed grasping organs from its-her otherwise limbless form, then absorbing them again.

"You may proceed, Captain," Blue Sphere announced after a time. "The Locrians intend no insult. Mere efficiency of communication is the most likely purpose. I suspect Ship-Commander is less fluent in Erthumat than this one. At any rate the Locrian's emotional aura is benign."

"But apprehensive," offered the other Naxian, Rosy Tetrahedron. "Definite anxiety is evident. The Locrian feels strong uncertainty as to Erthuma motivations or intentions in this sector of space."

"Fine," Wing-Marra said. "If they're as nervous about us as we are about them, there's hope for working something out. Reciprocity is the mother of security, eh, Sanoclaro? Eh? Old diplomatic proverb."

Sanoclaro didn't smile. But he hadn't really expected her to.

He killed the image-stasis and the screen came to life again. The Locrian could have walked away from the transmitter while Wing-Marra's colloquy with the Naxians was going on, but it was still there. At least Wing-Marra assumed that it was the same one. He stared at it. What he saw was a fleshless angular head much longer than it was wide, a lipless V-shaped beak of a mouth, a single giant glaring eye shielded by a clear bubble-like plate hinged at each side, a thin tubular neck sprouting out of a flimsy, skeletal six-limbed trunk.

The Locrian looked for all the world like a giant insect, a dry parched chitinous thing that would probably crunch if you hit it with the edge of your hand. Very likely they had evolved from some kind of low-phylum insect-like arthropods on their dry, chilly home world, which belonged to an orange K5 sun in the Cygnus arm of the galaxy. But there was nothing low-phylum about them now. They were chordate vertebrates with tough siliceous spinal columns to support their scaly gray-green exoskeletons. And they had tough, shrewd brains in their narrow, elongated skulls.

The moment the stasis broke the Locrian said, "We request clarification, Erthuma-representative. Do we speak with Diplomacy or Administration?"

"Administration. I am Hayn Wing-Marra, captain, Erthuma of Hesperia in St. Dominic's Star system."

The Locrian made a crackling sound that seemed like displeasure. "We request Diplomacy. It is a point of protocol. Transspecies discussions are protocol matters."

Wing-Marra felt like screaming. The last thing he wanted was to have to conduct this discussion by way of Ayana Sanoclaro, considering the wild suspicions she had just been voicing. But the Locrian was right: contact across species lines in open space had to follow protocol. Reluctantly Wing-Marra beckoned to Sanoclaro, who gave him a little smirk of triumph and stepped into the pale yellow glow of the communications field.

"What we want to know, Speaker-to-Erthumoi," she said without preamble, "is whether you're staking a claim to the solar system that lies adjacent to our present position."

"Negative," said the Locrian immediately. Though the two ships were eighty-eight million kilometers apart at that moment, the communications field—a modulated-neutrino carrier wave operating through hyperspace—permitted instantaneous communication between them. For that matter, it would have permitted communication at essentially the same response time even if the ships had been at opposite ends of the galaxy. "No claim to this system has been recorded."

Wing-Marra held up both his hands. Making two circles out of his thumbs and forefingers, he moved them in an elaborate pantomime that he hoped would suggest the orbital relationship of the second planet and its huge moon. But Sanoclaro, without even looking at him, had already begun to ask the obvious next question.

"Are you claiming just the second planet, then? Or its moon?"

"Is there Erthuma interest in the second planet?" the Locrian countered.

The Naxian who called it-herself Blue Sphere moved outside the field's scanner range and signaled to Wing-Marra that it was picking up increased ambiguities and uncertainties. Wing-Marra, peering at the screen, sought to detect some change in the Locrian's expression, but Speaker-to-Erthumoi's rigid features showed not a flicker of movement. An integument that chitinous wasn't capable of much movement, or perhaps of any at all. Whatever clues the Naxians used in doing their little trick, facial expressions didn't seem to play an important role.

Sanoclaro looked to Wing-Marra for a cue. He indicated the spectrometer screen, ablaze with drifting hydrocarbon masses.

"We are purely a scientific mission," Sanoclaro told the Locrian. "We're here to study the molecular cloud. We have no territorial intentions whatsoever."

"Nor do we," said Speaker-to-Erthumoi. "We require

only unhindered completion of our research."

Wing-Marra frowned. He was beginning to wonder if any of this was any business of his at all. If the only thing the Locrians wanted was to be left alone to snoop around the second world, and all that he wanted was to be left alone to study the molecular cloud—

No. The directives were very clear. When an Erthuma ship encountered a ship belonging to any of the other five races in open space, the Erthuma vessel, regardless of its own purpose, was required to file a report on the activities of the other spacecraft. Even though no one saw any serious risk of anything so farfetched and implausible as interstellar warfare breaking out, it behooved the Erthumoi—as the youngest and least experienced of the six starfaring peoples—to keep close watch on everything that their rivals might be up to. Assuming that their activities would never be anything but benign, regardless of the generally peaceful relationships that had prevailed among the Six Races since the first Erthuma entry into interstellar space, was folly.

He needed more information.

Making the planet-and-moon gesture again, Wing-Marra tried to depict the orbiting Locrian ship by moving his nose in a circle around the equator of the finger-and-thumb that represented the planet. Sanoclaro shot him a mystified look. Abandoning the pantomime, Wing-Marra whispered angrily, "Try to find out what the hell they're doing here, will you?"

Sanoclaro said, "May we inquire into the nature of your mission?"

Blue Sphere, still out of scanner range, signaled that increased agitation was coming from the Locrian. Or so Wing-Marra thought the Naxian was trying to tell him.

It was maddening for the captain to have to deal through

this many intermediaries. Every ship carried a Diplomacy as a matter of course, but Wing-Marra hadn't expected to need to make use of Sanoclaro's services in this remote region. And the Naxians, though they were valuable interpreters of non-verbal messages in tricky situations like this one, weren't always easy for non-Naxians to understand.

Speaker-to-Erthumoi said after a long pause, "Our mission is exploratory also."

Wing-Marra pantomimed drunkenness.

Sanoclaro looked puzzled again. Then, smiling to show that she understood, she said, "But surely a high-oxygen world such as the one nearby can be of little practical use to Locrians."

Speaker-to-Erthumoi was silent.

"May we inquire whether the nature of your exploration is exploratory?" Sanoclaro said. "Or is there perhaps some other purpose?"

"Other," said the Locrian.

"Other than scientific?"

"Other, yes."

"Is its nature such that our presence here will disrupt your work?"

"Not necessarily."

"Then it is proper to conclude that the representative of the Galactic Sphere of Locria has no objection to our continuing to remain in this region?"

Another long silence.

"No objection," Speaker-to-Erthumoi replied finally.

Both Naxians now signaled that they were picking up *distress, resentment, suspicion, general contradiction-of-spoken-statement.*

Wing-Marra fumed. He hoped Sanoclaro didn't think that having obtained the Locrians' permission for them to stay here was any sort of wonderful achievement. This was, after all, open territory.

He said under his breath, "I need to know what they're up to!"

Sanoclaro said, "Our captain instructs me to obtain data from you concerning the nature of your mission."

"I will reply shortly," said Speaker-to-Erthumoi. There was yet another lengthy pause. Then the image froze. This time it was the Locrians who had imposed the stasis, no doubt so Speaker-to-Erthumoi could engage in a quick off-screen strategy session with Ship-Commander.

Wing-Marra said to Sanoclaro, "If it's just a routine mapping mission, they shouldn't be as edgy as the Naxians say they are. When they come back on, see if you can pin them down about their reasons for landing scouts on that planet and its moon."

"What do you think I'm trying to do?"

"What I think," said Linga Hyath, "is that they probably were just on a routine mapping mission, but they found something on the second world or its moon that was way out of the ordinary, and so they're sticking around to take a close look at it, and they wish we'd get the hell out of here before we find it too."

"Thank you," Wing-Marra told the Cosmography. "Your grasp of the obvious is extraordinarily profound."

Hyath glared and began to reply.

"Save it," said Wing-Marra. The screen was alive again.

Speaker-to-Erthumoi—if that indeed was who was on the screen now—looked astonishingly transformed, as though it had been wearing a mask before and now had removed it. The hard, sharp-angled gray chitin of its all-but-featureless face had been opened back like the two doors of a cabinet, and what was visible now was the bare surface of its great staring glassy inner eye, the immensely penetrating organ that Locrians revealed only when they needed to see with particular clarity. Facing that eye was like facing fifty Naxians at once. It seemed to be seeing right into him. Wing-Marra felt stripped bare, down to bone and tendon. He had never seen a Locrian in full percept mode before, and he didn't like it.

To hell with it, he thought. I don't have anything to hide.

He met the glare of that terrible eye without flinching.

The Locrian said, "Ship-Commander requests face-to-face contact with Erthuma-captain in order to continue the discussion in a more fruitful way. He proposes stochastic choice to determine which ship is to be the site of the meeting."

Sanoclaro looked inquiringly toward Wing-Marra, who nodded at once.

"Agreed," the Diplomacy told the alien. "Shall we flip a coin?"

"That method is acceptable."

"Do you want us to flip one?"

"We prefer to do that," said the Locrian.

Again Wing-Marra nodded. His irritation was mounting rapidly. Let them use a coin with two heads, for all he cared. What did it matter whether the meeting took place on his ship or theirs? He just wanted to get on with his work.

"Select your choice," said Speaker-to-Erthumoi. It held up its claw, revealing a shining six-edged coin of some bright coppery metal grasped between two of its numerous many-jointed fingers. One face of the coin showed some Locrian's beaky big-eyed head, and when the alien turned it over Wing-Marra saw jagged abstract patterns on the reverse.

"I'll take tails," Wing-Marra said.

"Tails?"

"The side that doesn't have the head."

"Ah."

Something happened off screen. Speaker-to-Erthumoi said, after a moment, "We have tossed the coin. Your selection proved to be correct. We will send a boarding party. How soon can you receive us?"

There was more grumbling, of course. Hyath and Sanoclaro, the suspicious ones, were convinced that the whole coin-tossing gambit had been nothing but a ploy to insinuate a Locrian force aboard the ship, perhaps so that they could seize it. Eslane Ree thought that was crazy, and said so. Mikoil Karpov, too, wanted to know why the two women were taking such an alarmist position. Even Murry-Balff, who usually went along with anything Wing-Marra said, thought it would have been a better idea to have sent the Diplomacy over to the alien vessel to conduct the conference. "If they're up to anything funny, better that they do it over there," Murry-Balff said. "And to her, not us."

Annoyed as he was by the paranoia of Sanoclaro and Hyath, Wing-Marra found nothing to amuse him in his old friend's frivolity. He was a cautious man but he saw no reason for fear. The risk was all on the Locrians' side. They were the ones who would be boarding a strange ship, after all. He couldn't bring himself to believe that they had anything so wild as an armed takeover in mind. No, the coin-toss had probably been honest, and the Locrians could probably be trusted. Or else they were working up something so devious that no sane person could be expected to be on guard against it.

Within the hour a beetle-like hypershuttle brought a

four-Locrian delegation across the gulf between the two ships. It popped back into normal space astonishingly close to the *Achilles* and coasted in for a docking.

Four Locrians came scrambling through the access lock. They were taller than the tallest of Erthumoi, but so light and frail were their bodies, six pipelike limbs and hardly any thorax, that they seemed little more than walking skeletons.

By way of protection against the intoxicating richness of the Erthuma ship's atmosphere, they were wearing translucent spacesuits that hung about them in loose, awkward folds, like old baggy skin. Anything beyond a 10 percent oxygen concentration was dizzying to them, and furthermore they preferred to breathe air that was thinned by a substantial neon component, which the *Achilles* was unable to supply.

The first thing the Locrians saw was the spherical golden grille and trembling corkscrew antennae of the simultrans machine that Murry-Balff had set up in the center of the meeting room. They obviously didn't like it.

"There is no real need to employ this device," said one of the Locrians coolly, giving the translating gadget a fiercely contemptuous stiff-necked glare. "Your language holds no mysteries for us."

Wing-Marra had expected that. The other races were *always* scornful of Erthuma artificial-intelligence gadgets, because in one way or another they were able to manage most things without such mechanical assistance. The simultrans was capable of rendering real-time translations of anything said in any of the six galactic languages into any or all of the other five. Erthumoi, notorious for their general incapacity to master the ancient and intricate languages of most alien species, found the machine extremely useful. The others didn't.

But Wing-Marra suspected there was more to the Locrian objections to the simultrans than simple racial prejudice. With the simultrans offering instantaneous translation of anything said, no members of either species would be able to speak with each other in surreptitious asides unintelligible to the other party. Wing-Marra saw that as a distinct advantage for him, since some or all of the Locrians appeared to be fluent in Erthumat, but no one aboard the *Achilles* understood more than a smattering of Locrian. Evidently the Locrians saw things the same way.

Smiling grandly, he said, "Ah, but we feel it is only courteous to offer you this small assistance. You are already under the stress of having come aboard a strange ship, and you are compelled to conduct this meeting clad in spacesuits that doubtless must cause you some discomfort. We would not burden you with the obligation to converse in an alien tongue as well."

"But it is not necessary that we—"

"Permit me to insist. I am overwhelmed by your unselfishness but I could not bear the shame of having inconvenienced you so deeply."

There was a frosty silence. The Locrian looked—so far as Wing-Marra was capable of telling—extremely annoyed.

But after a moment the Locrian said, "Very well. Let us use the translator. You know me as Speaker-to-Erthumoi. I am accompanied by Ship-Commander and Recorder."

Three names, four Locrians, no indication of what was what or which was whom. Wing-Marra didn't even try to get an explanation.

"I am Captain Wing-Marra," he said. "This is my Diplomacy, Ayana Sanoclaro. These Naxians travel with us and will observe. They call themselves Blue Sphere and Rosy Tetrahedron. Jorin Murry-Balff, my Communications, will record our conversation. With your permission, of course."

"Granted," said Speaker-to-Erthumoi.

Within the helmet of its suit its head split open, revealing the great luminous beacon of its inner eye.

Wing-Marra shivered.

One of the other Locrians opened its eye also. Wing-Marra could not decide whether that one was Recorder or Ship-Commander. Did it matter? Perhaps they were all Recorder. Or all four were Ship-Commander.

Aliens, he thought. Go and figure.

The other two remained sealed. A safety measure, Wing-Marra suspected. Locrians were terribly vulnerable when their inner eye was exposed. The slightest pressure against it—the touch of a hand—could blind or even kill. Therefore they opened their facial hinges only when they deemed it absolutely necessary to do so.

Even in normal visual mode, Wing-Marra had heard, Locrians saw three-dimensionally, penetrating into the interiors of things. With the inner eye unveiled, he imagined that they could see right into his soul.

The two unveiled ones were watching him from opposite sides, as though trying to read all aspects of him. It was like being in the crossfire of two brilliant lasers. Wing-Marra understood now why they had asked for this face-to-face meeting. They wanted a chance to evaluate the nature of the Erthuma they were dealing with in a way that long distance conversation via neutrino-wave could not provide.

Well, let them look, Wing-Marra thought. Let them look as long and as hard and as deep as they like.

The silent surveillance went on and on and on.

After a time he stopped finding it merely disagreeable and began to find it worrisome. He glanced toward the Naxians for an opinion. But they were calm. They lay motionless, placidly coiled side by side in a corner of the room, watching with unblinking eyes. They were in their limbless relaxation-state. Evidently they saw no cause for alarm in this peculiar wordless interrogation.

At length one of the unveiled Locrians—not the one who had identified itself as Speaker-to-Erthumoi—said, "We believe that you are trustworthy."

"I am deeply grateful for that," Wing-Marra said, trying hard not to sound sarcastic.

"These are delicate matters in which we find ourselves enmeshed," another of the Locrians intoned. "We must operate from a position of absolute assurance that you will not abuse our confidence."

"Of course," Wing-Marra said.

"Let us come to the point, Captain Wing-Marra," said the fourth alien. "What we would prefer is that you leave this region at once, making no further investigation."

Ayana Sanoclaro uttered a muffled, undiplomatic grunt of surprise and anger. Wing-Marra's own reaction was closer to amusement. Was that why they had given him this elaborate scrutiny? That seemed a preposterous build-up for such a straightforward, almost simpleminded demand. Did they think he was a child?

But he restrained himself.

Carefully he said, "We have come a great distance, and we have significant research goals that we wish to carry out. Leaving here now is out of the question for us."

"Understood. You will not leave and we do not expect you to. As we have said, the problem we face here is delicate, and we would prefer to handle it without the complications that the intrusion of another galactic species can bring. But we state only a preference."

Wing-Marra nodded. He had forgotten how literal-minded Locrians could be.

"Aside from our going away from here right away, then, what is it you really want from us?" he asked.

The two Locrians who had not opened their inner eyes now drew back the hinges of their faces. Wing-Marra found himself confronting four great blazing orbs. Within the translucent helmets, four sharp-edged alien beaks were slowly opening and closing—a sign, he supposed, of intense concentration. But he suspected also that it might connote Locrian tension, disquietude, malaise. Something about their stance suggested that: they held themselves even more stiffly than usual, practically motionless, limbs rigid.

The Naxians too now seemed distressed, probably from having picked up jittery auras from the Locrians. They had uncoiled and lay stretched taut, side-by-side, their eyes gleaming and bulging, their little transient flipper-limbs shooting in and out of their sides.

"It may be the case," said one of the Locrians finally, just as the silence had begun to seem interminable, "that we are not able to deal with the problem that we see here unaided. Indeed, we are quite certain of this. What we propose, therefore, is an alliance."

"What?"

"We will recapitulate. There is a problem in this solar system that causes us much concern. We would rather conceal it from you than share it with you; but because we have come to feel that we are incapable of solving the problem without assistance, specifically without Erthumoi assistance, we are willing to regard the arrival of Erthumoi at just this moment as providential. And invite you to work with us toward a solution."

Wing-Marra felt a faintly sickening sensation, as though he were teetering on the rim of an infinitely deep mine shaft. What, he wondered, was he getting into here?

He looked from one Locrian to the next, four fleshless, forbidding insectoid heads whose alien eyes blazed like frightful torches.

"All right," he said. "Tell me something about this problem of yours."

"Let us show you," said the Locrian who was Speaker-to-Erthumoi.

The alien gestured to another of the Locrians—perhaps it was Recorder—who drew from the folds of its spacesuit a small brassy-looking metallic object that Wing-Marra recognized as a Locrian image-projecting device. The Locrian set it on the floor in front of itself.

"We came here," said Speaker-to-Erthumoi, "much as you did, simply to explore. We had no military or economic purpose in mind. As you already recognize, the planets of this solar system would be of little value to us. But in the course of our reconnaissance, we came upon something in the vicinity of the second world that aroused our curiosity. We investigated more closely, and this is what we observed."

Speaker-to-Erthumoi nodded. Recorder—if that was who it was—stared at the image-projector until a warm golden glow, like that of a little sun, began to come from it. The device, Wing-Marra knew, was tuned to the Locrian's brain waves.

Suddenly the room blossomed into vivid color. A three-dimensional scene, so immediate in its presence that it seemed almost as though the wall of the *Achilles* had opened to reveal another world just outside, took form before Wing-Marra's eyes.

It *was* another world. Heavy-bellied orange clouds hung

low in a deep-turquoise sky. The vantage point at which Wing-Marra found himself was just below the clouds, perhaps a kilometer above the surface. He saw dense blue-green forests below, broad rivers, a chain of huge shimmering lakes.

Far off on the horizon a smallish G-type sun was setting, streaking the air with brilliant bands of violet and gold. On the opposite side of the sky a moon had already begun rising, huge and oppressively close, perhaps no more than 100,000 kilometers away. Its bare, smooth, gleaming face was marked with the dark rugged lines of what must surely be immense mountain ranges ringing shining ovals that might have been the beds of long-dry seas.

"What you see is the second world of the nearby system on a summer evening," Speaker-to-Erthumoi announced. "It is not an agreeable place. The mean temperature at the altitude of observation is approximately 315 K. It is slightly cooler at ground level, but still unpleasantly warm, at least by our standards. The atmosphere is composed almost entirely of nitrogen and oxygen, with substantial water vapor and minor components of argon and carbon dioxide. The atmospheric pressure is equally displeasing, approximately seven times as great, at surface level, as on Locrian-norm worlds. There are strong tidal effects, caused by the proximity of a satellite unusually large in relation to its primary, and a vortex of relatively cool air descending permanently from the poles creates constant strong cyclonic winds. Ordinarily we would not have continued our observations of such a planet beyond this point. However—"

The other Locrian made a barely perceptible movement. The focal intensity of the image changed, and Wing-Marra abruptly found himself looking at the second world from a point not far above the tangled canopy of a tropical jungle.

Winged creatures were moving slowly through the air.

"Native life?" Wing-Marra asked.

"No. Look again."

He narrowed his eyes against the brightness of the sky, doubly lit by the spectacular sunset and the cold white glory of the gigantic shining moon. What had seemed to him at first quick glance to be huge birds now appeared something quite other: humanoid figures with small stubby legs and two slender arms held close against their chests. From bulging humps below their shoulders rose two powerful limblike projections heavily banded with muscle and anchored by jutting keels on their chests; and out of those came the giant fleshy wings, far larger in area than the creatures themselves, whose steady stately flapping motions held them aloft.

Then one of the flying creatures turned so that its narrow, tapering head was clearly outlined against the sky, and Wing-Marra could plainly see the great curving bony crest rising from its forehead and the equally astonishing jut of its elongated chin. He had no further doubt. Another of the galactic races had preceded both Locrians and Erthumoi to this place.

"Crotonites?" he said, with a little involuntary shudder.

"Indeed. See, now, their base." Focus shifted once again, and Wing-Marra beheld the elaborate web-work weave of a Crotonite nest, spreading through the treetops to cover perhaps a hectare. The winged aliens, equipped with breathing masks to help them deal with an atmosphere whose chemistry was not much to their liking, moved busily back and forth, swooping down to land, disappearing within the strands of the delicate structure, emerging again and rising skyward with strong, unhurried strokes of their great wings.

"If there are Crotonites here," Wing-Marra said, "why haven't we detected any signs of a Crotonite starship in the vicinity?"

"No doubt it has been here and gone," said the Locrian. "So far as we can determine, the Crotonite base here has been established for quite some time. We regard it a semi-permanent outpost."

Wing-Marra looked toward Sanoclaro. The Diplomacy's expression was solemn.

She said, "It might just be a world they could use, I suppose. Thick atmosphere, warm climate. Though the atmosphere doesn't seem poisonous enough to make them really happy, but they could work out some kind of adaptation to help them cope with all that oxygen. They seem to be doing all right with those breathing masks. Well, if they've filed a claim, we'll have to apply to them for permission if we want to make a landing and set up a base. But not if we're only going to make a ship survey of the molecular cloud. This solar system lies completely outside the cloud. Their claim wouldn't give them any rights to adjacent space."

"They have filed no claim," Speaker-to-Erthumoi said.

Wing-Marra frowned. "No?"

"Nothing. Nor have they made any response to our presence here. They seem to be making an elaborate point of ignoring us. It is as though they have not noticed us. Or you, we presume, since you evidently have not heard from them. They simply go about their business, setting out every day from that base and exploring the planet in an ever widening circle."

"Then I fail to see the difficulty," the Erthuma captain said. "If they don't care that others are here, why should you care so much that they are? This whole solar system's a free zone for everybody. And in any case there doesn't seem to be much here of any importance."

"You have not heard the entire story yet," said Speaker-to-Erthumoi. "They also have a base on the moon."

Another tiny movement by the Locrian operating the projector, and the lush tropical scene vanished in an instant. Its place was taken by something far more harsh: the barren, airless landscape of the second planet's moon. Now Wing-Marra found himself at the edge of what must have been an ancient sea. A shallow, barren basin of some white limy rock stretched to the horizon. Colossal mountains, their lofty summits unexpectedly eroded and rounded as they might have been on a world that had an atmosphere, rose to one side. The dazzling green bulk of the second world hung close overhead, filling the sky, terrifyingly near, seemingly about to plunge down upon him.

The Crotonites had woven a seven-sided Crotonite dwelling that sprawled over the brightly lit plain just at the edge of the mountains' shadow. And Crotonites, swaddled in individual pressure-bubbles that covered them, wings and all, from crested heads to stubby legs, were driving about in land-crawlers.

But their movements were incomprehensible. They seemed to be circling a big empty area a dozen or so kilometers from their base. From time to time one of the crawlers would abruptly disappear, as though it had been devoured by some unseen lurking monster; or one would wink suddenly into existence in the middle of the plain, as if popping out of nowhere.

"I don't understand," Wing-Marra said. "Where are they going? Where are they coming from?"

"We ask ourselves the same thing," said Speaker-to-Erthumoi. "Our answer is that the Crotonites believe they must go to great pains to conceal whatever they are doing on that lunar plain. And so they have generated a zone of invisibility around it."

"Can they do such a thing?" Wing-Marra asked, surprised.

"It would appear that they can. We see nothing; and yet we feel the presence of living beings in that empty zone."

Murry-Balff said, "What do your instrument readings show? If there are Crotonites moving around out there, you'd be getting infrared output. And if they've set up some kind of invisibility gadget, there might be some measurable light-wave distortion around its edges. Or various other forms of data corruption."

"We do not have instruments capable of measuring what cannot be seen," replied the Locrian, and there was a distinctly icy edge to its flat, unemotional voice. "What we detect is the emanations of intelligent beings, radiating in the Crotonite mind-spectrum, coming from a place that seems to be uninhabited and uninhabitable."

Wing-Marra said, "What do you think they're trying to hide? A weapons factory? A center for espionage activities? A laboratory for secret scientific research?"

"We have considered all those possibilities. They have varying orders of probability. But what we think is most probable of all is that they have discovered something of great value on that moon, and do not want any other galactic race to know what they have."

"That might explain why they haven't filed a claim to this system," Sanoclaro said. "Even though their occupation of the planet and the moon would ordinarily validate any claim. Maybe they didn't want to call this place to anybody's attention even to the extent of claiming it. They gambled instead that nobody else would find it."

"This is our belief also," said the Locrian.

Sanoclaro shook her head. "Bad luck for them that not one but *two* different galactic races stumbled on it right after them, against all odds. But sometimes it does happen that the needle in the haystack gets found."

Speaker-to-Erthumoi said, "What it is the Crotonites have discovered here, we have no idea, any more than we know how they are able to conceal it. But Crotonites would not remain in so hostile an environment without strong motivation. We wish to know what that motivation is: that is, what it is that they are concealing."

Wing-Marra laughed. "We thought *you* were the ones who had found something valuable here."

"What we found was Crotonites working here secretly in a zone of mystery. We wish to know what that zone of mystery contains. And so we invite you to enter into partnership with us."

"So you've already told us. But just what kind of partnership do you mean?"

"We have one asset to offer: the discovery that the Crotonites are hiding something. But we are unable to proceed beyond that. You Erthumoi can provide, perhaps, the asset we lack: the technology by which the Crotonites' shield of concealment can be penetrated. Let us work together to expose and exploit their secret. And we will share, half and half, in such profits as come from the venture."

"Half and half?" Wing-Marra said. "If there's something valuable on that moon, don't you think the Crotonites are entitled to a share, too? Or are you planning to cut them out of it altogether?"

"To be sure," said Speaker-to-Erthumoi. "We may have to divide the profits in thirds."

The discussion aboard the *Achilles* that followed the departure of the Locrian boarding party was very possibly the loudest and most vociferous that Wing-Marra had ever known in all the eleven cycles of his life.

Sanoclaro, of course, was horrified at the notion of entering into any kind of deal with Locrians, and urged Wing-Marra to head for the nearest Erthuma world at once and turn the affair over to the authorities there. But her friend Linga Hyath, to everyone's amazement, disagreed completely with her: she was all for finding out without any delay what it was that the Crotonites were hiding on the second planet's moon. If the cool and unemotional Locrians were so churned up over it, she said, then it was important to know what they had. Mikoil Karpov took the same position, and so did Murry-Balff, who was already bubbling with notions of how to break through the Crotonite data-screen.

Eslane Ree, though, was on Sanoclaro's side. "This is simply none of our business," the Navigation said quietly, and, when Hyath and Murry-Balff took issue with her, she said it again less quietly, and then very loudly indeed. For a small woman she was capable of astonishing ferocity when she thought the occasion warranted it, and apparently she thought this one did. "We're here to do scientific research. Not to strike bargains with aliens."

"You look on aliens as enemies?" Karpov asked.

"I don't look on them as friends," Eslane Ree shot back. "They tolerate us in the galaxy because they have no choice. We came muscling into a system that they had carved up into five nice slices while we were still using stone axes, and demanded our piece of it. Well, because interstellar war is currently obsolete, and the galaxy is so big that even the Five Races hadn't had time to explore it all, they graciously allowed us to become the Sixth Race. But they don't trust us and they don't like us, and they all think they're a whole lot wiser than we are, and maybe they are. We haven't been out in the galaxy long enough to know."

"We have achieved so much in such a very short time," said Karpov ponderously. "Is that not—"

Eslane Ree glared at him.

"In a short time, yes, we've figured out black holes and pulsars and hyperdrives and neutrino-wave communication, and maybe all that makes us think we're pretty hot stuff. But when it comes to galactic politics we're still strictly novices. If the Locrians want to do something dirty to the Crotonites, let them. Why should we risk getting drawn in? Because the Locrians tell us they'll cut us in on the profits? *What* profits? When have the bugs ever gone out of their way to cut us in on anything? How do we know what they're really up to? What they want to do is use us. And when they're through using us, they might very well get rid of us, if it turns out what we've stumbled across is something that's inconvenient for us to know."

"Madness," Karpov muttered.

"I don't think you have any right—"

"Please," said Septen Bolangyr. "It is my turn to speak."

Bolangyr, who usually was indifferent to discussions of policy, also argued in favor of keeping out of potential trouble. "We don't understand much about Locrian psychology and we don't even begin to understand the Crotonites," he argued. "All we know, really, is that both of them are older and probably shrewder races than ours, and that, as Eslane Ree says, neither of them have much respect or liking for us. Eslane Ree is correct. We're likely to find ourselves way over our heads if we get mixed up in some squabble between them."

"Wrong!" Karpov cried. "Such a great opportunity to

learn! We must not turn our backs! Not only the mystery of this moon, but the mystery of Locrians, the mystery of Crotonites! Go among them, is what we must do! Engage them! Entangle ourselves! How else can we learn? How can we simply turn our backs at such a time?"

"Easily," said Eslane Ree. "We're scientists, not spies."

"And to involve ourselves in any such irregular trans-species dealings is completely unwise," said Ayana Sanoclaro.

"And for all we know the bugs are the bad guys and the bats are the good guys," said Septen Bolangyr. "We'll be putting our noses into something we don't remotely understand. That doesn't feel very healthy to me."

"But can't you see—"

"Won't you realize—"

"If you'd only stop to consider—"

And so on until Wing-Marra, running out of patience at last, cut through the uproar to say, "I make it three in favor, three against. All right. I cast the tie-breaking vote. We go in with the Locrians."

"No!" The word came from Eslane Ree and Ayana Sanoclaro in the same instant. "Impossible! Unthinkable!"

"And very stupid," said Bolangyr.

"Those who don't like it," Wing-Marra replied, "can place formal objections on file. We will take official notice and proceed as planned." To Eslane Ree he said, "This is a scientific mission, yes. But it's also an Erthuma spaceship, and all Erthuma ships have the responsibility of protecting Erthuma interests in space, which sometimes involves monitoring the activities of the other five stargoing species. That's what we're supposed to do, and that's what we're going to do. Clear? Good. Murry-Balff, I want to talk to you about what instruments we're going to use to scan the Crotonite lunar base. Sanoclaro, put together a Crotonite master psychological profile for me. I need to know what makes those bats tick. You have twenty minutes. Eslane Ree, park us around that second planet's moon and compute a landing orbit that'll put our groundship down somewhere in the neighborhood of the Crotonite base. Bolangyr, run the usual maintenance checks on all extravehicular-activity equipment. I think that's all for now." He paused a moment. "No. There's one thing more. Hyath, go down below and tell the snakes—excuse me, the Naxians—what we've just decided. Ask one of them to volunteer for the landing party."

"And me?" Mikoil Karpov asked.

Wing-Marra realized that he had provided an assignment for everyone except Biochemistry. But he couldn't see any immediate role for Karpov in any of this.

Then, with a pang, the captain remembered that they had all come to this obscure corner of the galaxy for a reason that had nothing to do with Locrians or Crotonites or galactic power politics. For a long sad moment he stared at the glowing screen of the spectrometer. Neglected though it was, it was still flashing bright-hued reports from the nearby molecular cloud. Through Wing-Marra's mind went roiling visions of esoteric hydrocarbons, life-giving amino acids, complex polyvalents of a thousand kinds, stirring about tantalizingly in that mysterious ocean of intricate gases that lay just beyond his reach.

He sighed.

"You keep an eye on the spectrometer screen," he told Karpov. "There's no telling what sort of significant stuff is going to turn up inside that cloud. And we aren't going to stop the whole mission dead in its tracks while we deal with this distraction. Not if I can help it. Okay? Okay. Adjourned."

★ ★ ★ ★ ★

They set up their camp in the long shadow of the great mountains, fifty kilometers from the Crotonite moon-base: close enough so that the curvature of the lunar surface would not interfere with Murry-Balff's instruments, but not so close that the Crotonites would come running right over to put up a fuss.

The first thing Wing-Marra did was to send out an all-frequencies neutrino-wave announcement telling the entire galaxy that a joint Erthuma-Naxian-Locrian expedition had landed to investigate certain "anomalies" on a moon of the second planet of an unclaimed main-sequence star in the W49 nebula, where a Crotonite exploration team appeared to be already at work.

Murry-Balff said quizzically, "Sir, is that such a good idea? The Crotonites can't fail to pick that message up. Should we really be letting them know we're here?"

"They already know we're here," Wing-Marra said, amused. "Do you think we can put a groundship down right in their back yard without their noticing? What the message does is tell everyone *else* that we're here. In case the Crotonites have any idea of defending their turf against intruders. If we were to attempt a secret landing, they might feel it was safe to respond with an immediate lethal attack."

"Against a trans-species ship? But that would be an act of war!" Murry-Balff exclaimed.

"Yes, it would. That's why I want to make it difficult for them to proceed with it. Most of us operate under the sane and reasonable assumption that one species will never attack another, but I suspect the Crotonites may operate under the assumption that they shouldn't attack another species unless they think they can get away with it. If everybody for 50,000 light-years around knows we've landed here, the Crotonites are less likely to undertake military action against us. Or so I hope."

In fact he had no real idea how the Crotonites were likely to react to anything, but he was prepared for the worst. The psychological profile of them that Ayana Sanoclaro had drawn up for him was profoundly disturbing in that regard.

Of the five senior races of the galaxy, the Crotonites were the least predictable and, potentially at least, the most dangerous. Only their preference for worlds with thick atmospheres heavily laced with ammonia and hydrogen cyanide, evidently, is what had kept them out of serious conflict with the other races. The worlds they inhabited were unendurable to the other species; the worlds they coveted were worlds that none of the others would want.

What set them apart from the other intelligent species of the galaxy, possibly even more than their metabolic differences, was the fact that they were the only one that had wings. Locrians and Erthumoi walked upright; Naxians were wrigglers; Cephallonians, aquatic; the ponderous Samians, when they deigned to move at all, rolled. But Crotonites were fliers.

On their home worlds they lived primarily airborne lives, moving slowly but with a strange grace through the heavy atmosphere, swooping and rising, rising and swooping. Lesser-winged creatures were their food, caught always while in flight. They had no cities, only small transient settlements fashioned of twisted fiber, which they abandoned after only short periods of occupation. How they had ever attained the technological capacity to achieve interstellar travel was hard for Erthumoi to understand; but, then, it was hard for Erthumoi to see how any of the Five Races, except perhaps the Locrians, had managed to cross that difficult-to-attain threshold. Yet they all had, where thousands of other intelligent species had not. Some force had driven them, often against all biological and mechanical probability, to reach outward not only to their neighboring worlds but to the stars themselves.

Could it be, Wing-Marra wondered, that the force that had impelled the Crotonites outward was hate?

Certainly they manifested plenty of that in their dealings with the other races. They scarcely troubled to conceal their contempt for beings who had no wings. "Ground-crawlers," they called them, or "mud-lickers," or "land-slugs." So great was their disdain for all things wingless that they could not bear even to eat the meat of the unwinged, predatory carnivores though they were: it was shameful, they explained, to incorporate the flesh of land-slugs into their own high-soaring bodies.

Once they had learned that various sorts of wingless mud-lickers had found a way of traveling between the stars, therefore, the Crotonites must have felt that they too would have to go forth into that vast darkness. And they had not rested until they also had solved the mysteries of hyperspace travel.

Once they did enter the community of starfaring races, they accepted the presence of those who already roamed the galaxy, because they had no choice about it. There was no way for them to maintain absolute isolation from the rest. Interstellar commerce requires a certain amount of contact with alien creatures, and it is economically suicidal to let racial prejudices get in the way of that. But they made it plain that they did no more than tolerate any of the others, and that in fact what they felt for them was loathing and enmity.

They did not, of course, carry those feelings to the extent of actual warfare. If there ever had been any such thing as interstellar warfare, it had gone out of fashion long before the first Erthumoi starfarers had come upon the scene. One reason for that was the logistical difficulty of waging war on a galactic scale, even with hyperdrive-equipped vessels. Another was that in a galaxy of effectively infinite size there was very little motive for serious territorial disputes among six intelligent life-forms whose environmental requirements were all mutually incompatible. But the main reason, probably, why the Crotonites never acted upon their hostility toward the wingless was that they knew the wingless would not permit war to break out. Nothing was apt to draw the separate races together more swiftly than any sort of conflict that might lead to war. War was an expensive nuisance; war was a messy disruption; war simply could not be allowed. The Crotonites probably knew that they would be annihilated at once by a united all-species force if they ever gave vent to their deepest emotions, and that helped to keep the galactic peace.

Instead they cheated wherever they could, they swindled, they behaved toward the wingless in all ways as though matters of morality were unimportant. The wingless in turn bore little love for them. Erthumoi, who had their own not very complimentary nicknames for each of the other galactic races, called the Crotonites "bats," or sometimes even "devils."

And now Wing-Marra found himself camped fifty kilometers from a nest of them.

"This moon can't have been airless very long," Linga Hyath was saying. "Probably it was just as habitable as its primary world, once upon a time."

"You think so?" Wing-Marra said.

They stood, spacesuit-clad, arrayed in a semi-circle around Murry-Balff as he bent over the bank of instruments that he had set up on the bed of the dry sea. There were eight in the group: Wing-Marra, Hyath, Sanoclaro, Murry-Balff, Eslane Ree, the Naxian Blue Sphere, and two of the Locrians. Septen Bolangyr, Mikoil Karpov, and Rosy Tetrahedron had remained behind on the *Achilles*.

Hyath indicated the towering mountain range that loomed behind them. "Those are very big mountains," she said. "The sort you'd expect to find on a moon like this. But look at the way they've been worn down. For most of their existence they've been subjected to wind and rain and the other geological forces of a living world. But of course an atmosphere will wander off into space if a world's not big enough to hold it by gravitational force and if it's warm enough so that the atmospheric molecules can move faster than the local escape velocity. There was a time when this place must have had an atmosphere pretty much like its primary's, I'd guess—these two are really a double-planet system, most likely with similar outgassing history—but the moon, large though it is, was too small, and too warm, to keep its air. Little by little the entire atmosphere was able to break free of the gravitational field here and escape. And eventually there was none left at all."

"How long ago did that happen, would you say?" Eslane Ree asked.

"Oh, quite recently, quite recently indeed," said Hyath. "Within the last two or three hundred million years, is my top-of-the-head answer."

Eslane Ree chuckled. "Oh. Only two or three hundred million years ago! That's your idea of quite recently?"

"Surely you understand that on the geological timescale that's only—"

"Hold it," Wing-Marra said. "I think Murry-Balff's got something."

The Communications had been leaning forward over his control panel, muttering to himself, shaking his head, tapping in data setups, wiping them out, tapping new ones in. Suddenly the board was alive with flashing lights.

"Okay," Murry-Balff said. "I think we have data capture."

Wing-Marra peered close. The readout was analog, but he could make comprehend nothing of the patterns he saw.

"What I've done," said Murry-Balff, "has been to plot light-wave deviation, first. That's this information here. Assuming there's a zone of significant surface mass in that supposedly empty zone, it ought to have at least some relativistic effects on photons traveling through its vicinity, regardless of the visual data corruption that the Crotonites are managing to throw up around it. Okay. There it is." He pointed to a pattern in green and red at the side of his panel. It meant nothing at all to Wing-Marra. Murry-Balff said, "It's next to imperceptible, but that's what you'd expect of any sort of mass smaller than a continent, anyway. But the fact is that it *isn't* imperceptible. What I'm picking up is the bending I expected, right here—and *here*—that's an inferred computation of the required size of whatever's causing the perturbation. Those are the boundaries of the concealed object, see?"

"Show me that again," Wing-Marra said.

Murry-Balff made a quick gesture with his light-pen.

"But that's enormous!" said Wing-Marra. "It's the size of a small city!"

"That's right. Not such a small one, either. The area is—umm—64 square kilometers, plus or minus four. Now, we get the sonar in there and we try to see whether it'll penetrate the Crotonite data shield, and we discover that we can, more or less, although the perimeter data is likewise corrupt and has to be factored for a standard distortion deviation, which the little brain here in this box has been kind enough to work out for me. We bounce the sound waves through the invisibility shield, and luckily for us, the shield doesn't screen them out once we're inside and so far as I can tell does not corrupt our data, but returns us a clean readout. Which gives us the horizon profile of the concealed object."

"Where?"

"Here. You see? These ups, these downs. The skyline, so to speak, of the hidden city. And the mean elevation is—well, rooftop level, I make out to be 11.5 meters, with a deviation of—umm—the tallest building is, let's say, 21.5 meters, but there aren't many of those, and most of the others are, well, single-story structures—"

"Structures?" Ayana Sanoclaro said. "You've got actual buildings showing on that screen?"

The two Locrians were murmuring now in their own harsh, clicking language. The Naxian, agitated, was rapidly thrusting its little flipper-limbs forth and retracting them.

"Didn't you hear me?" Murry-Balff said. "There's a city under the Crotonite screen. Now that I'm past their corruption line, I'll have the whole thing mapped out for you in less than fifteen minutes."

"A city?" Sanoclaro said in wonder. "The Crotonites have built a city on this airless moon? Under some sort of dome, do you mean?"

Murry-Balff looked up at her. "Did I say it was a Crotonite city? Do the Crotonites even build cities? There's no dome that I can see, at least not an actual physical one, though of course all I'm getting is shadow-images, and it's possible that a dome viewed edge-on might somehow not show up on my screen. I can check that out from another angle. But you can see the building profiles, can't you?" He waved his hands grandly over the panel, which was still entirely incomprehensible to Wing-Marra. "There's nothing Crotonite-looking here. Look, these are streets and avenues. Crotonites don't ordinarily have streets and avenues, do they? And those are solid, rounded structures with vaulted roofs. I don't have the foggiest idea what they are, but Crotonite they aren't."

"But who—?" Sanoclaro demanded, gesturing bewilderedly. "It isn't one of ours, or we'd have had records of a landing here. It can't be Locrian. The Cephallonians would hardly build a settlement on a world that doesn't have a drop of water. The Samians—the Naxians—"

"Why does it have to be a city belonging to any of the Six Races?" Wing-Marra asked suddenly.

Everyone stared at him.

"What are you saying?" asked Eslane Ree. "That there's a seventh interstellar race somewhere that nobody knows about yet?"

"I don't know," Wing-Marra told her. "Right now all I can do is ask questions, not answer them." To Hyath he said, "You believe that this place once was as habitable as its companion planet, but that it's been airless like this for—how long? Three hundred million years?"

"Plus or minus a hundred million," said Hyath.

"Same difference." He closed his eyes a moment. Then, turning to the Locrians, he said, "You people were the first of the Six Races to achieve star travel, right? How long ago was that?"

"It was in the Eighteenth Era," one of the Locrians began.

"Translate that into Galactic Standard Years. Please."

After a moment the Locrian said, "You would think of it

as approximately 315,000 years before the present time."

Wing-Marra nodded. By Linga Hyath's geological way of reckoning things, that was only a heartbeat ago.

He said, "And when you first got out into interstellar space, did you encounter any other starfaring races then, older races that are extinct now?"

"No," said the Locrian. "We did, of course, come upon the ruins of ancient civilizations which perhaps had been galactic in nature, though we do not believe that they were. But of living galactic races—no, no, we were the first of our epoch. And perhaps the first in the history of this galaxy."

"I'm not so sure of that," said Wing-Marra, half to himself.

His mind was racing. Knowledge he had not called upon in hundreds of years came bubbling now out of its deep hiding place.

In the second cycle of his life, flushed with the new youth of his first rejuvenation, he had turned his attention toward the remote past with much the same intensity as he had much later taken up organic chemistry. Archaeology then had been the center of his energies, and for decades he had pored backward into the yesterdays of his species, digging into the few hundred years of history that his native world of Hesperia could provide, then onward, deeper, to Earth, the mother world of all Erthumoi, where antiquity was measured in hundreds of centuries: Chichén Itzá, Pompeii, Babylon, Troy, Luxor, Lascaux. But even that had not satisfied his hunger for antiquity, for Earth was a young world as galactic worlds went, and the Erthumoi a very young race: the mother planet offered no more than 30,000 or 40,000 years of past that had the richness and complexity he sought, and beyond that lay nothing but stray scraps of bone, scatterings of stone tools, the charred ashes of ancient hearths.

So he had gone out into the galaxy again, digging on worlds beyond the Erthuma sphere. At least 10,000 of the worlds of the galaxy had evolved intelligent life-forms. Only a relative handful of those had gone on to develop technological civilizations, and some of those were extinct: dead by their own hands, so it would appear. Of the survivors, only five, before the Erthumoi, had reached the level of interstellar travel. It was not generally thought that any of the extinct races had succeeded in traveling beyond their own solar systems. A widely held theory argued that there was a critical technological threshold that every race had to pass: the ability to achieve self-destruction invariably came sooner than the ability to attain interstellar flight, and only those races able to master their own self-destructive impulses would last long enough to master the mysteries of hyperspace travel. Many had not.

Wing-Marra had probed the ruins of dead alien civilizations in a dozen different star-systems. But they too were disappointing to someone seeking vivid and immediate insight into the look and texture of the distant past. Even in the best preserved of them, not much had withstood the inroads of time: a faint line of stone foundations here, an empty burial vault there, some shattered walls, a battered fragment or two of strange jewelry, perhaps a bit of some unfamiliar and unrecognizable fossil, and not much more. That was all that remained. The youngest of those lost civilizations was 100,000 Galactic Standard Years old, according to his dating instruments; the oldest was five times as ancient as that. Mere traces, outlines in the sand.

But now—on a world where no one could have lived for hundreds of millions of years—

A city? A complete city, with a discernible street plan, and buildings still so intact, after whole geological eras, that roofs still remained and the number of stories could be counted? No, that was archaeological nonsense, Wing-Marra thought. Whatever lay out there on that dead plain, it could not possibly be a settlement that went back to a time when this world still had air and water and vegetation.

But what, then? Perhaps, in the stillness and void of this lifeless moon, the familiar forces of erosion would not operate as they did elsewhere, and whatever was built here would remain through all the ages, undecayed. Why would anyone bother, though, to build a fair-sized city on so absolutely inhospitable a place as this world had become once its atmosphere had fled? And who would have done it? None of the Five Races, that seemed certain. And surely not Erthumoi.

A seventh galactic race, unknown to all the others?

It had to be.

It could not be.

This makes no sense, Wing-Marra thought. None whatsoever.

"What are you thinking?" Sanoclaro asked.

"A lot of things," said Wing-Marra. "But I don't have enough information. Do you know what we need to do now? We need to get into our buggies and ride over across there to take a close look at whatever it is that the Crotonites don't want us to see."

It was, of course, an outrageous thing to be doing. The ground vehicles were equipped with weaponry, and both Wing-Marra and Murry-Balff were carrying hand-model blasters, which were not uncommon items of male ornamental dress on their home world. The Locrians, too, were armed. But in all the cycles of his life Wing-Marra had never once had occasion to use his blaster against another living creature, and he doubted that Murry-Balff had either. As for using it against a member of one of the other galactic races—no, no, it was unthinkable for a member of one race to injure a member of another.

He was counting on the fact that the Crotonites were likely to feel the same way.

Besides, this solar system was unclaimed. If the Crotonites had taken the trouble to claim it, they could have closed both the second planet and its moon to all other races, and backed that up, if necessary, by force. But they had filed no claim. Whether they had chosen that course for some unfathomable sneaky Crotonite reason, or simply because they had been too confident that no other race would find this place, was something Wing-Marra did not know. Either way, as things stood, they had no legal right to bar anyone else from landing here.

They could, naturally, keep trespassers from entering any base they had established themselves. But Wing-Marra had no intention of going anywhere near the Crotonite base. All he wanted to inspect was that big empty place out on the bed of the vanished lunar sea. That was no Crotonite base, was it? That was simply an empty place. How could they stop him from driving right up to it? From peering in? From entering it, if he could?

They would have to admit that there was something there, after all, before they could keep him from trying to look at it.

At first, it seemed as though the Locrians would not buy any of his reasoning and were going to refuse to accompany him into the plain. They were afraid of some violation of Crotonite territorial rights that would lead to big political trouble. The Naxian, too, was uneasy about going along. Naxians, because of their keen intuitive sense of what might be going on in any organism's mind, were usually confident of their ability to handle themselves in all sorts of bothersome situations. But Blue Sphere, like the Locrians, indicated that it-she would just as soon stay away from the Crotonite outpost.

Wing-Marra was unhappy about that. He wanted the Locrians and the Naxian along for a show of solidarity—the Crotonites were less likely to commit some hostile act if they saw that they'd be stirring up trouble with three of the Six Races at once—and also he valued Naxian intuition and Locrian cold-blooded intellectuality. But they would not give in.

"Very well," Wing-Marra said finally. "We'll just have to go without you, I guess."

Which broke the impasse, for the Locrians did not trust their Erthuma partners sufficiently to want them to get first look at the enigma on the plain without them, and Blue Sphere, although it-she plainly suspected that Wing-Marra was bluffing, apparently did not want to take the risk that he was crazy enough to mean what he said. So in the end they all went: a tri-species expedition, setting out in two ground-vehicles across the hard flat limestone floor of the ancient dry sea.

They were still twenty kilometers or so from the zone of mystery when Eslane Ree pointed out a Crotonite landcrawler coming up on their left.

"Everyone into defensive mode," Wing-Marra ordered. "All weaponry armed and ready, but don't get overanxious. Let's just see what they do."

What the Crotonites did was to swing into a path parallel to theirs at a distance of perhaps half a kilometer, and ride alongside them. A little while later, a second Crotonite vehicle took up the same escort position on the right. Then a third appeared, hanging back to the rear. All three maintained constant distances from the Erthuma vehicles as they traveled over the plain.

"The bats watch us, and we watch the bats," Wing-Marra said. "And neither side makes the first move. All right. We wait and see, and so do they. How far are we from the edge of the zone, Murry-Balff?"

"Seven hundred meters."

"Well, we'll have some answers pretty soon."

"Here," Murry-Balff said. "This is it."

Wing-Marra signaled and the caravan came to a halt. They seemed to be in the middle of nowhere. Behind them, far behind, lay the mountains and their camp, and some distance off to the south the Crotonite camp. Ahead of them, stretching out almost endlessly, was the bright, chalky, almost featureless plain that once had been the floor of a prehistoric ocean. The green second world, hanging overhead, seemed closer than ever, a massive, looming weight, and its brilliant light cast an eerie, chilling glow.

Right in front of us, Wing-Marra thought, is a city that may be half a billion years old. And we can't see a damned thing.

"Here come the Crotonites," Eslane Ree said.

"Yes. I'm aware of them. Let's get out and sniff around a little."

He was the first out of the vehicle. After a moment, one of the Locrians jumped out also, and then the other. Sanoclaro and Eslane Ree followed. Murry-Balff remained with his instruments. Blue Sphere, looking fidgety and troubled, stayed in the vehicle also. Wing-Marra beckoned to it-her to get out. Murry-Balff could do his work from the vehicle, if he wanted to, but Wing-

Marra needed the Naxian by his side.

He took a few steps forward, wondering if he would feel resistance. But there was nothing. Nothing at all.

"Am I near it?" he asked.

"Another ten meters," Murry-Balff replied. "But the Crotonites—"

"Yes. I know."

From the right, the left, the rear, the three Crotonite landcrawlers came zeroing in, and pulled up in an open arc around the two Erthuma vehicles. Wing-Marra, though he knew the gesture was preposterous, let his hand rest lightly on the blaster strapped to the side of his spacesuit. God help us all, he told himself, if it comes down to stuff like that. But he felt he had at least to make the gesture.

The Crotonites were out of their land-crawlers, now, six of them, approaching him in the peculiarly dismaying waddling shuffle that they employed when they were forced to walk on the surface of a world. Seen close up, they were less frightful-looking than when flying like devils through the air, because their huge wings were furled and swaddled within their pressure-suits. That way, they appeared as short, plump, almost comical little beings, standing no more than waist-high to an Erthuma. But they were, Wing-Marra thought, pretty evil looking all the same. The great ungainly bulk of the folded wings behind them provided an ominous reminder of their true forms, and their long sharp-featured heads, crested and bony-chinned, had a harsh, repellent, monstrous look.

"Turn on the simultrans," Wing-Marra said to Murry-Balff.

The Crotonites, he knew, would never deign to speak Erthumat. And he knew only seven words in Crotoni, four of them obscene and the others profane.

"Who is the leader here?" asked the shortest and fiercest-looking of the Crotonites, one with diabolical yellow eyes streaked with bands of red.

Wing-Marra raised his hand. "I am. Captain Hayn Wing-Marra of the Erthuma research vessel *Achilles*."

"I am Hiuptis," said the Crotonite. "What are you doing here, Captain Wing-Marra?"

"Why, we've been out for a drive. And now we're taking a little walk."

"I mean what are you doing in this solar system."

"Carrying out chemical research. We're studying the molecular cloud nearby."

"And does the molecular cloud extend to the surface of this moon?"

"Not at all. But while we were in orbit up there we ran into some old friends from Locria, who suggested that we all come down here for a little rest and relaxation."

"Indeed," said the Crotonite coldly. "This moon is an extremely relaxing place. But I suggest that you enjoy yourselves elsewhere. If you continue in the direction you are traveling, you will very shortly be trespassing on a research center established by and operated for the exclusive use of the Galactic Sphere of Crotonis."

"Will we?" Wing-Marra said. "A research center, you say? Where? I don't see anything here at all." He took a deep breath and began to move forward, indicating with a small movement of his hand that the others should come with him. "It's absolutely empty out here, so far as I can tell."

Murry-Balff said softly, "You're within two meters of the shield perimeter now, sir."

"Yes. I know."

Wing-Marra took another step.

The Crotonites began to look extremely agitated. Their bright, beady eyes gleamed and flickered, and they shifted their weight awkwardly from one to the other of their short, birdlike legs. Wing-Marra imagined that they would be flapping their wings, too, if their wings were not pinioned within their pressure suits. As he walked forward, the Crotonites hopped along beside him, keeping pace.

"One meter, sir," Murry-Balff said.

Wing-Marra nodded and stepped across the invisible line.

It was like walking through a wall. Inside, everything was different. He was standing in a kind of antechamber, an open space that curved off to either side at a wide angle. Behind him was the barren plain, still visible, and straight ahead of him, perhaps fifty meters ahead, lay a zone of absolute blackness, so dense and dark that it could well have been the outer boundary of the universe. The space between the invisible wall to his rear and the blackness ahead formed the antechamber, which was brightly lit by drifting clusters of glowfloats and cluttered everywhere with alien-looking instruments. It was full of Crotonites, too, who were staring at him with a look on their demonic bony faces that was surely the Crotonite equivalent of the most extreme astonishment.

Murry-Balff, still monitoring everything from the vehicle, said, "There's a second shielded zone within the first one, sir."

"I'm looking right at it. It's black as the pit."

"It's totally light-absorbent. But the sonar goes through. The city starts just on the other side."

The Crotonite who called itself Hiuptis tapped Wing-Marra urgently on his thigh. "Now do you see, Captain? Plainly this is a research zone, and delicate observations are in progress."

"Fascinating," said Wing-Marra. "I never would have believed it."

"You concede that we are carrying on research here?"

"Yes. Yes, of course you are. That's plain to see."

"Then I call upon you to cease this trespass at once!"

"Ah, but we're not trespassing, are we?" Wing-Marra said lightly. "We're only visiting. It's a purely social thing. This is such a forlorn dead place, this moon. It's good to have the company of one's fellow creatures for a little while in a place like this. And as long as we're here, you really don't mind if we look around a bit, do you? What sort of research did you say you were doing, by the way? I don't seem to recall."

Hiuptis turned to the Locrians. "Ship-Commander!" the Crotonite cried sharply. "Will you be a party to this detestable intrusion also? I warn you that you will thereby involve the Galactic Sphere of Locria in the culpability, and our inevitable demand for reparations will extend to your sphere as well as that of Erthuma. You have been warned."

"We take note of the warning," said one of the Locrians solemnly. "To which we reply that we are here only because we wish to pay our respects to the representatives of the Galactic Sphere of Crotonis, now that we have become aware that you too are present in this unknown and unclaimed solar system where both we and the Erthumoi have separately been carrying out research programs of our own."

The Locrian's emphasis on *unclaimed* was subtle but unmistakable. Hiuptis made a sputtering sound. It was shifting from foot to foot again, so quickly that it seemed almost to be hopping.

Wing-Marra glanced around. The Crotonites within the research station were unarmed, but the six who had come out to intercept the Erthuma vehicles carried blasters. He wondered what the chance was that they would use them if he continued to press forward. Certainly Hiuptis seemed furious, but so far the only threat it had made was that there would be a demand for reparations. Did that mean the Crotonites were ruling out any kind of attempt to end the intrusion by force? Or was Hiuptis merely trying to lull him with some slippery Crotonite sleight-of-tongue?

He looked toward Blue Sphere. The Naxian seemed to be aware of what Wing-Marra needed to know. It-she signaled relative calm: the Crotonites were angry, were, in fact, fuming mad, but there seemed to be no immediate danger of actual violence.

Of course, even Naxians weren't infallible. But Wing-Marra decided to risk it.

He began to move forward again, toward the strange zone of blackness that lay before him.

Hiuptis and the other five blaster-equipped Crotonites hopped frantically along at his side. "Captain Wing-Marra! Captain Wing-Marra! Captain Wing-Marra!" Hiuptis cried, again and again, in increasingly excited tones.

The other Crotonites, those who had been operating the myriad scanning devices that were aimed toward the wall of darkness, were staring at him, frozen with astonishment.

"Do you mean to go in *there?*" Hiuptis asked. "Surely not! Surely not, Captain Wing-Marra!"

Wing-Marra turned toward his Naxian again. Blue Sphere looked troubled now.

They are afraid, it-she told Wing-Marra silently. They are angry that you are in here where they do not want you to go, but they are afraid, also, of what may happen if you go in there. It is for your sake that they are afraid.

"Murry-Balff?" Wing-Marra said. "Do you have any reading on what's going on on the other side of the inner screen? Do you pick up the presence of any Crotonites over there?"

"I don't, sir, no. But that doesn't mean there aren't any, only that the sonar doesn't—"

"Right," Wing-Marra said. He looked toward the Locrians. "What about you? Can you try to see through that darkness and tell me what's behind there?"

The Locrians, after a moment's hesitation, unveiled their inner eyes, and turned their piercing three-dimensional vision toward the black void ahead.

"Buildings," reported one of the Locrians, its voice sounding oddly strangled.

"Buildings, yes," said the other. "Streets. A whole city is there."

"No Crotonites?"

"No living thing at all," the first Locrian said. "It is very quiet in there. It is extremely still."

"Fine," Wing-Marra said. "I'll take a look."

"Captain!" Eslane Ree cried, in horror. "No!"

"Captain Wing-Marra!" said Hiuptis, practically squawking with rage and frustration. "I forbid—I utterly forbid—"

"Excuse me," Wing-Marra said. "I'll be right back, I promise you."

Quickly, before he could change his mind, he stepped into the zone of darkness.

The first thing he noticed on the far side was that he was still alive. He had been prepared to die—eleven cycles might well be quite enough, he had often thought—but that had not happened.

The second bit of information that came to him was the amber glow on the arm-monitor of his suit that told him he was now in the presence of an atmosphere. An oxygen-based atmosphere, at that. He could probably take his spacesuit off altogether in here, though he did not intend to. This place was like a world unto itself, sealed off within the screens that shielded it. Perhaps the atmosphere in here was the one the city had had when this moon was still alive.

Then, as his vision adapted to the low light level within the inner shield, he saw the city.

It was stunning beyond his comprehension. Low buildings, yes—Murry-Balff's readouts had been right about that. In a perfect state of preservation, absolutely new-looking, and so totally strange in their architecture that he felt as though he had wandered into a land of dreams. Everything seemed to melt and flow: domes became parapets, walls became balconies, windows turned to arches. All was fluid, and yet everything was fixed, solid, eternal.

Unfamiliar colors teased his eyes. He could almost have believed that he was seeing in some far corner of the spectrum, that these were the hues beyond violet, or perhaps the ones below red.

Wonderstruck, he moved forward, down a narrow street that seemed to widen invitingly as he entered it.

The movement, he realized, was an illusion. Nothing moved here. All was in stasis: timeless, silent, free from any sort of decay. There was no dust. There were no cracks in the walls. This was a city outside time, shielded against all harm. No tectonic movement within the depths of this moon had left its mark on these flawless structures. No meteors had come plunging through the airless sky to crash through these roofs. No spider had spun here. Moth and rust were strangers here. An eternity and a half might have passed since the builders of this place had taken their leave of it, but nothing about it had changed.

How was that possible? What spell of enchantment kept this place invulnerable against the tooth of time?

He went close, peering through windows that seemed opaque and translucent at the same time. There were objects in the buildings: artifacts, mechanisms. He saw things on shelves that baffled and awed and astounded him. Wing-Marra began to tremble. Should he go in? No, he thought. Not now. Not yet. He might be pushing his luck too far. Who knew what traps awaited him in there, to guard those ancient treasures against intruders? And yet, to think that all the wonders of an unknown technology were just on the far side of those shimmering walls—

He was choking with amazement. There was no place to compare with this in all the galaxy.

He touched a wall. It seemed to give slightly against the pressure of his fingertips. And then suddenly the sky above him was ablaze with the whirling snakes of the Kekule ring. The fiery vision of a gigantic organic molecule danced before him. It was none that he had ever seen or even imagined before, immense, bewilderingly intricate, joined in a thousand places, holding forth the possibility of infinite complexity. He stared into it and it was like staring into a new universe. After a time he let go of the wall and took a few tottering steps backward.

The vision faded at once and was gone.

But the impact, lingering, was overwhelming. Wing-Marra's mind throbbed. He had to get away. He needed to come to terms with what he had seen. He could not bear to remain in this place any longer.

He swung about and ran through the silent streets toward the blackness, and burst through it, and stumbled out into the antechamber. The bright lights dazzled him painfully and he shrank away from them, covering his face for a moment, closing his eyes. When he felt able to open them again, he saw them all staring at him in wonder, Crotonites, Locrians, his own people, all of them appalled, all of them aghast.

"You are alive?" Hiuptis whispered.

"Alive, yes. How long was I in there?"

Eslane Ree said, "A minute or so. No more."

"It seemed like years."

"What was in there?" Ayana Sanoclaro asked.

Wing-Marra gestured. "Go in and see for yourself."

"Are you serious?"

"Go in!" he cried. "All of you! You've never imagined anything like that! I wasn't hurt—why should you be?" He looked down at the Crotonite commander. "You mean to say that you never went in there, not once, not any of you?"

"No," Hiuptis murmured. "Never. We thought it was too dangerous. We only scanned it from outside, and nothing more. The shields—we were not sure if they were lethal. Finally we risked a penetration of the outer one. But the other—the other—"

"So you didn't put the shields up yourselves?"

The Crotonite made a gesture of negation.

"No," Wing-Marra said. "Naturally you didn't. Neither the invisibility shield nor the decay-proof shield inside it. We couldn't figure out how you had done it, and of course you hadn't done it. You don't have the technology for that. Nobody in the galaxy does. You just stumbled on the whole thing, and you've been dancing around the edges of it. Well, go on in now! All of you! Go and see! My God, there are miracles in there! And who can even guess how old it all is? Fifty million years? A billion? It can sit like that forever . . . right to the end of time."

"Captain—" It was Linga Hyath. "Captain, you're getting too excited."

"Damned right I am!" Wing-Marra cried. "Go in there and see! Go in, will you? See for yourselves!"

Afterward, when everyone had come stumbling out, hushed and dazed and dumfounded, a strained silence fell. The vastness of the wonders that they had seen seemed to have overcome them all.

Only the Locrians appeared able to come to terms immediately with that grand and staggering experience. To Wing-Marra's amazement they joined hands and pranced about in a weird, jubilant dance, rubbing their antennae together as they cavorted. No doubt they were already counting the profits that could be mined from the hoard of treasure beyond the shield.

It was then that Hiuptis came to Wing-Marra and said, in a dark, cold tone the Erthuma had not heard from it before, "You wingless ones will leave our research center now, and you will not return. You will obey without further discussion."

There was insistence in Hiuptis's crackling voice, and menace, and something else: the implication, perhaps, that everyone there needed a time to retreat and digest the meaning of the discovery. But mainly there was menace and insistence. Wing-Marra suspected that there might be real violence, despite all taboos, if they tried to remain any longer; and Blue Sphere backed up his suspicions with the blunt warning that the Crotonites were reaching a point of exasperation that might prove explosive.

"Don't worry," Wing-Marra told Hiuptis. "We're going to go. You can have the place to yourselves again."

The Locrians halted their strange dance instantly. One of them turned to Wing-Marra in amazement, its great eye gleaming, and said, "But our agreement—!"

Wing-Marra met its glare with one of his own. "We can discuss that later. I'm calling for a withdrawal. I'm not ready to take any further steps here. You can do as you please."

"Leaving this find to them?" the Locrian said, astounded. "Incredible! You actually mean to withdraw and let them have—"

"For the time being," said Wing-Marra. "Only for the time being."

The Locrian rose to its full height and waved its forelimbs furiously in protest. But Wing-Marra, turning quickly away, began to walk toward the perimeter of the outer screen, toward the ground-vehicles waiting just outside it.

Sanoclaro came up beside him. "Are you serious? You're really just going to pull out, now?"

He whirled to face her. "What do you think I'm going to do? Start a war with Crotonis over it? These Crotonites are half crazy with confusion and rage and greed and outraged pride and God knows what other emotions, all of them dangerous. They're right at the point where they'll kill to get us out of here, now. Do you want to see if they will?"

"But to allow them sole possession of such a find—"

"For the moment," said Wing-Marra. "Only for the moment. They're in possession, but they don't have ownership. Nobody does. They discovered it, sure. But they didn't claim it, which they probably thought was very clever. Then the Locrians found out about it and got us involved. I went in on my own hook, which the Crotonites hadn't dared to do, and discovered that it's accessible and full of incredible things. You understand this sort of stuff: you can see how muddled the claim is by this time. Let higher authorities figure it out now. The only thing that's certain is that nothing's ever going to be the same again in this galaxy."

"But what do you think the city is?" Sanoclaro asked.

"Something left behind by a race greater than any of the Six," said Wing-Marra quietly. "That's all I know. I couldn't begin to guess who they were. Or are."

"*Are?* But you said the site might be a billion years old!"

"It might, yes. Or a million. And its builders might have become extinct before there was vertebrate life on Earth. Or they might still be out there somewhere, hidden away in some unexplored arm of the galaxy, or in some other galaxy entirely. Maybe we'll stumble upon them. Or maybe they'll come back from wherever they are and pay *us* a visit. Or maybe they'll never be heard from again. In any case, the damage is done."

"The damage?"

"There's a city full of a superior alien technology sitting here. Now that we know what to look for, we may find that there are fifty more invisible cities just like it stashed around the galaxy too, or five hundred, full of the most astounding gadgets anyone has ever dreamed of. You can bet that all that technology, if anybody can figure out what to use it for, is going to destabilize the equilibrium among the Six Races that keeps this galaxy peaceful. Or worse: suppose the builders themselves ever come back and decide to play with us—choosing sides among the Six Races, picking allies, making enemies, maybe looking for vassals—can you imagine what that will do?"

"Yes," said Sanoclaro quietly. "I can."

They reached the ground-vehicle. Wing-Marra turned for one last look at the place where the city lay hidden.

He saw nothing. Nothing at all, only the bare bright expanse of the flat stark plain, and a few Crotonite groundcrawlers. He shook his head.

Everything will be different from now on, he thought. Nothing will ever be the same again.

"Let's get back to the ship," he said wearily. All his people stood waiting by the vehicles, each one of them seemingly lost in astonished recollection of the vision they had seen. "I need to put together some sort of a report," he said. "The whole Erthuma sphere will know about this place by tomorrow. The whole damned galaxy, I suppose."

"And then?" Eslane Ree asked. "What will we do after that?"

"Who knows? That's not my concern right now. I've had enough excitement. I've got other work to do, you know. I still want to see what sort of hydrocarbons are floating around in that molecular cloud." He allowed his eyes to close, and the alien city sprang to life behind his lids, strange dreamlike buildings stretching on and on to the horizon, and every one of them laden with implements and devices of unknown and perhaps unknowable use. He saw the vision again, bearing promise of chemistries beyond any chemistry he had ever known. His whole being throbbed with the recollection of what he had seen and felt behind that wall of darkness. A magical place, he thought. A place of wonders. And, maybe, of terrors. Time would tell.

Yes, he thought, everything is going to be different now, all throughout the galaxy. And, he suspected, he, too, would never be quite the same again. After such a vision, how could he be?

He smiled. Eleven cycles old, and he could still feel a little shiver of wonder now and then. That wasn't so bad. Of course, it took something pretty spectacular to get that kind of response out of him: a cloud thirty light-years wide loaded with complex organic molecules, say, or an alien city a billion years old. But he had lived eleven lifetimes, after all. After eleven cycles he couldn't be expected to react in a big way to anything ordinary. He had seen all the ordinary things before, too many times.

He shrugged. It would be interesting to stick around for another cycle or two, and see what was going to happen next.

"Okay," he said, beckoning them all to get back into the ground-vehicles. "I think we're finished here for the time being. Let's go."

This Is the Road

Leaf, lolling cozily with Shadow on a thick heap of furs in the airwagon's snug passenger castle, heard rain beginning to fall and made a sour face: very likely he would soon have to get up and take charge of driving the wagon, if the rain was the sort of rain he thought it was.

This was the ninth day since the Teeth had begun to lay waste to the eastern provinces. The airwagon, carrying four who were fleeing the invaders' fierce appetites, was floating along Spider Highway somewhere between Theptis and Northman's Rib, heading west, heading west as fast as could be managed. Jumpy little Sting was at the power reins, beaming dream commands to the team of six nightmares that pulled the wagon along; burly Crown was amidwagon, probably plotting vengeance against the Teeth, for that was what Crown did most of the time; that left Leaf and Shadow at their ease, but not for much longer. Listening to the furious drumming of the downpour against the wagon's taut-stretched canopy of big-veined stickskin, Leaf knew that this was no ordinary rain, but rather the dread purple rain that runs the air foul and brings the no-leg spiders out to hunt. Sting would never be able to handle the wagon in a purple rain. What a nuisance, Leaf thought, cuddling close against Shadow's sleek, furry blue form. Before long he heard the worried snorting of the nightmares and felt the wagon jolt and buck: yes, beyond any doubt, purple rain, no-leg spiders. His time of relaxing was just about over.

Not that he objected to doing his fair share of the work. But he had finished his last shift of driving only half an hour ago. He had earned his rest. If Sting was incapable of handling the wagon in this weather—and Shadow too, Shadow could never manage in a purple rain—then Crown ought to take the reins himself. But of course Crown would do no such thing. It was Crown's wagon, and he never drove it himself. "I have always had underbreeds to do the driving for me," Crown had said ten days ago, as they stood in the grand plaza of Holy Town with the fires of the Teeth blazing in the outskirts.

"Your underbreeds have all fled without waiting for their master," Leaf had reminded him.

"So? There are others to drive."

"Am I to be your underbreed?" Leaf asked calmly. "Remember, Crown, I'm of the Pure Stream stock."

"I can see that by your face, friend. But why get into philosophical disputes? This is my wagon. The invaders will be here before nightfall. If you would ride west with me, these are the terms. If they're too bitter for you to swallow, well, stay here and test your luck against the mercies of the Teeth."

"I accept your terms," Leaf said.

So he had come aboard—and Sting, and Shadow—under the condition that the three of them would do all the driving. Leaf felt degraded by that—hiring on, in effect, as an indentured underbreed—but what choice was there for him? He was alone and far from his people; he had lost all his wealth and property; he faced sure death as the swarming hordes of Teeth devoured the eastland. He accepted Crown's terms. An aristocrat knows the art of yielding better than most. Resist humiliation until you can resist no longer, certainly, but then accept, accept, accept.

Refusal to bow to the inevitable is vulgar and melodramatic. Leaf was of the highest caste, Pure Stream, schooled from childhood to be pliable, a willow in the wind, bending freely to the will of the Soul. Pride is a dangerous sin; so is stubbornness; so too, more than the others, is foolishness. Therefore, he labored while Crown lolled. Still, there were limits even to Leaf's capacity for acceptance, and he suspected those limits would be reached shortly.

On the first night, with only two small rivers between them and the Teeth and the terrible fires of Holy Town staining the sky, the fugitives halted briefly to forage for jellymelons in an abandoned field, and as they squatted there, gorging on ripe succulent fruit, Leaf said to Crown, "Where will you go, once you're safe from the Teeth on the far side of the Middle River?"

"I have distant kinsmen who live in the Flatlands," Crown replied. "I'll go to them and tell them what has happened to the Dark Lake folk in the east, and I'll persuade them to take up arms and drive the Teeth back into the icy wilderness where they belong. An army of liberation, Leaf, and I'll lead it." Crown's dark face glistened with juice. He wiped at it. "What are your plans?"

"Not nearly so grand. I'll seek kinsmen too, but not to organize an army. I wish simply to go to the Inland Sea, to my own people, and live quietly among them once again. I've been away from home too many years. What better time to return?" Leaf glanced at Shadow. "And you?" he asked her. "What do you want out of this journey?"

"I want only to go wherever you go," she said.

Leaf smiled. "You, Sting?"

"To survive," Sting said. "Just to survive."

* * * * *

Mankind had changed the world, and the changed world had worked changes in mankind. Each day the wagon brought the travelers to some new and strange folk who claimed descent from the old ancestral stock, though they might be water-breathers or have skins like tanned leather or grow several pairs of arms. Human, all of them, human, human, human. Or so they insisted. If you call yourself human, Leaf thought, then I will call you human too. Still, there were gradations of humanity. Leaf, as a Pure Stream, thought of himself as more nearly human than any of the peoples along their route, more nearly human even than his three companions; indeed, he sometimes tended to look upon Crown, Sting, and Shadow as very much other than human, though he did not consider that a fault in them. Whatever dwelled in the world was without fault, so long as it did no harm to others. Leaf had been taught to respect every breed of mankind, even the underbreeds. His companions were certainly no underbreeds: they were solidly midcaste, all of them, and ranked not far below Leaf himself. Crown, the biggest and strongest and most violent of them, was of the Dark Lake line. Shadow's race was Dancing Stars, and she was the most elegant, the most supple of the group. She was the only female aboard the wagon. Sting, who sprang from the White Crystal stock, was the quickest of body and spirit, mercurial, volatile. An odd assortment, Leaf thought. But in extreme times one takes one's traveling companions as they come. He had no complaints. He found it possible to get along with all of them, even Crown. Even Crown.

The wagon came to a jouncing halt. There was the clamor of hooves stamping the sodden soil; then shrill high-pitched cries from Sting and angry booming bellowings from Crown; and finally a series of muffled hissing explosions. Leaf shook his head sadly. "To waste our ammunition on no-leg spiders—"

"Perhaps they're harming the horses," Shadow said. "Crown is rough, but he isn't stupid."

Tenderly Leaf stroked her smooth haunches. Shadow tried always to be kind. He had never loved a Dancing Star before, though the sight of them had long given him pleasure: they were slender beings, bird-boned and shallow-breasted, and covered from their ankles to their crested skulls by fine dense fur the color of the twilight sky in winter. Shadow's voice was musical and her motions were graceful; she was the antithesis of Crown.

Crown now appeared, a hulking figure thrusting bluntly through the glistening beaded curtains that enclosed the passenger castle. He glared malevolently at Leaf. Even in his pleasant moments Crown seemed angry, an effect perhaps caused by his eyes, which were bright red where those of Leaf and most other kinds of humans were white. Crown's body was a block of meat, twice as broad as Leaf and half again as tall, though Leaf did not come from a small-statured race. Crown's skin was glossy, greenish-purple in color, much like burnished bronze; he was entirely without hair and seemed more like a massive statue of an oiled gladiator than a living being. His arms hung well below his knees; equipped with extra joints and terminating in hands the size of great baskets, they were superb instruments of slaughter. Leaf offered him the most agreeable smile he could find. Crown said, without smiling in return, "You better get back on the reins, Leaf. The road's turning into one big swamp. The horses are uneasy. It's a purple rain."

Leaf had grown accustomed, in these nine days, to obeying Crown's brusque orders. He started to obey now, letting go of Shadow and starting to rise. But then, abruptly, he arrived at the limits of his acceptance.

"My shift just ended," he said.

Crown stared. "I know that. But Sting can't handle the wagon in this mess. And I just killed a bunch of mean-looking spiders. There'll be more if we stay around here much longer."

"So?"

"What are you trying to do, Leaf?"

"I guess I don't feel like going up front again so soon."

"You think Shadow here can hold the reins in this storm?" Crown asked coldly.

Leaf stiffened. He saw the wrath gathering in Crown's face. The big man was holding his natural violence in check with an effort; there would be trouble soon if Leaf remained defiant. This rebelliousness went against all of Leaf's principles, yet he found himself persisting in it and even taking a wicked pleasure in it. He chose to risk the confrontation and discover how firm Crown intended to be. Boldly he said, "You might try holding the reins yourself, friend."

"Leaf!" Shadow whispered, appalled.

Crown's face became murderous. His dark, shining cheeks puffed and went taut; his eyes blazed like molten nuggets; his hands closed and opened, closed and opened, furiously grasping air. "What kind of crazy stuff are you trying to give? We have a contract, Leaf. Unless you've suddenly decided that a Pure Stream doesn't need to abide by—"

"Spare me the class prejudice, Crown. I'm not pleading Pure Stream as an excuse to get out of working. I'm tired and I've earned my rest."

Shadow said softly, "Nobody's denying you your rest, Leaf. But Crown's right that I can't drive in a purple rain. I would if I could. And Sting can't do it either. That leaves only you."

"And Crown," Leaf said obstinately.

"There's only you," Shadow murmured. It was like her to take no sides, to serve ever as a mediator. "Go on, Leaf. Before there's real trouble. Making trouble like this isn't your usual way."

Leaf felt bound to pursue his present course, however perilous. He shook his head. "You, Crown. You drive."

In a throttled voice Crown said, "You're pushing me too far. We have a contract."

All Leaf's Pure Stream temperance was gone now. "Contract? I agreed to do my fair share of the driving, not to let myself be yanked up from my rest at a time when—"

Crown kicked at a low wickerwork stool, splitting it. His rage was boiling close to the surface. Swollen veins throbbed in his throat. He said, still controlling himself, "Get out there right now, Leaf, or by the Soul I'll send you into the All-Is-One!"

"Beautiful, Crown. Kill me, if you feel you have to. Who'll drive your damned wagon for you then?"

"I'll worry about that then."

Crown started forward, swallowing air, clenching fists.

Shadow sharply nudged Leaf's ribs. "This is going beyond the point of reason," she told him. He agreed. He had tested Crown and he had his answer, which was that Crown was unlikely to back down; now enough was enough, for Crown was capable of killing. The huge Dark Laker loomed over him, lifting his tremendous arms as though to bring them crashing against Leaf's head. Leaf held up his hands, more a gesture of submission than of self-defense.

"Wait," he said. "Stop it, Crown. I'll drive."

Crown's arms descended anyway. Crown managed to halt the killing blow midway, losing his balance and lurching heavily against the side of the wagon. Clumsily he straightened. Slowly he shook his head. In a low, menacing voice he said, "Don't ever try something like this again, Leaf."

"It's the rain," Shadow said. "The purple rain. Everybody does strange things in a purple rain."

"Even so," Crown said, dropping onto the pile of furs as Leaf got up. "The next time, Leaf, there'll be bad trouble. Now go ahead. Get up front."

Nodding to him, Leaf said, "Come up front with me, Shadow."

She did not answer. A look of fear flickered across her face.

Crown said, "The driver drives alone. You know that, Leaf. Are you still testing me? If you're testing me, say so and I'll know how to deal with you."

"I just want some company, as long as I have to do an extra shift."

"Shadow stays here."

There was a moment of silence. Shadow was trembling. "All right," Leaf said finally. "Shadow stays here."

"I'll walk a little way toward the front with you," Shadow said, glancing timidly at Crown. Crown scowled but said nothing. Leaf stepped out of the passenger castle; Shadow followed. Outside, in the narrow passageway leading to the midcabin, Leaf halted, shaken, shaking, and seized her. She pressed her slight body against him and they embraced, roughly, intensely. When he released her she said, "Why did you try to cross him like that? It was such a strange thing for you to do, Leaf."

"I just didn't feel like taking the reins again so soon."

"I know that."

"I want to be with you."

"You'll be with me a little later," she said. "It didn't make sense for you to talk back to Crown. There wasn't any choice. You *had* to drive."

"Why?"

"You know. Sting couldn't do it. I couldn't do it."

"And Crown?"

She looked at him oddly. "Crown? How would Crown have taken the reins?"

From the passenger castle came Crown's angry growl: "You going to stand there all day, Leaf? Go on! Get in here, Shadow!"

"I'm coming," she called.

Leaf held her a moment. "Why not? Why couldn't he have driven? He may be proud, but not so proud that—"

"Ask me another time," Shadow said, pushing him away. "Go. Go. You have to drive. If we don't move along we'll have the spiders upon us."

On the third day westward they had arrived at a village of Shapechangers. Much of the countryside through which they had been passing was deserted, although the Teeth had not yet visited it, but these Shapechangers went about their usual routines as if nothing had happened in the neighboring provinces. These were angular, long-legged people, sallow of skin, nearly green in hue, who were classed generally somewhere below the midcastes, but above the underbreeds. Their gift was metamorphosis, a slow softening of the bones under voluntary control that could, in the course of a week, drastically alter the form of their bodies, but Leaf saw them doing none of that, except for a few children who seemed midway through strange transformations, one with ropy, seemingly boneless arms, one with grotesquely distended shoulders, one with stiltlike legs. The adults came close to the wagon, admiring its beauty with soft cooing sounds, and Crown went out to talk with them. "I'm on my way to raise an army," he said. "I'll be back in a month or two, leading my kinsmen out of the Flatlands. Will you fight in our ranks? Together we'll drive out the Teeth and make the eastern provinces safe again."

The Shapechangers laughed heartily. "How can anyone drive out the Teeth?" asked an old one with a greasy mop of blue-white hair. "It was the will of the Soul that they burst forth as conquerors, and no one can quarrel with the Soul. The Teeth will stay in these lands for a thousand thousand years."

"They can be defeated!" Crown cried.

"They will destroy all that lies in their path, and no one can stop them."

"If you feel that way, why don't you flee?" Leaf asked.

"Oh, we have time. But we'll be gone long before your return with your army." There were giggles. "We'll keep ourselves clear of the Teeth. We have our ways. We make our changes and we slip away."

Crown persisted. "We can use you in our war against them. You have valuable gifts. If you won't serve as soldiers, at least serve us as spies. We'll send you into the camps of the Teeth, disguised as—"

"We will not be here," the old Shapechanger said, "and no one will be able to find us," and that was the end of it.

As the airwagon departed from the Shapechanger village, Shadow at the reins, Leaf said to Crown, "Do you really think you can defeat the Teeth?"

"I have to."

"You heard the old Shapechanger. The coming of the Teeth was the will of the Soul. Can you hope to thwart that will?"

"A rainstorm is the will of the Soul also," Crown said quietly. "All the same, I do what I can to keep myself dry. I've never known the Soul to be displeased by that."

"It's not the same. A rainstorm is a transaction between the sky and the land. We aren't involved in it; if we want to cover our heads, it doesn't alter what's really taking place. But the invasion of the Teeth is a transaction between tribe and tribe, a reordering of social patterns. In the great scheme of things, Crown, it may be a necessary process, preordained to achieve certain ends beyond our understanding. All events are part of some larger whole, and everything balances out, everything compensates for something else. Now we have peace, and now it's the time for invaders, do you see? If that's so, it's futile to resist."

"The Teeth broke into the eastlands," said Crown, "and they massacred thousands of Dark Lake people. My concern with necessary processes begins and ends with that fact. My tribe has nearly been wiped out. Yours is still safe, up by its ferny shores. I will seek help and gain revenge."

"The Shapechangers laughed at you. Others will also. No one will want to fight the Teeth."

"I have cousins in the Flatlands. If no one else will, they'll mobilize themselves. They'll want to repay the Teeth for their crime against the Dark Lakers."

"Your western cousins may tell you, Crown, that they prefer to remain where they are safe. Why should they go east to die in the name of vengeance? Will vengeance, no matter how bloody, bring any of your kinsmen back to life?"

"They will fight," Crown said.

"Prepare yourself for the possibility that they won't."

"If they refuse," said Crown, "then I'll go back east myself, and wage my war alone until I'm overwhelmed. But don't fear for me, Leaf. I'm sure I'll find plenty of willing recruits."

"How stubborn you are, Crown. You have good reason to hate the Teeth, as do we all. But why let that hatred cost you your only life? Why not accept the disaster that has befallen us, and make a new life for yourself beyond the Middle River, and forget this dream of reversing the irreversible?"

"I have my task," said Crown.

Forward through the wagon Leaf moved, going slowly, head down, shoulders hunched, feet atickle with the urge to kick things. He felt sour of spirit, curdled with dull resentment. He had let himself become angry at Crown, which was bad enough; but worse, be had let that anger possess and poison him. Not even the beauty of the wagon could lift him: ordinarily its superb construction and elegant furnishings gave him joy, the swirl-patterned fur hangings, the banners of gossamer textiles, the intricate carved inlays, the graceful strings of dried seeds and tassels that dangled from the vaulted ceilings, but these wonders meant nothing to him now. That was no way to be, he knew.

The airwagon was longer than ten men of the Pure Stream lying head to toe, and so wide that it spanned nearly the whole roadway. The finest workmanship had gone into its making: Flower Giver artisans, no doubt of it, only Flower Givers could build so well. Leaf imagined dozens of the fragile little folk toiling earnestly for months, all smiles and silence, long, slender fingers and quick, gleaming eyes, shaping the great wagon as one might shape a poem. The main frame was of lengthy pale spars of light, resilient wingwood, elegantly laminated into broad curving strips with a colorless fragrant mucilage and bound with springy withes brought from the southern marshes. Over this elaborate armature tanned sheets of stickskin had been stretched and stitched into place with thick yellow fibers drawn from the stick-creatures' own gristly bodies. The floor was of dark shining nightflower-wood planks, buffed to a high finish and pegged together with great skill. No metal had been employed in the construction of the wagon, nor any artificial substances: nature had supplied everything. Huge and majestic though the wagon was, it was airy and light, light enough to float on a vertical column of warm air generated by magnetic rotors whirling in its belly; so long as the earth turned, so would the rotors, and when the rotors were spinning the wagon drifted cat-high above the ground, and could be tugged easily along by the team of nightmares.

It was more a mobile palace than a wagon, and wherever it went it stirred excitement: Crown's love, Crown's joy, Crown's estate, a wondrous toy. To pay for the making of it Crown must have sent many souls into the All-Is-One, for that was how Crown had earned his livelihood in the old days, as a hired warrior, a surrogate killer, fighting one-on-one duels for rich eastern princelings too weak or too lazy to defend their own honor. He had never been scratched, and his fees had been high; but all that was ended now that the Teeth were loose in the eastlands.

Leaf could not bear to endure being so irritable any longer. He paused to adjust himself, closing his eyes and listening for the clear tone that sounded always at the center of his being. After a few minutes he found it, tuned himself to it, let it purify him. Crown's unfairness ceased to matter. Leaf became once more his usual self, alert and outgoing, aware and responsive.

Smiling, whistling, he made his way swiftly through the wide, comfortable, brightly lit midcabin, decorated with Crown's weapons and other grim souvenirs of battle, and went on into the front corridor that led to the driver's cabin.

Sting sat slumped at the reins. White Crystal folk such as Sting generally seemed to throb and tick with energy; but Sting looked exhausted, emptied, half dead of fatigue. He was a small, sinewy being, narrow of shoulder and hip, with colorless skin of a waxy, horny texture, pocked everywhere with little hairy nodes and whorls. His muscles were long and flat; his face was cavernous, beaked nose and tiny chin, dark mischievous eyes hidden in bony recesses. Leaf touched his shoulder. "It's all right," he said. "Crown sent me to relieve you." Sting nodded feebly but did not move. The little man was quivering like a frog. Leaf had always thought of him as indestructible, but in the grip of this despondency Sting seemed more fragile even than Shadow.

"Come," Leaf murmured. "You have a few hours for resting. Shadow will look after you."

Sting shrugged. He was hunched forward, staring dully through the clear curving window, stained now with splashes of muddy tinted water.

"The dirty spiders," he said. His voice was hoarse and frayed. "The filthy rain. The mud. Look at the horses, Leaf. They're dying of fright, and so am I. We'll all perish on this road, Leaf, if not of spiders then of poisoned rain, if not of rain then of the Teeth, if not of the Teeth then of something else. There's no road for us but this one, do you realize that? This is the road, and we're bound to it like helpless underbreeds, and we'll die on it."

"We'll die when our turn comes, like everything else, Sting, and not a moment before."

"Our turn is coming. Too soon. Too soon. I feel death-ghosts close at hand."

"Sting!"

Sting made a weird ratcheting sound low in his throat, a sort of rusty sob. Leaf lifted him and swung him out of the driver's seat, setting him gently down in the corridor. It was as though he weighed nothing at all. Perhaps just then that was true. Sting had many strange gifts. "Go on," Leaf said. "Get some rest while you can."

"How kind you are, Leaf."

"And no more talk of ghosts."

"Yes," Sting said. Leaf saw him struggling against fear and despair and weariness. Sting appeared to brighten a moment, flickering on the edge of his old vitality; then the brief glow subsided, and, smiling a pale smile, offering a whisper of thanks, he went aft.

Leaf took his place in the driver's seat.

Through the window of the wagon—thin, tough sheets of stickskin, the best quality, carefully matched, perfectly transparent—he confronted a dismal scene. Rain dark as blood was falling at a steep angle, scourging the spongy soil, kicking up tiny fountains of earth. A bluish miasma rose from the ground, billows of dark, steamy fog, the acrid odor of which had begun to seep into the wagon. Leaf sighed and reached for the reins. Death-ghosts, he thought. Haunted. Poor Sting, driven to the end of his wits.

And yet, and yet, as he considered the things Sting had said, Leaf realized that he had been feeling somewhat the same way, these past few days: tense, driven, haunted. *Haunted.* As though unseen presences, mocking, hostile, were hovering near. Ghosts? The strain, more likely, of all that he had gone through since the first onslaught of the Teeth. He had lived through the collapse of a rich and intricate civilization. He moved now through a strange world, all ashes and seaweed. He was haunted, perhaps, by the weight of the unburied past, by the memory of all that he had lost.

A rite of exorcism seemed in order.

Lightly he said, aloud, "If there are any ghosts in here, I want you to listen to me. *Get out of this cabin.* That's an order. I have work to do."

He laughed. He picked up the reins and made ready to take control of the team of nightmares.

The sense of an invisible presence was overwhelming.

Something at once palpable and intangible pressed clammily against him. He felt surrounded and engulfed. It's the fog, he told himself. Dark blue fog, pushing at the window, sealing the wagon into a pocket of vapor. Or was it? Leaf sat quite still for a moment, listening. Silence. He relinquished the reins, swung about in his seat, carefully inspected the cabin. No one there. An absurdity to be fidgeting like this. Yet the discomfort remained. This was no joke now. Sting's anxieties had infected him, and the malady was feeding on itself, growing more intense from moment to moment, making him vulnerable to any stray terror that whispered to him. Only with a tranquil mind could he attain the state of trance a nightmare-driver must enter; and trance seemed unattainable so long as he felt the prickle of some invisible watcher's gaze on the back of his neck. This rain, he thought, this damnable rain. It drives everybody crazy. In a clear, firm voice Leaf said, "I'm altogether serious. Show yourself and get yourself out of this cabin."

Silence.

He took up the reins again. No use. Concentration was impossible. He knew many techniques for centering himself, for leading his consciousness to a point of unassailable serenity. But could he achieve that now, jangled and distracted as he was? He would try. He had to succeed. The wagon had tarried in this place much too long already. Leaf summoned all his inner resources; he purged himself, one by one, of every discord; he compelled himself to slide into trance.

It seemed to be working. Darkness beckoned to him. He stood at the threshold. He started to step across.

"Such a fool, such a foolish fool," said a sudden dry voice out of nowhere that nibbled at his ears like the needle-toothed mice of the White Desert.

The trance broke. Leaf shivered as if stabbed and sat up, eyes bright, face flushed with excitement.

"Who spoke?"

"Put down those reins, friend. Going forward on this road is a heavy waste of spirit."

"Then I wasn't crazy and neither was Sting. There *is* something in here!"

"A ghost, yes a ghost, a ghost, a ghost!" The ghost showered him with laughter.

Leaf's tension eased. Better to be troubled by a real ghost than to be vexed by a fantasy of one's own disturbed mind. He feared madness far more than he did the invisible. Besides, he thought he knew what this creature must be.

"Where are you, ghost?"

"Not far from you. Here I am. Here. Here." From three different parts of the cabin, one after another. The invisible being began to sing. Its song was high-pitched, whining, a grinding tone that stretched Leaf's patience intolerably. Leaf still saw no one, though he narrowed his eyes and stared as hard as he could. He imagined he could detect a faint veil of pink light floating along the wall of the cabin, a smoky haze moving from place to place, a shimmering film like thin oil on water, but whenever he focused his eyes on it the misty presence appeared to evaporate.

Leaf said, "How long have you been aboard this wagon?"

"Long enough."

"Did you come aboard at Theptis?"

"Was that the name of the place?" asked the ghost disingenuously. "I forget. It's so hard to remember things."

"Theptis," said Leaf. "Four days ago."

"Perhaps it was Theptis," the ghost said. "Fool! Dreamer!"

"Why do you call me names?"

"You travel a dead road, fool, and yet nothing will turn you from it." The invisible one snickered. "Do you think I'm a ghost, Pure Stream?"

"I know what you are."

"How wise you've become!"

"Such a pitiful phantom. Such a miserable drifting wraith. Show yourself to me, ghost."

Laughter reverberated from the corners of the cabin. The voice said, speaking from a point close to Leaf's left ear, "The road you choose to travel has been killed ahead. We told you that when you came to us, and yet you went onward, and still you go onward. Why are you so rash?"

"Why won't you show yourself? A gentleman finds it discomforting to speak to the air."

Obligingly the ghost yielded, after a brief pause, some fraction of its invisibility. A vaporous crimson stain appeared in the air before Leaf, and he saw within it dim, insubstantial features, like projections on a screen of thick fog. He believed he could make out a wispy white beard, harsh glittering eyes, lean curving lips; a whole forbidding face, a fleshless torso. The stain deepened momentarily to scarlet and for a moment Leaf saw the entire figure of the stranger revealed, a long narrow-bodied man, dried and withered, grinning ferociously at him. The edges of the figure softened and became mist. Then Leaf saw only vapor again, and then nothing.

"I remember you from Theptis," Leaf said. "In the tent of Invisibles."

"What will you do when you come to the dead place on the highway?" the invisible one demanded. "Will you fly over it? Will you tunnel under it?"

"You were asking the same things at Theptis," Leaf replied. "I will make the same answer that the Dark Laker gave you then. We will go forward, dead place or no. This is the only road for us."

They had come to Theptis on the fifth day of their flight—a grand city, a splendid mercantile emporium, the gateway to the west, sprawling athwart a place where two great rivers met and many highways converged. In happy times any and all peoples might be found in Theptis, Pure Streams and White Crystals and Flower Givers and Sand Shapers and a dozen others jostling one another in the busy streets, buying and selling, selling and buying, but mainly Theptis was a city of Fingers—the merchant caste, plump and industrious, thousands upon thousands of them concentrated in this one city.

The day Crown's airwagon reached Theptis much of the city was ablaze, and they halted on a broad stream-split plain just outside the metropolitan area. An improvised camp for refugees had sprouted there, and tents of black and gold and green cloth littered the meadow like new nightshoots. Leaf and Crown went out to inquire after the news. Had the Teeth sacked Theptis as well? No, an old and sagging Sand Shaper told them. The Teeth, so far as anyone had heard, were still well to the east, rampaging through the coastal cities. Why the fires, then? The old man shook his head. His energy was exhausted, or his patience, or his courtesy. If you want to know anything else, he said, ask *them*. They know everything. And he pointed toward a tent opposite his.

Leaf looked into the tent and found it empty; then he looked again and saw upright shadows moving about in it, tenuous figures that existed at the very bounds of visibility and could be perceived only by tricks of the light as they changed place in the tent. They asked him within, and Crown came also. By the smoky light of their tent fire they were more readily seen: seven or eight men of the Invisible stock, nomads, ever mysterious, gifted with ways of causing beams of light to travel around or through their bodies so that they might escape the scrutiny of ordinary eyes. Leaf, like everyone else not of their kind, was uncomfortable among Invisibles. No one trusted them; no one was capable of predicting their actions, for they were creatures of whim and caprice, or else followed some code the logic of which was incomprehensible to outsiders. They made Leaf and Crown welcome, adjusting their bodies until they were in clear sight, and offering the visitors a flagon of wine, a bowl of fruit. Crown gestured toward Theptis. Who had set the city afire? A red-bearded Invisible with a raucous rumbling voice answered that on the second night of the invasion the richest of the Fingers had panicked and had begun to flee the city with their most precious belongings, and as their wagons rolled through the gates the lesser breeds had begun to loot the Finger mansions, and brawling had started once the wine cellars were pierced, and fires broke out, and there was no one to make the fire wardens do their work, for they were all underbreeds and the masters had fled. So the city burned and was still burning, and the survivors were huddled here on the plain, waiting for the rubble to cool so that they might salvage valuables from it, and hoping that the Teeth would not fall upon them before they could do their sifting. As for the Fingers, said the Invisible, they were all gone from Theptis now.

Which way had they gone? Mainly to the northwest, by way of Sunset Highway, at first; but then the approach to that road had become choked by stalled wagons butted one up against another, so that the only way to reach the Sunset now was by making a difficult detour through the sand country north of the city, and once that news became general the Fingers had turned their wagons southward. Crown wondered why no one seemed to be taking Spider Highway westward. At this a second Invisible, white-bearded, joined the conversation. Spider Highway, he said, is blocked just a few days' journey west of here: a dead road, a useless road. Everyone knows that, said the white-bearded Invisible.

"That is our route," said Crown.

"I wish you well," said the Invisible. "You will not get far."

"I have to get to the Flatlands."

"Take your chances with the sand country," the red-bearded one advised, "and go by way of the Sunset."

"It would waste two weeks or more," Crown replied. "Spider Highway is the only road we can consider." Leaf and Crown exchanged wary glances. Leaf asked the nature of the trouble on the highway, but the Invisibles said only that the road had been "killed," and would offer no amplification. "We will go forward," Crown said, "dead place or no."

"As you choose," said the older Invisible, pouring more wine. Already both Invisibles were fading; the flagon seemed suspended in mist. So, too, did the discussion become unreal, dreamlike, as answers no longer followed closely upon the sense of questions, and the words of the Invisibles came to Leaf and Crown as though swaddled in thick wool. There was a long interval of silence, at last, and when Leaf extended his empty glass the flagon was not offered to him, and he realized finally that he and Crown were alone in the tent. They left it and asked at other tents about the blockage on Spider Highway, but no one knew anything of it, neither some young Dancing Stars nor three flat-faced Water Breather women nor a family of Flower Givers. How reliable was the word of Invisibles? What did they mean by a "dead" road? Suppose they merely thought the road was ritually impure, for some reason understood only by Invisibles. What value, then, would their warning have to those who did not subscribe to their superstitions? Who knew at any time what the words of an Invisible meant? That night in the wagon the four of them puzzled over the concept of a road that has been "killed," but neither Shadow's intuitive perceptions nor Sting's broad knowledge of tribal dialects and customs could provide illumination. In the end Crown reaffirmed his decision to proceed on the road he had originally chosen, and it was Spider Highway that they took out of Theptis. As they proceeded westward they met no one traveling the opposite way, though one might expect the eastbound lanes to be thronged with a flux of travelers turning back from whatever obstruction might be closing the road ahead. Crown took cheer in that; but Leaf observed privately that their wagon appeared to be the only vehicle on the road in either direction, as if everyone else knew better than to make the attempt. In such stark solitude they journeyed four days west of Theptis before the purple rain hit them.

* * * * *

Now the Invisible said, "Go into your trance and drive your horses. I'll dream beside you until the awakening comes."

"I prefer privacy."

"You won't be disturbed."

"I ask you to leave."

"You treat your guests coldly."

"Are you my guest?" Leaf asked. "I don't remember extending an invitation."

"You drank wine in our tent. That creates in you an obligation to offer reciprocal hospitality." The Invisible sharpened his bodily intensity until he seemed as solid as Crown; but even as Leaf observed the effect he grew thin again, fading in patches. The far wall of the cabin showed through his chest, as if he were hollow. His arms had disappeared, but not his gnarled long-fingered hands. He was grinning, showing crooked close-set teeth. There was a strange scent in the cabin, sharp and musky, like vinegar mixed with honey. The Invisible said, "I'll ride with you a little longer," and vanished altogether.

Leaf searched the corners of the cabin, knowing that an Invisible could always be felt even if he eluded the eyes. His probing hands encountered nothing. Gone, gone, gone, whisking off to the place where snuffed flames go, eh? Even that odor of vinegar and honey was diminishing. "Where are you?" Leaf asked. "Still hiding somewhere else?" Silence. Leaf shrugged. The stink of the purple rain was the dominant scent again. Time to move on, stowaway or no. Rain was hitting the window in huge murky windblown blobs. Once more Leaf picked up the reins. He banished the Invisible from his mind.

These purple rains condensed out of drifting gaseous

clots in the upper atmosphere—dank clouds of chemical residues that arose from the world's most stained, most injured places and circled the planet like malign tempests. Upon colliding with a mass of cool air such a poisonous cloud often discharged its burden of reeking oils and acids in the form of a driving rainstorm; and the foulness that descended could be fatal to plants and shrubs, to small animals, sometimes even to man.

A purple rain was the cue for certain somber creatures to come forth from dark places: scuttering scavengers that picked eagerly through the dead and dying, and larger, more dangerous things that preyed on the dazed and choking living. The no-leg spiders were among the more unpleasant of these.

They were sinister spherical beasts the size of large dogs, voracious in the appetite and ruthless in the hunt. Their bodies were plump, covered with coarse, rank brown hair; they bore eight glittering eyes above sharp-fanged mouths. No-legged they were indeed, but not immobile, for a single huge fleshy foot, something like that of a snail, sprouted from the underbellies of spiders and carried them along at a slow, inexorable pace. They were poor pursuers, easily avoided by healthy animals; but to the numbed victims of a purple rain they were deadly, moving in to strike with hinged, poison-barbed claws that leaped out of niches along their backs. Were they truly spiders? Leaf had no idea. Like almost everything else, they were a recent species, mutated out of the-Soul-only-knew-what during the period of stormy biological upheavals that had attended the end of the old industrial civilization, and no one yet had studied them closely, or cared to.

Crown had killed four of them. Their bodies lay upside down at the edge of the road, upturned feet wilting and drooping like plucked toadstools. About a dozen more spiders had emerged from the low hills flanking the highway and were gliding slowly towards the stalled wagon; already several had reached their dead comrades and were making ready to feed on them, and some of the others were eyeing the horses.

The six nightmares, prisoners of their harnesses, prowled about uneasily in their constricted ambits, anxiously scraping at the muddy ground with their hooves. They were big, sturdy beasts, black as death, with long feathery ears and high-domed skulls that housed minds as keen as many humans, sharper than some. The rain annoyed the horses but could not seriously harm them, and the spiders could be kept at bay with kicks, but plainly the entire situation disturbed them.

Leaf meant to get them out of here as rapidly as he could.

A slimy coating covered everything the rain had touched, and the road was a miserable quagmire, slippery as ice. There was peril for all of them in that. If a horse stumbled and fell it might splinter a leg, causing such confusion that the whole team might be pulled down; and as the injured nightmares thrashed about in the mud the hungry spiders would surely move in on them, venomous claws rising, striking, delivering stings that stunned, and leaving the horses paralyzed, helpless, vulnerable to eager teeth and strong jaws. As the wagon traveled onward through this swampy rain-soaked district Leaf would constantly have to steady and reassure the nightmares, pouring his energy into them to comfort them, a strenuous task, a task that had wrecked poor Sting.

Leaf slipped the reins over his forehead. He became aware of the consciousness of the six fretful horses.

Because he was still awake, contact was misty and uncertain. A waking mind was unable to communicate with the animals in any useful way. To guide the team he had to enter a trance state, a dream state; they would not respond to anything so gross as conscious intelligence. He looked about for manifestations of the Invisible. No, no sign of him. Good. Leaf brought his mind to dead center.

He closed his eyes. The technique of trance was easy enough for him, when there were no distractions.

He visualized a tunnel, narrow-mouthed and dark, slanting into the ground. He drifted toward its entrance.

Hovered there a moment.

Went down into it.

Floating, floating, borne downward by warm, gentle currents: he sinks in a slow spiral descent, autumn leaf on a springtime breeze. The tunnel's walls are circular, crystalline, lit from within, the light growing in brightness as he drops toward the heart of the world. Gleaming scarlet and blue flowers, brittle as glass, sprout from crevices at meticulously regular intervals.

He goes deep, touching nothing. Down.

Entering a place where the tunnel widens into a round smooth-walled chamber, sealed at the end. He stretches full-length on the floor. The floor is black stone, slick and slippery; he dreams it soft and yielding, womb-warm. Colors are muted here, sounds are blurred. He hears far-off music, percussive and muffled, *rat-a-rat, rat-a-rat, bllllooom, bllllooom.*

Now at least he is able to make full contact with the minds of the horses.

His spirit expands in their direction; he envelops them, he takes them into himself. He senses the separate identity of each, picks up the shifting play of their emotions, their prancing fantasies, their fears. Each mare has her own distinct response to the rain, to the spiders, to the sodden highway. One is restless, one is timid, one is furious, one is sullen, one is tense, one is torpid. He feeds energy to them. He pulls them together. Come, gather your strength, take us onward: this is the road, we must be on our way.

The nightmares stir.

They react well to his touch. He believes that they prefer him over Shadow and Sting as a driver: Sting is too manic, Shadow too permissive. Leaf keeps them together, directs them easily, gives them the guidance they need. They are intelligent, yes, they have personalities and goals and ideals, but also they are beasts of burden, and Leaf never forgets that, for the nightmares themselves do not.

Come, now. Onward.

The road is ghastly. They pick at it and their hooves make sucking sounds coming up from the mud. They complain to him. *We are cold, we are wet, we are bored.* He dreams wings for them to make their way easier. To soothe them he dreams sunlight for them, bountiful warmth, dry highway, an easy trot. He dreams green hillsides, cascades of yellow blossoms, the flutter of hummingbirds' wings, the droning of bees. He gives the horses sweet summer, and they grow calm; they lift their heads; they fan their dream-wings and preen; they are ready now to resume the journey. They pull as one. The rotors hum happily. The wagon slides forward with a smooth coasting motion.

Leaf, deep in trance, is unable to see the road, but no matter; the horses see it for him and send him images, fluid, shifting dream-images, polarized and refracted and diffracted by the strangenesses of their vision and the distortions of dream communication, six simultaneous and individual views. Here is the road, bordered by white birches whipped by an angry wind. Here is the road, an earthen swath slicing through a forest of mighty pines bowed down by white new snow. Here is the road, a ribbon of fertility, from which dazzling red poppies spring wherever a hoof strikes. Fleshy-finned blue fishes do headstands beside the road. Paunchy burghers of the Finger tribe spread brilliantly laundered tablecloths along the grassy margin and make lunch out of big-eyed reproachful oysters. Masked figures dart between the horses' legs. The road curves, curves again, doubles back on itself, crosses itself in a complacent loop. Leaf integrates this dizzying many-hued inrush of data, sorting the real from the unreal, blending and focusing the input and using it to guide himself in guiding the horses. Serenely he coordinates their movements with quick confident impulses of thought, so that each animal will pull with the same force. The wagon is precariously balanced on its column of air, and an unequal tug could well send it slewing into the treacherous thicket to the left of the road. He sends quicksilver messages down the thick conduit from his mind to theirs. Steady there, steady, watch that boggy patch coming up! Ah! Ah, that's my girl! Spiders on the left, careful! Good! Yes, yes, ah, yes! He pats their heaving flanks with a strand of his mind. He rewards their agility with dreams of the stable, of newly mown hay, of stallions waiting at journey's end.

From them—for they love him, he knows they love him—he gets warm dreams of the highway, all beauty and joy, all images converging into a single idealized view, majestic groves of wingwood trees and broad meadows through which clear brooks flow. They dream his own past life for him, too, feeding back to him nuggets of random autobiography mined in the seams of his being. What they transmit is filtered and transformed by their alien sensibilities, colored with hallucinatory glows and tugged and twisted into other-dimensional forms, but yet he is able to perceive the essential meaning of each tableau: his childhood among the parks and gardens of the Pure Stream enclave near the Inland Sea, his wanderyears among the innumerable, unfamiliar, not-quite-human breeds of the hinterlands, his brief, happy sojourn in the fog-swept western country, his eastward journey in early manhood, always following the will of the Soul, always bending to the breezes, accepting whatever destiny seizes him, eastward now, his band of friends closer than brothers in his adopted eastern province, his sprawling lakeshore home there, all polished wood and billowing tented pavilions, his collection of relics of mankind's former times—pieces of machinery, elegant coils of metal, rusted coins, grotesque statuettes, wedges of imperishable plastic—housed in its own wing with its own curator. Lost in these reveries he ceases to remember that the home by the lake has been reduced to ashes by the Teeth, that his friends of kinder days are dead, his estates overrun, his pretty things scattered in the kitchen-middens.

Imperceptibly, the dream turns sour.

Spiders and rain and mud creep back into it. He is reminded, through some darkening of tone of the imagery pervading his dreaming mind, that he has been stripped of everything and has become, now that he has taken flight, merely a driver hired out to a bestial Dark Lake mercenary who is himself a fugitive.

Leaf is working harder to control the team now. The horses seem less sure of their footing, and the pace slows; they are bothered about something, and a sour, querulous anxiety tinges their messages to him. He catches their mood. He sees himself harnessed to the wagon alongside the nightmares, and it is Crown at the reins, Crown wielding a terrible whip, driving the wagon frenziedly forward, seeking allies who will help him fulfill his fantasy of liberating the lands the Teeth have taken. There is no escape from Crown. He rises above the landscape like a monster of congealed smoke, growing more huge until he obscures the sky. Leaf wonders how he will disengage himself from Crown. Shadow runs beside him, stroking his cheeks, whispering to him, and he asks her to undo the harness, but she says she cannot, that it is their duty to serve Crown, and Leaf turns to Sting, who is harnessed on his other side, and he asks Sting for help, but Sting coughs and slips in the mud as Crown's whip flicks his backbone. There is no escape. The wagon heels and shakes. The right-hand horse skids, nearly falls, recovers. Leaf decides he must be getting tired. He has driven a great deal today, and the effort is telling. But the rain is still falling—he breaks through the veil of illusions, briefly, past the scenes of spring and summer and autumn, and sees the blue-black water dropping in wild handfuls from the sky—and there is no one else to drive, so he must continue.

He tries to submerge himself in deeper trance, where he will be less readily deflected from control.

But no, something is wrong, something plucks at his consciousness, drawing him toward the waking state. The horses summon him to wakefulness with frightful scenes. One beast shows him the wagon about to plunge through a wall of a fire. Another pictures them at the brink of a vast impassable crater. Another gives him the image of giant boulders strewn across the road; another, a mountain of ice blocking the way; another, a pack of snarling wolves; another, a row of armored warriors standing shoulder to shoulder, lances at the ready. No doubt of it. Trouble. Trouble. Trouble. Perhaps they have come to the dead place in the road. No wonder that Invisible was skulking around. Leaf forces himself to awaken.

There was no wall of fire. No warriors, no wolves, none of those things. Only a palisade of newly felled timbers facing him some hundred paces ahead on the highway, timbers twice as tall as Crown, sharpened to points at both ends and thrust deep into the earth one up against the next and bound securely with freshly cut vines. The barricade spanned the highway completely from edge to edge; on its right it was bordered by a tangle of impenetrable thorny scrub; on its left it extended to the brink of a steep ravine.

They were stopped.

Such a blockade across a public highway was inconceivable. Leaf blinked, coughed, rubbed his aching forehead. Those last few minutes of discordant dreams had left a murky, gritty coating on his brain. This wall of wood seemed like some sort of dream too, a very bad one. Leaf imagined he could hear the Invisible's cool laughter somewhere close at hand. At least the rain appeared to be slackening, and there were no spiders about. Small consolations, but the best that were available.

Baffled, Leaf freed himself of the reins and awaited the next event. After a moment or two he sensed the joggling rhythms that told of Crown's heavy forward progress through the cabin. The big man peered into the driver's cabin.

"What's going on? Why aren't we moving?"

"Dead road."

"What are you talking about?"

"See for yourself," Leaf said wearily, gesturing toward the window.

Crown leaned across Leaf to look. He studied the scene an endless moment, reacting slowly. "What's that? A *wall?*"

"A wall, yes."

"A wall across a highway? I never heard of anything like that."

"The Invisibles at Theptis may have been trying to warn us about this."

"A wall. A wall." Crown shook with perplexed anger. "It violates all the maintenance customs! Soul take it, Leaf, a public highway is—"

"—sacred and inviolable. Yes. What the Teeth have been doing in the east violates a good many maintenance customs too," Leaf said. "And territorial customs as well. These are unusual times everywhere." He wondered if he should tell about the Invisible who was on board. One problem at a time, he decided. "Maybe this is how these people propose to keep the Teeth out of their country, Crown."

"But to block a public road—"

"We were warned."

"Who could trust the word of an Invisible?"

"There's the wall," Leaf said. "Now we know why we didn't meet anyone else on the highway. They probably put this thing up as soon as they heard about the Teeth, and the whole province knows enough to avoid Spider Highway. Everyone but us."

"What folk dwell here?"

"No idea. Sting's the one who would know."

"Yes, Sting would know," said the high, clear, sharp-edged voice of Sting from the corridor. He poked his head into the cabin. Leaf saw Shadow just behind him. "This is the land of the Tree Companions," Sting said. "Do you know of them?"

Crown shook his head. “Not I,” said Leaf.

“Forest-dwellers,” Sting said. “Tree-worshippers. Small heads, slow brains. Dangerous in battle—they use poisoned darts. There are nine tribes of them in this region, I think, under a single chief. Once they paid tribute to my people, but I suppose in these times all that has ended.”

“They worship trees?” Shadow said lightly. “And how many of their gods, then, did they cut down to make this barrier?”

Sting laughed. “If you must have gods, why not put them to some good use?”

Crown glared at the wall across the highway as he once might have glared at an opponent in the dueling ring. Seething, he paced a narrow path in the crowded cabin. “We can't waste any more time. The Teeth will be coming through this region in a few days, for sure. We've got to reach the river before something happens to the bridges ahead.”

“The wall,” Leaf said.

“There's plenty of brush lying around out there,” said Sting. “We could build a bonfire and burn it down.”

“Green wood,” Leaf said. “It's impossible.”

“We have hatchets,” Shadow pointed out. “How long would it take for us to cut through timbers as thick as those?”

Sting said, “We'd need a week for the job. The Tree Companions would fill us full of darts before we'd been chopping an hour.”

“Do you have any ideas?” Shadow said to Leaf.

“Well, we could turn back toward Theptis and try to find our way to Sunset Highway by way of the sand country. There are only two roads from here to the river, this and the Sunset. We lose five days, though, if we decide to go back, and we might get snarled up in whatever chaos is going on in Theptis, or we could very well get stranded in the desert trying to reach the highway. The only other choice I see is to abandon the wagon and look for some path around the wall on foot, but I doubt very much that Crown would—"

"Crown wouldn't," said Crown, who had been chewing his lip in tense silence. "But I see some different possibilities."

"Go on."

"One is to find these Tree Companions and compel them to clear this trash from the highway. Darts or no darts, one Dark Lake and one Pure Stream side by side ought to be able to terrify twenty tribes of pinhead forest folk."

"And if we can't?" Leaf asked.

"That brings us to the other possibility, which is that this wall isn't particularly intended to protect the neighborhood against the Teeth at all, but that these Tree Companions have taken advantage of the general confusion to set up some sort of toll-raising scheme. In that case, if we can't force them to open the road, we can find out what they want, what sort of toll they're asking, and pay it if we can and be on our way."

"Is that Crown who's talking?" Sting asked. "Talking about paying a toll to underbreeds of the forest? Incredible!"

Crown said, "I don't like the thought of paying toll to anybody. But it may be the simplest and quickest way to get out of here. Do you think I'm entirely a creature of pride, Sting?"

Leaf stood up. "If you're right that this is a toll station, there'd be some kind of gate in the wall. I'll go out there and have a look at it."

"No," said Crown, pushing him lightly back into his seat. "There's danger here, Leaf. This part of the work falls to me." He strode toward the midcabin and was busy there a few minutes. When he returned he was in his full armor: breastplates, helmet, face mask, greaves, everything burnished to a high gloss. In those few places where his bare skin showed through, it seemed but a part of the armor. Crown looked like a machine. His mace hung at his hip, and the short shaft of his extensor sword rested easily along the inside of his right wrist, ready to spring to full length at a squeeze. Crown glanced toward Sting and said, "I'll need your nimble legs. Will you come?"

"As you say."

"Open the midcabin hatch for us, Leaf."

Leaf touched a control on the board below the front window. With a soft, whining sound a hinged door near the middle of the wagon swung upward and out, and a stepladder sprouted to provide access to the ground. Crown made a ponderous exit.

Sting, scorning the ladder, stepped down: it was the special gift of the White Crystal people to be able to transport themselves short distances in extraordinary ways.

Sting and Crown began to walk warily toward the wall. Leaf, watching from the driver's seat, slipped his arm lightly about the waist of Shadow, who stood beside him, and caressed her smooth fur. The rain had ended; a gray cloud still hung low, and the gleam of Crown's armor was already softened by fine droplets of moisture. He and Sting were nearly to the palisade, now, Crown constantly scanning the underbrush as if expecting a horde of Tree Companions to spring forth. Sting, loping along next to him, looked like some agile little two-legged beast, the top of his head barely reaching to Crown's hip.

They reached the palisade. Thin, late-afternoon sunlight streamed over its top. Kneeling, Sting inspected the base of the wall, probing at the soil with his fingers, and said something to Crown, who nodded and pointed upward. Sting backed off, made a short running start, and lofted himself, rising almost as though he were taking wing. His leap carried him soaring to the wall's jagged crest in a swift blurred flight. He appeared to hover for a long moment while choosing a place to land. At last he alighted in a precarious, uncomfortable-looking position, sprawled along the top of the wall with his body arched to avoid the timber's sharpened tips, his hands grasping two of the stakes and his feet wedged between two others. Sting remained in this desperate contortion for a remarkably long time, studying whatever lay beyond the barricade; then he let go his hold, sprang lightly outward, and floated to the ground, a distance some three times his own height. He landed upright, without stumbling. There was a brief conference between Crown and Sting. Then they came back to the wagon.

"It's a toll-raising scheme, all right," Crown muttered. "The middle timbers aren't embedded in the earth. They end just at ground level and form a hinged gate, fastened by two heavy bolts on the far side."

"I saw at least a hundred Tree Companions back of the wall," Sting said. "Armed with blowdarts. They'll be coming around to visit us in a moment."

"We should arm ourselves," Leaf said.

Crown shrugged. "We can't fight that many of them. Not twenty-five to one, we can't. The best hand-to-hand man in the world is helpless against little forest folk with poisoned blowdarts. If we aren't able to awe them into letting us go through, we'll have to buy them off somehow.

But I don't know. That gate isn't nearly wide enough for the wagon."

He was right about that. There was the dry scraping squeal of wood against wood—the bolts were being unfastened—and then the gate swung slowly open. When it had been fully pushed back it provided an opening through which any good-size cart of ordinary dimensions might pass, but not Crown's magnificent vehicle. Five or six stakes on each side of the gate would have to be pulled down in order for the wagon to go by.

Tree Companions came swarming toward the wagon, scores of them—small, naked folk with lean limbs and smooth blue-green skin. They looked like animated clay statuettes, casually pinched into shape: their hairless heads were narrow and elongated, with flat sloping foreheads, and their long necks looked flimsy and fragile. They had shallow chests and bony, meatless frames. All of them, men and women both, wore reed dart-blowers strapped to their hips. As they danced and frolicked about the wagon they set up a ragged, irregular chanting, tuneless and atonal, like the improvised songs of children caught up in frantic play.

"We'll go out to them," Crown said. "Stay calm, make no sudden moves. Remember, these are underbreeds. So long as we think of ourselves as men and them as nothing more than monkeys, and make them realize we think that way, we'll be able to keep them under control."

"They're men," said Shadow quietly. "Same as we. Not monkeys."

"Think of them as like monkeys," Crown told her. "Otherwise we're lost. Come, now."

They left the wagon, Crown first, then Leaf, Sting, Shadow. The cavorting Tree Companions paused momentarily in their sport as the four travelers emerged; they looked up, grinned, chattered, pointed, did handsprings and headstands. They did not seem awed. Did Pure Stream mean nothing to them? Had they no fear of Dark Lake? Crown, glowering, said to Sting, "Can you speak their language?"

"A few words."

"Speak to them. Ask them to send their chief here to me."

Sting took up a position just in front of Crown, cupped his hands to his mouth, and shouted something high and piercing in a singsong language. He spoke with exaggerated, painful clarity, as one does in addressing a blind person or a foreigner. The Tree Companions snickered and exchanged little yipping cries. Then one of them came dancing forward, planted his face a handsbreadth from Sting's, and mimicked Sting's words, catching the intonation with comic accuracy. Sting looked frightened, and backed away half a pace, butting accidentally into Crown's chest. The Tree Companion loosed a stream of words, and when he fell silent Sting repeated his original phrase in a more subdued tone.

"What's happening?" Crown asked. "Can you understand anything?"

"A little. Very little."

"Will they get the chief?"

"I'm not sure. I don't know if he and I are talking about the same things."

"You said these people pay tribute to White Crystal."

"Paid," Sting said. "I don't know if there's any allegiance any longer. I think they may be having some fun at our expense. I think what he said was insulting, but I'm not sure. I'm just not sure."

"Stinking monkeys!"

"Careful, Crown," Shadow murmured. "We can't speak their language, but they may understand ours."

Crown said, "Try again. Speak more slowly. Get the monkey to speak more slowly. The chief, Sting, we want to see the chief! Isn't there any way you can make contact?"

"I could go into trance," Sting said. "And Shadow could help me with the meanings. But I'd need time to get myself together. I feel too quick now, too tense." As if to illustrate his point he executed a tiny jumping movement, blur-snap-hop, that carried him laterally a few paces to the left. Blur-snap-hop and he was back in place again. The Tree Companion laughed shrilly, clapped his hands, and tried to imitate Sting's little shuttling jump. Others of the tribe came over; there were ten or twelve of them now, clustered near the entrance to the wagon. Sting hopped again: it was like a twitch, a tic. He started to tremble. Shadow reached toward him and folded her slender arms about his chest, as though to anchor him. The Tree Companions grew more agitated; there was a hard, intense quality about their playfulness now. Trouble seemed imminent. Leaf, standing on the far side of Crown, felt a sudden knotting of the muscles at the base of his stomach. Something nagged at his attention, off to his right out in the crowd of Tree Companions; he glanced that way and saw an azure brightness, elongated and upright, a man-size strip of fog and haze, drifting and weaving among the forest folk. Was it the Invisible? Or only some trick of the dying daylight, slipping through the residual vapor of the rainstorm? He struggled for a sharp focus, but the figure eluded his gaze, slipping ticklingly beyond sight as Leaf followed it with his eyes. Abruptly he heard a howl from Crown and turned just in time to see a Tree Companion duck beneath the huge man's elbow and go sprinting into the wagon. "Stop!" Crown roared. "Come back!" And, as if a signal had been given, seven or eight others of the lithe little tribesmen scrambled aboard.

There was death in Crown's eyes. He beckoned savagely to Leaf and rushed through the entrance. Leaf followed. Sting, sobbing, huddled in the entranceway, making no attempt to halt the Tree Companions who were streaming into the wagon. Leaf saw them climbing over everything, examining, inspecting, commenting. Monkeys, yes. Down in the front corridor Crown was struggling with four of them, holding one in each vast hand, trying to shake free two others who were climbing his armored legs. Leaf confronted a miniature Tree Companion woman, a gnomish bright-eyed creature whose bare lean body glistened with sour sweat, and as he reached for her she drew not a dart-blower but a long narrow blade from the tube at her hip, and slashed Leaf fiercely along the inside of his left forearm. There was a quick, frightening gush of blood, and only some moments afterward did he feel the fiery lick of the pain. A poisoned knife? Well, then, into the All-Is-One with you, Leaf. But if there had been poison, he felt no effects of it; he wrenched the knife from her grasp, jammed it into the wall, scooped her up, and pitched her lightly through the open hatch of the wagon. No more Tree Companions were coming in, now. Leaf found two more, threw them out, dragged another out of the roof beams, tossed him after the others, went looking for more. Shadow stood in the hatchway, blocking it with her frail arms outstretched. Where was Crown? Ah. There. In the trophy room. "Grab them and carry them to the hatch!" Leaf yelled. "We're rid of most of them!"

"The stinking monkeys," Crown cried. He gestured angrily. The Tree Companions had seized some treasure of Crown's, some ancient suit of mail, and in their childish buoyancy had ripped the fragile links apart with their tug-of-war. Crown, enraged, bore down on them, clamped one hand on each tapering skull—*"Don't!"* Leaf shouted, fearing darts in vengeance—and squeezed, cracking them like nuts. He tossed the corpses aside and, picking up his torn trophy, stood sadly pressing the sundered edges together in a clumsy attempt at repair.

"You've done it now," Leaf said. "They were just being inquisitive. Now we'll have war, and we'll be dead before nightfall."

"Never," Crown grunted.

He dropped the chain-mail, scooped up the dead Tree Companions, carried them dangling through the wagon, and threw them like offal into the clearing. Then he stood defiantly in the hatchway, inviting their darts. None came. Those Tree Companions still aboard the wagon, five or six of them, appeared empty-handed, silent, and slipped hastily around the hulking Dark Laker. Leaf went forward and joined Crown. Blood was still dripping from Leaf's wound; he dared not induce clotting nor permit the wound to close until he had been purged of whatever poison might have been on the blade. A thin, straight cut, deep and painful, ran down his arm from elbow to wrist. Shadow gave a soft little cry and seized his hand. Her breath was warm against the edges of the gash. "Are you badly injured?" she whispered.

"I don't think so. It's just a question of whether the knife was poisoned."

"They poison only their darts," said Sting. "But there'll be infection to cope with. Better let Shadow look after you."

"Yes," Leaf said. He glanced into the clearing. The Tree Companions, as though thrown into shock by the violence that had come from their brief invasion of the wagon, stood frozen along the road in silent groups of nine or ten, keeping their distance. The two dead ones lay crumpled where Crown had hurled them. The unmistakable figure of the Invisible, transparent but clearly outlined by a dark perimeter, could be seen to the right, near the border of the thicket: his eyes glittered fiercely, his lips were twisted in a strange smile. Crown was staring at him in slack-jawed astonishment. Everything seemed suspended, held floating motionless in the bowl of time. To Leaf the scene was an eerie tableau in which the only sense of ongoing process was supplied by the throbbing in his slashed arm. He hung moored at the center, waiting, waiting, incapable of action, trapped like others in timelessness. In that long pause he realized that another figure had appeared during the melee, and stood now calmly ten paces or so to the left of the grinning Invisible: a Tree Companion, taller than the others of his kind, clad in beads and gimcracks but undeniably a being of presence and majesty.

"The chief has arrived," Sting said hoarsely.

The stasis broke. Leaf released his breath and let his rigid body slump. Shadow tugged at him, saying, "Let me clean that cut for you." The chief of the Tree Companions stabbed the air with three outstretched fingers, pointing at the wagon, and called out five crisp, sharp, jubilant syllables; slowly and grandly he began to stalk toward the wagon. At the same moment the Invisible flickered brightly, like a sun about to die, and disappeared entirely from view. Crown, turning to Leaf, said in a thick voice, "It's all going crazy here. I was just imagining I saw one of the Invisibles from Theptis skulking around by the underbrush."

"You weren't imagining anything," Leaf told him. "He's

been riding secretly with us since Theptis. Waiting to see what would happen to us when we came to the Tree Companions' wall."

Crown looked jarred by that. "When did you find that out?" he demanded.

Shadow said, "Let him be, Crown. Go and parley with the chief. If I don't clean Leaf's wound soon—"

"Just a minute. I need to know the truth. Leaf, when did you find out about this Invisible?"

"When I went up front to relieve Sting. He was in the driver's cabin. Laughing at me, jeering. The way they do."

"And you didn't tell me? Why?"

"There was no chance. He bothered me for a while, and then he vanished, and I was busy driving after that, and then we came to the wall, and then the Tree Companions—"

"What does he want from us?" Crown asked harshly, face pushed close to Leaf's.

Leaf was starting to feel fever rising. He swayed and leaned on Shadow. Her taut, resilient little form bore him with surprising strength. He said tiredly, "I didn't know. Does anyone ever know what one of them wants?" The Tree Companion chief, meanwhile, had come up beside them and in a lusty, self-assured way slapped his open palm several times against the side of the wagon, as though taking possession of it. Crown whirled. The chief coolly spoke, voice level, inflections controlled. Crown shook his head. "What's he saying?" he barked. "Sting? *Sting?*"

"Come," Shadow said to Leaf. "Now. Please."

She led him toward the passenger castle. He sprawled on the furs while she searched busily through her case of unguents and ointments; then she came to him with a long green vial in her hand and said, "There'll be pain for you now."

"Wait."

He centered himself and disconnected, as well as he was able, the network of sensory apparatus that conveyed messages of discomfort from his arm to his brain. At once he felt his skin growing cooler, and he realized for the first time since the battle how much pain he had been in: so much that he had not had the wisdom to do anything about it. Dispassionately he watched as Shadow, all efficiency, probed his wound, parting the lips of the cut without squeamishness and swabbing its red interior. A faint tickling, unpleasant but not painful, was all he sensed. She looked up, finally, and said, "There'll be no infection. You can allow the wound to close now." In order to do that Leaf had to reestablish the neural connections to a certain degree, and as he unblocked the flow of impulses he felt sudden startling pain, both from the cut itself and from Shadow's medicines; but quickly he induced clotting, and a moment afterward he was deep in the disciplines that would encourage the sundered flesh to heal. The wound began to close. Lightly Shadow blotted the fresh blood from his arm and prepared a poultice; by the time she had it in place, the gaping slash had reduced itself to a thin raw line. "You'll live," she said. "You were lucky they don't poison their knives." He kissed the tip of her nose and they returned to the hatch area.

Sting and the Tree Companion chief were conducting some sort of discussion in pantomime, Sting's motions sweeping and broad, the chief's the merest flicks of fingers, while Crown stood by, an impassive column of darkness, arms folded somberly. As Leaf and Shadow reappeared Crown said, "Sting isn't getting anywhere. It has to be a trance parley or we won't make contact. Help him, Shadow."

She nodded. To Leaf, Crown said, "How's the arm?"

"It'll be all right."

"How soon?"

"A day. Two, maybe. Sore for a week."

"We may be fighting again by sunrise."

"You told me yourself that we can't possibly survive a battle with these people."

"Even so," Crown said. "We may be fighting again by sunrise. If there's no other choice, we'll fight."

"And die?"

"And die," Crown said.

Leaf walked slowly away. Twilight had come. All vestiges of the rain had vanished, and the air was clear, crisp, growing chill, with a light wind out of the north that was gaining steadily in force. Beyond the thicket the tops of tall ropy-limbed trees were whipping about. The shards of the moon had moved into view, rough daggers of whiteness doing their slow dance about one another in the darkening sky. The poor old shattered moon, souvenir of an era long gone: it seemed a scratchy mirror for the tormented planet that owned it, for the fragmented race of races that was mankind. Leaf went to the nightmares, who stood patiently in harness, and passed among them, gently stroking their shaggy ears, caressing their blunt noses. Their eyes, liquid, intelligent, watchful, peered into his almost reproachfully. *You promised us a stable,* they seemed to be saying. *Stallions, warmth, newly mown hay.* Leaf shrugged. *In this world,* he told them wordlessly, *it isn't always possible to keep one's promises. One does one's best, and one hopes that that is enough.*

Near the wagon Sting has assumed a cross-legged position on the damp ground. Shadow squats beside him; the chief, mantled in dignity, stands stiffly before them, but Shadow coaxes him with gentle gestures to come down to them. Sting's eyes are closed and his head lolls forward. He is already in trance. His left hand grasps Shadow's muscular furry thigh; he extends his right, palm upward, and after a moment the chief puts his own palm to it. Contact: the circuit is closed.

Leaf has no idea what messages are passing among the three of them but yet, oddly, he does not feel excluded from the transaction. Such a sense of love and warmth radiates from Sting and Shadow and even from the Tree Companion that he is drawn in, he is enfolded by their communion. And Crown, too, is engulfed and absorbed by the group aura; his rigid martial posture eases, his grim face looks strangely peaceful. Of course it is Sting and Shadow who are most closely linked; Shadow is closer now to Sting than she has ever been to Leaf, but Leaf is untroubled by this. Jealously and competitiveness are inconceivable now. He is Sting, Sting is Leaf, they all are Shadow and Crown, there are no boundaries separating one from another, just as there will be no boundaries in the All-Is-One that awaits every living creature, Sting and Crown and Shadow and Leaf, the Tree Companions, the Invisibles, the nightmares, the no-leg spiders.

They are getting down to cases now. Leaf is aware of strands of opposition and conflict manifesting themselves in the intricate negotiation that is taking place. Although he is still without a clue to the content of the exchange, Leaf understands that the Tree Companion chief is stating a position of demand—calmly, bluntly, immovable—and Sting and Shadow are explaining to him that Crown is not at all likely to yield. More than that Leaf is unable to perceive, even when he is most deeply enmeshed in the larger consciousness of the trance-wrapped three. Nor does he know how much time is elapsing. The symphonic interchange—demand, response, development, climax—continues repetitively, indefinitely, reaching no resolution.

He feels, at last, a running-down, an attenuation of the experience. He begins to move outside the field of contact, or to have it move outside him. Spiderwebs of sensibility still connect him to the others even as Sting and Shadow and the chief rise and separate, but they are rapidly thinning and fraying, and in a moment they snap.

The contact ends.

The meeting was over. During the trance-time night had fallen, an extraordinarily black night against which the stars seemed unnaturally bright. The fragments of the moon had traveled far across the sky. So it had been a lengthy exchange; yet in the immediate vicinity of the wagon nothing seemed altered. Crown stood like a statue beside the wagon's entrance; the Tree Companions still occupied the cleared ground between the wagon and the gate. Once more a tableau, then: how easy it is to slide into motionlessness, Leaf thought, in these impoverished times. Stand and wait, stand and wait; but now motion returned. The Tree Companion pivoted and strode off without a word, signaling to his people, who gathered up their dead and followed him through the gate. From within they tugged the gate shut; there was the screeching sound of the bolts being forced home. Sting, looking dazed, whispered something to Shadow, who nodded and lightly touched his arm. They walked haltingly back to the wagon.

"Well?" Crown asked finally.

"They will allow us to pass," Sting said.

"How courteous of them."

"But they claim the wagon and everything that is in it."

Crown gasped. "By what right?"

"Right of prophecy," said Shadow. "There is a seer among them, an old woman of mixed stock, part White Crystal, part Tree Companion, part Invisible. She has told them that everything that has happened lately in the world was caused by the Soul for the sake of enriching the Tree Companions."

"Everything? They see the onslaught of the Teeth as a sign of divine favor?"

"Everything," said Sting. "The entire upheaval. All for their benefit. All done so that migrations would begin and refugees would come to this place, carrying with them valuable possessions, which they would surrender to those whom the Soul meant should own them, meaning the Tree Companions."

Crown laughed roughly. "If they want to be brigands, why not practice brigandage outright, with the right name on it, and not blame their greed on the Soul?"

"They don't see themselves as brigands," Shadow said. "There can be no denying the chief's sincerity. He and his people genuinely believe that the Soul has decreed all this for their own special good, that the time has come—"

"Sincerity!"

"—for the Tree Companions to become people of substance and property. Therefore they've built this wall across the highway, and as refugees come west, the Tree Companions relieve them of their possessions with the blessing of the Soul."

"I'd like to meet their prophet," Crown muttered.

Leaf said, "It was my understanding that Invisibles were unable to breed with other stocks."

Sting told him, with a shrug, "We report only what we

learned as we sat there dreaming with the chief. The witch-woman is part Invisible, he said. Perhaps he was wrong, but he was doing no lying. Of that I'm certain."

"And I," Shadow put in.

"What happens to those who refuse to pay tribute?" Crown asked.

"The Tree Companions regard them as thwarters of the Soul's design," said Sting, "and fall upon them and put them to death. And then seize their goods."

Crown moved restlessly in a shallow circle in front of the wagon, kicking up gouts of soil out of the hard-packed roadbed. After a moment he said, "They dangle on vines. They chatter like foolish monkeys. What do they want with the merchandise of civilized folk? Our furs, our statuettes, our carvings, our flutes, our robes?"

"Having such things will make them equal in their own sight to the higher stocks," Sting said. "Not the things themselves, but the possession of them, do you see, Crown?"

"They'll have nothing of mine!"

"What will we do, then?" Leaf asked. "Sit here and wait for their darts?"

Crown caught Sting heavily by the shoulder. "Did they give us any sort of time limit? How long do we have before they attack?"

"There was nothing like an ultimatum. The chief seems unwilling to enter into warfare with us."

"Because he's afraid of his betters!"

"Because he thinks violence cheapens the decree of the Soul," Sting replied evenly. "Therefore he intends to wait for us to surrender our belongings voluntarily."

"He'll wait a hundred years!"

"He'll wait a few days," Shadow said. "If we haven't

yielded, the attack will come. But what will you do, Crown? Suppose they were willing to wait your hundred years. Are you? We can't camp here forever."

"Are you suggesting we give them what they ask?"

"I merely want to know what strategy you have in mind," she said. "You admit yourself we can't defeat them in battle. We haven't done a very good job of awing them into submission. You recognize that any attempt to destroy their wall will bring them upon us with their darts. You refuse to turn back and look for some other westward route. You rule out the alternative of yielding to them. Very well, Crown. What do you have in mind?"

"We'll wait a few days," Crown said thickly.

"The Teeth are heading this way!" Sting cried. "Shall we sit here and let them catch us?"

Crown shook his head. "Long before the Teeth get here, Sting, this place will be full of other refugees, many of them, as unwilling to give up their goods to these folk as we are. I can feel them already on the road, coming this way, two days' march from us, perhaps less. We'll make alliance with them. Four of us may be helpless against a swarm of poisonous apes, but fifty or a hundred strong fighters would send them scrambling up their own trees."

"No one will come this way," said Leaf. "No one but fools. Everyone passing through Theptis knows what's been done to the highway here. What good is the aid of fools?"

"*We* came this way," Crown snapped. "Are we such fools?"

"Perhaps we are. We were warned not to take Spider Highway, and we took it anyway."

"Because we refused to trust the word of Invisibles."

"Well, the Invisibles happened to be telling the truth, this time," Leaf said. "And the news must be all over

Theptis. No one in his right mind will come this way now."

"I feel marchers already on the way, hundreds of them," Crown said. "I can sense these things, sometimes. What about you, Sting? You feel things ahead of time, don't you? They're coming, aren't they? Have no fear, Leaf. We'll have allies here in a day or so, and then let these thieving Tree Companions beware." Crown gestured broadly. "Leaf, set the nightmares loose to graze. And then everybody inside the wagon. We'll seal it and take turns standing watch through the night. This is a time for vigilance and courage."

"This is a time for digging graves," Sting murmured sourly as they clambered into the wagon.

Crown and Shadow stood the first round of watches while Leaf and Sting napped in the back. Leaf fell asleep at once and dreamed he was living in some immense brutal eastern city—the buildings and street plan were unfamiliar to him, but the architecture was definitely eastern in style, gray and heavy, all parapets and cornices—that was coming under attack by the Teeth.

He observed everything from a many-windowed gallery atop an enormous square-sided brick tower that seemed like a survival from some remote prehistoric epoch. First, from the north, came the sound of the war song of the invaders, a nasty unendurable buzzing drone, piercing and intense, like the humming of high-speed polishing wheels at work on metal plates. That dread music brought the inhabitants of the city spilling into the streets—all stocks, Flower Givers and Sand Shapers and White Crystals and Dancing Stars and even Tree Companions, absurdly garbed in mercantile robes as though they were so many fat citified Fingers—but no one was able to escape, for there were so many people, colliding and jostling and stumbling and falling in helpless heaps, that they blocked every avenue and alleyway.

Into this chaos now entered the vanguard of the Teeth; shuffling forward in their peculiar bent-kneed crouch, trampling those who had fallen. They looked half-beast, half-demon: squat thick-thewed flat-headed long-muzzled creatures, naked, hairy, their skins the color of sand, their eyes glinting with insatiable hungers. Leaf's dreaming mind subtly magnified and distorted them so that they came hopping into the city like a band of giant toothy frogs, thump-thump, bare fleshy feet slapping pavement in sinister reverberations, short powerful arms swinging almost comically at each leaping stride. The kinship of mankind meant nothing to these carnivorous beings. They had been penned up too long in the cold, mountainous, barren country of the far northeast, living on such scraps and strings as the animals of the forest yielded, and they saw their fellow humans as mere meat stockpiled by the Soul against this day of vengeance. Efficiently, now, they began their round-up in the newly conquered city, seizing everyone in sight, cloistering the dazed prisoners in hastily rigged pens: these we eat tonight at our victory feast; these we save for tomorrow's dinner; these become dried meat to carry with us on the march; these we kill for sport; these we keep as slaves. Leaf watched the Teeth erecting their huge spits. Kindling their fierce roasting-fires. Diligent search teams fanned out through the suburbs. No one would escape. Leaf stirred and groaned, reached the threshold of wakefulness, fell back into dream. Would they find him in his tower? Smoke, gray and greasy, boiled up out of a hundred parts of town. Leaping flames. Rivulets of blood ran in the streets. He was choking. A terrible dream. But was it only a dream? This was how it had actually been in Holy Town hours after he and Crown and Sting and Shadow had managed to get away, this was no doubt as it had happened in city after city along the tormented coastal strip, very likely something of this sort was going on now in—where?—Bone Harbor? Veduru? Alsandar? He could smell the penetrating odor of roasting meat. He could hear the heavy galloping sound of a Teeth patrol running up the stairs of his tower. They had him. Yes, here, now, now, a dozen Teeth bursting suddenly into his hiding place, grinning broadly—Pure Stream, they had captured a Pure Stream! What a coup! Beasts. Beasts. Prodding him, testing his flesh. Not plump enough for them, eh? This one's pretty lean. We'll cook him anyway. Pure Stream meat, it enlarges the soul, it makes you into something more than you were. Take him downstairs! To the spit, to the spit, to the—

"Leaf?"

"I warn you—you won't like—the flavor—"

"Leaf, wake up!"

"The fires—oh, the stink!"

"Leaf!"

It was Shadow. She shook him gently, plucked at his shoulder. He blinked and slowly sat up. His wounded arm was throbbing again; he felt feverish. Effects of the dream. A dream, only a dream. He shivered and tried to center himself, working at it, banishing the fever, banishing the shreds of dark fantasy that were still shrouding his mind.

"Are you all right?" she asked.

"I was dreaming about the Teeth," he told her. He shook his head, trying to clear it. "Am I to stand watch now?"

She nodded. "Up front. Driver's cabin."

"Has anything been happening?"

"Nothing. Not a thing." She reached up and drew her fingertips lightly along the sides of his jaws. Her eyes were warm and bright, her smile was loving. "The Teeth are far away, Leaf."

"From us, maybe. Not from others."

"They were sent by the will of the Soul."

"I know, I know." How often had he preached acceptance! This is the will, and we bow to it. This is the road, and we travel it uncomplainingly. But yet, but yet—he shuddered. The dream mode persisted. He was altogether disoriented. Dream-Teeth nibbled at his flesh. The inner chambers of his spirit resonated to the screams of those on the spits, the sounds of rending and tearing, the unbearable reek of burning cities. In ten days, half a world torn apart. So much pain, so much death, so much that had been beautiful destroyed by relentless savages who would not halt until, the Soul only knew when, they had had their full measure of revenge. The will of the Soul sends them upon us. Accept. Accept. He could not find his center. Shadow held him, straining to encompass his body with her arms. After a moment he began to feel less troubled, but he remained scattered, diffused, present only in part, some portion of his mind nailed as if by spikes into that monstrous ash-strewn wasteland that the Teeth had created out of the fair and fertile eastern provinces.

She released him. "Go," she whispered. "It's quiet up front. You'll be able to find yourself again."

He took her place in the driver's cabin, going silently past Sting, who had replaced Crown on watch amidwagon. Half the night was gone. All was still in the roadside clearing; the great wooden gate was shut tight and nobody was about. By cold starlight Leaf saw the nightmares browsing patiently at the edge of the thicket. Gentle horses, almost human. If I must be visited by nightmares, he thought, let it be by their kind.

Shadow had been right. In the stillness he grew calm, and perspective returned. Lamentation would not restore the shattered eastland, expressions of horror and shock would not turn the Teeth into pious tillers of the soil. The Soul had decreed chaos: so be it. This is the road we must travel, and who dares ask why? Once the world had been whole and now it is fragmented, and that is the way things are because that is the way things were meant to be. He became less tense. Anguish dropped from him. He was Leaf again.

Toward dawn the visible world lost its sharp starlit edge; a soft fog settled over the wagon, and rain fell for a time, a light, pure rain, barely audible, altogether different in character from yesterday's vicious storm. In the strange light just preceding sunrise the world took on a delicate pearly mistiness; and out of that mist an apparition materialized. Leaf saw a figure come drifting through the closed gate—*through* it—a ghostly, incorporeal figure. He thought it might be the Invisible who had been lurking close by wagon since Theptis, but no, this was a woman, old and frail, an attenuated woman, smaller even than Shadow, more slender. Leaf knew who she must be: the mixed-blood woman. The prophetess, the seer, she who had stirred up these Tree Companions to block the highway. Her skin had the White Crystal waxiness of texture and the White Crystal nodes of dark, coarse hair; the form of her body was essentially that of a Tree Companion, thin and long-armed; and from her Invisible forebears, it seemed, she had inherited that perplexing intangibility, that look of existing always on the borderland between hallucination and reality between mist and flesh. Mixed-bloods were uncommon; Leaf had rarely seen one, and never had encountered one who combined in herself so many different stocks. It was said that people of mixed blood had strange gifts. Surely this one did. How had she bypassed the wall? Not even Invisibles could travel through solid wood. Perhaps this was just a dream, then, or possibly she had some way of projecting an image of herself into his mind from a point within the Tree Companion village. He did not understand.

He watched her a long while. She appeared real enough. She halted twenty paces from the nose of the wagon and scanned the entire horizon slowly, her eyes coming to rest at last on the window of the driver's cabin. She was aware, certainly, that he was looking at her, and she looked back, eye to eye, staring unflinchingly. They remained locked that way for some minutes. Her expression was glum and opaque, a withered scowl, but suddenly she brightened and smiled intensely at him and it was such a *knowing* smile that Leaf was thrown into terror by the old witch, and glanced away, shamed and defeated.

When he lifted his head she was out of view; he pressed himself against the window, craned his neck, and found her down near the middle of the wagon. She was inspecting its exterior workmanship at close range, picking and prying at the hull. Then she wandered away, out to the place where Sting and Shadow and the chief had had their conference, and sat down cross-legged where they had been sitting. She became extraordinarily still, as if she were asleep, or in trance. Just when Leaf began to think she would never move again, she took a pipe of carved bone from a pouch at her waist, filled it with a gray-blue powder, and lit it. He searched her face for tokens of revelation, but nothing showed on it; she grew ever more impassive and unreadable. When the pipe went out, she filled it again, and smoked a second time, and still Leaf watched her, his face pushed awkwardly against the window, his body growing stiff. The first rays of sunlight now arrived, pink shading rapidly into gold. As the brightness deepened the witch-woman imperceptibly became less solid; she was fading away, moment by moment, and shortly he saw nothing of her but her pipe and her kerchief, and then the clearing was empty. The long shadows of the six nightmares splashed against the wooden palisade. Leaf's head lolled. I've been dozing, he thought. It's morning, and all's well. He went to awaken Crown.

They breakfasted lightly. Leaf and Shadow led the horses to water at a small clear brook five minutes' walk toward Theptis. Sting foraged awhile in the thicket for nuts and berries, and, having filled two pails, went aft to doze in the furs. Crown brooded in his trophy room and said nothing to anyone. A few Tree Companions could be seen watching the wagon from perches in the crowns of towering red-leaved trees on the hillside just behind the wall. Nothing happened until midmorning. Then, at a time when all four travelers were within the wagon, a dozen newcomers appeared, forerunners of the refugee tribe that Crown's intuitions had correctly predicted. They came slowly up the road, on foot, dusty and tired-looking, staggering beneath huge untidy bundles of belongings and supplies. They were square-headed muscular people, as tall as Leaf or taller, with the look of warriors about them; they carried short swords at their waists, and both men and women were conspicuously scarred. Their skins were gray, tinged with pale green, and they had more fingers and toes than was usual among mankind.

Leaf had never seen their sort before. "Do you know them?" he asked Sting.

"Snow Hunters," Sting said. "Close kin to the Sand Shapers, I think. Midcaste and said to be unfriendly to strangers. They live southwest of Theptis, in the hill country."

"One would think they'd be safe there," said Shadow.

Sting shrugged. "No one's safe from the Teeth, eh? Not even on the highest hills. Not even in the thickest jungles."

The Snow Hunters dropped their packs and looked around. The wagon drew them first; they seemed stunned by the opulence of it. They examined it in wonder, touching it as the witch-woman had, scrutinizing it from every side. When they saw faces looking out at them, they nudged one another and pointed and whispered, but they did not smile, nor did they wave greetings. After a time they went on to the wall and studied it with the same childlike curiosity. It appeared to baffle them. They measured it with their outstretched hands, pressed their bodies against it, pushed at it with their shoulders, tapped the timbers, plucked at the sturdy bindings of vine. By this time perhaps a dozen more of them had come up the road; they too clustered about the wagon, doing as the first had done, and then continued toward the wall. More and more Snow Hunters were arriving, in groups of three or four. One trio, standing apart from the others, gave the impression of being tribal leaders; they consulted, nodded, summoned and dismissed other members of the tribe with forceful gestures of their hands.

"Let's go out and parley," Crown said. He donned his best armor and selected an array of elegant dress weapons. To Sting he gave a slender dagger. Shadow would not bear arms, and Leaf preferred to arm himself in nothing but Pure Stream prestige. His status as a member of the ancestral stock, he found, served him as well as a sword in most encounters with strangers.

The Snow Hunters—about a hundred of them now had gathered, with still more down the way—looked apprehensive as Crown and his companions descended from the wagon. Crown's bulk and gladiatorial swagger seemed far more threatening to these strong-bodied warlike folk than they had been to the chattering Tree Companions, and Leaf's presence too appeared disturbing to them. Warily they moved to form a loose semicircle about their three leaders; they stood close by one another, murmuring tensely and their hands hovered near the hilts of their swords.

Crown stepped forward. "Careful," Leaf said softly. "They're on edge. Don't push them."

But Crown, with a display of slick diplomacy unusual for him, quickly put the Snow Hunters at their ease with a warm gesture of greeting—hands pressed to shoulders, palms outward, fingers spread wide—and a few hearty words of welcome. Introductions were exchanged. The spokesman for the tribe, an iron-faced man with frosty eyes and hard cheekbones, was called Sky; the names of his co-captains were Blade and Shield. Sky spoke in a flat, quiet voice, everything on the same note. He seemed empty, burned out, a man who had entered some realm of exhaustion far beyond mere fatigue. They had been on the road for three days and three nights almost without a halt, said Sky. Last week a major force of Teeth had started westward through the midcoastal lowlands bound for Theptis, and one band of these, just a few hundred warriors, had lost its way, going south into the hill country. Their aimless wanderings brought these straying Teeth without warning into the secluded village of the Snow Hunters, and there had been a terrible battle in which more than half of Sky's people had perished. The survivors, having slipped away into the trackless forest, made their way by back roads to Spider Highway, and, numbed by shock and grief, had been marching like machines toward the Middle River, hoping to find some new hillside in the sparsely populated territories of the far northwest. They could never return to their old home, Shield declared, for it had been desecrated by the feasting of the Teeth.

"But what is this wall?" Sky asked.

Crown explained, telling the Snow Hunters about the Tree Companions and their prophetess, and of her promise that the booty of all refugees was to be surrendered to them. "They lie in wait for us with their darts," Crown said. "Four of us were helpless against them. But they would never dare challenge a force the size of yours. We'll have their wall smashed down by nightfall!"

"The Tree Companions are said to be fierce foes," Sky remarked quietly.

"Nothing but monkeys," said Crown. "They'll scramble to their treetops if we just draw our swords."

"And shower us with their poisoned arrows," Shield muttered. "Friend, we have little stomach for further warfare. Too many of us have fallen this week."

"What will you do?" Crown cried. "Give them your swords, and your tunics and your wives' rings and the sandals off your feet?"

Sky closed his eyes and stood motionless, remaining silent for a long moment. At length, without opening his eyes, he said in a voice that came from the center of an immense void, "We will talk with the Tree Companions and learn what they actually demand of us, and then we will make our decisions and form our plans."

"The wall—if you fight beside us, we can destroy this wall, and open the road to all who flee the Teeth!"

With cold patience Sky said, "We will speak with you again afterward," and turned away. "Now we will rest, and wait for the Tree Companions to come forth."

The Snow Hunters withdrew, sprawling out along the

margin of the thicket just under the wall. There they huddled in rows, staring at the ground, waiting. Crown scowled, spat, shook his head. Turning to Leaf he said, "They have the true look of fighters. There's something that marks a fighter apart from other men, Leaf, and I can tell when it's there, and these Snow Hunters have it. They have the strength, they have the power; they have the spirit of battle in them. And yet, see them now! Squatting there like fat frightened Fingers!"

"They've been beaten badly," Leaf said. "They've been driven from their homeland. They know what it is to look back across a hilltop and see the fires in which your kinsmen are being cooked. That takes the fighting spirit out of a person, Crown."

"No. Losing makes the flame burn brighter. It makes you feverish with the desire for revenge."

"Does it? What do you know about losing? You were never so much as touched by any of your opponents."

Crown glared at him. "I'm not speaking of dueling. Do you think my life has gone untouched by the Teeth? What am I doing here on this dirt road with all that I still own packed into a single wagon? But I'm no walking dead man like these Snow Hunters. I'm not running away, I'm going to find an army. And then I'll go back east and take my vengeance. While they—afraid of monkeys—"

"They've been marching day and night," Shadow said. "They must have been on the road when the purple rain was falling. They've spent all their strength while we've been riding in your wagon, Crown. Once they've had a little rest, perhaps they—"

"Afraid of *monkeys!*"

Crown shook with wrath. He strode up and down before the wagon, pounding his fists into his thighs. Leaf feared that he would go across to the Snow Hunters and attempt by bluster to force them into an alliance. Leaf understood the mood of these people: shattered and drained though they were, they might lash out in sudden savage irritation if Crown goaded them too severely. Possibly some hours of rest, as Shadow had suggested, and they might feel more like helping Crown drive his way through the Tree Companions' wall. But not now. Not now.

The gate in the wall opened. Some twenty of the forest folk emerged, among them the tribal chief and—Leaf caught his breath in awe—the ancient seeress, who looked across the way and bestowed on Leaf another of her penetrating comfortless smiles.

"What kind of creature is that?" Crown asked.

"The mixed-blood witch," said Leaf. "I saw her at dawn, while I was standing watch."

"Look!" Shadow cried. "She flickers and fades like an Invisible! But her pelt is like yours, Sting, and her shape is that of—"

"She frightens me," Sting said hoarsely. He was shaking. "She foretells death for us. We have little time left to us, friends. She is the goddess of death, that one." He plucked at Crown's elbow, unprotected by the armor. "Come! Let's start back along Spider Highway! Better to take our chances in the desert than to stay here and die!"

"Quiet," Crown snapped. "There's no going back. The Teeth are already in Theptis. They'll be moving out along this road in a day or two. There's only one direction for us."

"But the wall," Sting said.

"The wall will be in ruins by nightfall," Crown told him.

The chief of the Tree Companions was conferring with Sky and Blade and Shield. Evidently the Snow Hunters knew something of the language of the Tree Companions, for Leaf could hear vocal interchanges, supplemented by pantomime and sign language. The chief pointed to himself often, to the wall, to the prophetess; he indicated the packs the Snow Hunters had been carrying; he jerked his thumb angrily toward Crown's wagon. The conversation lasted nearly half an hour and seemed to reach an amicable outcome. The Tree Companions departed, this time leaving the gate open. Sky, Shield, and Blade moved among their people, issuing instructions. The Snow Hunters drew food from their packs—dried roots, seeds, smoked meat—and lunched in silence. Afterward, boys who carried huge water-bags made of sewn hides slung between them on poles went off to the creek to replenish their supply, and the rest of the Snow Hunters rose, stretched, wandered in narrow circles about the clearing, as if getting ready to resume the march. Crown was seized by furious impatience. "What are they going to do?" he demanded. "What deal have they made?"

"I imagine they've submitted to the terms," Leaf said.

"No! No! I need their help!" Crown, in anguish, hammered at himself with his fists. "I have to talk to them," he muttered.

"Wait. Don't push them, Crown."

"What's the use? What's the use?" Now the Snow Hunters were hoisting their packs to their shoulders. No doubt of it; they were going to leave. Crown hurried across the clearing. Sky, busily directing the order of march, grudgingly gave him attention. "Where are you going?" Crown asked.

"Westward," said Sky.

"What about us?"

"March with us, if you wish."

"My wagon!"

"You can't get it through the gate, can you?"

Crown reared up as though he would strike the Snow Hunter in rage. "If you would aid us, the wall would fall! Look, how can I abandon my wagon? I need to reach my kinsmen in the Flatlands. I'll assemble an army; I'll return to the east and push the Teeth back into the mountains where they belong. I've lost too much time already. I *must* get through. Don't you want to see the Teeth destroyed?"

"It's nothing to us," Sky said evenly. "Our lands are lost to us forever. Vengeance is meaningless. Your pardon. My people need my guidance."

More than half the Snow Hunters had passed through the gate already. Leaf joined the procession. On the far side of the wall he discovered that the dense thicket along the highway's northern rim had been cleared for a considerable distance, and a few small wooden buildings, hostelries or depots, stood at the edge of the road. Another twenty or thirty paces farther along, a secondary path led northward into the forest; this was evidently the route to the Tree Companions' village. Traffic on that path was heavy just now. Hundreds of forest folk were streaming from the village to the highway, where a strange, repellent scene was being enacted. Each Snow Hunter in turn halted, unburdened himself of his pack, and laid it open. Three or four Tree Companions then picked through it, each seizing one item of value—a knife, a comb, a piece of jewelry, a fine cloak—and running triumphantly off with it. Once he had submitted to this harrying of his possessions, the Snow Hunter gathered up his pack, shouldered it, and marched on, head bowed, body slumping. Tribute. Leaf felt chilled. These proud warriors, homeless now, yielding up their remaining treasures to—he tried to choke off the word, and could not—to a tribe of monkeys. And moving onward, soiled, unmanned. Of all that he had seen since the Teeth had split the world apart, this was the most sad.

Leaf started back toward the wagon. He saw Sky, Shield, and Blade at the rear of the column of Snow Hunters. Their faces were ashen; they could not meet his eyes. Sky managed a half-hearted salute as he passed by.

"I wish you good fortune on your journey," Leaf said.

"I wish you better fortune than we have had," said Sky hollowly, and went on.

Leaf found Crown standing rigid in the middle of the highway, hands on hips. "Cowards!" he called in a bitter voice. "Weaklings!"

"And now it's our turn," Leaf said.

"What do you mean?"

"The time's come for us to face hard truths. We have to give up the wagon, Crown."

"Never."

"We agree that we can't turn back. And we can't go forward so long as the wall's there. If we stay here, the Tree Companions will eventually kill us, if the Teeth don't overtake us first. Listen to me, Crown. We don't have to give the Tree Companions everything we have. The wagon itself, some of our spare clothing, some trinkets, the furnishings of the wagon—they'll be satisfied with that. We can load the rest of our goods on the horses and go safely through the gate as foot-pilgrims."

"I ignore this, Leaf."

"I know you do. I also know what the wagon means to you. I wish you could keep it. I wish I could stay with the wagon myself. Don't you think I'd rather ride west in comfort than slog through the rain and the cold? But we can't keep it. *We can't keep it,* Crown, that's the heart of the situation. We can go back east in the wagon and get lost in the desert, we can sit here and wait for the Tree Companions to lose patience and kill us, or we can give up the wagon and get out of this place with our skins still whole. What sort of choices are those? We have no choice. I've been telling you that for two days. Be reasonable, Crown!"

Crown glanced coldly at Sting and Shadow. "Find the chief and go into trance with him again. Tell him that I'll give him swords, armor, his pick of the finest things in the wagon. So long as he'll dismantle part of the wall and let the wagon itself pass through."

"We made that offer yesterday," Sting said glumly.

"And?"

"He insists on the wagon. The old witch has promised it to him for a palace."

"No," Crown said. *"NO!"* His wild roaring cry echoed from the hills. After a moment, more calmly, he said, "I have another idea. Leaf, Sting, come with me. The gate's open. We'll go to the village and seize the witch-woman. We'll grab her quickly, before anyone realizes what we're doing. They won't dare molest us while she's in our hands. Then, Sting, you tell the chief that unless they open the wall for us, we'll kill her." Crown chuckled. "Once she realizes we're serious, she'll tell them to hop to it. Anybody that old wants to live forever. And they'll obey her. You can bet on that. They'll obey her! Come, now." Crown started toward the gate at a vigorous pace. He took a dozen strides, halted, looked back. Neither Leaf nor Sting had moved.

"Well? Why aren't you coming?"

"I won't do it," said Leaf tiredly. "It's crazy, Crown. She's a witch, she's part Invisible—she already knows your scheme. She probably knew of it before you knew of it yourself. How can we hope to catch her?"

"Let me worry about that."

"Even if we did, Crown—no. No. I won't have any part of it. It's an impossible idea. Even if we did seize her. We'd be standing there holding a sword to her throat, and the chief would give a signal, and they'd put a hundred darts in us before we could move a muscle. It's insane, Crown."

"I ask you to come with me."

"You've had your answer."

"Then I'll go without you."

"As you choose," Leaf said quietly. "But you won't be seeing me again."

"Eh?"

"I'm going to collect what I own and let the Tree Companions take their pick of it, and then I'll hurry forward and catch up with the Snow Hunters. In a week or so I'll be at the Middle River. Shadow will you come with me, or are you determined to stay here and die with Crown?"

The Dancing Star looked toward the muddy ground. "I don't know," she said. "Let me think a moment."

"Sting?"

"I'm going with you."

Leaf beckoned to Crown. "Please. Come to your senses, Crown. For the last time—give up the wagon and let's get going, all four of us."

"You disgust me."

"Then this is where we part," Leaf said. "I wish you good fortune. Sting, let's assemble our belongings. Shadow? Will you be coming with us?"

"We have an obligation toward Crown," she said.

"To help him drive his wagon, yes. But not to die a foolish death for him. Crown has lost his wagon, Shadow, though he won't admit that yet. If the wagon's no longer his, our contract is voided. I hope you'll join us."

* * * * *

He entered the wagon and went to the midcabin cupboard where he stored the few possessions he had managed to bring with him out of the east. A pair of glistening boots made of the leathery skins of stick-creatures, two ancient copper coins, three ornamental ivory medallions, a shirt of dark red silk, a thick, heavily worked belt—not much, not much at all, the salvage of a lifetime. He packed rapidly. He took with him a slab of dried meat and some bread; that would last him a day or two, and when it was gone he would learn from Sting or the Snow Hunters the arts of gathering food in the wilderness.

"Are you ready?"

"Ready as I'll ever be," Sting said. His pack was almost empty—a change of clothing, a hatchet, a knife, some smoked fish, nothing else.

"Let's go, then."

As Sting and Leaf moved toward the exit hatch, Shadow scrambled up into the wagon. She looked tight-strung and grave; her nostrils were flared, her eyes downcast. Without a word she went past Leaf and began loading her pack. Leaf waited for her. After a few minutes she reappeared and nodded to him.

"Poor Crown," she whispered. "Is there no way—"

"You heard him," Leaf said.

They emerged from the wagon. Crown had not moved. He stood as if rooted, midway between wagon and wall. Leaf gave him a quizzical look, as if to ask whether he had changed his mind, but Crown took no notice. Shrugging, Leaf walked around him, toward the edge of the thicket, where the nightmares were nibbling leaves. Affectionately he reached up to stroke the long neck of the nearest horse, and Crown suddenly came to life, shouting, "Those are my animals! Keep your hands off them!"

"I'm only saying goodbye to them."

"You think I'm going to let you have some? You think I'm that crazy, Leaf?"

Leaf looked sadly at him. "We plan to do our traveling on foot, Crown. I'm only saying goodbye. The nightmares were my friends. You can't understand that, can you?"

"Keep away from those animals! *Keep away!*"

Leaf sighed. "Whatever you say." Shadow, as usual, was right: poor Crown. Leaf adjusted his pack and moved off toward the gate, Shadow beside him, Sting a few paces to the rear. As he and Shadow reached the gate, Leaf looked back and saw Crown still motionless, saw Sting pausing, putting down his pack, dropping to his knees. "Anything wrong?" Leaf called.

"Tore a bootlace," Sting said. "You two go on ahead. It'll take me a minute to fix it."

"We can wait."

Leaf and Shadow stood within the frame of the gate while Sting knotted his lace. After a few moments he rose and reached for his pack, saying, "That ought to hold me until tonight, and then I'll see if I can't—"

"*Watch out!*" Leaf yelled.

Crown erupted abruptly from his freeze, and, letting forth a lunatic cry, rushed with terrible swiftness toward Sting. There was no chance for Sting to make one of his little leaps: Crown seized him, held him high overhead like a child, and, grunting in frantic rage, hurled the little man toward the ravine. Arms and legs flailing, Sting traveled on a high arc over the edge; he seemed to dance in midair for an instant, and then he dropped from view. There was a long diminishing shriek, and silence. Silence.

Leaf stood stunned. "Hurry," Shadow said. "Crown's coming!"

Crown, swinging around, now rumbled like a machine of death toward Leaf and Shadow. His wild red eyes glittered ferociously. Leaf did not move; Shadow shook him urgently, and finally he pushed himself into action. Together they caught hold of the massive gate and, straining, swung it shut, slamming it just as Crown crashed into it. Leaf forced the reluctant bolts into place. Crown roared and pounded at the gate, but he was unable to force it.

Shadow shivered and wept. Leaf drew her to him and held her for a moment. At length he said, "We'd better be on our way. The Snow Hunters are far ahead of us already."

"Sting—"

"I know. I know. Come, now."

Half a dozen Tree Companions were waiting for them by the wooden houses. They grinned, chattered, pointed to the packs. "All right," Leaf said. "Go ahead. Take whatever you want. Take everything, if you like."

Busy fingers picked through his pack and Shadow's. From Shadow the Tree Companions took a brocaded ribbon and a flat, smooth green stone. From Leaf they took one of the ivory medallions, both copper coins, and one of his stickskin boots. Tribute. Day by day, pieces of the past slipped from his grasp. He pulled the other boot from the pack and offered it to them, but they merely giggled and shook their heads. "One is of no use to me," he said. They would not take it. He tossed the boot into the grass beside the road.

The road curved gently toward the north and began a slow rise, following the flank of the forested hills in which the Tree Companions made their homes. Leaf and Shadow marched mechanically, saying little. The bootprints of the Snow Hunters were everywhere along the road, but the Snow Hunters themselves were far ahead, out of sight. It was early afternoon, and the day had become bright, unexpectedly warm. After an hour Shadow said, "I must rest."

Her teeth were clacking. She crouched by the roadside and wrapped her arms about her chest. Dancing Stars, covered with thick fur, usually wore no clothing except in the bleakest winters; but her pelt did her no good now.

"Are you ill?" he asked.

"It'll pass. I'm reacting. Sting—"

"Yes."

"And Crown. I feel so unhappy about Crown."

"A madman," Leaf said. "A murderer."

"Don't judge him so casually, Leaf. He's a man under sentence of death, and he knows it, and he's suffering from it, and when the fear and pain became unbearable to him he reached out for Sting. He didn't know what he was doing. He needed to smash something, that was all, to relieve his own torment."

"We're all going to die sooner or later," Leaf said. "That doesn't generally drive us to kill our friends."

"I don't mean sooner or later. I mean that Crown will die tonight or tomorrow."

"Why should he?"

"What can he do now to save himself, Leaf?"

"He could yield to the Tree Companions and pass the gate on foot, as we've done."

"You know he'd never abandon the wagon."

"Well, then, he can harness the nightmares and turn around toward Theptis. At least he'd have a chance to make it through to the Sunset Highway that way."

"He can't do that either," Shadow said.

"Why not?"

"He can't drive the wagon."

"There's no one left to do it for him. His life's at stake. For once he could eat his pride and—"

"I didn't say *won't* drive the wagon, Leaf. I said *can't*. Crown's incapable. He isn't able to make dream contact with the nightmares. Why do you think he always used hired drivers? Why was he so insistent on making you drive in the purple rain? He doesn't have the mind-power. Did you ever see a Dark Laker driving nightmares? Ever?"

Leaf stared at her. "You knew this all along?"

"From the beginning, yes."

"Is that why you hesitated to leave him at the gate? When you were talking about our contract with him?"

She nodded. "If all three of us left him, we were condemning him to death. He has no way of escaping the Tree Companions now unless he forces himself to leave the wagon, and he won't do that. They'll fall on him and kill him, today, tomorrow, whenever."

Leaf closed his eyes, shook his head. "I feel a kind of shame. Now that I know we were leaving him helpless. He could have spoken."

"Too proud."

"Yes. Yes. It's just as well he didn't say anything. We all have responsibilities to one another, but there are limits. You and I and Sting were under no obligation to die simply because Crown couldn't bring himself to give up his pretty wagon. But still—still—" He locked his hands tightly together. "Why did you finally decide to leave, then?"

"For the reason you just gave. I didn't want Crown to die, but I didn't believe I owed him my life. Besides, you had said you were going to go, no matter what."

"Poor, crazy Crown."

"And when he killed Sting—a life for a life, Leaf. All vows are cancelled now. I feel no guilt."

"Nor I."

"I think the fever is leaving me."

"Let's rest a few minutes more," Leaf said.

It was more than an hour before Leaf judged Shadow strong enough to go on. The highway now described a steady upgrade, not steep but making constant demands on their stamina, and they moved slowly. As the day's warmth began to dwindle, they reached the crest of the grade, and rested again at a place from which they could see the road ahead winding in switchbacks into a green, pleasant valley. Far below were the Snow Hunters, resting also by the side of a fair-size stream.

"Smoke," Shadow said. "Do you smell it?"

"Campfires down there, I suppose."

"I don't think they have any fires going. I don't see any."

"The Tree Companions, then."

"It must be a big fire."

"No matter," Leaf said. "Are you ready to continue?"

"I hear a sound—"

A voice from behind and uphill of them said, "And so it ends the usual way, in foolishness and death, and the All-Is-One grows greater."

Leaf whirled, springing to his feet. He heard laughter on the hillside and saw movements in the underbrush; after a moment he made out a dim, faintly outlined figure, and realized that an Invisible was coming toward them, the same one, no doubt, who had traveled with them from Theptis.

"What do you want?" Leaf called.

"Want? Want? I want nothing. I'm merely passing through." The Invisible pointed over his shoulder. "You can see the whole thing from the top of this hill. Your big friend put up a mighty struggle, he killed many of them, but the darts, the darts—" The Invisible laughed. "He was dying, but even so he wasn't going to let them have his wagon. Such a stubborn man. Such a foolish man. Well, a happy journey to you both."

"Don't leave yet!" Leaf cried. But even the outlines of the Invisible were fading. Only the laughter remained, and then that too was gone. Leaf threw desperate questions into the air and, receiving no replies, turned and rushed up the hillside, clawing at the thick shrubbery. In ten minutes he was at the summit, and stood gasping and panting, looking back across a precipitous valley to the stretch of road they had just traversed. He could see everything clearly from here: the Tree Companion village nestling in the forest, the highway, the shacks by the side of the road, the wall, the clearing beyond the wall. And the wagon. The roof was gone and the sides had tumbled outward. Bright spears of flame shot high, and a black, billowing cloud of smoke stained the air. Leaf stood watching Crown's pyre a long while before returning to Shadow.

They descended toward the place where the Snow Hunters had made their camp. Breaking a long silence, Shadow said, "There must once have been a time when the world was different, when all people were of the same kind, and everyone lived in peace. A golden age, long gone. How did things change, Leaf? How did we bring this upon ourselves?"

"Nothing has changed," Leaf said, "except the look of our bodies. Inside we're the same. There never was any golden age."

"There were no Teeth, once."

"There were always Teeth, under one name or another. True peace never lasted long. Greed and hatred always existed."

"Do you believe that, truly?"

"I do. I believe that mankind is mankind, all of us the same whatever our shape, and such changes as come upon us are trifles, and the best we can ever do is find such happiness for ourselves as we can, however dark the times."

"These are darker times than most, Leaf."

"Perhaps."

"These are evil times. The end of all things approaches."

Leaf smiled. "Let it come. These are the times we were meant to live in, and no asking why, and no use longing for easier times. Pain ends when acceptance begins. This is what we have now. We make the best of it. This is the road we travel. Day by day we lose what was never ours, day by day we slip closer to the All-Is-One, and nothing matters, Shadow, nothing except learning to accept what comes. Yes?"

"Yes," she said. "How far is it to the Middle River?"

"Another few days."

"And from there to your kinsmen by the Inland Sea?"

"I don't know," he said. "However long it takes us is however long it will take. Are you very tired?"

"Not as tired as I thought I'd be."

"It isn't far to the Snow Hunters' camp. We'll sleep well tonight."

"Crown," she said. "Sting."

"What about them?"

"They also sleep."

"In the All-Is-One," Leaf said. "Beyond all trouble. Beyond all pain."

"And that beautiful wagon is a charred ruin!"

"If only Crown had had the grace to surrender it freely once he knew he was dying. But then he wouldn't have been Crown, would he? Poor Crown. Poor crazy Crown." There was a stirring ahead, suddenly. "Look. The Snow Hunters see us. There's Sky. Blade." Leaf waved at them and shouted. Sky waved back, and Blade, and a few of the others. "May we camp with you tonight?" Leaf called. Sky answered something, but his words were blown away by the wind. He sounded friendly, Leaf thought. He sounded friendly. "Come," Leaf said, and he and Shadow hurried down the slope.